ZOOT-FIRE SHOOTOUT!

Ryder knew there was still one F-15 Agressor out there in the dark night sky. He checked the Phantom's fuel and weapons load. Both half full. He flipped on the massive air-search radar, tipped the F-4 over and began a steep dive toward the darkended earth. Down to 5,000 feet in seconds, he pulled up in a series of quick jerks that nearly cut his rib cage in two. He was bathed in sweat and suddenly his helmet felt two sizes too small. *Damn, he loved this kind of stuff!*

Had the F-15 called it quits? He doubted it. Split seconds later the Agressor streaked out of the night and sent a barrage of Zoot cannon shells raining down on where he thought a Zoot SAM battery was located. The distinctive red flashes of the holographic bullets seemed to rip up the rocky terrain on top of the ridge.

The F-15 passed so close to Ryder, he could see the outline of the pilot by the light of his cockpit panel. Ryder turned the Phantom over on its back and put himself on the F-15's tail.

It was time to get that fourth notch on his belt.

WHILE SUPPLIES LAST!

MACK MALONEY

WAR HEAVEN

ZEBRA BOOKS
KENSINGTON PUBLISHING CORP.

ZEBRA BOOKS

are published by

Kensington Publishing Corp.
475 Park Avenue South
New York, NY 10016

First printing: June, 1991

Printed in the United States of America

Foreword

Roswell Army Air Field, Roswell, New Mexico, July 1947

Lightning flashes lit up the entire northern horizon.

With each crash of thunder, the windows in the control tower rattled dangerously close to the point of shattering. The rain pelting the fifty-foot-high tower was so intense, the six men inside could feel it swaying in the tempest.

But the possibility of the plywood-and-concrete-block tower collapsing was actually the least of their problems. Out there, somewhere, in the stormy New Mexico night were two B-29 Superfortresses trying to find their way home. Each airplane was carrying twelve crew members on board.

Each was also carrying an atomic bomb.

The airplanes were on the last leg of a 250-mile round trip to the White Sands Atomic Testing Ground. Their mission, launched from Roswell shortly after sunset, called for the airplanes to drop their single-bomb payload on a target etched out of the dry desert of White Sands, one of the first such atomic-bomb drops attempted at night.

The mission had seemed snakebitten from the start. Originally three airplanes were scheduled to participate; one had to drop out almost immediately after taking off due to mechanical problems. The remaining two B-29s fought high winds and were plagued with radio interference all the way to the target area, only to find once they got there that the test had been cancelled by the White Sands technical people because of bad weather over the target.

Now the two B-29s were coming back to Roswell trying to ride

5

through the same band of fierce storms that had moved across a wide area of south central New Mexico and were now racing east toward their home base.

Under normal circumstances, any other two B-29s would have been diverted to another air base, or even a municipal airport to save them from the harrowing experience of riding through the typically-violent summer night storms. But Roswell Army Air Field was unlike any other base in the United States. Its unit, the 509th Bomb Group, was the only one in the country equipped to carry, handle, and care for atomic bombs. For security reasons, as well as technical ones, the planes had to return to Roswell.

A strange incident earlier in the night was now almost forgotten.

While the B-29s were still more than an hour out from Roswell, the base's radar systems had picked up an unidentified blip on their screens. At about the same time, an F-51 Mustang fighter plane, which was acting this night as a chase escort plane for the two bombers, had been sent ahead to the base to literally plot a course through the storms on the idea that it would double back and lead the bombers home. The Mustang was diverted toward the unidentified blip under strict rules to identify it, attempt to turn it away from the highly restricted airspace over Roswell, and, failing that, to shoot it down.

The Mustang pilot had bumped in for a landing twenty minutes ago, his fuel tanks dry from pursuing the unidentified bogey out on the northern perimeter of the base. In a brief conversation with the tower, the Mustang pilot claimed he'd shot at something out on the range, that he'd hit it, and that it had gone down. To the men in the Roswell Control Tower, it was a minor point at the moment. They still had two bombers out there, flying through a violent thunderstorm, each one carrying a bomb that held the destructive power of the one that obliterated Hiroshima.

The windows in the Roswell Tower were rattling harder than ever when the base chaplain came through the door. He was soaking wet, his usually finely combed gray-white hair mussed beyond hope, his ruddy complexion made pale by the wind and rain.

"What's the situation?" he asked the officer in charge of the control tower.

"They're still out there," the officer replied, as he watched over three other men who were simultaneously trying to raise the two bombers on three different radios and three different frequencies.

"I suppose a prayer is in order?" the chaplain asked.

"For us or them?" the tower officer replied.

Twenty minutes later, the two B-29s finally arrived over the base.

Each one circled twice and then came in for a jittery but successful landing on the long rain-swept runway. The tower personnel breathed a collective sigh of relief as each bomber slowed to a crawl and taxied to its assigned hangar where the atomic bombs would be dethroned and stored away.

A long night was slowly coming to an end.

The base flight surgeon appeared in the doorway of the tower just as all hands were gathered around the overworked coffeepot. He was here to find the chaplain.

"Father, if you have a minute, could you go down to the infirmary?"

"Sure . . . why?"

"Talk to the kid who flew the Mustang chase plane tonight," was the reply. "He's a little shaky."

"Are you sure it's my department?" the chaplain asked, dumping four spoonfuls of sugar in his coffee.

"Yours more than mine," the doctor replied.

There was another bright flash of lightning, followed by a crash of thunder, this one powerful enough to rattle the empty coffee cups hanging near the overheated pot.

The storm would continue on into the night.

Part 1

1

Over the Nevada desert

The F-16XL "Cranked Arrow" jet fighter tore through the cloudless late-afternoon sky at more than 1000 mph.

Its afterburning engine in full supersonic scream, the delta-winged airplane banked hard to the left and streaked by a pair of oncoming Soviet-built MiG-29 Fulcrums like they were standing still. Rolling once, the 'XL then did a full overhead loop, which effectively placed it behind the Fulcrums. Two well-placed bursts of fire from the 'XL's nose a second later instantly dispatched the hapless MiGs. As they both plunged smoking toward the ground, the 'XL performed a quick victory roll and then pulled back up on its tail.

Following a mile behind the highly-experimental F-16XL was a souped-up F-15 Eagle fighter. Its pilot, USAF Colonel Ryder Long, watched as the Cranked Arrow thundered straight up and out of sight, leaving behind only a wisp of white exhaust and a pair of wingtip contrails.

Not bad, he thought, *Not bad at all . . .*

He pulled back on his own control stick, at the same time opening up his throttles and boosting the F-15's powerful engines past Mach 1. In an instant, the Eagle was also rocketing upward, chasing the twin vapor trails of the F-16XL to 20,000 feet.

"Base, this is Eagle Chase One," Ryder called into his helmet's lip mike as he leveled off. "Phase-two sequence is ready to commence."

His radio crackled once. "Roger, Eagle Chase. You are go for phase-two sequence . . ."

The red, white, and blue F-16XL performed a series of tight circles and then turned to engage a chevron of six MiG-27 Floggers

9

coming toward it from the north. Once again, six streams of frighteningly-bright yellow light flashed out from the 'XL's nose as it streaked head-on into the Floggers. The MiGs scattered frantically—but it was too late. One by one the Soviet fighters began to fall, smoke and flames billowing from their tails, victims to the 'XL's awesome pyrotechnics.

Ryder counted the striken aircraft as they spiraled downward, reporting back to Base as he did so: "Red Three down . . . Red Four ditto . . . Five and Six . . ."

"Roger, Eagle Chase . . ." his radio crackled. "We read sequence two complete. You are now go for sequence three . . ."

Ryder tried his best to keep on the tail of the F-16XL as its pilot put the rocketship-like airplane into a screaming dive—but the effort was not completely successful. The Cranked Arrow was simply much faster than the F-15.

With reluctant admiration, Ryder watched as the 'XL pilot roared straight down, his control not wavering an instant until he finally pulled out of the screeching dive barely a hundred feet above the hard Nevada deck.

An entire battalion of Soviet-built T-72 battle tanks was waiting for the Cranked Arrow, their twin plumes of dust and engine exhaust creating the trademark ministorm of an armored column in full desert charge.

Ryder took two deep gulps of oxygen and mimicked as best he could the 'XL pilot's gut-wrenching pull-up maneuver. By the time he leveled off at 100 feet, the 'XL was already sowing a cloud of antiarmor bomblets from a weapons dispenser attached to its fuselage onto the armored column. With frightening efficiency the tanks began exploding in twos and threes, the resulting flames and sparks lighting up the already-sun-drenched desert for miles.

All it took were four quick passes by the F-16XL and the tanks were reduced to little more than two dozen flaming, sparkling hulks—some smoking heavily, some careening wildly in the desert, others simply gone in a vapor. In all, the annihilation took less than a minute.

Leaving the decimated armored column in its wake, the 'XL continued its low-level supersonic rampage. Ahead of it waited a line of SAM batteries ribboned into the side of a long, shallow ravine. To Ryder, still hard-pressed to stay on the tail of the 'XL, it appeared as if all the SAMs launched at once, each one streaking toward the futuristic F-16 variant. Yet the 'XL pilot weaved his way effortlessly through the antiaircraft missiles like a serpent through a patch of flaming reeds. Not a single SAM even came close to the jinking superfighter.

Beyond the line of SAMs, a squadron of Soviet Hind helicopter gunships rose as one from the protection of a red-sanded butte. Though armed to the hilt with dangerous Aphid air-to-air missiles, the nine fierce-looking Soviet choppers were no match for the firepower of the F-16XL. They were systematically destroyed in a matter of seconds, falling prey to the 'XL's combined barrage of cannon fire and Sidewinder missiles.

His work done, the F-16XL pilot put the jet into another steep, twisting climb, leveling out at exactly 12,500 feet. Then, by opening a specially installed water line attached to the rear of his engine, the pilot was able to induce a long thick white-vapor trail in the wake of his amazing airplane.

With the sweep of an artist, the F-16XL pilot began to carve a huge *W* in contrails across the dry Nevada sky.

All the while, off in the distance, a line of four AC-130 Hercules gunships were following the 'XL's action, their open-window weapons bays filled not with their usual computer-driven Gatling guns but with 70-millimeter movie cameras.

Once the miles-long *W* was completed, the F-16XL circled it once, then roared off to the west, quickly disappearing over the horizon and into the setting sun.

At that moment, Ryder's radio once again came to life: "Okay, *cut!* That's a take, everybody . . ."

He immediately pushed his radio send button for confirmation.

"Base, do I read the sequences' completion command?"

"Roger, Chase One," came the reply. "Sequences complete. Good work. Return to base . . ."

Twenty minutes later, Ryder brought the F-15 in for a landing at Nellis Air Force Base, the huge installation located near the gambling mecca of Las Vegas in southern Nevada.

Taxiing over to an isolated part of the base, Ryder saw the F-16XL was already there, its engine shut down, its specially trained ground

11

crew well into its postflight maintenance checks. The 'XL's pilot was nowhere to be seen, though. He'd been whisked away to a nearby motor home/dressing room by a squad of production assistants immediately upon landing. Once again Ryder was deprived of getting a good look at the man who, in his opinion, was the best fighter pilot he'd ever seen.

His own ground crew appeared as soon as he taxied the F-15 up to its designated hardstand, close by two sun-bleached hangars. The six men in regular Air Force work suits were a welcome sight for him. They were his kind of people. This entire section of Nellis was lousy with film-crew types—dozens of cameramen, lighting men, sound technicians, producers, movie extras, and gofers—all of them scurrying around with determined scowls on their faces, all of them doing their best to look important. Ryder had done *his* best to avoid them at all times. They were definitely *not* his kind of people. He'd yet to meet one who wasn't just oozing with show-biz bullshit.

Ryder was the senior in-flight technical adviser for the *Top Gun*-like film, a $100-million, still-unnamed epic that was set in the near future and centered on the adventures of a somewhat mysterious, heroic fighter pilot. It had seemed like such a choice assignment when he'd first received the special orders to work on the film. And piloting the F-15 chase plane through the expertly choreographed flying sequences *had* been exciting—at first. The 70-mm camera installed in the F-15's nose had already shot thousands of feet of exciting, action-packed film, just as the cameras on the four AC-130 support planes and the dozens of stationary cameras set up out in the desert had shot many thousands of feet more.

But the assignment had lost most of its glamour very quickly. The endless takes and boring delays between camera shoots had turned it into a grind for everyone in the two-hundred-man Air Force support crew after just the first week.

Now, twenty-one days into the anticipated two-month-long duty, Ryder was already itching for something new.

He spent several minutes shutting down the F-15's flight systems, and secured the cockpit before finally climbing out of the fighter. One of Nellis's public-affairs officers was waiting for him as he stepped down from the access ladder. Next to this officer was a deeply tanned, heavily made-up, leathery faced middle-aged woman. She was holding a tape recorder in one hand and a small notepad in the other.

"Colonel Ryder? Do you have a moment, sir?" the public-affairs officer asked him somewhat wearily, his just-doing-my-job look wearing thin.

"Just about that," Ryder replied as politely as possible.

"I would like to introduce you to Evie Walker from the *Star*," the PA officer said, "She's doing a story about the making of the movie . . ."

Ryder was familiar with the Hollywood reporter; he'd seen her many times on the film's location over the past three weeks, talking to anybody who would talk to her. Now it appeared that it was his turn. But he'd been flying since six that morning and it was now close to four in the afternoon. He was tired, sweaty, and hungry. A cold beer, a hot shower, and a good meal awaited him, in that order. The last thing he wanted to do was get hooked by a show-business tabloid reporter.

He shifted his helmet and oxygen mask to his left hand and shook hands with the bleached-blonde woman.

"You're quite a hero yourself, Colonel," she told him, her eyes narrowing almost to slits. "Maybe they should be making this movie about *you* . . ."

Ryder smiled uneasily.

"The hero in this movie comes from a paperback novel," he told her. "I'm just an ordinary pilot, flying a camera plane."

The women slyly snapped on her tape recorder.

"Don't be modest, Colonel," she chided him. "You're very well known in this country. You were all over the news shows last year. . . ."

Ryder could only shake his head and stare at the ground. She was right – almost a year ago he'd been part of a top-secret mission called Distant Thunder whose aim was to destroy a hidden ICBM missile base built in the wilds of Burma by a mad Vietnamese terrorist named Colonel Toon. It had been a dicey operation from the start, and at its climax, Toon had actually launched an ICBM carrying a highly-radioactive nuclear warhead toward San Diego. Flying a U.S. Navy F-14 Tomcat, Ryder and his partner, D. J. Woods, had destroyed the missile just seconds before it could reach its critical altitude, thus averting a major catastrophe. Once the mission was completed and Toon's plans squashed, the U.S. government broke the story to the media in a grand style, hoping to underscore the ever-present threat of terrorist organizations gaining nuclear launch capability.

Ryder and Woods became instant celebrities in the process.

"I really think everything's been covered about Distant Thunder," he told the reporter. "With all the other things that are going on in the world, people must be tired of hearing about it by now."

But the wily, veteran reporter was not to be deterred that easily.

"My idea, Colonel, was to do a story on the difference between real combat and what's being depicted here for this movie," she pressed on. "After all, it *is* one of the largest budgets ever for a Hollywood film, not even counting the Soviet government's assistance. *Have* there been any problems?"

Ryder shrugged and again shook his head. He'd been asked the same question a dozen times already by other reporters covering the shoot.

"No problems that I know of," he began his well-rehearsed, stock reply. "It is somewhat interesting that we are able to use so much actual Soviet equipment. As you know, with the dissolving of the Warsaw Pact, there is a large surplus of it these days and I understand the Soviets were very happy to sell us some for this film. I also find it interesting that so many Soviet reservists were able to come over and work in the film as extras. Obviously this would not have happened even a few years ago.

"However, I think it's important to remember that while the airplanes and tanks and other weapons shown in the film are real, they have been heavily modified. They are now little more than special-effects pieces, remotely controlled by radio to fly and shoot their weapons and be destroyed by computer-controlled time bombs and delayed explosives. Everything—from the flying sequences to the land battles—has been laid out perfectly to achieve a realistic look. But real combat is not so cut and dried. All this is fascinating. Real war is rather frightening."

The woman squinted her eyes at him again, silently sizing him up. He was tall, not yet thirty, and had the good looks of a major-league baseball player. He was also a fair actor. She knew the answer was one he'd given many times before—and yet he'd delivered it with the subtle aplomb of a thespian. Her conclusion: there'd be little more forthcoming about any technical problems with the film.

So she quickly switched tactics.

14

"Are you dating any of the actresses in the cast?"

Caught off-guard, Ryder was saved the pains of replying by the appearance of a large black Air Force staff car. The Pontiac screeched to a halt in front of the F-15 and a captain climbed out. He quickly walked over to Ryder.

"Excuse me, sir, you're wanted at the central base personnel office," the no-nonsense African-American officer told him. "Immediately . . ."

Ryder turned back to the reporter. "Sorry, ma'am," he said. "This sounds important."

She grudgingly nodded and snapped off her recorder.

"Well, if duty calls, I suppose," she said. "But I'd still like to do an in-depth interview with you. Maybe we'll go to lunch?"

Ryder shook her hand again and gratefully headed for the staff car. "Lunch?" he said. "Yeah, maybe . . ."

Just as he was climbing into the Pontiac, a parade of limousines rolled by. Ryder knew that the middle one—it being the longest and most elaborate of the group—carried the man who'd so expertly piloted the F-16XL during the day's filming.

As the limos went past him, Ryder finally caught a glimpse of the star pilot sitting in the rear seat of the middle car, looking out at him.

Their eyes met briefly and the mysterious flyer gave him a thumbs-up.

Then in the wink of an eye, the column of limos had passed by.

Ryder shook his head and watched as they roared off toward the main gate.

"Who *is* that guy?" he wondered aloud.

Randolph Air Force Base, Texas

The USAF officer in room 88-R4 lit his first cigarette of the day and blew out a series of perfectly formed smoke rings.

He checked his watch. It was 1630 hours—4:30 in the afternoon. The half-dozen enlisted people in his command had already left for the day.

Time to get to work, he thought.

Stretched out before him was a bank of computers that held many of the personnel files for the U.S. Air Force's fighter pilot corps.

15

Now, with the door to this computer room securely locked and checked, he booted up a small desktop computer and typed in a series of top-secret security codes. Within a minute, he'd gained access to a computer file that contained the names and service records of a select group of Air Force fighter pilots.

Typing in another command, he pushed the computer's return button and a single personnel file materialized on the screen before his eyes.

It read: *J. Ryder Long, Colonel.*

The officer then picked up his phone and dialed a number in the 703 area code. Hearing the appropriate beep, he placed the phone into his computer's modem and typed in yet another computer command. Two more beeps told him that the file was now being accessed by the person on the other end of the phone.

The officer sat back and watched with dry fascination as major portions of the personnel file were erased by invisible fingers. Words such as *troublesome* and *rebellious* simply disappeared, to be replaced with words like *dedicated* and *loyal*. Substantial parts of the pilot's family background data were also changed, giving the impression that the man had no close family. The only major area not altered was the pilot's actual in-flight performance record. One look told the personnel officer that this could very well stand on its own.

The whole operation took less than five minutes. Once it was finished, the phone connection was quickly terminated and the modem disconnected. The officer pushed the appropriate buttons to return the altered file back into the data base, sealing it inside with a final special security code.

His role thus completed, the officer shut off the small computer, put on his jacket, and went home.

2

Nellis

The late afternoon sun was just beginning to set when Ryder Long finally arrived back at his small off-base apartment and dragged himself inside.

He had spent the last hour tramping all over the base personnel office, looking for the recently relocated officer-assignment section. Once he found the place—in the basement of another building—he learned that no one actually wanted to see him. Rather a message from the Department of the Air Force Central Assignment Headquarters at Randolph Air Force Base in Texas had come in for him. It told him to expect a telephone call to his home at exactly 1730 hours—five-thirty, or ten minutes from then.

At this point, Ryder had barely enough energy to reach inside his icebox and crack open a beer. His dreams of a long shower had to be put on hold for a while, as were the ones for a big steak down at the local cafe. All he could do now was sip the Budweiser and wait for the phone to ring.

The fact that the call was coming at all was fairly intriguing. There was only one reason why the Central Assignment HQ would want to talk to him: to give him new orders.

He slowly drained his beer and was getting up to retrieve another when the phone rang. He checked his watch: it was exactly 1730 hours. Right on time, he thought. This must be serious.

He answered on the second ring.

"Colonel Long?" the voice on the other end asked. "Are you alone? Can you talk?"

17

Ryder froze for a moment, unable to reply. He thought he recognized the voice. High-pitched, nasal, a mouthful of Southern drawl.

"Yeah, I'm alone," Ryder finally replied. "Who's this?"

Now there was a short pause on the other end of the line.

"You know better than to ask that, Colonel," the caller finally said.

That was all Ryder needed to hear. The voice was now matched with the face. The caller was definitely a man he knew as Lieutenant Moon.

Moon was a U.S. intelligence agent who had been a crucial player during the training phase of Distant Thunder. After the mission was over, Ryder learned that Moon—who was not a lieutenant at all—was considered one of the country's top intelligence operatives.

But Moon didn't work for the CIA. Rather he was employed by the National Security Agency, the vast, virtually unknown bigger cousin of the CIA. The NSA had been instrumental in planning and implementing Distant Thunder. And although that operation had been far from trouble-free, Ryder had developed a respect for the NSA, understanding why it was known among inner government circles as "the only U.S. intelligence agency that worked."

"Okay, you're right," Ryder said, implying that he knew who was on the other end. "Go ahead . . ."

There was a slight burst of static on the line. "Excuse the connection," the caller said. "but I'm talking on a secure-scramble phone. You know how they can be."

"I can hear you fine," Ryder said, stealing a sip from his second beer. "What can I do for you?"

"We need your help again, Colonel," the caller said. "Even more so than last time . . ."

The words instantly began burning themselves into Ryder's consciousness. Moon's tone was dead serious.

He took a longer slug of beer.

"What's the duty?" he asked.

"I can't get specific," Moon replied, "Not even on a scrambler. I'll brief you in person, when the time comes . . ."

"What's the timetable?" Ryder asked, making sure to choose his words carefully.

"Immediately," was the quick reply. "The first elements are already in place."

Ryder crossed his fingers. "What about my current duty?" he asked. "This movie thing is real high priority."

"Forget the movie—you've already been relieved of that duty, Colonel," Moon replied. "Be ready to go for an indefinite amount of time by 0800 hours tomorrow. A car will pick you up at your billet."

Once again, Ryder knew he had to phrase his next question carefully.

"Can you at least tell me what kind of weather conditions I can expect? I've still got to pack the right gear . . ."

The pause at the other end of the line was so extended, Ryder momentarily wondered if the connection had somehow been broken.

Finally, Moon's voice came back on.

"Be prepared for time in the desert, Colonel," the man told him. "You're going back to War Heaven."

War Heaven. Just the name was enough to pierce the heart or freeze the spine.

The place almost defied description. It was located in the middle of the Nevada desert, yet even an expert would have a hard time finding it. To build it—if that was the right word—cost billions of dollars. Yet should an uninitiated person wander into it, they could conceivably pass right through without noticing anything more than desert, scrub bushes, and an occasional butte. And even though thousands of American servicemen had rotated through the place, it was said that not even the President himself was privy to *everything* that went on there.

In many ways, War Heaven wasn't so much a distinct place as it was a state of mind. Its official title was the Nevada Special Weapons Testing Range. Its evolution began in the late 1970s after the disastrous attempt to rescue the American hostages being held by Ayatollah Khomeini's Iran. After that debacle, the more rational elements inside the Pentagon decreed that special elite troops taking part in similar operations in the future would train under conditions so realistic that they "should feel the fire on their asses when someone shoots at them."

At about the same time that a much smaller training ground for regular troops called the National Training Center was opened in the Mojave Desert, work secretly commenced on War Heaven, about 150 miles to the north. Thus began a highly classified, wide-ranging "black program" to simulate an authentic, highly-realistic and multi-environment battlefield for use only by the country's most select military units. Just as the U.S. Navy pilots who went through the famous Top Gun fought electronically controlled dogfights against so-called "Aggressor" aircraft (many of which were U.S. built airplanes made to look like those of potential enemies), the special troops deployed in War Heaven faced a baffling array of potential adversaries: on the ground as well as from the air.

During Ryder's first tour inside "the Range," his tiny unit found itself on the wrong end of squadrons of Aggressor aircraft as well as a crazy quilt of ground forces—the Blue, Gray and Green armies—whose allegiances could switch at a moment's notice depending on the orders of the day.

The elaborate war games inside War Heaven went on twenty-four hours a day, seven days a week. Just who was fighting who was determined by the brains of the place: Command Central, known to all simply as C2. Using a top-secret Cray supercomputer, C2 not only ran every operation within War Heaven, it kept score on the various engagements not unlike a bookie kept bets. Units who achieved certain objectives were rewarded with "points." These points were in turn exchanged for the necessities of life inside the Range: food, fuel, supplies, and special ammunition. Those units who failed to meet their objectives quickly went bankrupt and were unceremoniously kicked out of the place, and usually assigned to far-off, unglamorous posts—Greenland was a favorite—where isolation and drudgery ensured a tight lip.

An oft-repeated phrase inside the Range was "Whoever has the most toys at the end, wins the game." And what toys they were! The quest to make the weaponry used inside War Heaven realistic had culminated in the creation of an amazing, highly-secret technology known to all as "Zoot." The result of a rumored unholy alliance between the Pentagon and the people who had made Mickey Mouse famous, Zoot technology used advanced, laser-generated holographics to make a host of simulated weapons—aerial bombs, artillery shells, surface-to-air missiles, mortars, machine guns, rifles, pistols—all frighteningly real. The combination of the holographic projection and the accompanying sound, blast pressure and special-effects-style flame and smoke was so real, it had actually induced heart attacks in some and soiled underpants in others.

A Zoot weapon could do everything but kill you—and Ryder could attest to the fact. He'd seen many War Heaven Zoot weapons in action during his first tour, and they so vividly mimicked the real thing, he still had nightmares about the damn things. Everything having to do with Zoots was interconnected. For example, if a Zoot mortar shell directly "impacted" on a truck or a tank, not only would a holographic explosion take place but the vehicle would cease to work, because the computer controlling its fuel intake would be automatically shut down by the Zoot detection device known as HILES, for Holographic Integrated Laser Engagement System. If a Zoot SAM "hit" an airplane, it would scramble the flight computer to such a point that the pilot had little choice but to head back to base—pronto. When used in conjunction with a wide variety of gas bombs—high strains of tear gas, nausea gas, itchy "crab" gas, hallucination gas, and the particularly nasty CX knock-out gas flowed freely inside War Heaven—the Zoots had the ability to scare the bejesus out of the staunchest warrior, while at the same time giving him the highest respect for the real thing.

And that, after all, was the whole point.

Ryder sat down on his couch and opened his third beer. The idea of going back into the computerized battlefield now made his work on the movie seem like a luxury in comparison. Plus, he was sure it was only a first step. War Heaven was a training ground, a place to prepare for something to come. Just what *that* duty might be had now entered the part of his brain where he stored all his nagging, unpleasant thoughts, dormant but ready to be activated at any moment.

He quickly drained his fresh beer and headed for the shower. He would take a long hot one—knowing that it would probably be the last time in a while that he'd be able to enjoy such a time-consuming luxury.

* * *

He stepped from the steamy bathroom twenty minutes later to find that his answering machine was flashing.

His first thought was that Moon had called back. But in the same instant he knew that security-obsessed NSA man would hardly have left a message.

He impatiently waited for the message tape to rewind, then spent another minute racing it ahead to the spot where the latest message had been left.

What he heard would change his life.

"Hi, Ry. This is Maureen. I'm calling you from TWA flight three-nine-two. I'm using the flight-to-ground telephone. This thing is amazing. Anyway, I'm over Oklahoma right now, I wish you were there to get this message. But maybe this is best, because it's bad news. No, not bad news, I should say, *sad* news. I was going to surprise you this weekend by flying in. I really was. But at the last minute, I got the go-ahead for the craziest story assignment. It's really nutty. I can't go into details. It's top secret, you know. But I'll call you as soon as I can. I wish you could call me back, but you can't. We're landing soon and I'm taking another private flight out right away, so you couldn't even page me if you wanted to. Anyway, I want to tell you, that . . . that I'm thinking of you and I hope we see each other soon. Bye."

Ryder was devastated.

He'd met Maureen via the most improbable circumstances during his involvement in Distant Thunder. She was smart, savvy, gorgeous. So much so that for the first time in his life, he believed he'd found someone he would actually consider marrying one day. But her work—she was a high-profile reporter for the *Washington Post*—and his, made spending a lot of time together nearly impossible. So they'd kept up the relationship by burning up the phone lines and keeping the post office in business for the better part of the year.

And now, he'd just missed a chance to see her in the flesh. Even more painful was the realization that even if she *had* made it out to Vegas on her surprise trip, he wouldn't have been able to see her anyway, due to his recent change in orders.

He sat down, naked and dripping, and tried to let the misery drain out of him. But it was no use. He and Maureen had somehow been attracted to each other *before* even meeting a year ago.

Now those same cosmic forces seemed to be conspiring to keep them apart.

3

Two hours later, Ryder was walking through the front doors of Caesar's Palace, probably the most popular casino on the famous Las Vegas Strip.

He was miserable. Despite Maureen's advice, he'd tried for two hours to track her down at several Texas airports, all to no avail. Calls to her office in Washington also proved unsuccessful. She was on a special, very confidential assignment, he was told, and wouldn't be back for weeks. Nor would she be calling in on a regular basis.

When he finally gave up, he had to fight back a nagging intuition that he might never see her again.

He had no desire to sit home on this, his last night in civilization; he wanted to immerse himself in a sea of strangers instead. This way he could suffer in peace without having to be alone.

Caesar's fit the bill. It was his favorite big casino. He almost never visited places like Circus Circus, the Flamingo, or the Thunderbird. Living in Las Vegas was a mixed blessing for any serviceman. A salary for a week, a month, a year, or more could evaporate in the throw of a single unfriendly card. The upside was that Las Vegas was probably the cheapest place to eat and drink in the civilized world. Caesar's usually laid out the best in free food and booze for its would-be gamblers, and this is why Ryder's internal compass always steered him here.

The place was packed tighter than usual—there was a big air-show scheduled for Nellis later that month, and the airplane enthusiasts, resplendent in their patch-happy jackets and hats, were already streaming into town to see the sights and lose some money. Ryder was an expert at bypassing the more crowded tables and quickly found a snoozy blackjack game in a somewhat isolated corner of the large gambling hall.

He watched a few hands from a discreet distance, and the dealer, pegging him as a military officer right away, gave him a friendly nod.

The two men in the first two seats were tourists, savvy with the cards, but nervously losing a bundle. The two seats to their immediate right were empty at the moment. Seat five was covered by a large black woman sitting behind a mountain of chips. Seat six held a man who appeared too drunk even to see the cards, never mind play with them. It was the slowest game of twenty-one Ryder had ever witnessed. No wonder the dealer was glad to see him.

He converted his money reserve of seventy-three dollars into chips and then plunked himself down into the third seat, much to the dealer's relief. Within a half minute, he was sucking on a free bourbon and ginger, and munching on complimentary hors d'oeuvres.

His filling of the third slot did little to alter the direction of the game. The tourists, actually two brothers from Milwaukee, were watching their hard-earned extra cash disappear, while the large black woman, who had a thick Jamaican accent, continued to win big and the drunk continued to drink.

Ryder's standard opening strategy—to bet his first hand with twenty dollars no matter what—failed when he busted on the improbable combination of two sevens down and an eight card up. This was an omen if there ever was one. Now down to fifty-three dollars, he began playing simple two-dollar hands, knowing all he had to do was win every third hand or so to ensure a steady stream of complimentary drinks.

It went on like this for an hour.

Win a hand, lose two, eat a few weenie wraps, and wave for another free drink. All the while, the casino continued to fill up, the regular sharks rubbing elbows with the wide-eyed tourists and the visiting airshow enthusiasts. Watching it all on the periphery were the ever-vigilant casino security people and, of course, the high-priced call girls.

Ryder was into his fourth drink when he looked up and found

one of these painted ladies settling into the seat next to him. Although prostitution was legal in most of Nevada, it was still against the law within Las Vegas itself. But apparently this *fille de joie* wasn't interested in working. She had sat down to gamble.

It was enough to raise the dealer's eyebrows briefly, a glance to his nearby security man telling him that the woman was not a regular. From her handbag she unloaded a pile of chips that rivaled those belonging to the woman from Jamaica, and boozily snapped her fingers for her free drink.

Ryder used his pilot's trained peripheral vision to study the call girl. She was bejeweled and well-dressed, and, like most of her sisters of the night, looked like a grown woman barely out of her teens. Her long red hair appeared to be natural, despite the decidedly unnatural streak of blonde running down the middle. She was petite but well-shaped and very attractive in a girl-next-door-gone-bad sort of way.

Her addition to the group completely altered the game's leisurely pace. The brother team from Milwaukee suddenly began seeing some modest regains. The winning machine from Jamaica increased her takes. Even the drunk started hitting.

Ryder, who had been winning just about a third of the time, suddenly hit a very hot streak. He was just drunk enough to throw back half of every pot, and kept on winning. In less than ten minutes, he'd suddenly amassed more than seven hundred dollars. The only one not winning was the beautiful newcomer. Throughout it all, she seemed almost distracted, betting haphazardly and several times almost folding on potentially prime hands.

Find all kinds in this town, Ryder thought, working his way into his fifth free drink and happily stacking his chips. *At least she'll be her own person tomorrow.*

It was just after ten P.M. when the man ran screaming through the casino.

At first it was just a single shout—almost like a cry for help. Ryder thought a fight had broken out near the front door—sometimes the sharks and tourists didn't mix quite right—and that the crack security people would have the misunderstanding cleaned up in seconds.

26

But the shouting got louder and closer, and when Ryder finally managed to spot the man running through the crowd, he froze to his seat. The man was maybe sixty or so, with a paunch and a shock of white hair. Yet the screams coming from his throat— wild, almost insane yelps and shrieks—seemed to be those of a young boy, or even a woman. It was frightening to see it and to hear it. He ran right by their table, security men on his heels, his nose running, a wild look in his eyes, a foam forming at the corners of his mouth.

Some patrons laughed, a few uproariously. Others simply watched in dazed confusion. Only the regulars in the crowd knew that this sort of thing didn't happen in Caesar's. The security people finally tackled him about fifteen feet from Ryder's table. Wrestling him to the floor, the plainclothes security men braced for a wild fight. Yet, as soon as the man went down, he went limp, slumped forward, and then, oddly, began kissing the dirty, liquor-sticky carpet.

"I'm back!" he yelled in triumph. "Jesus Christ! I'm home at last!"

More security men arrived, some of them uniformed, and a call went out for the regular Las Vegas cops. The man had pulled himself up into a happy crouch and was alternately laughing and singing wildly: "Hey, I'm home! *I'm finally home!*"

The incident was now becoming a major embarrassment for the casino's management as more people wanted to watch the strange scene than to gamble. To counter this, a security manager crouched down beside the man and began to quietly speak to him.

"Had too much to drink, pal?" he asked the man in a comforting, friendly manner. "Eat a bad steak at the Flamingo?"

The man never stopped laughing. "They took me," he sang out. "They took me, and poked me, and filed my skin and squeezed my nuts . . . But now I'm home. Damn, I'm back home!"

"Who took you?" the security man asked.

The man was almost white by now with laughter.

"A flying saucer," he yelled wildly, at the same time soundly oddly matter-of-fact. "A bunch of little dudes from a UFO! They snatched me three days ago. And they just let me go!"

The security man smiled authentically for the first time. He had finally pegged the man's neurosis. He was a UFO nut. He'd seen little green men from Mars.

"A flying saucer, you say?" the security man yelled loud enough for half the casino to hear. "They must be doing the late show at the Hilton!"

The bad joke had the intended effect: it loosened the crowd of nervous patrons troubled by the intrusion. Conversation started up again, dealers began dealing cards, and waitresses flooded the immediate area with free booze. Soon everyone was back to spending money and drinking freely. And most everyone was laughing, even at Ryder's table.

Everyone except the call girl.

4

New Mexico, the next day, 6:30 A.M.

It was getting hot.

The helicopter pilot was concerned that the stagnant, dry morning air would make it difficult for him to restart his engine—intense heat could play tricks on chopper blades. So he left the engine on idle while he helped his passenger unload her gear.

"Are you sure this is the right place?" he asked the woman, yelling over the racket of the idling engine. "I'm not even sure we're even still in New Mexico . . ."

Maureen O'Brien looked around at the barren terrain, now lit by the magnificent sunrise, and then checked a small photomap she'd unfolded from her pocket.

"This is it," she confirmed, yelling back. "Those hills over there look right. That rise to the south. That dry riverbed."

The chopper pilot wiped the sweat from his brow and scratched his chin. She was gorgeous—blonde, blue eyes, the body of a *Playboy* model. As such, she was not the kind of person he felt comfortable about leaving out in the middle of nowhere.

"I'm having second thoughts about all this . . ." he told her, checking that all her gear was off the chopper. "Are you sure you're going to be okay?"

"I've done a lot worse than this," she assured him, lightly touching his arm.

The chopper pilot involuntarily shivered with excitement at her touch. She looked better than a movie star, more like a woman in

29

a rock video, he decided. She also seemed to be smart, determined, and confident. And well-prepared, as her two well-packed knapsacks and string of canteens attested.

Still . . .

"Do you have a gun?" he asked her.

"I don't need a gun," she replied. "I've got this . . ."

She held up an aerosol can of a Mace-like substance, the kind that women carry to ward off muggers. The chopper pilot had to admit it was an industrial-strength–size can.

He finally shrugged with resignation. "I hope you know what you're doing."

She reached out and touched his arm again, freezing him for a moment.

"I do," she replied.

Five minutes later, the chopper was gone, fading like a mirage in the haze and finally disappearing over the northern horizon. At last, she was on her own.

Maureen strapped on her knapsacks and canteen belt and checked her map once again.' Then she began walking south.

She was glad the helicopter pilot hadn't recognized her. In anticipation of this adventure, she'd purposely changed her appearance over the past few weeks. New hairdo, fake designer glasses, different makeup. Apparently it had been worth the effort.

Her major scoop the year before on the Distant Thunder operation had made her one of the country's most high-profile journalists—much to the delight of her primary employer, *The Washington Post*. Her picture had appeared in all the big magazines—*People, Newsweek, TV Guide*—and in hundreds of newspapers. She'd done the talk show circuit twice. She'd appeared on *CNN, Meet the Press, Face the Nation,* and *Nightline*. She'd received lucrative offers to host her own Washington-based news show, her own nationally syndicated talk show, and to play herself in the proposed movie. She had even been approached to pose in *Playboy*.

The opportunities had come so fast and furious that she had been forced to hire an agent, who was still sorting through it all. Theoretically, she was still considering all the opportunities—except the one from Hef. Nevertheless, the agent estimated that she could make a million dollars in the next eight months alone.

She was reluctant to dive into any of them too quickly, though. She knew the flash-in-the-pan syndrome had to be avoided at all costs. So she had a plan: if she kept on getting the big scoops, she could have the best of both worlds. The opportunities would not dry up, and she could continue to be an active journalist.

This was the line of reasoning that had brought her to this southeast corner of New Mexico, wearing her slight disguise. Somewhere over the horizon, she knew, could be the biggest scoop in the history of mankind.

She walked on for two hours.

It wasn't as unpleasant as she'd expected. It was very hot, certainly—but her ample water supply and her specially designed lightweight clothes and underwear prevented it from sapping her strength. Besides, she'd trained for this trek for weeks, walking around in the broiling heat of Washington, D.C., a few hours each weekday and taking off for the wilds of the Virginia mountains on the weekends for a series of solitary overnight mountain-climbing trips. She'd researched desert survival techniques and knew all of the safety procedures by heart. Plus she'd packed a powerful two-way radio, a smaller but reliable backup and distress beacon whose signal was tied into an international airplane crash and recovery system.

And if all else failed, she knew she could always count on her father. A retired but still influential Army general with hundreds of top-level friends in the Pentagon, he'd have half the Air Force out looking for her if she didn't report in at the predesignated times.

There were no surprises along her hike. She saw only few animals—mostly mice—all of which scurried away at her approach. The terrain was rockier than she expected at first, but after ninety minutes or so, the coarse earth began giving way to clumps of grass and vegetation. When she reached point C, as indicated on her map, the terrain had evolved into one vast rolling plain of dried grass. By the time she'd reached point D, approximately two thirds of the way to her destination, she was walking through the ankle-high grass of pastureland.

She celebrated this milestone by taking a ten-minute break and

31

drinking half a canteen of water. It was now coming up on nine A.M.; she was right on schedule. And the map had been impeccable. When she returned to Washington, she would happily reward the military intelligence agent who'd given it to her.

Her long walk was not out of necessity, per se. Her destination, though isolated, was accessible to vehicles with appropriately strengthened shock absorbers and springs. Rather her approach was one intended to mislead anyone she might "innocently" run into. If and when that happened, she had to *look* like she'd been hiking for several hours. If not, then all the effort would have been for nothing.

It was nine-thirty when she reached point G, a high rise that overlooked a small, brown grass valley. Here she saw her first sign of civilization: a winding dirt road, muddied by an earlier isolated morning shower and already dried back to a hard crust. Beyond the road was a deep, dry wash, the remains of an ancient line shack, and a row of equally-antique fence pickets.

On the other side of the pickets was a circle of truck campers and Winnebagos.

Maureen quickly retrieved her Nikon and began snapping off photos. Long shots, zoom-ins, wide-angles—she took two dozen pictures in all, detailing the immediate area, with the emphasis on the ring of vehicles about three quarters of a mile away.

She replaced the depleted roll of film with a fresh one and buried the Nikon deep inside one of her knapsacks. Then she made a quick coded call on her primary radio to a small newspaper office near White Sands, New Mexico, where a part-time correspondent for the *Post* worked. This done, she buried the radio even deeper in her pack than the camera.

Then she removed her shirt.

She was wearing what had to be the sexiest piece of hiking apparel on the market. It was a white bra-like garment, knitted from lightweight cooling fibers into a fishnet design. She'd been both amazed and happy when she found it in the Banana Republic mail-order catalog. The thing was actually pretty functional; it had supported and cooled her well-developed breasts with barely a hint of perspiration throughout the trip.

It would also play another, more subtle role in her overall plan. Tying her shirt around her waist, she crossed her fingers for luck and then walked down the hill and toward the circle of campers.

They spotted her just as she came up out of the dry wash and passed between two battered fence posts.

She counted twelve people in all—eleven men and one woman. A few of the men were older and looked like members of academia. The rest were in their twenties—typical age of graduate students. Off to the left of the campers were a series of freshly-dug ditches, slits, and squared-off trenches. Many of these holes were covered with large sifting screens. Dozens of digging tools, both large and small, were scattered about, as were water jugs, beach umbrellas, and radio sets. Two still cameras on tripods marked one side of the site, a battery-packed video camera guarded another.

It was everything Maureen had expected, right down to the elaborately placed lines of yellow string that cordoned off the holes as well as the entire dug-up area. She had "stumbled" into what was unquestionably an archaeological dig.

Two men ran out to meet her; their agitated expressions were tempered somewhat by her good looks and scant dress. Already the hiking bra had proved its worth.

"Sorry, miss," the older of the two men called out to her. "I'm afraid this area is off limits . . ."

Maureen dutifully stopped in her tracks and lowered her knapsacks with a huff of relief.

"I'm sorry," she said, "I was just wondering if you could give me some directions . . ."

Both men stopped about ten feet away from her. Their expressions showed they couldn't believe someone else was walking around out in the isolated plain, never mind someone dressed like her.

"Where are you going?" one asked.

She looked in every direction except toward the dig site.

"I'm not sure," she told them, not altogether untruthfully. "I think I might be lost . . ."

5

The A-7 Corsair II rumbled through the morning Nevada sky, flying low and twisting its way between the occasional buttes and small mountain ranges along its flight path.

Ryder Long was at the controls of the subsonic jet, his slightly hung-over brain functioning just well enough to allow his hands and feet to go through the motions of flying the airplane.

The A-7 was known by pilots and ground personnel as "the SLUF," a nonaffectionate acronym for "Slow Little Ugly Fucker." It was an appropriate nickname. The snub-nosed plane *was* slow with a top-speed of only about 500 mph. It *was* little—in appearance it resembled a chopped-down, carved-up version of the legendary F-8 Crusader of the 1950s and 1960s. Thus, the A-7 was an ugly fucker.

Used by both the Air Force and the Navy mostly as a light ground-attack plane during Vietnam and subsequent conflicts, the A-7 began retiring from the front lines in the late 1980s. Many had been refitted as trainers, chase planes, and taxi craft, used for moving pilots from one location to another. As such, it was probably the most *un*glamorous combat plane in the American arsenal.

For Ryder, flying the A-7 was like the owner of a Ferrari driving an old Volkswagen. But the mode of his transport was far from his mind at the moment. His thoughts were on other matters.

The events at the casino the night before had stayed with him through his sleep and into the morning. Just like coming upon a bad car accident or witnessing a fatal house fire, seeing a man crack up in public like that was unnerving. It was almost enough to make him forget that he'd walked out of the casino with $856 in winnings, and that was after he'd tipped his dealer $25.

Not having the time to go to the bank, he now had all that money—mostly small bills—stuffed into various parts of his flight suit.

His upcoming assignment was also very much on his mind.

An unmarked car had picked him up at his apartment shortly after 0800 as promised. The man in civilian clothes behind the wheel had driven him into Nellis, where he was pointed toward the SLUF and given a flight plan that would carry him right into War Heaven.

He was due to land at a place called Area 61 within the half hour. One of several super-secret air bases within the Range—Tonopah AFB, also known as Area 51, being another, more northernly base—Area 61 served as an ingress point for many visitors to War Heaven.

He knew that Area 61 was also home to many secret aircraft designs. He was hoping then that whatever mission awaited him there or inside War Heaven itself would involve his flying something hotter than the SLUF.

The list of these potential aircraft was a short but intriguing one. Oddly, exotic planes like the F-117A Stealth "fighter" (it was actually a ground attack plane) and the B-2 Stealth bomber would probably not make such a list. True, both had plied the highly restricted skies above central Nevada for years—the F-117 had flown at night over the Tonopah area for nearly a decade before its existence was officially confirmed by the Air Force. But these no-longer-secret "radar-invisible" airplanes were old hat now. For the most part, the B-2s sat unused in their very expensive air-conditioned hangars out in California, and many of the F-117s had deployed to Holloman AFB in New Mexico. This only meant that something else had taken their place.

Ryder's list of alternatives broke down into three parts. Experimental aircraft such as the Lockheed F-22 and the Northrop F-23 Advanced Tactical Fighters fell into the first category. Their existence was known to the world—the ATF competition had been widely reported in the press for several years. But there were only a few copies of each plane at present, and as much as Ryder would have loved to strap into one of the ATFs—both were rumored to be far beyond anything ever built to fly in both design and handling—he doubted that the NSA would drag him all the way to War Heaven just for him to do what any one of a dozen test pilots available in the U.S. could do just as well, or better.

This only made his second list of the potential aircraft—those *not* known to the world—even more intriguing. There were always rumors of something new and strange flying out on the Range. There was the F-120, reportedly a Stealth craft that truly was a fighter, and a supersonic one to boot. There was the A-14, another Stealth ground-attack plane that might or might not be able to take off and land vertically, like an AV-8 Harrier. There were rumblings of a new spy plane—one that would replace the still-mysterious, prematurely retired Mach 4 SR-71 "Blackbird." The new version was said to be able to actually fly in low space, at incredible speeds, using advanced ramjets as well as employing Stealth technologies.

Then, of course, there was the third list: the one consisting of secret aircraft that no one had even heard rumors about.

He checked his position and his flying time. He was exactly thirty minutes out of Nellis and about fifteen minutes from Area 61. A threshold of sorts awaited him, the point where he would pass from Nellis air control into the highly restricted airspace above War Heaven. Once he was past this point, in many ways, neither he nor his airplane would officially exist.

Then the real adventure would begin.

He braced himself, both physically and mentally, for this transition. He tried to transfer all thoughts of life on the "outside"—the tit duty during the filming of the movie, the weirdness at the casino, his missed opportunity with Maureen, the $856 in his suit—into his brain's hold/waiting file. From this point on, everything had to be focused on what lay ahead, and for the most part, his consciousness cooperated. However, he knew from experience that thoughts of Maureen were hard to squirrel away for very long.

He flashed by the departure point and took a deep gulp of pure oxygen. Although there were no mileposts or outward signs, he knew he was now back in War Heaven. He could almost *feel* it. The desert below didn't look much different, but he knew that certain parts were wired to the max, that hidden cameras and exotic Zoot technology were everywhere and that a grand Big Brother of a supercomputer was watching over it all, ministered by the men of C2.

He punched his radio send button and officially bid good-bye to Nellis. Then with the switch of a dial, he changed his radio's frequency to the obscure Channel 10 255.3 setting. This was the electronic grapevine of the Range.

"Six to Zero-Plus-Three," Ryder said simply into his helmet's lip microphone. "Requesting landing clearance . . ."

"Zero-Plus-Three to Six," came the oddly echoed reply. "You are cleared to land on runway two, southeast. Wind is at five knots."

"Roger."

He soon cleared the last mountain range and got a good visual on the air base. Strictly speaking, it was an extremely small place—at least, what could be seen of it. It was built near the side of some low mountains, and except for the pair of crossed runways, it could have passed for a mining operation or something just as banal.

There were no aircraft lined up along the runways, of course—after all, there were still Soviet spy satellites capable of passing overhead, and there was no sense in inviting temptation in thawing times. There were a few buildings hard by the main mountain's base, all of them painted drab gray and surrounded by high fences. Scattered individual structures could be seen here and there on the periphery of the facility, as well as a satellite dish or two. But that was it. Super-secret as it may be, no one had ever accused the place of looking glamorous.

He pulled the A-7 around into a long, slow turn and brought the small jet in for a landing on runway two, southeast. A small white van appeared at the end of the airstrip, its four-way flashes silently telling Ryder to follow its lead. He did so, trailing the van to an isolated hardstand. A ground crew emerged from a small hut nearby, all of them dressed in casual civilian clothes.

The lead guy gave Ryder the signal to cut his engine, which he did immediately. It took him another few seconds to shut down the rest of the A-7's systems, and then he finally was able to pop the canopy.

He was hit with a strong blast of scorching wind, its velocity

37

whipped by the curve of the small mountain and the ever-climbing morning temperatures. He took in a couple deep breaths to acclimate his lungs from the cool pure oxygen of his plane to the dry air of Area 61. Then he unstrapped and climbed down the access ladder.

Two men were waiting for him. Both wore white tee shirts, faded blue jeans, and sneakers; no uniforms were needed here. There were no introductions. Just a couple quick handshakes and a request that he join them in the van.

Ryder was only too happy to comply. The van was air- conditioned and he welcomed the relief from the blazing heat, even though he'd been subjected to its intensity for less than a minute. Ha climbed into the rear seat of the truck and let the cool, motorized air wash over him. His two hosts—both amiable, friendly sorts—climbed into the front seat, and reminded him to fasten his seat belt. Then they were off.

They rode past the base's largest exposed building. It was a combination meeting place/operations center/PX. It didn't matter that Ryder had all the gambling money on him—he knew from experience that every item on the shelves of the PX was free.

They slowly passed by the front of the building, and he studied the two well-trimmed lawns in front of the place. Despite the blazing sun, the lawns were so bright and green, they seemed painted with emerald sparkles. It was probably the time-diverting passion of a few residents of this strange place, he thought. The challenge: How do we not only grow great grass in the desert, how do we make it the greenest fucking grass in the world?

There was a small wooden sign stuck in the middle of the right-side lawn, one that if placed on a typical suburban lawn would have asked, "PLEASE KEEP OFF THE GRASS."

This one instead read, "REMEMBER, YOU ARE NOT REALLY HERE."

6

It had always struck Ryder as being odd that for all its blanketing top security, Area 61 sometimes seemed to be one of the worst-kept secrets in the world.

It had been written about frequently in the U.S. press over the years. Tabloids like the *National Enquirer, The Star,* and *Weekly World News* covered supposed activities there on a more or less regular basis and the place was even more of a staple for stories in the "fringe" publications.

Though it was frequently confused with Tonopah, which, while secret, actually lay next to a small but robust civilian area, Area 61 had also been featured on TV shows like *Hard Copy, Inside Edition,* and *A Current Affair;* and Oprah, Phil, and Geraldo had all mentioned the place more than once.

According to these stories, Area 61 actually went by several names: S-4. Military Parcel 17-A. Hangar 52.

But there was one name that stuck, maybe because it seemed to sum it up the best: Dreamland.

According to these less-than-reliable sources, Dreamland was more than a proving ground for the military's top-secret experimental weapons. It was, they claimed, the most mystical and mystifying of places. It was where Hitler's brain was stored. It was where JFK was being kept alive. It was home to Elvis and Bigfoot. The remains of crashed UFOs were hidden nearby. One hangar was a morgue for the bodies of alien spacemen. Another held more gold than Fort Knox.

It was a conspiracy buff's dream, for if everything that had been written about it were true, then all the missing pieces to all of the

39

world's most notorious puzzles could eventually be found in Dreamland.

It seemed somehow appropriate then—at least to someone like Ryder, who had actually passed through the place—that Area 61/S-4/Parcel 17-A/Hangar 52 served as a kind of capital city for the authentically-mysterious War Heaven.

Less than an hour after landing at Area 61, Ryder was speeding along a paved road in the back seat of a Hummer, the four-wheeled do-it-all machine (sometimes also called a HumVee) that had replaced the jeep as the military's general-purpose vehicle. Two officers in nondescript uniforms sat up front, keeping the talk to a friendly minimum. That was fine with him. There was little need for chitchat inside War Heaven. It was a paradise for a Type A personality—all business, no bullshit. The schmoozers on the Nellis movie crew wouldn't last a day in this place, he thought.

The time he'd actually spent at the Area 61 air base had been surprisingly uneventful. He'd gone through a routine yet thorough check of his clearance paper, the processing officer telling him that he wouldn't be spending much time in Area 61 after all. His still-secret orders called for him to be driven much deeper into War Heaven itself. He was then issued a nondescript field uniform—a desert-brown camouflage outfit—and a small but impressive survival kit. A quick walk over to the unusual PX resulted in a free toothbrush. A sandwich from a vending machine there was surprisingly good, as was the similarly dispensed coffee. Both were also free.

Now racing northward, away from Area 61 and into the heart of the weapons range, he recalled the first time he'd been deployed to War Heaven. It was on a C-130 Hercules cargo plane, which had circled endlessly through an entire night, its windows ominously blacked out, before landing at an isolated airstrip under simulated enemy Zootfire.

He was glad he was entering the Disneyland of war gaming in a more dignified manner this time. It gave him the opportunity to relax and enjoy the view.

They were traveling on a thoroughfare that was known on the

Range as Eternity Road, because sometimes it seemed to go on forever. Running for more than four hundred miles, it served as the main highway for the weapons range. It had two major arteries—Mountain 101 and Desert 66—and many little ones. Mountain 101 twisted and turned around the buttes, mesas, and small tree-covered mountains that dotted the northern and western edges of the weapons range. Desert 66 ran through the vast, open spaces on the eastern edge. These two main roadways were interconnected by secondary roads at various, frequently-congested locations.

Ryder's Hummer had turned onto the 101 artery shortly after leaving Area 61. The winding narrow roadway had already passed by dozens of FSTEEs—Full-Scale Training Exhibit Environments—which were the vital organs of War Heaven itself. Known to the troops simply as Fitzies, each one mimicked to a frightening degree a potential battleground that elite U.S. troops might face around the world.

There was, for instance, the German village. Hard by a small mountain and built to full scale, it featured narrow, twisting urban streets and European-style, cookie-cutter houses. There was jungleland, tucked away in a small valley, lush with artifically-grown, thick vegetation, synthetic grass huts, and man-made rice paddies; it was right out of the Mekong Delta. Next canyon over was the Caribbean airstrip, complete with a potholed runway and hangars bearing faded Cuban Air Force markings.

The further one traveled on 101, the more bizarre and elaborate the Fitzies became. An Alpine ski lodge, complete with real-looking yet fake snow, was built in the shadows of one of the biggest mountains. The Black Sea fishing village was constructed next to an large artificial lake that featured artificially created waves and winds. The small Subcontinent-like town was filled with wandering cows and large fat scavenger birds, and located atop a hot, dusty plateau. There was even a Fitzie simply called Small City which was a chillingly realistic re-creation of a small American Midwestern town.

On and on it went, beyond amazing, beyond mysterious, beyond adequate description, even those of the wildest tabloids. Like some kind of landscape from a mild nightmare, disconcerting in layout, slightly toylike in form, looking for all the world like an amusement park gone mad.

Even more astonishing, the entire weapons range had a roof on it. An invisible roof, actually. Someone somewhere had discovered that by bouncing a series of laser beams around to precise locations at precise high-intensity amplifications, the whole place could be electronically masked and therefore rendered all but invisible to the lenses of any Soviet satellites passing high overhead. A leftover from the Star Wars program, this system alone had cost close to $5 billion.

As for possible intruders flying closer to the earth, there were two squadrons of specially equipped F-16 interceptors—one secretly based at NAS Fallon in the north, the other scattered about on small, two-aircraft airfields located along the periphery of the Range itself.

These airplanes quietly patrolled the borders of the place. Their standing orders were clear: they were to shoot down any unauthorized aircraft—be it a Piper Cub or any airliner—that wandered into the vast restricted airspace and couldn't be turned around by less belligerent means.

The Hummer continued along 101 for another half hour before switching over to a feeder road that brought it onto Desert 66.

Gradually the fantasyland of valleys and protective mountain ranges disappeared and the terrain turned back into the high, dry desert. Here the Fitzies were more scattered, but no less abundant. Many were mock-ups of potential desert warfare environments, of course. Miles of trenches, sand berms, and concrete bunkers made up dozens of "Arab world" FSTEES, though a few urban, third world, or even futuristic training exhibits could be seen set off from the road here and there. There was an elaborately scaled, commercial airport—known as Entebbe Two to the troops—which had two life-sized commuter terminals, a baggage center, three parking areas, and actual, working TWA, Pan Am, and Delta passenger jets. There were two nuclear power plant mock-ups, (at least Ryder *thought* they were mock-ups), a mock hydroelectric dam site, and even a full-scale but apparently nonworking space-shuttle launch site.

As with the mountain route, this roadway was dotted with working air bases of all kinds—from simple, one-hangar, single-runway fields to large, multirunway, multihangar complexes. Most of these air bases also supported barracks, warehouses, fuel depots, and small gas-turbine power plants. Some were bristling with activity. Others looked like they'd been closed for months.

Ryder's vehicle passed many convoys along the way, several consisting solely of M-1A1 tanks, rumbling along at top speed. Others were made up of M-2 or M-3 Bradley fighting vehicles, light armored vehicles, various mobile artillery pieces, multiple-launch rocket systems, support trucks pulling things like Patriot missile batteries and dozens of Hummers. Most of these vehicles were painted either blue, gray or green and marked with a distinctive red stripe, indicating that a holographic Zoot weapon was on board.

Just as the desert highway was busy with various troop and equipment movements, the sky above the weapons range was also alive with activity. Helicopters of all types—Apaches, Cobras, Chinooks, Hueys—were constantly dashing about. America's front-line jet fighters—F-14s, F-15s, F-16s, F/A-18s—and attack planes like the A-6s and A-10s crisscrossed the sky. Frequently a big boy like a B-52 or a B-1 would be spotted, racing overhead in the middle altitudes. They shared airspace with prop-driven E-2C electronic-warfare aircraft, KC-10 air-refuel tankers, and C-130 cargo and support aircraft.

Above it all, long-winged TR-1 recon jets—the successor to the famous U-2—hovered like all-seeing hawks.

Despite all this activity, Ryder nevertheless found himself dozing off after a while, his body repairing the last of the hangover damage from the night before. Even with the constant jostling of the Hummer, it turned out to be a pleasant slumber.

It would be his last refreshing sleep for some time.

7

It was two hours later when he was nudged awake by one of the officers in the front seat of the Hummer.

Wiping the deep sleep from his eyes, Ryder tried to get his bearings.

They were parked on the edge of a small town. Not much more than a collection of nondescript 1950s-style houses with a dusty street running through its middle, the town lay in a ravine that was squeezed in between two tall craggy mountains. As these twin peaks served to cut off most of the sunlight in all directions, it appeared that the town was destined to be perpetually bathed in shadows, giving it a somber, spooky feel.

Ryder crawled out of the vehicle and stretched. The place looked absolutely deserted.

He turned back to his drivers. "What now, guys?"

Both men gave him a friendly shrug.

"We're heading back to Sixty-one, sir," one explained. "Our only orders were to drop you off here . . ."

With that, they both climbed back into the Hummer and drove away.

Ryder watched the vehicle disappear down the road, wondering what the hell came next. He was out in the middle of nowhere, with no provisions, no radio, nothing. It was enough to unnerve some people — but he had to remind himself he was in War Heaven. Things like this happened all the time.

He walked down the middle of the street, surveying the dilapidated houses. Most were boarded up; others were simply in disrepair. It didn't appear that the town was a typical Fitzie: there were no wires running about, no telltale Zoot-computer terminals or engagement sensors anywhere.

At the end of the street was a small white-shingled church. It seemed slightly less neglected than the rest of the buildings. An announcement board out front had cracked, yellowed letters that spelled out the message PRAY FOR OUR COUNTRY.

Ryder walked up to the front of the church, slowly opened the door, and peeked inside. There was a man kneeling in the front pew, head bowed, hands to his face, apparently deep in prayer.

The squeak of the door attracted the man's attention; he turned around and looked at Ryder.

The pilot immediately recognized the face in the dull, colored light of a stained-glass window. It was the NSA triggerman, Lieutenant Moon.

"Come in, Colonel. I've been waiting for you."

Ryder walked up to the front pew. They shook hands rather stiffly.

"Good to see you again, Colonel," Moon said, forcing his friendly, lopsided smile.

"I didn't know you were a religious man, Lieutenant," Ryder told him.

"I'm not," the diminutive agent replied. "At least, I wasn't until recently."

They sat down in the front pew, Moon placing his small briefcase between them.

"You must be wondering what's up, I suppose?" Moon asked him.

"I'm curious," Ryder replied with deliberate understatement.

"Okay, I'll give it to you straight, then," Moon said somberly. "We have a grave crisis here—inside the Range. It could have dire consequences for the whole country."

Ryder braced himself; apparently the message on the church board outside was not a total coincidence.

Moon took a deep breath and let it out slowly.

"A small group of military officers and civilians has taken over War Heaven . . ."

He paused for a moment to allow his words to sink in.

"They've gone way off the beam. They are running their own programs. They have their own agenda. They've even defied a direct presidential order."

"Sounds serious," Ryder said. "Who are they?"

Moon seemed to lower his voice a notch. "They're part of a group called the ISC . . ."

"Never heard of it."

"I'm not surprised," Moon said. "The Vice President doesn't even know about it. ISC stands for the Intelligence Security Committee. It's the most secret of all our intelligence groups. The people in it were drawn from the other agencies: CIA, DIA, NSA. All of the services' intelligence groups. They're all supposed to be best and the brightest."

"I'm with you so far . . ." Ryder told him.

"One of the things the ISC does is run War Heaven," Moon went on. "They've got the keys to the supercomputer. They control all the Zoot stuff. They decide who goes up against who, who gets the points, the works. They are, in effect, Command Central . . ."

"C-Two is powerful people," Ryder observed.

"That's only half of it," Moon went on. "Their other mission is to make sure all of the country's most sensitive military secrets stay that way. And I'm not talking about things like the Stealth fighter or the B-2. I mean the *real* secrets. The crazy stuff. The deepest, the blackest programs. Stuff that just can't be believed."

"Sounds like the two jobs go together . . ." Ryder said wryly.

"They do—that's the problem," Moon agreed. "There are only about thirty people in the ISC and most are headquartered right here, on the Range itself."

Moon paused a moment, as if to collect his thoughts.

"As hard as it is to believe," he began again, slowly, "we've reached the conclusion that many of these guys have possibly gone nuts—literally, insane."

"What?"

"It's true. It started about nine months ago. Little things began popping up. Weird things. It took a while for people to notice. But when they did, everything got out of control, real quick. The ISC started issuing strange memos. Holding secret meetings. Not responding to direct orders. They were moving people around in here that made no sense to anyone who would recognize such things. They did some very *irrational* things. And with the stuff

46

these guys know, and the technology they have at their control, well, it's damn frightening . . ."

"What have they done exactly?" Ryder asked. "Give me a concrete example."

Moon reached into his briefcase and came up with a tabloid newspaper called the *World News*. It was especially sensationalistic and tacky, all black-and-white photos, with blaring 60-point-type headlines and crude, garish illustrations.

He handed it to Ryder. "Look at this . . ."

The headline read: GOVERNMENT SAYS UFO WAR IS COMING! Beneath it was a cartoonish drawing of a pair of outlandish flying saucers blasting each other with "death rays" while a smoking, flaming Earth hung in the background. Two blurry photos bracketed the drawing. One photo showed an almost angelic humanoid with a caption that read: *A good alien.* The other photo showed a small, devious ET-type figure with a bulbous head, big eyes, and no mouth. Its caption read: *An evil alien.* The gist of the article was that the good aliens would soon be battling the evil aliens for no less than control of the universe.

"Yeah, so," Ryder said with a shrug. "It's a crazy story in a crazy newspaper. What's it have to do with anything?"

Moon took the tabloid newspaper back from Ryder.

"See the name of the writer?" he asked. " 'Garibaldi Olsen.' "

"Yeah, weird name. So?"

" 'Garibaldi Olsen' is a pseudonym for a guy named G. Vogel Haas," Moon explained. "He was, up until a year ago, one of the most respected researchers in this country. I mean *the top*. This guy was into fusion power. Quantam mechanics. Quarks. Squarks. Wormholes. Cosmic strings. Way-out stuff like shooting laser beams in between individual atoms in different elements. Using computers to measure stuff called old time, and new time. Sideways time. This is high-concept physics we're talking about. The works, baby . . ."

"So what's he doing writing this crap?"

"That's just it," Moon said. "It isn't crap. Not all of it, anyway."

"You're losing me," Ryder told him. "You're not saying this nutty story is true . . ."

"I know it sounds incredible," Moon replied, "but there is some very, very sensitive information in this story. Stuff that only the

ISC guys would know."

He turned to the wild UFO story's jump page.

"See these numbers in the last few paragraphs?" he said, pointing to a series of figures at the end of the article. "According to the story, these are supposed to show the 'attack coordinates' of these evil aliens."

Ryder quickly glanced at the numbers. "So?"

"So, have you ever heard of the NSSS?" Moon asked.

Ryder had. "The Navy Space Surveillance System," he confirmed. "It keeps tabs on all the satellites and space junk floating around in orbit . . ."

"Correct," Moon said. "It's part of the overall Space Surveillance Network. As you can imagine, a lot of it is extremely classified."

"And?"

"And," Moon continued, "these figures, in this crazy story, contain *actual* readouts from the Navy Space Surveillance System main computer. We checked."

"God damn . . ." Ryder whispered, giving the story a second look. "How did this Garibaldi guy get them? And what the hell's he doing putting it into this kind of newspaper?"

Moon shook his head.

"We just don't know," he admitted. "We've been looking for him everywhere. But so far, no luck. He'd published in every top physics journal in the country over the last ten years. When we went to a few of the editors that he used to work with—guys at MIT, *Scientific American,* and others—they told us that this Haas guy had really gone off the deep end lately. Booze. Cheap broads. Pissing away money. He went nuts. Started making some wild statements to the wrong people. Stuff not too far from what's in this story. UFOs and aliens. The invasion is coming. Said he had proof.

"Well, these egghead editors didn't cotton to this stuff, as you can imagine. A couple of them felt bad for him, figured he just snapped. They gave him some money and told him to go away. Others just told him to go away. He turned around and claimed someone was trying to ruin him. That he was being blackmailed by the government because he knew too much. When we got in touch with the publishers of these crazy tabloids, they told us that he turned to writing this kind of stuff just to stay in beer and butts. By the time we caught on, he'd written a couple stories and then he disappeared. He was last seen in a barrio in L.A. On skid row . . ."

"That's a long way to fall," Ryder observed. "Very strange."

"It gets stranger," Moon told him.

He pulled another tabloid newspaper from his briefcase, called the *International Examiner*. Its headline screamed: "SPY SATELLITES SPOT UFO FLEET!" and showed a blurry photo of a satellite superimposed on another fantastic drawing of a stream of huge flying saucers heading toward Earth.

"That's a photo of a KH-33A spy satellite," Moon told Ryder. "There's only one in existence and it went up right before Desert Storm. It's so secret, no more than three photos were ever taken of it, and they're all in the care of the ISC."

"And one of them made it into this nutty newspaper?" Ryder asked, studying the photo.

"Exactly . . ." Moon said grimly. "Same way. Some guy who used to be a top-notch military science researcher started making outlandish claims, trying to publish way-out stuff. He got shut out, hit the skids and turned to writing garbage. Wrote two stories and then, *poof!* he was gone, too."

"And the photo?" Ryder asked.

Moon shrugged. "He either stole it, or someone gave it to him."

Moon pulled out a handful of tabloid clips.

"We've got more than a dozen other stories like this," he said. "All of them in crazy newspapers, all of them written by top guys that have bounced, all of them containing bits of incredibly sensitive information that only the ISC has access to."

"This makes no sense," Ryder said, looking over the bizarre clippings. "Why would they be doing this? Are they leaking the information to the Russians, like for money?"

"No, it's not that," Moon replied. "I hate to say it, but the Russians know about a lot of this stuff. And what they don't know, they wouldn't be able to understand anyway. None of our potential enemies would. So blatant espionage is not the angle."

"Then, what *is* the angle?" Ryder asked.

Moon could only shake his head.

"No one knows," he said. "It's all so fucking weird. We've got to assume these researchers had some contact with the ISC, somewhere along the way. But it's got to be more than that. A cover for something else. Something connected to the ISC taking over War Heaven . . ."

Ryder stared at the church ceiling.

"But how could the country's top intelligence group go so screwy, so fast?" he asked finally.

"No one is sure," Moon admitted. "Obviously this whole compartmentalization of the country's super-secret stuff just got way out of control. These ISC guys were given too much power, too much access. I suppose that was inevitable after the Cold War supposedly ended, but they were able to do just about anything they wanted and get away with it."

"Power is one thing," Ryder observed. "But doing insane things is another. Does anyone have an idea what might have happened to them?"

"There's no shortage of theories on that," Moon said. "I've heard everything: Booze. Drugs. Embezzlement. A fundamentalist religious angle. Someone thought it might be a plot by New Age channeling kooks. Or maybe some kind of survivalist cult, like the big one up in Wyoming. The background checks on these ISC guys were extensive to begin with. Now, since all this shit has gone down, we've gone back over their records with a fine-tooth comb . . ."

"And what's been found?"

"That's just it," Moon replied. "There *is* no common thread. Some of them are inclined to be boozers, but not all of them. Some could be closet drug addicts, but not all of them. Some are fundamentalist born-again Christians, but some are artsy-fartsy atheists from Ivy League schools. The strange thing is, these wacked-out researchers fit the same profile—which is, no profile at all.

"There *is* a theory that the Cray supercomputer is affecting them somehow—something to do with the semiconductor chips or even the electromagnetism. And that's not as far-out as it sounds. Scientists have been studying things just like that for years, especially the electromagnetic angle. They already know that a lot of electromagnetism can fuck up your blood cells. So why not the brain cells, too? And no one disputes the fact that these guys have been hanging around the Cray computer a lot . . ."

"So you know exactly where they are?" Ryder asked.

"Sure we do," Moon replied. "They're sitting inside the mountain next to Area 61. But they've made it quite clear that if they're interfered with, if we make the slightest move against them, they'll blow up the supercomputer, the files, the Zoot stuff, the works. With an A-bomb, yet . . ."

Ryder rolled his eyes in disbelief. "Christ, they've got a nuclear bomb, too?"

Moon nodded gravely. "A pretty big one," he said. "Twenty megatons . . ."

Ryder whistled with astonishment. "How did they get it?"

"They *ordered* it," Moon told him. "Specially-made, right down at Sandia National Labs. They got the fusing stuff from Livermore. By the time anyone figured out what was going on, it was too late. I guess it makes for a real weird combination. From what I hear, what they've got is more like a device used for an A-bomb test than as a weapon. But the explosion it can make will be very authentic."

"And are they nutty enough to use it?" Ryder asked. "I mean, would they really set off a nuke? They'd be killing themselves in the process, wouldn't they?"

"Not necessarily," Moon replied. "I mean, putting aside the possibility of mass suicide for a moment, you realize that Area Sixty-one is practically A-bomb–proof to begin with. Well, they've reinforced it again. They've doubled the concrete, doubled the steel. Even doubled the EMP pulse protection. They also brought in air purifiers, extra fuel, food, and supplies. They've got their own electrical power sources, redundant computer lines, communications gear that runs five levels deep. They could set off an atomic blast on the surface and survive in their bunker under that mountain for six months, a year, even more . . ."

Ryder let out a long, low whistle. "Any chance they're bluffing?" he asked.

"I seriously doubt it," Moon replied angrily. "They sent a fucking memo to the President, for God's sake, outlining their threats. They told him, straight out, 'We're working on something very heavy here. Don't get in our way or the balloon goes up.' He fired back a presidential order, telling them to desist immediately. They ignored it. That doesn't sound like they're bluffing to me."

"Then, why not just go in and get them?" Ryder asked. "We're sitting in the middle of some of the best elite troops in the world. Get some the Rangers or some SEALs and pull a lightning strike and–"

Moon held up his hand and cut him off mid-sentence.

"That would be impossible," he said. "Because the ISC controls the Range, they control the movement of every Gray grunt, every Green trooper, every guy in Blue, every chopper, airplane, truck, and tank. They control the Zoots, therefore they control everything. So no unit inside here can do anything against them. They'd see a movement of Range troops toward them in a minute. And then we'd be pushing them to make good on their threats.

"The alternative is to use outside troops, but that's impossible, too. These guys are plugged into every computer the Pentagon owns. They'd see a mobilization by any regular outside forces in a minute.

"So for us to use force against them—*real* force—we'd need a sanitized unit. *And* we'd have to do it under the rules of the Range."

"What do you mean?" Ryder asked.

"It's complicated," Moon said. "But, you see, even though they've gone around the bend, the ISC still has to take care of the business of operating War Heaven, at least until the time is up on whatever the hell they're doing. So they have to continue assigning operations. Awarding points. Doing the supply drops. In many ways, this place *is* their power. It's in their best interest to keep it running on an even keel.

"Now, if we could figure out a way to chip away at that power—well, then we might be able to make some headway. But that's going to take a lot of time and we'll need a sanitized force, one that the ISC hasn't got a plug into. There's just not one of those available as we speak . . ."

Ryder almost hated to ask the next question.

"So where do I come in?"

Moon gave him the lopsided smile again.

"I'm afraid you're the joker in the deck, Colonel," Moon replied. "Very few people know that the ISC has flipped out. Now, crazy things are happening inside here, but that's business as usual as far as the troops on the Range are concerned.

"But we know one thing for sure: the ISC guys have been re-cruiting a few inside individuals to use for God knows what. All of them pilots."

"That's just fucking great . . ." Ryder moaned.

"They're very clever about doing it, too," Moon went on. "They're especially interested in guys with good records. Guys who will follow orders and keep their mouths shut."

"Oh, well, then, that *does* leave me off the hook," Ryder said, only half-kidding. He knew that when it came to discipline, his service record was a mess.

"Not quite," Moon told him. "We pulled a lot of strings to have you brought back here, and to do so, we had to alter your service record. Cleaned it up, so to speak. You are now a loyal, unques-tioning pilot. The guy who saved Distant Thunder. We're putting you back in here and twisting a few lines and hoping the ISC takes the bait. If they do, then it will be up to you to get in their pants and figure out what's going on."

Ryder was astonished.

"But why me?" he asked. "There's got to be a hundred other guys who could—"

Moon held his hand up and once again cut him off.

"It's you because you're a damn hero, Long," he told him through gritted teeth. "You saved the fucking day a year ago and now you have to do it again. It's that fucking simple."

"And what the hell do I do when I've figured it all out?" he shot back at Moon. "Who do I tell? You?"

"Tell no one," Moon said urgently. "Remember, they've made it quite clear that if anyone on the inside here does anything against them, then the lid goes off. They insist on being left alone and allowed to work on their own agenda—whatever that is.

"So all you can do, once you get to the bottom of it, is try to stop it, as quickly as you can."

"And where the hell are you going to be?"

"I don't know," the NSA agent told Ryder. "But I will not be able to contact you once you begin duty."

"Why the hell not?"

"Because the ISC might realize the extent of our knowledge of their activities by that time," Moon said. "After that, all bets will be off. For us to be even seen talking might blow the whole thing . . ."

Ryder stared at the shadowy NSA agent for a long time. Then a stray thought crossed his mind.

"You know, how do I know *you're* on the level, Moon?" he asked in all seriousness. "How do I know this just isn't another nutty exercise set up by you NSA guys? Or even one big drill for the whole Range?"

Moon just looked at the church's altar.

"You don't," he said finally. "And I don't expect you to take my word. All I can expect from you is to go about your duty here. Do what's expected of you. Fly your missions and go with the flow. And when the crazy stuff starts happening, *then* you'll know . . ."

Ryder was shaking his head.

"But you said it yourself," he told Moon. "Crazy stuff happens in here all the time. How the hell will I know when something starts going wrong?"

Moon looked at him for a long time, and then nodded.

"Believe me," he said. "You'll know . . ."

Ryder just shook his head. He had a hundred questions flashing through his mind.

"But what happens if they transfer me out of here?" he asked. "I mean, no one stays on the Range forever—it's a training ground. Everyone eventually gets deployed somewhere out in the real world."

"If that happens, you'll have no choice but to go where they send you," Moon told him. "And then, I guess, when the time is right or it looks like things are coming to a head, you'll just have to try and get back in."

Ryder almost laughed in his face. *"Get back in?"* he said. "This is the most restricted place on Earth!"

Moon just shook his head again. "I didn't say it was going to be easy," he replied. "But obviously there's a lot at stake here."

They were both silent for a moment; the eerie quiet was amplified by the stillness of the church.

"Do I have a choice at all in any of this, Moon?" Ryder finally asked.

The agent shook his head.

"Not really," he replied frankly. "This has been inside the Oval

54

Office for the past month. The President is gravely concerned about the whole affair—as you can imagine. For all we know, these ISC guys are plotting a coup. A military takeover of this government. Or something even *crazier*. Is that enough of an incentive for you?"

Ryder just stared back up at the church's ceiling. It was full of holes, and a few stray beams of sunlights were leaking in.

"Two days ago, the President cut an executive order that had your name all over it," Moon went on. "I don't think it would be wise at this point to question a direct order from your Commander in Chief. Do you?"

Ryder looked sidelong at him. "Very persuasive," he said dryly.

Moon shrugged. "It's my business . . ."

"And mine is putting my ass on the line," Ryder told him. "That's why I've got to have something in return."

Moon was taken aback, but just for a moment.

"Such as what?" he asked.

Ryder's mind was racing at Mach 1. What should he ask for? A million dollars? A promotion? Early retirement with full pension?

"Actually, I want two things," he said. "One, I want some help on this mission. Two heads are better than one, and should anything happen to me—well, you'd still have one of us standing . . ."

Moon was floored by Ryder's request.

"Are you kidding?" he asked. "Who can we trust to help you? Especially at this late juncture?"

"The same guy you trusted for Distant Thunder," Ryder replied pointedly. "I want to work with my old partner, D. J. Woods."

Moon pondered this for a moment, then asked, "And what the hell is the second thing?"

"Try to find a woman friend of mine," Ryder told him. "And if you do, give her a message for me . . ."

Ten minutes later, they left the small town in Moon's Hummer.

They moved quickly onto Desert 66, passing dozens of other military vehicles, containing soldiers who had no idea that War Heaven had become the center of a very bizarre situation.

Ryder soon began recognizing some of the terrain. The waves of high-desert scrub bushes, the craggy hills, the occasional dry river wash. Soon they turned onto a winding dirt road that carried them into a small valley. Coming over a rise, Ryder began picking out specific landmarks.

To the left of the vehicle were some battered buildings; beyond them, some barren hills. To the right there was a large open field with a jagged line of cliffs behind. In front of him was a gradually sloping valley floor and a potholed runway.

He knew this place quite well. He'd been deployed here just a year before during his first tour inside War Heaven.

It was called Spookbase.

Puny by War Heaven standards, Spookbase was little more than the one battered runway; the three dilapidated Quonset-style hangars, and a ramshackle operations building. He'd spent some of the most terrifying moments of his life here—and some of the most exhilarating ones, too.

"My home away from home," he told Moon dryly.

"It hasn't been active since you guys left," Moon replied "We were able to slip in an odd little training mission to cover your presence here. We figured this was as good a place as any to operate."

They pulled up to the front of the ops building and climbed out of the vehicle. There were several ground-crew types moving around, all wearing the same sand camouflage uniform as Ryder.

"None of these guys is hip to what's going on," Moon told him quietly. "You'll just have to go along with the mission we've conjured up and wait for something to happen. The sooner the better, of course . . ."

"Yeah, great," Ryder said, looking around the desolate airstrip. "And just what is this mission?"

"I'll show you," Moon replied.

They walked over to the first hangar, which was chained and padlocked shut. Ryder could detect the telltale odor of jet fuel coming from underneath the hangar doors. It smelled particularly sweet.

Was this a tip-off that something could be salvaged from this gloomy iconoclastic task? Was there a hot-shot F-22 or F-23 ATF waiting for him behind the corrugated steel doors? Or maybe an aircraft completely different—like a small ramjet-powered fighter or an invisible, supersonic Stealth craft?

He waited impatiently as Moon worked the lock. Finally, the key turned and the padlock snapped open. Moon drew the chains out and, with one great lunge, set the rolling doors opening.

Ryder took one look and couldn't believe his eyes.

There was no sophisticated ATF inside, or a ramjet speed-demon or a new, super-invisible Stealth fighter. Inside was nothing more than a well-worn, somewhat battered F-4 Phantom, painted in Vietnam-era green camouflage and wearing the insignia of the Tennessee Air National Guard.

Moon read his reaction right away and managed a final thin, lopsided smile.

"Good to have you back, Colonel," he said.

8

Eighty miles from Spookbase, one hour later

The mud-splattered civilian-type Jeep Cherokee made its way up the winding, narrow road, all four of its tires struggling to get traction on the loose, sandy gravel.

The well-worn road got steeper as it ran up to the top of the small ridge, and the extreme angle, combined with the softness of the roadbed itself, had spelled doom for many a transmission in the past four and half decades. Still, the Jeep pressed on, slowly creeping upward, its clutch smoking madly, its forward progress measured in inches.

It was almost 1545 hours—three forty-five in the afternoon—and the Nevada sun was at last beginning to wane. The temperature across the weapons range was slowly dropping into the more manageable eighties. The Jeep's driver was bathed in sweat, though—he'd been on the road for nearly six hours, having left Las Vegas shortly after ten that morning. A six-hour return trip awaited him, but at least it would take place in the cooler temperatures of the desert night.

Once again he was amazed how well his passenger had endured the long, hot, and dusty drive up from Vegas. She looked as cool, calm, and collected as ever. *How does she do it?* he'd asked himself over and over, never daring to put the question to her directly. *How can anyone not sweat in this heat?*

She had spent the time as always, reading fashion magazines, drinking Evian water from the bottle, and ignoring him whenever possible. He'd been taking her on these weekly trips for almost a year now, yet he doubted that she even knew his first name. Not that it made a difference. Things had been tense between them for months.

He had developed a mighty crush on her early on, around the second month or so. And who could blame him? She was absolutely stunning: very early twenties, fair skin, a great little body, red hair with a streak of blonde running through it.

But like everything else in the desert, the infatuation quickly evaporated—especially after she'd turned down his amateurish proposition cold. In that embarrassing moment, he realized she wasn't interested in love and romance. Not when it was her business to *simulate* the same. After that first rebuff, he knew he was destined to be her driver and nothing more.

The Cherokee finally gained the upper hand on the gravel road and soon reached the top of the ridge. Turning left, the driver followed a more benign pathway down into a slight dip and then back up toward the jagged overhanging cliff that marked the southern end of the plateau. Here the sun was blazing bright again; the shadows themselves seemed to be sizzling. It made no difference to the driver—he had at least four hours to relax before the return trip commenced.

His passenger, on the other hand, still had her work ahead of her.

They turned the last corner and finally reached their destination: an unusual structure located precariously close to the edge of the cliff.

The house—if it could be called that—looked like an architect's nightmare. One section, the oldest, was a large well-worn log cabin, which dominated the base of the dwelling. It was the eight separate attachments—additions put on over the last forty-five years or so—that gave the place its bizarre appearance. One addition was built entirely of glass, its windows crammed with hundreds of green plants, ferns, and cacti. Another was constructed in white cement and rose like a tower guarding the southern approach. Another looked like it belonged on the back of a beach house—sliding glass doors and a teakwood sun deck, with a half-dozen strings of gaudy, multicolored party lights that had been in style back in the 1950s.

Still another addition was almost mosquelike in appearance.

Built of intricately smoothed stucco, with blue, gold, and green tiles laid in, its candy-kisser-shaped dome would more likely be found in Dhahran than Nevada. Almost in an effort of equal religious representation, the addition to its immediate right was nothing less than a board-for-board reconstruction of a tiny wedding chapel, similar to those that dominated downtown Las Vegas.

The sixth addition anchored the back end of the house and it was built of plain drab cement, featured no windows, no fancy attachments. It looked like a fallout shelter built aboveground. Additions seven and eight were actually added side by side to the top floor of the original log cabin. Both looked like elaborate tree houses, each one held up by sturdy telephone-pole supports covered in desert scrub vines. Atop of one of these towers was a baffling array of TV satellite dishes.

Its official name was "Casa Fantastica," really loose Spanish for Crazy House. Its nickname, though, was "Close to the Edge," an apt description of both its design and the person who lived within. The Jeep driver had seen this place once a week for the past year, yet it never failed to amaze and amuse him. Even in a place like War Heaven, where the unusual was the norm, the strange building close to the edge of the cliff stood out as the strangest item of all.

He parked the Jeep and shut off its engine. The passenger gave herself a spray of perfume, adjusted her tight jeans, and climbed out of the Jeep.

"Anything going in?" she asked.

"No, not this time." the driver replied.

She took a deep breath of the still-heated air and sighed. "I'll be out by seven, I hope . . ."

The driver leaned back and stretched. "Enjoy yourself," he said slyly.

She grabbed her suitcase, gave him a "fuck you" look, and headed for the dwelling's front door.

There were three security devices arrayed to the left of the massive steel-reinforced oak door: a thumbprint analyzer, a retina analyzer, and a voice-identification system. The woman pressed her thumb against the appropriate glass panel. It beeped instantly. She then put her left eye up against the periscope-type device, and it too beeped almost immediately. Finally, she recited a seven-digit number into the nearby boom microphone. Five seconds later, she could hear the electronic locks on the massive door click open.

It was dark inside today, the only light being generated from the two dozen color TV sets that dominated the far wall of the main hallway. Each TV set was tuned to a different channel. As always, sports shows dominated the barrage of flickering screens, though there were a few news programs in evidence, as well as several science shows. Beneath each TV was a VCR, grinding away, taping the particular broadcast above, but she knew the chances of any of the tapes ever being played back and viewed were close to nil.

Next to the bank of TV screens was a large personal computer whose own screen was flashing various forms of betting information on such things as horse racing, jai alai, and baseball games. To the left of the computer was a telephone receiver placed securely into a modem. She didn't understand the particulars, but she *did* know that this elaborate setup was electronically sending preprogrammed wagers over the phone lines to a private betting club up near Reno.

"Are you here?" she called out.

There was no reply.

She walked toward the middle of the main hall where a line of bookshelves stood like huge dominoes. The shelves did not contain books. Instead they held a massive collection of videotapes—more than five thousand in all. Each one was elaborately color-coded and meticulously labeled with titles like: "First Year Operating Characteristics of the F-101 Engine," "F/A-18 Gear Performance; the First 100 Hours," and "Advanced Avionics for F-117C."

The woman sniffed at the sight of the videotapes. She knew the roll of technical titles actually masked a vast collection of pornographic movies. Some of them were homemade by amateurs. Others came from any one of the dozen or so big X-rated video mail-order houses. Many more of them had been produced overseas. She had viewed a number of the selections on several occasions, but for some reason, they always made her feel uneasy.

"Is anyone home?" she called, again to no reply.

A peek into the mini-mosque found it empty—so too the small chapel, although she could tell the dozens of lilies that enveloped the place had been watered recently. She walked back into the main hall through the rambling, somewhat-untidy work area. A Macintosh PC stood ready for word processing atop a grand computer table, but significantly no printer was attached to it. A glance of the Mac's screen revealed the beginning verses of yet another original prayer: *"Oh, Heavenly Father. You, Who are the Fire of the Desert . . ."*

She turned right, into the library. It held only about a hundred books, as well as a few authentically technical videos. But it was the walls of the place that were oddly fascinating. They were covered with photos, more than two hundred in all. Each one was expensively framed, deliberately hung. Each one depicted the same person: Albert Einstein.

The woman stopped to look at two new additions to the gallery. One showed Einstein shaking hands with FDR; the other showed him wielding a brightly chromed shovel, obviously as part of some ground-breaking ceremony. What always struck the woman as funny about all the photos was Einstein's hair. Though at first glance it seemed unruly and unattended, it looked *exactly* the same in every one of the photographs, almost as if the late genius had set it and brushed it that way.

She walked on through the concrete bunker addition, and stopped to study the vast quantity of prescription bottles that were stored on several tables there. Many of them were bodily-function-inducing agents. Others were for the treatment of high blood pressure, angina, calcium deficiencies. One table was devoted to barbiturates, though, and the woman took a sample pill from several bottles. Another table held only amphetamines, and she likewise took one pill from about a half dozen bottles.

Putting the pills into her well-worn pill case, she walked down into the beach house addition and finally dropped her suitcase next to the spiral staircase that led up into one of the towers.

"Are you here or not?" she called out with some exasperation.

She heard a rustling at the top of the stairs and then saw the thin, wrinkled face of the man looking down the well at her. He was in his late sixties. His thinning gray hair was long and pulled back into a pony tail. His face showed the beginnings of yet another beard. He was dressed, as always, in a clean but tattered U.S. Army uniform and worn-out sneakers.

"What did you say?" he asked, his mischievous voice slightly raspy but still displaying a warm Texas accent.

She looked up at him as if he were a petulant child.

"I said, 'Are you here or not?' "

His weak, sad smile revealed a set of yellowed teeth.

"I'm *always* here," he replied.

9

New Mexico

The campfire was roaring by the time the food was put on.

Ten pieces of boned chicken, a half dozen beef steaks, and some kind of odd vegetarian "sausage" were skewered between pink onions and green tomatoes and crackling just above the mesquite-fueled flames.

"Smells wonderful, doesn't it?" someone asked.

"Just like the old days," came the reply, "except for the sausage . . ."

Maureen had to agree. The campfire. The darkened hills. The howling coyotes. The rustling wind. It was all very authentically Old West. Except the sausage.

It hadn't taken her long to convince the archaeologists that she was an amateur hiker and indeed lost and low on supplies. Relieved that no one in the digging party recognized her, she so expertly played confused for several hours that by early afternoon, the concerned archaeologists had invited her to spend the night with them. She had quickly accepted, of course.

Maureen was the first person they'd seen since setting up camp two weeks before. Once it was settled that she'd be with them for the night, she was able to engage several of them in some "innocent" conversation.

Though absolutely silent on exactly what they were digging for—and Maureen was careful not to press the question directly— the members confirmed that they were all from the University of Chicago and that they'd been planning this particular dig for three years. The majority of this time had been spent quietly trying to get funding for the project. It had proved to be a difficult task, for this was not the usual broken-pot-and-arrowhead expedition.

Maureen never let on what she knew about them: That this was the first major dig for many of them, and that there was a lot of security surrounding the project. She knew each of the five professors and seven graduate students had been selected from a pool of about a hundred on the basis of two criteria: their knowledge of archaeology and their ability to keep their mouths shut. She knew each member had also gone through an extensive background check. Anyone with relatives in the military, federal service, the legal profession, or the media would not be allowed to go.

She also knew that the ramifications of what would happen should the wrong people learn about the dig had been upmost in the minds of the organizers.

But fourteen days out in the wilds of New Mexico had tempered their xenophobia a bit—thus the invitation for Maureen to stay the night.

It was quite clear, however, that though they were polite, many of the diggers were still quietly suspicious of her motives. Damsels in distress found wandering in the desert usually meant trouble, and it was obvious that despite the outward friendliness, the archaeologists were a tight-knit, tight-lipped group.

And this had to change if Maureen's mission was to succeed.

So as soon as the food was taken off the roaring fire and distributed, she decided it was time for an old-fashioned truth session.

She waited until everyone had their plate of food in front of them and the jugs of ice water had been passed around. Then she took a single bite of chicken, washed it down with a slug of water, and rose up on her knees.

"I have a confession to make," she announced rather suddenly, "I wasn't just hiking out here on the range. I was actually looking for you . . ."

Several of the dig members dropped their plates in surprise and anger. Whispers of "I knew it!" flew around the campfire.

"I'm a journalist," Maureen pressed on, "and I heard about your expedition from a friend. I did some investigating and . . . well, here I am."

The grumbling around the fire became more heated.

The leader of the group was the senior professor, named Dr. Ernie Pascullo. Verbose, friendly, and fairly well-known in his own academic circles, he had told Maureen earlier that he'd been wanting to dig in this particular spot for more than fifteen years.

Now Dr. Ernie was very upset with her.

"We didn't invite a member of the press for a specific reason," he said heatedly. "And that was, we didn't want to turn this into a circus."

Maureen cringed at his rebuke; there was little evidence of the former politeness in the man's voice.

"I can assure you I have no intention of doing that," Maureen told them. "But I *do* know you might have an interesting story here. I think it's important to tell it properly . . ."

"Is your name even really Maureen?" asked Dr. Ernie's first assistant, a pretty brunette woman named Vanessa.

"Yes, it is. Maureen O'Brien."

"Oh, no . . ." a voice on the other side of the fire said. *"I told you she looked familiar*—she's the one that's been all over the TV . . ."

"Damn, this whole thing is blown now," came another anonymous comment.

"She'll have a camera crew here by the morning!"

"No, I won't . . ." Maureen interjected emphatically.

"But how can we believe you now?" Dr. Ernie asked. "You've misrepresented yourself . . ."

"I didn't," she protested. "Not really . . ."

This was not going well. Maureen could feel the anger building around the campfire. No one was eating their meals. No one was drinking their water.

She stood up for effect. "Look, if I had wanted to do a big exposé, I would have come here with a dozen helicopters filled with stuff," she explained.

"They could be hiding right over the hill," Vanessa said. "Or waiting to drop down on us at any moment . . ."

"No, *please,"* Maureen pleaded with them. "I'm not that type of journalist, no matter what you might have heard. I don't cut and slash and then move on. I'm looking for small stories that have potential to become big ones. *Important* ones. That's what I think is happening here. Don't you want this all to be told correctly?"

An uneasy silence fell over the diggers. Maureen hadn't expected it to be smooth going, but at the moment, she had no idea which way the crowd was going to turn. Not only was no one eating their well-deserved meal, but the second helping was burning to a crisp over the fire. She suddenly felt ashamed, like someone who had crashed a very, very private party.

"I can't force myself upon you," she continued, kneeling back down and taking a token bite of her meal, hoping the gesture would ease things. "But I will promise you this: If you allow me to stay, I will report on what you find here as accurately and as truthfully as possible. I don't want to pat myself on the back, but I'm not some vampire from the *Enquirier* or from a tabloid TV show. I work for the *Washington Post*, one of the most prestigious newspapers in the country. It's read by anyone who is anybody in Washington, from the President on down. *They'll believe what I report.*

"And I ask you again: Isn't that what you want? Credibility?"

There was a chorus of grumbling and murmuring around the smoke and flames. She sensed that it wasn't quite as angry as a few moments before.

"Besides," she went on, continuing to build her case, "The one way you can be sure that I *don't* leak all of this is to keep me here—right?"

Now all discussion stopped as her statement began to sink in. It was a slightly underhanded declaration, but she felt the tide was turning her way.

"We really have little choice," Vanessa said finally. "You're forcing us to take you at your word."

"I promise you that if you do, I won't screw you," Maureen said sincerely. "I mean that . . ."

People began eating again, and someone rescued the second course from the fire.

"What the hell," someone called out between bites. "Let her stay. We might need the publicity at some point."

Dr. Ernie asked for a show of hands. The quick count looked unanimous.

"Do you have any archaeological experience at all?" Ernie asked her.

"Took two semesters of it in college," Maureen replied happily.

"And I've done digs at Gettysburg and Antietam."

"Well, we're not digging for musket balls out here," Dr. Ernie replied. "You realize that if we find what we're looking for, it could change everything. And I mean *everything*. Religion. Physics. All of world history."

"I know that," Maureen told them. "Believe me, I know . . ."

10

Spookbase

Ryder gunned the F-4's twin engines and began a long slow taxi to the end of the battered, cracked runway.

He'd never flown a Phantom before—most of them were being phased out of front-line service even before he joined the Air Force. Damn, they were being retired even before he was old enough to drive a car!

He knew it was bad luck to bitch about any airplane he was about to fly—but he couldn't help himself. The F-4 wasn't known as "Rhino" for nothing. It was big, heavy, and drove like a dump truck. Its upturned wingtips and downturned stabilizers made it look very, *very* ugly. Like someone had slammed the hangar doors on it—not once, but twice. Its success against Soviet-built MiGs during the Vietnam War was attributed more to its durability and superior climb rate than to its speed, nimbleness, or sleekness. And even these factors didn't work all the time—that's what bothered him the most. His own father had been shot down over Hanoi in 1967. He had been flying an F-4 at the time.

Ryder finally reached the end of the runway and went through his preflight instrument checks. The Phantom's twin engines were rumbling so much that his rear end was numb from the vibration. Whiffs of exhaust and fuel fumes had already infiltrated into the cockpit and were even leaking in through his mask.

What a shitbox, he thought.

He had a brief conversation with the Spookbase control tower, which was little more than a two-story wooden building overcrowded with old radios and outmoded radar gear. His takeoff wouldn't happen until after sundown, still ten minutes away. So he had little to do but sit back and try to work some blood circulation back into his paralyzed assbone.

Moon was long gone, of course. He'd left Ryder standing at the hangar staring at the beat-up F-4. He had said little more about the quixotic mission facing Ryder, other than that the pilot should keep a low profile, complete his forthcoming orders, and wait for the ISC to make their move.

No sooner had Moon's Hummer disappeared over the hill when a C-130 Hercules began circling Spookbase. It came in for landing and disgorged a thirty-six-man ground-support unit, under the command of an Air Force captain named Norton. The young black officer carried with him orders for the operation of Spookbase for the next three weeks. They called for the majority of his men to get various and outmoded equipment up and running at the small base and to prepare the F-4 for flight. Meanwhile a twelve-man contingent would take to the nearby hills and activate the string of Zoot SAM sites located there.

This was all done in a quick and efficient manner by Norton's men despite the obvious disadvantages inherent at the isolated base.

The officer also carried orders for Ryder. They called for him to fly a series of routine "night intercept" flights against a squadron of Aggressor aircraft deployed nearby.

Just why he was flying a Phantom marked with the insignia of the Tennessee Air National Guard he didn't know, and neither did Norton. Neither did they have a clue why the rear seat of the Rhino had been yanked out (it usually housed a radar-and-weapons officer) and replaced with a spare fuel tank.

Whatever the reason, Ryder knew he had to put these things on the back burner for now. What lay ahead was just a job: takeoff, intercept the incoming numerically-superior Aggressors, put up a fight, and then fly back. Trying to figure out if it had anything to do with his overall mission was useless.

The next ten minutes were excruciatingly slow. He checked his flight instruments over and over, just for something to do. His engines were still rumbling but right, his avionics were all lit green, and the Zoot weapons—a Zoot nose cannon and four Zoot

Sidewinders—were triggered and ready.

"Tower to Spook Flight . . ." his radio finally crackled. It was Norton. "You are now cleared for takeoff . . ."

"Roger, Tower," Ryder acknowledged, getting his mind back on the matter at hand. "Do you have intercept coordinates?"

"Negative, Spook Flight," came Norton's reply, "Your on-board radar systems will have to provide these coordinates."

Ryder received a brief weather-condition report and then signed off to the tower. He took a few deep gulps of the bad-tasting oxygen, popped his brakes, and pushed his throttles to maximum takeoff power.

A few seconds later, he was rumbling down the bumpy runway.

The four F-15 Aggressor aircraft tightened up their four-abreast battle formation and leveled off at 5000 feet above the darkened desert.

These airplanes were from the toughest Aggressor unit on the Range—the hated Tango Squadron. One indication of Tango's preeminence was that they alone among the half dozen Aggressor squadrons within the Range drove souped-up, specially-adapted F-15X Eagles. Painted black and resembling, to some degree, a cross between a Soviet-built MiG-29 Fulcrum and the Su-27 Flanker, these F-15s represented the dominating bird of prey in the skies above War Heaven, right down to their Soviet Air Force Red Star markings.

Their simulated target—the one-runway airfield known as Spookbase—was now a mere thirty-two miles ahead. Already, their threat-warning devices were beginning to key in on the radar waves emanating from the string of Zoot SAM sites that ringed the high country around Spookbase. On the flight leader's signal, each pilot snapped on his aircraft's ECM pod, the high-tech electronic countermeasures device that was used to scramble the survellience radars on the antiaircraft missile batteries.

The Aggressor formation had two tasks ahead of it. The Zoot SAM sites would provide targets for two of the F-15s, specifically ships Tango Three and Tango Four. They were carrying Zoot versions of the HARM missile, a powerful antiradiation weapon that keyed in on the enemy radar beams.

71

The plan called for Tangos Three and Four to go in first and take out as many of the Zoot SAMs as possible. This would clear the way for Tangos One and Two to come in at low altitude and bombard the base with far more insidious weapons.

Among the many military units mustering in and out of War Heaven, the Aggressor squadrons were by far the most disliked. The reason for this was simple: Of all the players in the immense, multibillion-dollar, ongoing war game, only the Aggressors carried weapons that could actually cause physical harm.

These were the gas bombs. The Aggressors had access to six types in all. The most widely used was called supertears, and as its name suggested, it was a particularly pungent form of tear gas. Second most prevalent were the stink bombs, a high-tech, pumped-up, air-deliverable version of the joke-shop capsules loved by adolescent pranksters everywhere.

Then came the crabs, an airburst, airborne skin irritant that was many times more vexing as its *insectum* namesake. Puke-gas bombs were self-explanatory. Z-gas bombs carried a powerful sleep-inducing agent. Finally there was the much-despised, but sparsely used Hal-Lou gas. One good whiff could cause terrifying hallucinations.

Tango One and Tango Two were both carrying one canister of supertears and one canister of puke gas apiece, as well as a full array of Zoot air-to-air missiles and a fully loaded Zoot cannon. Besides hauling the Zoot HARMs, Three and Four were also packing holographically generated antiaircraft missiles and cannons.

"Ten miles to target," the Aggressor's flight leader called over the radio. "Initiate combat formation now . . ."

On cue, Tangos Three and Four broke away from the four line and streaked up to 10,000 feet, kicking in their powerful afterburners as they did so. At the same moment, the pilots of Tangos One and Two reduced their airspeed to a subsonic crawl and began a long slow sweep to the west.

Tangos Three and Four quickly reached 10,000 feet. At this point, Tango Three became the flight leader.

"Arm all weapons," he called over to Four, at the same time snapping on his own arming switches. He immediately heard the reassuring whir of the holograph generator batteries beginning

72

to charge up. Within seconds, all of his Zoot weapons were ready to fire.

"I am total 'green,' " was the message from his wingman, Tango Four. "All weapons armed and charged."

"Roger, Four," the leader replied. "Let's go . . ."

The two black F-15s tightened up their formation and then put their aircraft into textbook attack dives, heading for Spookbase's Zoot SAM sites.

But suddenly every light inside Tango Four's cockpit blinked on and began flashing furiously. An instant later, there was a bright flash off the airplane's right wing, the intensity of which nearly blinded the pilot.

"Jesuzz! *What was that?*"

With frozen hands he instinctively yanked back on the F-15's control stick and applied throttle. But the airplane did not respond. Instead its flight computer reduced the jet's airspeed to barely 200 knots, leveled it out at 7500 feet, and put it in a slow turn back toward its home base. It also disarmed all of the plane's weapons.

It had all happened in the matter of a few seconds, but the fun was over for the pilot of Tango Four. He'd just been blasted by a Zoot Sidewinder.

"Damn it!" the pilot yelled into his microphone, breaking a long-standing regulation against obscenities on the air that still applied in War Heaven. *"Where did that come from?"*

His now-solitary flight leader did not reply. He was too busy putting his own airplane through a series of wild maneuvers in an attempt to avoid meeting the same embarrassing fate as his erstwhile partner.

As he was spinning through the night sky, the Tango leader pilot managed to switch his highly advanced look-up/look-down radar detection unit from homing in on ground signals to those emanating from airborne threats. Immediately a large blip appeared on his tracking screen, one that appeared to be in front and high above him.

He quickly checked the arming switches on his Zoot Sidewinders. There was a Spookbase interceptor out there, somewhere, and unless he was neutralized, the attack on the Zoot SAM batteries—as well as the target base itself—would become a very hazardous thing indeed.

After leveling out at 3000 feet, the Tango Three pilot glanced back at his radar scope. It was empty.

Where the hell did he go?

He tightened the focus on his radar screen and just by chance saw the faintest blip streak by in a highly unusual manner across the sweep field.

"Damn . . ." he whispered. "He's diving . . . Going down like a rock . . ."

The enemy pilot was losing altitude so quickly that the F-15's detection radar could barely get a reading on him. Just then an odd jolt ran through the Tango Three pilot. He suddenly realized that he recognized the somewhat reckless but usually effective maneuver.

Could it be?

As he watched the enemy blip fall off his screen completely, he quickly put his own plane into a screaming climb, intent on putting as much distance as possible between himself and the mysterious interceptor.

The pilots of Tangos One and Two had been watching the drama above them with growing trepidation.

Both knew the anticipated tidy air strike on Spookbase was now an impossibility. Not only was the runway's antiaircraft protection ring still intact, but the base personnel were no doubt alerted to their impending approach and had probably taken cover by now.

But the bombing raid would have to continue. Success or failure inside War Heaven was based on the system of points earned by the engaging forces: the better the operation, the more points a unit received. More points meant more supplies of food, fuel, and Zoot ammunition needed to sustain the unit and allow it to attack again. A string of successful attacks meant a largesse of booty for the Aggressors, a traditional state of affairs for them, as in many ways the rules were stacked in their favor.

Even dropping one of their gas bombs would result in some points and, to a degree, would prevent any lasting damage on the Tango Aggressor pilots' substantial reputation.

"Switch to Delay One strike plan . . ." Tango One radioed to

Tango Two. "I'll go in first . . ."

The Delay One plan was simple. Instead of both F-15s roaring over the Spookbase at the same time—a good idea if the Zoot SAMs had been suppressed—they would go over in a staggered fashion, Tango One about sixty seconds ahead of Tango Two. The chances of inflicting the most damage were reduced by this plan, but so were the chances of being bagged by a Zoot SAM.

Of course, there was still the problem of the Spookbase's guardian angel.

Tango One kicked in his afterburner and brought the F-15 down to 600 feet. Flying that low could be hazardous in this part of the desert, especially at night. But the F-15X was especially good at low-level flight due to its various terrain guidance/avoidance gear. So the Tango One pilot had done this many times before, under all conditions.

He switched on his target indicator display and powered up his Pave-Penny laser range finder. Once released, the lightweight gas canisters would be guided down the laser beam to the target, courtesy of the laser-activated guidance system in their nose cones.

He then switched over to his main situation display and called up his FLIR—the forward-looking infrared device. Instantly a thermal image of Spookbase materialized before his eyes. Nothing was moving anywhere in the field of his infrared vision. Prewarned, the base was locked up tight.

One mile away from the target, he reduced his speed by a third and zeroed his laser beam onto the largest structure at the base— the battered ops building. He was sure that the majority of Spooks were huddled in there, hoping the sealed windows and prevailing winds would spare them from whatever dropped out of the sky.

At a half mile out, he locked the laser beam onto the target and pushed the prerelease/ready button for his canister of supertears. Another button pressed, and operation of the jet was taken over by the main flight computer. If everything was right, the computer would carry him directly over the target, launch the gas bomb at the precise moment, and then exit the F-15X out of the area by the safest and most expeditious means.

But everything wasn't right . . .

Just seconds before the supertears canister was to be automatically released, a large, hulking shadow flashed in front of him.

"Christ!" Tango One pilot yelled, making it two radio violations for the mission in as many minutes.

He kicked out the main computer in a heartbeat and instinctively put the F-15X into a stomach-crunching climb. The next thing he knew, he was heading straight up at the nearly full moon above him.

And outlined in silouette against the moon was the nightmarish shape of an F-4 Phantom, coming directly at him.

The pilot of Tango Two, trailing his leader by about five miles, saw the brilliant Zoot flash directly to his south.

He immediately switched on his helmet mike.

"Tango One! Tango One! *Hostile* fire . . ."

There was no immediate reply.

"Tango One, what is your condition?"

Still nothing.

"Tango One . . . are you still battle-worthy?"

His radio crackled a second later.

"That's a negative, Tango Two . . ." came the rushed, sullen reply. "I'm back to base the short way . . . I think."

Tango Two couldn't believe what he was hearing. Tango One was the most experienced pilot in his unit. And he had just been taken out no more than 2500 feet—or mere seconds—from the target. He doubted anything even close to that had ever happened to Tango One before.

Still, Tango Two had to press on.

He began switching on his own attack systems: Pave-Penny FLIR and laser-beam generator. He also rechecked his Zoot cannon. The problem was, he couldn't attack the base and defend himself at the same time. If he went in low, and along the same flight path as Tango One, he might soon be taking the humiliating short way back to the base himself. But to postpone the attack and search for the Spookbase's aerial defender would also waste time, fuel, and possibly kill the mission altogether.

He was just fifteen miles out now. He yanked back on his throttles and slowed his speed, giving him more time to think. He switched over to his air-defense radar but saw no sign of the interceptor. This only deepened his concern.

At ten miles to target, he hit upon an idea. Switching off his elaborate laser targeting devices, he pulled back on the control stick and kicked in his afterburner. Inside of ten seconds he was approaching Spookbase at 1000 feet and pulling full military power.

His improvised plan was to flash over the small airstrip at top speed, and eyeball both his gas canisters somewhere within its perimeter. Then, in a surprise move that might key some extra points, he would strafe the nearest Zoot SAM battery on his pullout with his holographic cannon. Should the Spook plane get in his way anywhere along the line, he could at least engage him with the readied nose gun.

Just as with his flight leader, Tango Two had confidence in his plan. What he didn't take into account was that the Spookbase's interceptor might show up in the least likeliest of positions. That was, directly behind him.

How'd he get there?

None of his cockpit warning devices had time to flash when the Spook plane sent a stream of Zoot cannon shells rocketing by him. The F-15 pilot twisted in his seat just enough to get a fleeting glimpse of the enemy plane's navigation lights flying less than 500 feet off the end of his tail.

This guy is nuts, the Tango Two pilot thought, realizing for the first time that his adversary was a hulking Phantom. He quickly yanked back once again on his control stick in an effort to put some much-needed altitude between him and the dangerously tailgating Spook plane.

He looked back and saw that the enemy pilot was coming right up the pipe with him.

Damn . . .

He had allowed himself to get into one of the few situations in which the Phantom had the advantage—a straight-up climb.

Tango Two took the Phantom's Zoot Sidewinder like a man. It flashed right by him on his left, the brilliance of the holographic explosion stinging his eyes for a moment.

Within seconds the majority of his cockpit lights began blinking out. The F-15's main flight computer took command of the airplane, leveling it out in a rather rough fashion and jamming on the brakes at the same time. Now a clock began ticking. The Tango Two pilot could do little but sit back and have the computer fly him home. The short way.

The only bright spot was that he'd have some time to figure what to tell the guys back at the base.

Ryder was sucking on his oxygen mask like crazy.

His heart was already pounding right out of his flight suit; with each gulp of Big O, the rate nearly doubled.

He hadn't pumped this much adreneline in a year, and the rush was both exhilarating him and quite possibly killing him. He was bathed in sweat and suddenly his helmet felt two sizes too small. *Damn, he loved this kind of stuff.*

He'd love it even more if it didn't kill him first.

He checked his fuel and weapons load. Both were half full. And there was still one last F-15 Aggressor out there.

He continued the straight-up climb until he reached the grand height of 35,000 feet. He leveled off and went into a tight circle. Finding the remaining Aggressor craft was number one on his list, but he couldn't help but take a moment to gaze out at the nighttime landscape of War Heaven.

It had a frightening beauty of its own. From this vantage point he could see the halos of blue and green light of the bigger Fitzies scattered among the hills and valleys all along the desert. They looked like a haphazard string of amusement-park rides that stretched as far as the eye could see.

Most of them were absolutely buzzing with the distinctive flashes of Zoot explosions—missiles or guided munitions going in, Zoot SAMs and simulated AA fire coming out. Some of these battles were tremendous. And there were so many of them, he realized how insignificant his little scrape was by comparison.

No matter. Big battles were won on individual merit, too. He tipped the F-4 over and began a steep dive back toward Spookbase.

Time to get that fourth notch on his belt.

He guessed that the lone Aggressor would have abandoned the idea of an attack directly on the base by this time and would instead be concentrating on taking out a Zoot SAM battery or two and then scooting for home.

Ryder flipped on the Phantom's massive but by-no-means-state-of-the-art air-search radar and began probing even as he was screeching toward the darkened earth. He saw that half of the six Zoot SAM sites had their radars running hot. This gave him the tip he needed.

The radar operators would never have the hot dishes turned on unless they were under threat of immediate attack. After all, the Aggressors' main anti-SAM weapon—the HARM—homed in on hot radars. The question was, could Ryder get to the remaining F-15 before the F-15 could get to the Zoot SAM site?

He was back down to 5000 feet in seconds, pulling the F-4 up in a series of quick jerks that nearly cracked his rib cage in two, yet served to put him in a fighting position quicker than a slower, more gradual pullout would have done.

Suddenly he found himself coming right up on Spookbase itself, approaching from the southeast, with the ridge line containing the Zoot SAMs almost directly ahead. He altered his course slightly and pulled his Zoot cannon arming switch.

Just then there was a bright Zoot flash at the far end of the ridge. A secondary blue flash told everyone within eyesight that the Zoot SAM site had been destroyed.

"Dammit!" Ryder yelled, lucky that his lip mike was turned off. "There goes the no-hitter . . ."

He was even more determined to get the F-15 now. He twisted the F-4 toward the stricken Zoot SAM and was roaring over it a few seconds later. He then turned back west and climbed, trying to mimic what he thought would be the enemy pilot's flight path. Yet when he scanned the sky in front of him, he found it empty.

Had the F-15 Aggressor called it quits and headed for home? He doubted it. That was just not the Aggressors' way. Would he now come back around and try for an attack on the base? Even a token strafing would help save the Aggressors' mission from being complete disaster. But once again, Ryder doubted it. If the F-15 could knock out one or even two more Zoot SAM sites, then referees who were watching the battle from ground level—called Zebras, they were everywhere—might allow the Aggressors to conduct a follow-up strike.

Therefore, he streaked out and around and came in over the

second lit-up Zoot SAM site. A wag of wings—or actually his running lights—transmitted a message the savvy Zoot SAM crew understood. They quickly blinked their radars off, sat back, and waited. Their fate was now in the hands of their guardian angel.

The battle was quickly joined. The F-15 streaked out of the night and sent a barrage of Zoot cannon shells raining down on where he thought the Zoot SAM battery was located. As it was, the stream of holographic bullets missed the mark only by a few feet, their distinctive red flashes seeming to rip up the rocky terrain on the top of the ridge.

The F-15 passed so close to Ryder's F-4, he could see the outline of the enemy pilot by the light of his cockpit panel. Ryder turned the Phantom over on its back and put himself on the F-15's tail just as he was pulling up to 3500 feet. The Aggressor neatly flipped over in a similar maneuver in an effort to shake Ryder's big Rhino.

The move was partially successful. The F-15 could turn rings around the F-4, and it also had a speed advantage. It took another, more-gut-wrenching turn by Ryder to keep in on the F-15's vunerable six o'clock position.

Not wanting to waste any more time, Ryder let go a stream of Zoot cannon fire into the F-15's tail. He saw some hits, but they were not enough to disable the enemy plane. He let loose another burst, this one longer, more concentrated, his hope being that even if the cannon missed, at least the long blazing fusillade would unnerve his opponent and cause the man to do something stupid.

He didn't. The F-15 pilot simply fell out of the way of the holographic barrage and sent his airplane spinning back toward the ground. Ryder let out a long gasp and yanked the F-4 ass over heels and back onto the Aggressor's tail. He fired another burst; the F-15 just barely got out of the way. They both turned, and the nimbler F-15 came around on his rear end. Now it was Ryder's turn to avoid getting plugged. He did so, and quickly gained the advantage again. Another turn, another burst, another near miss on the F-15.

It went on like this for minutes. Up to heights as high as 36,500 feet and down to toe-curling deck scrapings below 200 feet, the two planes parried, slashed, feinted, and slashed again, all the while firing their Zoot cannons with little more than wild abandon. It was both exhilarating and exhausting—and definitely the longest ACM Ryder had ever participated in. But it seemed that for every move he made, the enemy pilot had a countermove. At the same time, Ryder was just barely escaping the F-15's concentrated attacks.

But Ryder had one ace up his sleeve that the Aggressor pilot did not. The extended dogfight was not only using up ammo on both sides, it was burning up fuel. The difference was that with Spookbase right below him, Ryder didn't have far to go. The F-15 did.

In the end, that fact decided the outcome of the titanic struggle. No pilot worth his salt would bolt such an exciting, *personal* furball, so the F-15 pilot stayed right to the end, fighting on way past his bingo point—the amount of fuel that would have gotten him back to his base safely—knowing that only a kill of the F-4 could salvage anything from the overall dismal Aggressor attack.

Ryder spent several minutes concentrating on being the mouse in this game, and when his own fuel light came on, he felt a weary smile spread across his face. The F-15 was bone-dry by this time. He had little other choice but to land at Spookbase.

Ryder couldn't control himself. He let out a yelp and buzzed the airfield just as the defeated and depleted F-15X was coming in for a landing. The place was all lit up by this time, and the meager contingent quickly surrounded this incredible prize of war as it reluctantly screeched to a halt. He couldn't imagine what a captured Aggressor craft would be worth in points, especially one of the exalted F-15X Tango models. Back during his first tour in War Heaven he and some others had captured an opponent's truck-borne SAM and had been rewarded for hours with drops of ammunition, food, and spare parts.

By this reasoning, they'd be parachuting the rewards in to Spookbase for days.

He made one long final turn, busting over the line of Zoot SAM sites in triumph before touching down on the bumpy airstrip just as his own fuel indicator flashed empty. He rolled the F-4 past the applauding crowd and jerked it to a halt about 100 feet before the F-15.

Quickly shutting down the engines, he was out of the cockpit in a flash. He'd just finished the ride of his life. Now, as he approached the Aggressor's airplane, he didn't know whether to expect a hearty handshake or a punch in the mouth from his defeated opponent. Either way, it really didn't matter. He had just captured an Aggressor warplane. Intact.

He watched the enemy pilot slowly emerge from his aircraft. He was dressed in all black, another part of the psychological edge that Aggressor pilots strutted like cock feathers. Even his helmet was black.

They approached each other now on the lighted tarmac, Ryder walking much faster and with more zip in his step than his opponent. The crowd had gathered a respectable distance away, content to wait and watch what would happen next.

When the two pilots were only about ten feet away, the Aggressor pilot finally paused long enough to remove his intimidating helmet. When he did, and had pushed the matted hair off his forehead, he squinted once and then stared at Ryder. Ryder immediately stopped dead in his tracks.

No, he thought, *it couldn't be . . .*

He took another tentative step forward. The Aggressor pilot did, too.

Ryder couldn't believe it. What were the chances?

The Aggressor pilot was now smiling broadly.

"How you been, partner?" he asked.

For one of the few times in his life, Ryder was authentically speechless.

The other pilot was his old friend, D. J. Woods.

11

Close to the Edge

The Jeep driver checked his watch—it was 2100 hours, nine P.M.

"Christ, what are they doing in there?" he wondered aloud. "A Chinese water torture?"

He lit his third cigarette of the hour and leaned back against the Jeep's windshield. He had passed most of the last few hours just like this, sitting on the hood of his vehicle watching the dozens of simulated, Zoot battles taking place all over War Heaven, as well as above it.

He'd seen action in both Grenada and Panama, and as realistic as the war-game amusement park might have made it seem, he knew there was nothing so horrifying as actual combat. Still, he found the holographic spectacle spread out before him to be perversely fascinating. The reds, blues, and greens shimmering against the night desert sky looked like a grand 1960s-style light show complete with the most massive fireworks display ever assembled.

All in all, it provided him a fair diversion while waiting for his woman passenger to emerge from inside the Casa Fantastica.

But still, he faced another six hours of driving before he would be able to lie down in his own bed again.

"Look at that one! God, the colors are beautiful, aren't they?"

The young woman—her professional name was Angel—ignored the old man's exclamations. They were sitting on the huge couch that dominated the top floor of the glass-room addition to Casa Fantastica. With its sweeping, 360-degree view, they were able to see just about all the huge Zoot explosions and fireworks-type displays going on around them.

She let out a long sigh and refilled her champagne glass. She'd been watching these weird bomb explosions—or whatever the hell they were!—once a week for the past year, and she was bored with them simply because she didn't understand them.

She was more concerned about the health—both physical and mental—of this, her most profitable client. Ever since she'd entered into this strange arrangement at the behest of a secret government agency, the old man's stability had seemed to be deteriorating by the week.

Sometimes he was quite lucid. He was funny, inventive, imaginative, and, despite his age, fairly sexual. At other times, he was quite the opposite. He was dark, moody, near-suicidal, sometimes rambling on for hours about some sort of cosmic nonsense. Booze only intensified the condition. On these occasions, when any kind of sex was out of the question, Angel was relegated to sit and listen to his rantings until he either threw her out or fell asleep.

At first, she'd convinced herself that if it hadn't been for the money—she was being paid $2500 *an hour* by the government—she would have jumped from this train almost immediately.

But over the past few months, she'd found herself becoming more and more involved. She was actually starting to care about the mysterious old man who lived in the strange house, more than anyone in her profession should ever allow themself to do.

And that was the problem.

Some of things he'd told her—in bed, or just sitting and watching the electronic fireworks—were absolutely frightening. They were secrets, top secrets of a nature so critical that on her worst nights she actually feared for her life, knowing that it would be easier for someone to put a bullet in her head than to try and deal with the problem of having a Las Vegas call girl being privy to some things her client claimed not even the President himself knew about.

"Do you want some more champagne?" she asked him, refilling his glass without waiting for a response.

He shifted his frail figure on the large leather couch and continued staring out the huge picture window at the intensifying holographic pyrotechnics on the desert floor below.

"Have I ever told you what my favorite invention is?" he asked her innocently.

Angel rolled her eyes. Yes, he had told her. Many times. But the essence of her job was in knowing when to lie. This was one of those times.

"I'll guess that it's the VCR," she told him, purposely snuggling up closer to him. "Either that or the invention of the X-rated videotape."

He didn't even take the moment to appreciate her oft-repeated joke.

"It's the lightning rod," he explained. "Do you know why?"

She gulped her champagne and quickly poured a refill.

"No," she said, "Tell me, please . . ."

He leaned back and stared at the thick glass ceiling for a moment.

"Before the lightning rod was invented," he began, "anyone who was unlucky enough to have their house or barn hit by lightning was accused of being witches by their neighbors. The prevailing belief was that lightning was actually generated from the fingertip of God, and that whoever's property it hit was being punished for some grievous sin. In some places way back then, people were burned or stoned to death if lightning hit anything they owned. That's how sure everyone was that the Almighty was behind it all – and that He was one vengeful bastard!"

He took a noisy swig of champagne.

"But with just one little thin piece of metal rod – and the idea behind it – all the nonsense about witches and Divine retributions went right out the window. The mighty hand of God was *grounded,* so to speak, both physically and psychically.

"What a grand invention! With one swipe, taking all that power away from the precious Almighty!"

Angel was now finishing off the champagne by drinking it right from the bottle. She'd heard the story so many times she could recite it from memory. She even knew where the man had first heard it all – on a radio lecture given by a famous science-fiction writer, years before.

But even after hearing it so many times, Angel still could not grasp the significance of it, if indeed there was any. She had grown up in L.A. and had lived in big cities all her life. As such, she had never even seen a lightning rod.

There was a particularly bright flash no more than a mile away from the house on the cliff. The attendant boom actually rattled the windows in the glass room.

"That was close!" the man yelped with glee. *"Damn* close!"

Angel took her hands away from her eyes and reached for a fresh bottle of Moët.

"Did I tell you I discovered a new star?" the man suddenly asked her.

"No, you didn't . . ."

"It's true," he said. "It's in the oddest position. Right on top of the moon—like at the twelve o'clock mark. I checked all of my star charts and it's not listed on any of them. I'm surprised—it's so bright, I don't know why no one has ever seen it before."

"Maybe it was just one of these crazy bombs or missiles or whatever they have out here," Angel told him, unwrapping the foil around the cork of the Moët.

"That would be impossible," he replied impatiently. "It's a star. I know it is. And I've already named it . . ."

"Really?" she asked, finally popping the cork on the new bottle of bubbly. "What did you call it?"

He turned and, for the first time in a long time, looked deeply into her eyes. He seemed to be on the verge of tears.

"I named it Angel, of course . . ."

Thirty minutes later, the young woman came out of the strange house and tossed her suitcase into the back of the Jeep.

"Done so soon?" the driver asked her cruelly.

She checked her watch and saw it was 9:45; she'd been on the clock since three. Six and three quarter hours equaled $16,875 for her, before taxes. Still, the thought of all that money in return for relatively little physical work failed to excite her. In some respects, she would have rather earned the money walking the streets or working a ranch.

She climbed into the vehicle and lit a cigarette.

"What do you know about the moon?" she asked the driver, staring up at the huge orange ball that was slowly rising above the desert.

The question caught him off-guard. It was the first conversational question she'd asked him since . . . well, since the "incident."

"I don't know," he replied. "They gave us the day off from school when men first landed on it . . ."

"Does it usually have stars around it?" she asked.

He looked back at her and then at the moon. "Are you kidding?" He laughed. "Look for yourself—it has *billions* of stars around it."

"No, I mean special stars," she pressed. "You know, ones that just stick around the moon, like exclusively."

The driver gunned the vehicle's engine to life.

"I don't know, Angel," he finally admitted, putting the vehicle in gear and heading back down the ridge road. "You're asking the wrong person."

Angel took a long drag on her cigarette, and tried to keep her eyes on the brilliant full moon.

"That's for sure," she said.

12

The sun rose on War Heaven at precisely 0505 hours the next day.

A single all-white Hummer was speeding down a dusty well-worn road, leaving a trail of early morning engine exhaust and dust in its wake. Ryder was at the wheel of the vehicle; D. J. Woods—"Woody" to his friends—was his passenger.

They were heading for the small town, located near the eastern edge of War Heaven, known as Jacks. There wasn't much to the place. A dozen rickety storefronts, all built on the same side of the street, they looked like location props for the movie classic, *Shane*.

In reality, Jacks *was* a closer kin to a movie set than to a "real" town. Exactly who first built it was a secret. The likely suspects included the CIA, the DIA, the NSA, the FBI, the DEA, or possibly some combination thereof. Over the past few years it had, on at least several occasions, been torn down, crated and shipped away, only to be hauled back some time later—a few days or a few months—and reconstructed in exactly the same spot. Why this was done was only known to the people who controlled War Heaven.

There were three main ground units deployed inside the weapons range: the Gray force, which was usually made up of one division of U.S. Army infantry units; the Green force, which usually consisted of two, 3500-man reinforced Marine regiments, plus several special units likes the SEALS; and the Blue force, usually made up of two battalions of crack airborne troops or Special Forces Green Berets. The Aggressor units and the Spooks—whose combined strength rarely numbered more than 150 men—made up the other main teams. At any given moment, on any given day, these units could be involved in tooth-and-nail battles with each other in any part of the vast weapons range. That was the whole idea behind the huge war gaming area, which in square mileage was almost as large as the state of Connecticut.

But the rules changed anytime any of these forces happened to be in the vicinity of Jacks.

Whenever the controllers of War Heaven determined that Jacks should put down stakes, then the surrounding area for exactly one mile around became absolutely neutral. No fighting was permitted within this circle; indeed, no Zoot weapons would function within the zone, and flying over it in a belligerent manner was strictly prohibited. Within this sanctuary, deployed units who would normally be battling each other with frighteningly realistic holographic weapons instead sat together and talked about sports, women, the military, and politics.

No surprise then that while most of the movable town consisted of small warehouses, refrigerated food storage bins, and a small fuel depot, the main building within Jacks was a saloon.

Jacks was also the only place in War Heaven where a soldier could get a cool beer or a hot meal that wasn't made from freeze-dried powder and water. It was also a place where leaders of the opposing forces could discuss "issues of mutual interest," as the diplomats might say.

For Ryder and Woody, the order this morning was to sample as many of the pleasures available at Jacks as humanly possible. First on their list, however, was a meeting with a referee unit captain and the commander of Woody's Aggressor squadron.

If nothing else, Woody's sudden appearance the night before had proved that Moon could still pull some mighty big strings. And fast.

Woody had been on a recruiting mission in Fresno for the Air Force—whipping up crowds by drag-racing National Hot Rod Association funny cars on a runway with a specially adapted F-5—when he was plucked out of a meet by a State Department helicopter.

"The next thing I know," Woody had told him, "I'm dressed in black, got a black helmet, and I'm flying a black F-15X. In the bigshot Tango Squadron. Against you! All in a matter of hours . . ."

From that point on, the strange mission Moon had handed Ryder had become more manageable by a factor of two. He and Woody had worked well together during Distant Thunder; they respected each other's abilities completely, and they had become close friends. His gut told him this would be crucial in the days ahead.

Woody had already gotten the same briefing from Moon: The ISC. Their weird agenda. The mystery of the cracked-up researchers. The ISC's outrageous blackmail threat against the government. Their nuclear bomb. Ryder and Woody had discussed the issue throughout the night, making sure they'd both gotten the story straight. Then, just as the sun was coming up, they'd agreed to keep any further discussion on their *real* mission to a minimum, for fear that the wrong ear—either human or electronic—might hear them.

They'd spent the rest of the time catching up on each other's lives since they last saw each other in the hospital at the U.S. Navy base on Subic Bay in the Philippines. It was there they'd recovered from the wounds sustained at the climax of Distant Thunder. When they were sufficiently healed, they'd both gone on to fairly exotic duty. Ryder as technical adviser for the Hero Pilot movie, and Woody, staging recruiting events like the drag-car race.

But although it had been almost a year since they'd bid farewell over in the Philippines, it seemed like no time had passed at all. Neither had ever expected to reenter War Heaven again—on that they had agreed. Now that they were back in, it seemed like they had never left.

"No offense, Woodman," Ryder told him as the buildings of Jacks finally came into view. "But can you imagine how many points they're going to deal me for capturing you and your hotshot airplane intact?"

"It doesn't bother me," Woody replied. "At least I didn't get shot down like those three other girls . . ."

They finally reached the small rickety town and as always found good parking to be scarce. The tiny street was cluttered with military vehicles ranging from zebra-striped referee jeeps to Gray army APCs to Green army LAVs to Blue army M-1A1 tanks. All of them were parked in the most haphazard fashions, cluttering the street and adding to the overall congestion problem.

"Still haven't got a traffic cop yet," Woody said as they drove through the town twice looking for a space to squeeze the Hummer into. They finally had to settle for a patch of muddy ground behind one of the refrigeration buildings.

"You'll have to wash this baby when you get back," Woody told

Ryder, kicking some of the muck off the Hummer's bumper.

"Maybe I'll get your squadron commander to do it for me," Ryder replied cockily, rightly feeling that he was about to be handed more points than Spookbase had ever been awarded for a single engagement. Maybe a few of them could be spent on an eat-crow car wash by the haughty F-15 Tango gang.

They swaggered into the main saloon, and though it was barely six a.m. the place was full of boisterous, beery soldiers.

"Got any money?" Ryder asked Woody, repeating the most-oft-told joke played on newcomers to the strange little town. The punchline was that just like the PX back at Area 61, no money was needed at Jacks.

They made their way through the crowd and to the bar and ordered two beers from the harried bartender. The beer came a few minutes later, warm and foamy, but acceptable for so early in the morning.

"See your boss anywhere?" Ryder asked Woody.

His partner did a quick scan of the crowded saloon and came back empty.

"Let's try one of the back rooms," he suggested.

They quickly drank their beers and ordered two more. Then they walked around the end of the bar and into the hallway, which led to a series of small private rooms in back.

The first three of these tiny apartments were empty. The fourth, it being a little larger and sporting a slightly better grade of cheap wood paneling, turned out to be the site of their meeting.

They walked in to find four men sitting around a table, drinking coffee and eating doughnuts. Two them were referees. A third was a regular U.S. Air Force colonel looking out of place in a dress uniform. The fourth man—he was sitting at the head of the table, wielding a coffee cup that was bigger than the others—was the commander of Woody's Aggressor unit, the much-ballyhooed Tango Squadron.

"Long? Woods?" the Aggressor officer asked upon seeing them.

"That's us," Ryder beamed, casually swigging his second beer of the early morning. "Hope we're not late . . ."

They walked in and grabbed the two seats nearest the Aggressor commander, who gruffly introduced himself to Ryder simply as "the Boss."

"Little early in the day to be drinking beer, isn't it, gentlemen?" the Boss asked them sternly.

Ryder immediately took a quick measure of the man. He was about fifty-five years old, built like a rolling fireplug with a wiffle cut so close to his skull that he appeared bald. His face wore the same stony expression that many hard-ass military officers strained so hard to perfect: eyes narrowed, brow furrowed, lips tight, nostrils flaring. It was supposed to relay a message of toughness, steely resolve, that kind of no-nonsense-type air.

To Ryder, it signaled that the guy was probably just another gung-ho shithead.

"We're kind of off the clock here, sir," Ryder told him politely. "You know, it's Jacks . . ."

"We have a very critical discussion ahead of us," the Boss fired back at him. "I should think you'd want to be sober for it."

Ryder and Woody quickly finished the beers and filled their glasses with coffee from the nearby pot.

"I assume we're here to discuss the action last night?" Ryder asked the Boss with a grin.

"Exactly, Colonel Long," the Boss replied, his voice sounding even angrier. "I understand you were piloting that Phantom last night?"

Ryder nodded triumphantly.

"Then, explain something to me," the Boss said through gritted teeth. *"What* in hell were you doing?"

Ryder was stunned. What was the problem here?

"I was performing an defensive intercept mission," he replied. "And I gained three planes killed and one . . . well, I guess you'd say one plane captured."

"And I suppose you think you're going to get a ton of points for this performance?" the Boss asked him, his teeth not yet moving an iota.

Ryder just shrugged. "That's the way it works around here, isn't it?"

A leaden silence descended on the room.

"Not exactly," one of the referees said finally. "Not in this case . . ."

Ryder felt a sudden sinking feeling in his stomach.

"I'm missing something here, aren't I?" he asked.

"You were supposed to *lose* that ACM last night," the Boss told him. "Lose it and *lose* it big!"

Ryder narrowed his eyes on the man. He had no idea what rank he was (few officers wore bars or stars in War Heaven), but only an Air Force general could outrank his own colonel status.

"Lose it?" he fired back. "What the hell for?"

"Because that was how it was supposed to be," the Boss replied, blinking slightly at Ryder's aggressive self-defense. "Four F-15s should beat up on an F-4 with no problem. Obviously that didn't happen . . ."

"Obviously," Ryder replied harshly. "And I'll say right now, that if for some reason, as part of one of your little games inside this kiddie park, you need a pilot to go up and start *losing* ACMs, well, you dragged the wrong boy way the hell out here."

A large vein on the Boss's forehead began pulsating furiously.

"Don't try to snow me, Long," he growled. "I just read your file. You're the luckiest bastard flying. By all rights you should be back driving C-130 humpjobs or, better yet, mustered out completely."

Ryder froze. Had the man read his real file? Or the newly sanitized version? Either way, he had to play the bluff.

"Did you read the entire file?" he asked him coolly.

"You mean, did I read about your service during Distant Thunder?" was the Boss's caustic reply, "Yeah, sure, I read it. And I say, no big deal. Okay? *No big deal.* You were brought here for only one reason, Long: You flew here before and you had the clearance. Okay? No heroics. No more grandstanding. You're here to provide training for my squadron. That means losing—a lot. Can you understand that?"

Ryder was astonished. The only thing holding him back from really lashing out at the man was one troubling question: Did this strange behavior have anything to do with Moon's apocalyptic ISC scenario?

"I can understand it," Ryder replied finally. "It's like that team that plays the Harlem Globetrotters all the time. They're paid to lose."

The Boss nodded belligerently. "Exactly, Colonel," he said.

Ryder just looked at Woody, who was rolling his eyes in disbelief.

"Okay, then," he said simply. "If that's the case, I want a transfer out."

"Even if it means going back to flying C-130s?" the regular Air

Force officer asked, speaking for the first time.

Ryder stood firm. "If that's how it has to be, yes," he replied.

Suddenly the Boss jumped up. He reached over toward Ryder and began shaking his hand, a smile a mile wide spreading across his formerly hardened features.

"Congratulations, Colonel," the man said excitedly.

Mystified, Ryder glanced at Woody, who could only shrug back. "Congratulations?" he asked. "What for?"

13

New Mexico

It was almost ten A.M. when Maureen finally woke up.

She was momentarily confused when she first opened her eyes. Her jeans were off and her blouse was undone, leaving her breasts partially exposed. Her bed was small and cramped; its mattress paper-thin. The ceiling—a piece of Formica adorned with gaudy silver stars—was not seven inches above her nose, and it sagged appreciably in the middle. A tiny window was next to her bed, but a small, closed grate prevented her from seeing outside.

It took only a few sleepy moments for her to realize she was sleeping in the upper deck of a truck camper, specifically the one owned by Vanessa, Doctor Ernie's assistant. Maureen had gratefully accepted the young woman's offer to the tiny bed after the long leisurely evening around the campfire had grown cold and the tired archaeology team members began drifting off to their own separate mobiles homes.

She *was* surprised though that she had slept so late. No reporter worth their salt ever slept past six A.M., no matter what time they had to go to work. And yet she had snoozed through four extra hours, an extravagance she hadn't enjoyed since her first year in college.

She quickly pulled on her jeans, buttoned up her blouse, then climbed down from the bed and into the undersized living space of the camper. There was no sign of Vanessa, but a small coffee pot was brewing on low and a cup had been left out for her. Maureen quickly filled it and took a few initial sips.

Slowly, the world began making more sense.

The time spent around the campfire had been very pleasant the night before—pleasant but guarded. No one spoke any further about what the dig team was looking for, and Maureen pointedly refrained from asking. Instead, they discussed the history-rich New Mexico plains, the plight of the endangered howling coyotes, the secret ingredients of the vegetarian sausage. Dr. Ernie then delighted the group with several authentically scary ghost stories, after which most people yearned to lock themselves away into their trailers where it was safe. Through it all, Maureen had come to like all of the diggers, and felt that they were well on their way to completely accepting her.

She was pouring a refill on her coffee when the camper door swung open and Vanessa walked in.

Her face was slightly flushed, as if she just returned from a rigorous exercise.

"I try to run five miles every day," she told Maureen, "I usually do ten back in the city. But in this heat, *cinco* is plenty . . ."

Maureen guessed that Vanessa was only a couple years younger than her, twenty-three at the most. She was very pretty, slender, and healthy-looking, but oddly she didn't have the physique of a person who ran ten miles a day. Rather her body appeared soft, and well rounded, not sharp and muscular.

Vanessa poured out a cup of coffee for herself.

"Did you sleep okay?" she asked Maureen. "I know it's kind of cramped up there."

"Fine," Maureen assured her. "This desert air must have some kind of an effect on me. I haven't slept this late in years."

"Same with me," Vanessa replied. "I sleep like a baby out here."

She produced a couple bowls, some milk, and a box of organic corn flakes.

"I discovered a small pond about a mile from here," Vanessa told her as they ate a quick breakfast. "The water is a lot better than what comes out of the tap in this thing. Do you want to drive over there with me and freshen up?"

It was an offer Maureen couldn't refuse.

They finished their meal, stored away all loose items, and then climbed out of the back of the camper. A quick scan of the area told

Maureen that the rest of the digging group was already at work, carefully spading out new plots, sifting through the loose dirt and gravel, and meticulously documenting any attendant information. Dr. Ernie gave them a friendly wave as they climbed into the cab of the Ford. As Vanessa started the engine and put the truck in gear, Maureen saw out of the corner of her eye, that one of diggers—a young man whose name she couldn't recall—was pointing a Polaroid instant camera toward them.

"Smile!" he yelled as they drove past.

Both Maureen and Vanessa complied, waving happily as the man took a picture of their departure.

The country out beyond the dig site was so spectacular, Maureen couldn't help being caught up in its beauty.

The recent rains had turned the fields a bright green. In some grazing areas, the grass was near a foot high and gently waving in the breeze.

They drove along in silence, Maureen content to admire the scenery while Vanessa steered the Ford along the bumpy, hilly roads.

Finally, after fifteen minutes or so, they reached the pond.

It was literally an oasis out in the middle of nowhere. The pond was about forty feet across, and fed a dozen or so trees on its periphery. Maureen could imagine that it had been a welcome sight to many a rider back in the days when this range land was truly wild and free.

Once again, it seemed as if Vanessa had changed her mind.

"I'll bet there were a lot of cowpokes happy to see this place after riding out around here years ago," she said, parking the Ford near the shallow end of the pond.

They got out and Vanessa retreated momentarily to the camper portion of the truck, returning with towels and two bars of soap.

"It's completely organic," she told Maureen, handing her one of the bars. "It won't hurt the water at all."

Maureen gratefully took the soap and a towel and walked to the edge of the pond. The water was so clean, the sandy bottom was clearly visible. She scooped up a handful of the water and pressed it to her lips. It tasted better than Evian.

Vanessa joined her on the small sandy beach and similarly tasted

97

the water. ·

"They could bottle it," she told Maureen. "Half the people in Chicago wouldn't be able to tell it from Perrier . . ."

Maureen kicked off her sneakers and immersed her feet in the cool water. For the moment, she was content to let the soothing water soak away the aches remaining from her long walk the day before.

"So, tell me what you know about why we are here," Vanessa asked her abruptly.

Immediately, Maureen went on guard. They had been dancing around the subject since her arrival. Now, Vanessa was broaching it in a very direct way.

Maureen knew she'd have to reply cautiously.

"Not much more than I explained at dinner last night," she finally said.

Vanessa stood up and removed her cowboy-style boots. "So you *do* know what we are digging for?"

"Well, I was hoping someone here would fill in the blanks for me," Maureen replied truthfully.

Vanessa slipped out of her long socks and then began unbuttoning her denim blouse.

"That would require quite a leap of faith on our part, wouldn't it?" she asked Maureen. "After all, many months of our lives went into preparing for this expedition. You can understand how we'd be reluctant to divulge everything to such a Johnny-come-lately . . ."

Maureen sensed the conversation turning cat-and-mouse. She wasn't in the mood for it.

She stood up and faced Vanessa, who had just finished unbuttoning her shirt.

"Let's make a deal," she told the young archaeologist. "I'll tell you what I know, if you tell me where I'm off base. Okay?"

Vanessa eyed her for a moment, then slowly took off her shirt, revealing her well-proportioned breasts held tightly in a soft cotton bra.

"Okay, it's a deal," she said.

Trying to ignore the fact that Vanessa was disrobing, Maureen pressed ahead.

"What I know about what happened here years ago comes mostly from news reports," she began.

"And that is?" Vanessa asked, casually unhitching her bra.

Maureen took a deep breath. The moment of truth had arrived.

"I know many people believe something crashed near here back in 1947," she said, measuring each word carefully. "A very mysterious aircraft of some kind. It came down on ranch land owned by a man named Mac Brazel, an area which I'm guessing is very close to where you are digging. Am I right so far?"

Vanessa had finally unloosened her bra clip and removed the garment completely.

"Yes, you are," she told Maureen, slowly rubbing her now-naked chest. "Go on . . ."

"This mysterious aircraft could have been an experimental military plane," Maureen continued slowly.

Vanessa was slowly unbuttoning her jeans. "Keep going," she said.

Maureen took another deep breath. "But maybe it wasn't. Maybe it didn't belong to our military. Or anybody's military. At least, not here on Earth."

Vanessa stepped out of her jeans to reveal a pair of shapely legs and hips as well as a well-curved bottom.

"So far, so good," she told Maureen, slipping out of her white cotton underpants.

"The rancher was the first to spot the wreckage and he notified the authorities," Maureen continued. "Soon afterward the wreckage of this aircraft, or whatever it was, was taken away by the military, specifically soldiers from an air base nearby . . ."

Now naked, Vanessa stretched luxuriously.

"No mistakes so far," she told Maureen, adding, "Aren't you going in?"

Maureen felt a breath catch in her throat. She couldn't help but eye the naked woman suspiciously. Was all this as innocent as it might seem?

Slowly Maureen began to undo her own buttons.

"Do you know about the press release?" Vanessa asked her.

"Yes," Maureen replied. "The day after they first saw the wreckage, a colonel at the nearby air base ordered his public-information officer to issue a statement to the newspapers. The press release said that the Air Force had gained possession of a flying disk through the cooperation of a local rancher."

Vanessa smiled as Maureen continued to undo her buttons.

"Very good," she said. "Almost verbatim . . . Then what happened?"

"Then the story hit the papers," Maureen went on, "and the higher authorities hit the roof. They immediately issued a second press release, saying the wreckage came from a weather balloon and not from a flying disk. That's when the cover-up supposedly began."

Maureen had finally fiddled with her buttons long enough. She had no choice but to pull off her shirt.

"What was the name of the unit stationed at the air base nearby?" Vanessa asked her.

"The 509th Bomb Group," Maureen answered quickly. "Part of the First Air Transport unit. It was the Air Force's only atomic-bomb unit at the time."

"Very good," Vanessa said. Maureen wondered: Was she talking about her information? Or the fact that she, too, had just removed her bra.

"The wreckage was flown on to Wright Air Field in Dayton," Maureen continued without prompting. "That's where the Army's Air Technical Intelligence Center was located."

"You obviously did some homework," Vanessa said, her eyes wandering to Maureen's naked breasts. "Do you know about the soil engineer?"

Maureen began tugging at her belt buckle. "His name was never officially released," she said. "But he claimed he came upon more wreckage shortly after the military came to Brazel's ranch, before they squashed the first press release. He said he found a . . . well, another part of a flying disk. This one much larger and more intact. And that there were four bodies on the ground around it. They had large heads and small bodies. Supposedly some college students on a field trip also saw this wreckage and the bodies before, once again, the military arrived and cleared the area."

Maureen had pulled off her own jeans by this time, but stopped short of removing her underpants. Vanessa stretched again, walked to the edge of the pond, and slowly entered the water. Soon she was lathering up her soap bar and spreading the suds across her shoulders and neck.

Maureen joined the woman in the water, being careful, though, to bathe a respectable distance away from her.

"Do you know anything about the materials that were recovered from the wreckage?" Vanessa asked her.

"Again, only what I've read," Maureen replied. "I've seen it described variously as 'plastic metal,' or 'metallic wood.' Supposedly it was very thin, but indestructible. It couldn't be burned. It couldn't be cut with a torch or an ax. It would crinkle like tin foil when crushed in a hand, but it would resume its shape almost immediately when released."

Vanessa dunked under the water and then soaped down her wet hair.

"Do you know about the glyphs?"

Maureen had now lathered her own body. She was also becoming more comfortable with Vanessa by the second.

"I've read that there was some writing on some of the wreckage," she said. "It was similar in some respects to Egyptian hieroglyphics, but was more geometric in shape. It was purplish in color, and seemed to be part of the metal itself, as opposed to being carved into it or drilled on."

Vanessa ducked under the water and rinsed her long brown hair.

"How about MJ-Twelve," she asked. "Have you heard of it?"

Maureen began lathering her own blond hair. "The document? Yes, I have . . ." she replied. "Supposedly, there was a group of scientists and military men appointed by the President some time after this alleged crash to investigate it. There were intelligence people in the group, as well is at least one man who later went out and presented himself to the press as a UFO debunker."

"As part of a disinformation campaign," Vanessa said, climbing out of the pond, her bath done.

"It would appear that way," Maureen replied, giving herself a final rinse off.

Vanessa had a towel waiting for her when Maureen emerged from the pond. They both quickly dried off, and then, still unclothed, sat again by the edge of the pond and let the hot morning sun warm them.

"That's really about all I know," Maureen said, wrapping the towel around her wet hair. "As I said last night, I was tipped that a group of scientists had returned to this area, under some rather unusual conditions. That's when I decided to come down and see for myself."

"So, I'll ask you again," Vanessa said. "Do you really know what our purpose here is?"

Maureen didn't move.

"Will you tell me?" she asked.

Vanessa suddenly wrapped the towel around her. She lowered her voice to a whisper.

"We're convinced that whatever crashed here was not of this Earth," she said. "In fact, all of the logical evidence points that way. Now, the military carted off what they could find, but that doesn't mean they got everything, especially around Brazel's property, where the wreckage was very widespread."

She took a long deep breath and let it out slowly.

"So we're looking for any remains or fragments that the military might have missed . . ."

The words took only a moment to echo in Maureen's ear. Then she smiled. Everything was falling into place.

"And if you *do* find something . . ." she began to say.

"Then we'll have substantial proof that UFOs exist," Vanessa finished for her. "And you'll have the biggest story of the century . . ."

14

Close to the Edge

The convoy ground its way up the side of the small mountain, each of the three vehicles trailing its own cloud of smoke and dust.

A Hummer was in the lead. It was carrying four members of a top-secret U.S. Marine Corps recon unit. Next came the Bradley fighting vehicle. It contained eight more troops—all of them U.S. Army Special Forces Green Berets. Bringing up the rear was a rare and expensive special combat vehicle. A cross between an old World War II half-track and an armored truck from the future, the heavily armed SCV—it carried six .50 caliber machine guns, a small howitzer, and several kinds of rocket launchers—was manned by a half-dozen members of the U.S. Air Force's crack base-security force.

The unusual parade reached the top of the ledge and moved down the rocky, bumpy road, rolling to a stop in front of Casa Fantastica. The security troops scrambled out of their vehicles and formed a tight semicircle around the front of the strange house. Most of the men carried M-16s, though a few sported small grenade launchers and Uzis. Each man wore the camouflaged field uniform of his respective service.

This unit—it being the epitome of interservice cooperation—was simply known as L-10. The soldiers in the highly-secret unit were not much different from the thousands deployed inside War Heaven—except in two very important ways: One, the men in L-10 took orders from members of the ISC. Two, they were armed with real weapons.

The only officer in the small unit was the Marine captain driving the Hummer. Satisfied that his forces were properly deployed, he reached for his hand-held radio and spoke three words into its mouthpiece. Not five seconds later, two near-silent, super-secret OH-9 helicopters rose up like phantoms from below the cliff on the far side of the house, where they'd been quietly lurking all along.

With his air cover now hovering in place, the Marine captain walked up to the front of the dwelling and quickly passed though the three "organic" security checks. This done, he reached inside his pocket and pulled out a crisp, newly printed twenty-dollar bill. Folding it in two, he knocked on the door twice and let himself in.

"Are you ready, sir?" he yelled once he reached the main hall. "It's time to go!"

He heard a shuffling sound coming from the library off to his right, and stepping forward, he saw the elderly man making his way toward him.

"Are you Marines?" the old man rasped at him, eyeing his uniform through thick, designer-rimmed glasses.

"Yes, sir," the officer answered with a casual salute.

"Where's the Army officer?" the old man demanded. "The guy who was here last week? He owes me twenty dollars . . ."

"He gave it to me to give to you, sir," the Marine told him, handing over the crisp twenty-dollar bill. "And asked me to give you his regards."

"I'm just as happy to take his money," the old man said with a creaky smile, putting the bill inside the breast pocket of his oft-mended uniform. "And yours, too. Are you a betting man, Marine? Horses? Fights? Baseball? You name the action, I'll match it, two to one."

The Marine captain smiled politely and shook his head. He'd been prewarned not to gamble with the man.

"No, sir," he said firmly. "But thanks anyway . . ."

The old man gave the officer a mischievous wink and then spun around toward the library.

"I've just got a swell new picture for my gallery," he told the officer. "Do you want to see it?"

"Of course I do, sir," the Marine replied.

He joined the old man at the far end of the low-lit library.

"Here it is," the old man said, pointing to a photo of Albert Einstein that showed the famous scientist posing in front of the Washington Monument. "It's a doozy, isn't it?"

"That it is, sir . . ."

"Got a couple new publications, too," the old man said, yanking the officer over to a nearby bookcase, which contained only books about Einstein, and pulling out two thinly-bound booklets. "This one is a bunch of papers he wrote while still in Switzerland. This one has to do with his first year at Princeton."

"Very impressive, sir," the Marine said, adding, "We should go now." The old man blew his nose.

"When are we due?" he asked the officer.

"We should be there no later than 1700 hours," the Marine replied, checking his watch. "It's now 1500 . . ."

The old man adjusted his service cap over his pony tail and straightened his sunglasses.

"Okay, if we must," he said. "Let's go."

The Marine officer escorted the man out the front door, where they both passed through the security devices and walked out into the sunshine of the small driveway.

"Hello, boys!" the old man let out with a yelp.

There was a quick, friendly chorus of reply from the surrounding L-10 security troops.

The old man then gave a salute to each of the quietly hovering helicopters. Both pilots acknowledged the gesture by dipping the nose of their respective aircraft.

On the Marine captain's hand signal, the coterie of protective troops slowly moved in, their highly trained eyes scanning everything from the nearby rocks to the far horizon, on guard to any threat that might come to the old man, as unlikely as such an attack might be.

The Marine officer checked the time—it was now 1505 hours. He said three more words into his walkie-talkie and the two choppers formed up 100 feet directly above the SCV. At the same time, the old man was led to the rear door of the huge vehicle and boosted inside by two burly Green Berets. Then the L-10 troops dashed to their proper mode of transport and the engines in all three vehicles roared to life almost simultaneously.

The convoy began to move again. After crawling back down the side of the mountain, it turned north, toward the deepest part of War Heaven.

15

Aggressor Base Tango

It was sunset.

A klaxon sounded three times, its haunting moan echoing across the darkened air base and through the nearby desert hills. The electronic wail served as the announcement that night had officially fallen.

Within seconds, the base began to come to life.

Four jet-black F-15Xs with Soviet Air Force markings were slowly towed out of their separate hangars and parked with solemn precision on the flight line. Two dozen men were waiting there. With one crisp order, these men — all of them mechanics, six for each plane — began swarming over the F-15Xs, making sure the jets were in proper flying condition.

The klaxon sounded three more times. On this signal, the ground crews began to switch on the engines for all four airplanes. They did this in a well-rehearsed sequence, the racket of each igniting jet engine growing in volume until the noise became one thunderous roar crashing through the eaves of the nearby hills.

A black van appeared at the far end of the flight line and began a slow trip toward the waiting aircraft. Finally reaching the group of warming jets, it came to a halt and four men stepped out.

Each was dressed in a jet black flight suit that bore the skull-and-crossbones patch of Aggressor unit Tango. Each was also carrying a futuristic helmet — also jet-black save for the Tango emblem. The helmet, which looked like a large insect head, had a multitude of wires flowing from its rear flap, as well as a spindly oxygen hook-up

106

hose.

The four men had a brief discussion among themselves, and then walked to their respective airplanes.

Two of the pilots—U.S. Air Force Colonel Arthur "Teddy" Williams and U.S. Navy Commander Lawrence "Crazy" Katt—were longtime veterans of the elite Aggressor unit. Williams, the senior officer, climbed into the first F-15X, traditionally called Tango One. Katt, his longtime wingman, strapped into Tango Two. Although their last mission had been unusually rocky, the two men were, quite conceivably, the best pilots inside War Heaven at the moment.

The other two pilots were newer to the game. The driver for Tango Three was Woody; he'd been part of the famous Tango unit for not even forty-eight hours.

The fourth pilot, the newest of them all, was Ryder.

He was shocked when he learned shortly after his meeting with the Boss at Jacks that he'd been assigned to the elite and much despised Tango Aggressor unit.

Shocked and more than a little confused.

How did it happen? They'd told him that the drill in the F-4 the night before had been his secret initiation rite into the Aggressor unit and that he'd passed with flying colors. But why the Tango Aggressors? Those who knew about the men who flew the Black F-15Xs considered them to be not only the best fighter pilots in War Heaven, but quite possibly the best in the world. Despite the nasty reputation, being assigned to the Tangos was a deployment secretly coveted by all the other pilots on the Range—and many on the outside as well. Dozens of top-notch pilots were considered for the assignment every year. But only two or three were chosen, and then only after an exhaustive security check.

Yet now here he was, plucked practically out of nowhere and, merely twelve hours later, strapping into Tango Four. But the bigger question was: *Why* did it happen? Was it part of his enigmatic mission to War Heaven? Was it the ISC making its move? Or was it just a fluke—another gamble of the crazy things that were always happening in War Heaven? He just didn't know—and there was no way for him to find out. For him to attempt to contact Moon was totally out of the question. In fact, he wouldn't know where to begin. And there was another mystery: Were the other two Tango Aggressor pilots working on the same mission? Was the Boss in on it? Or could they all be actually working *against* him and Woody?

He sank deeper into his seat, hooked up his oxygen mask to the cockpit's internal system, and and took a deep gulp of the Big O. He knew it was useless to spend time thinking about it all. Inside this strange world in the middle of the Nevada desert, finding answers only brought on more questions. Truth—"real" truth—was a rare commodity indeed.

There was one consolation: The F-15X was by far the most advanced fighter he'd ever seen, way beyond the aircraft he'd flown during the filming of the movie. It sported more powerful engines, and the avionics and weapons systems, both for dogfighting and ground attack, were absolutely state of the art. There were practically no switches to throw or buttons to push. Just about every control worked by heat-touch flat panels, which were ultrasophisticated versions of a modern elevator call button. His Zoot weapons display alone offered a mind-boggling range of armament, free-fall ordnance, air-to-air missiles, and, of course, a wide variety of gas bombs.

He plugged in his helmet activation wire and instantly his visor came to life with a thermal image of the darkening world outside. This was nightvision at its most advanced; everything was in such sharp, well-lit focus, he figured his sight, both for detail and distance, was improved by at least one hundred percent.

The plane's main flight computer was out of this world—literally. Woody had tipped him earlier that the Aggressor aircraft's main brains were direct relatives to ones developed for the orphaned Star Wars program. The computer could do everything: fly the plane, fire the Zoot weapons, track targets, handle communications, regulate fuel, watch over the survival systems, *and* keep track of the flight systems of every other plane in the flight—with a couple million bytes of capacity left over.

His thoughts were interrupted by the sound of the ground crew chief climbing up the F-15X's access ladder. Although Ryder had already taken a brief orientation flight in the aircraft earlier in the day, he still paid close attention as the crew chief ran down the critical flight systems.

The next few minutes passed while he occupied himself with double-checking his flight computer and inputting the latest weather updates. Their mission this night was to intercept a flight of eight

Marine F/A-18 Hornets flying for the Green forces out of a small base to the west and "aggressively engage" them.

Despite the two-to-one advantage, Ryder knew it would be far from a fair fight. Besides the fact that the F-15X aircraft was superior to the Hornet, the Aggressor intelligence network knew everything there was to know about the unsuspecting Marine flight: its heading, altitude, weapons load, even the names of the individual pilots and a reading on their ACM experience.

So, as always, the odds were stacked in the Aggressor unit's favor. All Ryder and the rest of his unit had to do was locate the Hornets, ambush them, and rack up the points.

At exactly 2000 hours, the klaxon sounded three more times.

The four black F-15Xs taxied out onto the base's single runway, Woody moving into the third spot and Ryder taking up the rear. One by one they screamed down the runway and took off.

Once they head reached a height of 10,500 feet, the F15Xs formed up into a fiercesome chevron battle line. Then they turned west, toward the still-brilliant fiery halo of the setting sun.

The hunt had begun.

Twenty miles north of Tango Base, located atop a barren, wind-ravaged butte, there was a place called the Eye.

Little more than a small cement bunker covered with desert-camouflage netting, it was actually the central point for one of the most sophisticated, and most secret, communications networks ever assembled on Earth. Yet the only evidence of this was the near-invisible gaggle of TV reception dishes that surrounded the bunker and its solitary 20-foot-high microwave FM radio antenna.

Inside the bunker was a large rectangular room measuring 75 feet by 50 feet, laid out not unlike a college amphitheater. A huge TV screen dominated one wall. Fifty plush seats, each with a small computer screen and an elaborate control panel attached to its right arm, were set up in a semicircle fashion facing this screen. Other than that, the room was empty save for a dusty American flag which hung limply from a pole in one corner and two computer screens which guarded another. Their low-lit monitors cast an eerie greenish glow around the bunker, providing its only significant illumination.

Sitting silently in the last row of seats, their faces all but lost in the green shadows in the otherwise darkened theater, were three men, each wearing a different military uniform. Two of them—one an Army officer, the other from the Navy—were sitting together. The third man was hunched over in his seat five chairs down from the other two. He was apparently asleep and snoring softly.

There was a small control room off to the side of the amphitheater, and behind its large, slightly tinted window sat a control console. Two men in civilian clothes were punching various programming commands into this console's computer, while a third spoke into a small headphone mike.

"We're up in five seconds," he announced into the main room. "Four . . . three . . . two . . . one. Now."

Suddenly the large TV screen flashed to life.

There were stars—thousands of them, burning bright, filling the screen. There was the moon, two days in retreat from being full, its white light reflecting like a ball of ice. Off in the distance was the silhouette of one of the rugged mountain ranges that ran the length of the secret weapons range. Beyond them, the barely discernible glow of Tango Base.

It was all there, up on the screen in incredible clarity like the world's best drive-in-movie screen. There was no noise, no static, no color distortion. Years beyond the electronic precision of the best high-definition TV, the video image was so clear, it was as if someone had thrown open a huge window on the side of the bunker to reveal the nighttime desert sky beyond.

"Quite of a picture," the Army officer whispered to his Navy counterpart.

"It's just amazing . . ." echoed the Navy man.

A few seconds passed, then eight red lights appeared in the upper right-hand corner.

"Incoming flight on screen," the man in the control room announced. "Mark 1850 hours . . ."

Suddenly the TV screen was electronically divided in two. On the left side was a condensed version of the original picture; on the right, a close-up shot of the approaching red lights.

"Going to full to close-up . . ."

The screen complied, and now with the closer, electronically enhanced nightvision view, it was quickly apparent the red lights were attached to eight F/A-18 Hornets, painted in green-gray camouflage

110

and wearing Marine Corps markings.

"Let's see some numbers," the Navy officer called out.

In an instant, rows of bright yellow numerals began appearing down the right-hand edge of the picture. These numbers told the observers that the Hornets were flying at 450 knots, at an altitude of 5000 feet, and were 35 miles away. Each airplane was using a full array of nighttime navigation equipment—including forward-looking infrared gear, or FLIR—and they were on a course that would take them directly over the bunker in ninety-two seconds.

"They put these guys together from the best of the jarhead Air Force," the Army officer explained. "Grenada. Panama. The Gulf. The Greens can't believe they were given such quality air cover."

"Too bad it won't last long," the other officer replied, sipping his coffee.

The picture flipped back to the original long shot, the rows of information numerals remaining on the right side of the picture.

"Tango intercept flight on screen now . . ." the director announced.

Suddenly four white lights flashed onto the upper left-hand corner of the screen, their video-enhanced silhouettes passing right in front of the nearly full moon.

"Well, there they are," the Army officer said, as another set of information numbers popped onto the far right of the screen. "Right on time . . ."

"Radar contact made between participants," the director announced, as the four white lights suddenly turned toward the F/A-18s. "We are engaging automatic sequential editing program now . . ."

The director punched one final button, then took off his headset. Lighting a cigarette, he leaned back in his chair and relaxed. His job was done for now.

For the next ten minutes everyone watching the huge screen witnessed an awesome display of nighttime air-to-air combat.

From the moment the four Tango flight F-15Xs had pounced on the Marine Hornets, the sky had been filled with Zoot flashes—holographic fire from simulated cannons and missiles. Not only could the men in the bunker see it all in crystal video clarity, they had the benefit of the information readouts decorating either side of the big TV screen, as well as a wide variety of special video effects, courtesy of the system's automatic sequential editing process.

This program followed the path of the aerial combatants, by automatically accessing the signal from hundreds of video cameras located within a twenty-square-mile area. Switching around from camera to camera, the computer selected and projected onto the screen the best shots of the combat between the Marines and the Aggressors, as well as providing various close-ups, replays, and slow-motion segments, much like the telecast director of a network football game, only ten times quicker.

But though the Marines fought valiantly, there was never any question who would win the engagement. It was obvious to the men watching the battle that the Tango F-15Xs were having no problems slicing up the Hornets, despite the numerical disparity. From heights as high as 25,000 feet to deck-scraping runs of barely 100 feet, the Tangos worked individually, as pairs, and occasionally as a full team, to systematically eliminate the Marines, scrambling their opponents' flight systems with well-timed blasts of Zoot holographic weapons, all the while taking no fatal hits on their own.

To their credit, the Marine pilots fought on to the last man. But it was over in less than fifteen minutes.

"Great flying," the Army man said, noting the message on the big screen that announced that all of the combatants were at that moment returning to their respective bases. "Those Tango guys *are* better than advertised."

"Let's see some replays," the Navy officer replied, his tone indicating that he needed more convincing. "We've got to make damn sure about this."

For the next half hour, the pair watched a computer-selected "greatest hits" package from the original just-completed broadcast. Maneuver after maneuver was projected onto the big screen, all of it in full-color, slow-motion video glory. From all angles, including startlingly clear shots from the participants' nose cameras, the pilots of jet black F-15Xs displayed astonishing nimbleness, cunning, and innovation amidst the natural confusion of the nighttime dogfight. Even the three men sitting at the control console paid close attention, though they'd witnessed hundreds of such encounters before.

When it was over, just about everyone in the bunker was very impressed. The F-15X Tango pilots were that good.

"It appears that these four guys are just what we've been looking for," the Army officer said. "Do you agree?"

"Have all of them passed the ten-level security check?" the Navy man asked.

"The main computer says they did," the other man replied after quickly accessing the information via the control panel on his chair arm. "Williams. Katt. Woods. Long. All of them clean. Good records. Not a troublemaker in the bunch."

"I hope that damn computer is right," the Navy officer grumbled. "One bad apple – snuck in under our noses – and this whole thing goes up like a bomb. And we go up with it . . ."

"They all own just the profile we want," the Army officer told him. "None are married. They have little or no contact with any other family members. They could disappear tomorrow and no one would notice."

The Navy man leaned back into his chair and rubbed his eyes.

"Okay," he said finally. "So they passed their first audition. I vote we put them through the Hell Week."

The Army officer leaned in closer to him.

"I do, too," he said. He punched up his computer again, and spent the next five minutes working his way through a myriad of security codes before finally calling up the document he wanted.

It was called "ISC Four/pre-'Operation Rapture.' "

With a flutter of fingers on the keyboard, he entered in a brief report on the dogfight just witnessed, including high praise for the pilots of Tango flight. He added two *Yes* votes next to a question that flashed: *Personnel Advancement Recommended?*

The Army officer then looked back up from the screen and turned back to the Navy man.

"What about him?" he asked, indicating the third figure five chairs down from them who had spent all of the time pretending that he was asleep. "Shouldn't we ask his opinion? After all, that's what he's here for . . ."

The Navy officer glanced over at the elderly man in the patched-up uniform and long gray pony tail and shrugged disdainfully.

"Why bother?" he asked.

16

New Mexico, six days later

Maureen was naked.

She was stretched out on a blanket next to the clear pond, letting the midmorning sun dry her body from her daily bath.

Vanessa was naked, too. She was combing out Maureen's long blonde hair, occasionally applying a dab of organic hair conditioner, a homemade mixture of yucca sap and milk.

Maureen hadn't felt so relaxed – so *comfortable* – in years. She'd become a working, valuable member of the dig team, pitching in on the sifting, measuring, and general work when needed, and conducting taped interviews with key members whenever time permitted.

With most of her initial suspicions dispelled, she and Vanessa had grown close over the past five days. As the only two females at the dig, they had quickly built a friendship that was akin to that between college roommates. They ate together, dug together, shared moisturizers. They'd spent much time filling in each other on their lives, from families to school to various jobs. To some degree, Vanessa seemed in awe of Maureen's high-profile success and her urban survival ethic. In turn, Maureen envied Vanessa's ability to enjoy what was essentially a simpler, more private life. Born in a small town in Iowa, she'd revealed to Maureen that she'd never been to a big city until she first went to Chicago to start undergraduate school at Northwestern at the age of nineteen.

Now, as the young woman continued to brush her drying hair, Maureen was certain that they would have been friends no matter what the circumstances of their meeting. The fact that they'd met literally out in the middle of nowhere only strengthened that feeling.

"Do you have a boyfriend now?" Vanessa asked her out of the blue.

Maureen hesitated a moment to consider her reply. Although they'd covered their past romances more than thoroughly, one thing they *hadn't* discussed was the current state of their romantic lives.

What to answer? Maureen thought.

"There is someone in my life," she finally replied. "I met him about a year ago. But I don't see him much. In fact, we were going to get together until this all came up."

"I'll bet he's handsome," Vanessa said sweetly, buffing a few drops of water from Maureen's back. "What does he do for a living?"

"He's a pilot," Maureen answered with a laugh.

"A pilot? *Really?*" Vanessa asked, her voice sounding like that of a wide-eyed schoolgirl. "What airline?"

Maureen laughed again as Vanessa's towel moved to the small of her back.

"He's not an airline pilot," she revealed. "He's in the Air Force."

Vanessa's towel stopped just short of Maureen's shapely rear.

"The Air Force?" she asked, after a moment's hesitation. "That's interesting . . ."

Maureen stretched, and ran her hands through her long blonde hair.

"He's really a nice guy," she said, more to herself than to Vanessa. "Sometimes I miss him a lot . . ."

She finally sat up and wrapped a towel around her still-damp hair.

Vanessa was rubbing her own body with suntan oil, a necessity in the hot New Mexico desert.

"You know," she said, putting a dab of the oil on Maureen's shoulder and lightly rubbing it in, "I've got a feeling that something big is going to happen today."

"You can never tell . . ." Maureen replied.

One hour later

It was shortly after nine A.M. when Dr. Ernie saw the glint of reflected light at the bottom of his sifting screen.

He'd almost missed it—in amongst the sand and soil, the screen was filled with small pieces of a common, shiny rock called gilineum. The combined reflection of this reflective mineral nearly masked the strange, bright silver object that had partially lodged in the corner of the screen.

Dr. Ernie froze as soon as he saw it. He actually tried to call out to the others working in a larger pit nearby, but just like in a dream, the words would not come out. Instead, he carefully lifted the object from the screen with his trowel and held it up to his good eye.

He'd never seen anything like it. It was about a half inch thick, two and half inches long, and an inch wide. In some ways it looked like a piece of aluminum, but it also looked like a piece of wood that had been spray-painted silver. It had a design to it, like it was a brace of some kind. Its finish seemed uniformly dulled, but oddly, it reflected the sun as intensely as a mirror.

It was Vanessa who was the first to share in the discovery. She'd come over to Dr. Ernie's isolated site to fetch him for coffee when she saw him turning the trowel every which way in front of his eyes.

"It's not another bottle cap, is it?" she asked him. They'd uncovered a dozen or so beer-bottle caps in the past few days, remnants no doubt of a range party held years before.

Dr. Ernie still couldn't speak. He was too absorbed in examining the object.

Maureen was on her way to the lunch camper when she saw Dr. Ernie and Vanessa hunkered down next to the small pit. She joined them and was immediately struck by the fascinating piece.

"Is it?" she asked, her tone hushed, as if actually talking about it would make it not so. "Could it really be?"

"It might be," Dr. Ernie said, finally summoning enough saliva into his mouth to talk. "Please, get the others . . ."

As Vanessa ran to gather the rest of the dig party, Maureen quickly retrieved her camera and began snapping photos.

"We have joint ownership of these pictures," she assured Dr. Ernie. "Any money resulting from them will be split evenly between the *Post* and your expedition . . ."

"Fine . . . fine," Dr. Ernie replied, obviously distracted. He was still balancing the object on the end of his small shovel, intent on examining every angle of it while being extra cautious that he didn't drop it.

Maureen went through her first roll of film in less than a minute. She was loading a second 36-frame roll into her Nikon when the others members of the team came running. They were expectantly excited over the find, their individual reactions ranging from giddy laughter to reverent prayer.

"Group shot!" Maureen called out as Dr. Ernie finally stood up and held the object out for all to see.

The dig team obediently lined up on either side of their leader, and Maureen snapped off another half roll.

"You get in here, Mo," Vanessa suggested, coming out to take the camera from her so Maureen could get in a few shots.

This done, half the people accompanied Ernie back to his Winnebago while the others threw another protective line of red tape around the pit where the object was found. Maureen retreated to the camper she'd been sharing with Vanessa to get her tape recorder and notebook. By the time she returned, most of the group was crowded into Ernie's mobile home.

The expedition leader had his microscope out and was now examining the object under the eyepiece. Several people nearby were taking notes; others were consulting large loose-leaf binders. Still others simply looked on with expressions of hopeful awe.

For her part, Maureen simply stuck her microphone into the middle of the crowd around Dr. Ernie's workbench and turned on her tape recorder.

"Fascinating," Ernie said over and over. "There are no imperfections on it at all. No scrapes. No pits. Certainly no signs of oxidation."

"Try bending it, Doctor," someone at the back suggested.

Ernie took two tweezers and, grasping the object on either side, attempted to bend it while it still rested on the specimen stand. To everyone's amazement, the material proved mysteriously pliable. It bent like rubber, yet it instantly returned to its original state when Dr. Ernie released the pressure of his tweezers.

"It has to be it!" someone yelled, with a tone equal to declaring "Eureka!"

"It must be . . ." someone else said.

Even the normally cautious Dr. Ernie was shaking his head, his face flush with pure joy.

"I think you might be right," he said, never taking his eye off the microscope's eyepiece. "I think we might have done it . . ."

Maureen felt her heart skip a beat. Already she was forming the lead to her story in her mind: "A team of archaeologists and UFO researchers digging near the city of Roswell, New Mexico, have found what they believe is a piece of a 'flying disk' that was rumored to have crashed in the area back in 1947 . . ."

But then suddenly there was a loud *boom!* and a flash of light. The Winnebago was suddenly shaking both from the frightening noise and from the combined movement of the startled people inside.

"What was that?" several people yelled at once.

Maureen was the nearest to the Winnebago's back door. She quickly opened it just in time to see a second flash of lightning, which was followed by another, louder thunderclap.

"That's quite a storm coming," she said, pointing out to the west at the large dark cloud heading straight for them. "We'd better button everything up . . ."

The team was out of the trailer at once, happily running around securing their tools and throwing sheets of plastic over the pit where the object had been found.

"How appropriate," Vanessa said to Maureen as they helped Dr. Ernie close all the windows in his Winnebago. "They say the saucer went down in an electrical storm like this. Maybe another one will crash . . ."

Maureen almost laughed at the statement, but caught herself at the last moment.

Suddenly, her thoughts were on Ryder.

She couldn't help wondering what he was doing at that exact moment . . .

17

Jacks

Ryder finished off the plate of scrambled eggs and drained his glass of warm beer, habitually checking his watch as he did so.

It was 8:45 A.M.

The saloon at Jacks was mobbed, of course.

As usual the Gray army troops outnumbered any other group, but there were also a fair number of Greens and Blues, along with a sprinkling of Aggressor pilots, Spookbase support personnel, and a few referees. Feeding and oiling this crowd was a major task, yet the overworked staff of waitresses and bartenders were dispensing glasses of whiskey, pitchers of beer, and plates of eggs with hurried aplomb.

Ryder was perched in the command chair at an enviable corner table, anchoring the fiercely determined Tango Base party team of Woody, Teddy Williams, and "Crazy" Katt. They'd held the strategic position for nearly twenty-four hours now, sleeping in alternating shifts in a small room they'd secured upstairs at Jacks for the dull hours, but fully manning the table when things were really hopping, which was most of the time.

They'd just finished their third full meal at the table—eggs three different ways—and had consumed dozens of beers. Now they decided to switch to whiskey and coffee.

Ryder signaled a waitress from across the crowded room. They had bribed her earlier in return for prompt service and the money had been well spent so far. Within a minute she arrived at the corner table with two bottles of unlabeled whiskey and a pot of piping hot coffee.

"I hope that stuff actually has booze in it," Woody said to her, pointing to the anonymous whiskey bottles.

"Don't worry about it," she replied. "The government can't afford that reduced-alcohol stuff."

"Damn. I love this country . . ." Woody declared.

"Amen," Ryder agreed, raising his cup with the three others in a mock toast.

They had just finished a very grueling week – and it would take more than a few beers and a cup of whiskey to help Ryder unwind from it.

He'd flown more times in the past six and half days than he had in the past year. Four flights during the day and two more at night had been the norm for a typical twenty-four-hour work period. Intercepts, ground attacks, armed recons, and a lot of ACM had taken place during these missions. In military parlance these missions were known as "turn and burns."

The last day of this grinding week of hell had been typical. It began at midnight, when the four Tango F-15Xs launched an attack on a large Gray army storage base located on the far eastern edge of the Range. After eliminating the base's Zoot SAM defense ring, they'd smothered the place with so many Supertears gas canisters that the referees finally called a halt to it. Returning to base, they'd fueled up, recharged their Zoot weapons, and launched again, this time flying a successful mission against a tank column of the Green forces. After more fuel and more Zoots, they surprised a flight of Blue Force Apache choppers roaming the range on a dawn patrol, bouncing all six in a matter of minutes.

After a quick chow break they flew a mission against a squadron of low-flying B-1s, "destroying" four. They refueled in flight, courtesy of a KC-10 aerial tanker, and then conducted a series of strafing attacks against a column of Green Forces attempting to move their mobile Patriot antimissile batteries from the mountains to the desert.

After a two-minute lunch, Ryder and Woody were scrambled on an intercept alert. They met up with eight Navy F-14s out of Fallon NAS and found themselves in the midst of a very uneven furball. But they had held their own long enough for Williams and Katt to come to their rescue. They returned the favor around three that afternoon when the two veteran Aggressor pilots were ambushed by a six-pack of Air Force F-16s and Ryder and Woody were scrambled to come to their aid. Their after-dusk sortie was yet another attack against a Gray force barracks and a Zoot Patriot missile battery.

Throughout the week, the four of them piled up an embarrassing number of points and were rewarded by so many supply drops—at one point they were coming in around the clock—that special takeoff and landing procedures had to be instituted around Tango Base in order to avoid an midair collison.

Despite the torturous pace, Ryder couldn't recall a time when he'd felt so content. He was a born flyer, and the last week had been like a dream come true. It was almost enough to make him forget exactly why he was in War Heaven in the first place.

They can point me in any direction they want to, he kept telling himself over and over. *All I want to do is fly.*

Exhilaration aside, all of them were glad when the orders came down that the seventh day would begin a period of rest. They'd left Tango an hour later and had been whooping it up at Jacks ever since.

As it turned out, their timing had been just right.

There'd been rumors for weeks all throughout War Heaven that Jacks was reviving one of its most vaunted institutions. Someone somewhere had labeled it the "Force Fraternization Program."

At Jacks, it was known simply as Happy Hour.

For whatever reason, the twice-daily Happy Hours had ended the last time Jacks had been torn down. When the town was finally rebuilt, the rooms upstairs stayed empty, virtually slicing off one of the things that had made Jacks so popular with the deployed troops in the first place.

But now, the word was that Happy Hours were back—and better yet, that the special kickoff was to happen at 9 A.M. on this very day.

Woody called out a time check. It was four minutes before nine. A hush came over the crowded bar.

"Ready, boys?" Ryder asked, taking a slug of his whiskey-laced coffee.

"I've been ready for about two fucking days," was Woody's anxious reply.

"Try two weeks," Williams said.

"Try two *months,*" Katt added.

"Three minutes to go," Woody informed them.

121

Ryder passed around a nearly depleted bottle of Old Spice and each man took a splash. Woody shared a pack of breath gum. Williams was meticulously pouring the contents of one of the whiskey bottles into four smaller containers, one for each Tango man, and Katt was busy scribbling out a schedule for use of the room upstairs. Assuming a minute of travel time from the table and back, plus a few minutes of small talk, each man would have the room for a lucky thirteen minutes.

"Two minutes . . ."

All eyes were now focused on the set of creaky stairs that ran along the far wall of the saloon. At the top of those stairs were the rooms that had remained locked for the past two months. Now, several of them were opened just a crack.

"One minute . . ."

It had been a long time, Ryder's inebriated brain was telling him. Too long. He considered himself a simple man. He needed so few things in life. Food. A bed. A shower. An airplane—preferably one that went very fast and could kick ass if needed. A car. Clean underwear. A regular paycheck. And . . .

"Five . . . four . . . three . . . two . . . one . . . *Showtime!*"

Suddenly the lights in the saloon dimmed. A well-worn tape cassette of canned honky-tonk piano music started up. All the windows were shuttered and the two main doors locked. There was a grateful burst of applause from those assembled.

The first door at the top of the stairs opened slowly and two women emerged. They were right out of central casting for saloon girls of a western movie. They wore brief, tacky, plunging-bodice dance-hall outfits, with black net stockings and buttoned-up half-ankle high-heel boots. Both were extremely attractive—in a sleazy sort of way.

The applause in the bar was now deafening. As the first two women made their way down the stairs, another pair—similarly dressed—came out of the second room. They paused at the top landing and then descended into the ocean of hooting, clapping soldiers. Two more came out of the third room, then two more out of the fourth.

Soon there was a flood of Jacks's famous, government-salaried saloon girls pouring down the stairs and into the open arms of the waiting troopers.

"Your tax money at work!" Woody howled as he scanned the line of painted beauties.

Ryder wished he had an oxygen mask to suck on; he was on the verge of passing out with excitement. There were blondes, brunettes, redheads. Most were Caucasian, some were black, some were Oriental, others a pleasant mix. Some were tall, some were slight. Some were "mature;" others, almost illegally youthful.

All were absolutely gorgeous.

"Start choosing, boys," Woody suggested as the saloon girls began pairing off with individual soldiers. "This only lasts an hour . . ."

Just how long *had* it been? Ryder boozily asked himself as he zoomed in on a luscious blonde who was gradually making her way toward them.

For some reason, he couldn't remember .

It didn't take a lot of thought. The blonde filled his bill. He signaled the indentured waitress, and with one smooth motion, she steered the blonde right onto Ryder's lap.

"Hi . . . I'm Colleen."

"Ryder Long."

"You're not a Gray, are you?"

"With this uniform?"

She stroked the neckline of his jet-black flight suit.

"You're in an Aggressor squadron?" she asked, with apparently authentic excitement.

"You've heard of us? " he asked.

"Who hasn't?" she cooed.

By this time, Woody, Katt, and Williams had also snagged companions of their own.

Now a clock was ticking. "You're first up, Ghost . . ." Woody told him over the near-deafening din of the newly-rejuvenated bar. "You've now got twelve minutes and thirty seconds . . ."

Ryder looked drunkenly into Colleen's eyes.

"Is this too sudden?" he asked her.

She hugged him and then kissed his cheek.

"You're so sweet," she whispered in his ear. "Are you sure you're in the Aggressors?"

One minute and five seconds later, Ryder ushered Colleen into the Team Tango's second-floor room.

Now it was just him, her, and the bed.

His inebriated brain cells teased him again: Just when *was* the last time he'd gotten his wheels greased?

The room was empty except for the creaky four-poster, a battered dressing table, and a faded mirror. Colleen produced two bar glasses from the dresser drawer and poured them both a drink from his canteen of quartered whiskey.

"Need to relax, soldier?" she asked.

Ryder flopped down the bed and stretched out.

"You bet I do . . ."

Colleen joined him on the squeaky bed and passed him his drink.

"We've got ten whole minutes," she purred, gently unzipping the front of his flight suit. "That can be a very long time . . ."

She continued to stroke his bare chest, while unsnapping the shoulder straps of her gown. A second later he was staring at two of the most beautiful bare breasts he'd ever seen. A pleasant shudder ran through him. The appropriate parts of his body were getting very interested.

"You see?" she whispered, gently squeezing her right breast. "And we've still got nine and a half minutes left . . ."

She stood up and seductively removed her gown, her shoes, her garters and stockings.

He took a slug from his drink and closed his eyes. He shuddered again as he felt her hands slowly moving down his chest. *When was the last* good *time?*

It had been in his recovery billet at San Diego, after the transfer from Subic Bay. It was early in the evening. A warm night. The sun had just dipped below the ocean. He was leaning back, just like this, and had about the same amount of booze inside him. Hands were running up and down his body, just like now.

He opened his eyes and for a moment thought he saw Maureen's beautiful face smiling down at him . . .

"Hey, Ghost . . ." Woody called out. "You're more than a minute late . . .,"

Ryder slipped back into his seat at the corner table, slightly out of breath, his hair mussed, his uniform newly wrinkled.

"Sorry, partner," he said, pulling Colleen back on to his lap with him. I owe you . . ."

It made no difference. Woody and his woman friend were already making their way across the crowded dance floor toward the stairs, nearly upending the woman dressed like an old-time Red Cross coffee girl who was dispensing packets of condoms to the troops.

"A beer would be great . . ." Colleen suggested.

Williams, Katt, and their two female companions seconded the motion. Ryder signaled their ever-reliable waitress and soon they were all gulping down reasonably cold beer.

"You've got a lot of memories, Mr. Aggressor," Colleen whispered in his ear. "I thought you guys were supposed to be so cool . . ."

"Are you complaining?" he asked.

She squeezed him once and kissed his lips. "Not at all," she replied. "I was complimenting you . . ."

Time passed. They ordered more beer, more whiskey, more coffee. Woody was back in twelve-five, wearing a sly smile and black garter belt around his neck. His companion—a redhead beauty named Wendy—looked even happier, if that was possible. She ceremoniously passed the key to the room to Katt, who was already sprinting toward the stairs, his lady friend in tow.

The area around their table was now very crowded, making the strategic location even more valuable. Ryder reached over the table to help the waitress deposit yet another pitcher of beer on its moist top when he noticed that someone had sat down in the empty seat next to him—the one vacated by Katt.

In the midst of the overcrowded saloon, appropriating such a valuable seat was like jumping someone's gold claim. Ryder immediately turned to evict the man.

But his opening volley suddenly got caught in his throat. This party-crasher was very unusual-looking, to say the least. He was wearing a dull silver-gray flight uniform with gold braiding. It was of no service Ryder had ever seen. The man was probably his own age—late twenties—yet his face was uncreased and entirely unblemished. Most unusual was his hair. Far removed from a regulation military haircut so prominent on the Range, it was long, blonde, and curly. It gave the man an oddly angelic look.

Woody and Williams were too busy nuzzling their dates to notice the man, but Colleen had dug her nails into his arm. The man had spooked her, too.

"You are from Tango base, correct?" the man asked Ryder.

125

"Who the fuck wants to know?" he drunkenly challenged the man.

"I have some news for you," the stranger continued, completely oblivious to Ryder's verbal assault. "At some point, your base will be attacked. Most of your aircraft will be totally destroyed. When that happens, you'll have exactly two hours to save the life of your best friend."

Ryder stared at him for a few long seconds and the strange man stared right back.

"I have something else for you," the stranger told him after a few uneasy moments.

He reached inside his uniform pocket and came up with a wrist watch. He gave it to Ryder.

Ryder took a moment to study the watch. It was a cheap-looking digital type; he couldn't imagine it costing more than a few bucks. What's more, it didn't even appear to be working. At the moment, its numbers were stuck on 00:00:00.

"You will find this very helpful," the man said.

"Who the hell are you?" Ryder finally asked him.

The man's eyes never wavered; the tone of his voice never changed.

"I think it's in your best interests to find that out yourself, Ghost," he replied calmly.

With that, the strange man got up and disappeared into the crowd.

18

Close to the Edge

"Are you really out of champagne?"

Angel got no reply, but that didn't surprise her. The old man was way up in the glass observatory, nearly on the other side of the rambling Casa Fantastica, and if she really wanted to talk to him from here, she'd have to use the intercom system.

Why bother? There was plenty of booze in the kitchen cabinet — whiskey, gin, vodka — and the wine cellar was, as always, fully stocked. She also had the option of raiding the old man's overflowing drug supply. The last handful of speed tablets she'd stolen from him had packed a pleasantly powerful punch — so much so, she'd vowed earlier to steal some more during this visit.

She grabbed a bottle of Glen Livet and climbed the spiral staircase up into her dressing room, which was a large, wide-windowed apartment located atop of one of the towers. Throwing her suitcase into a corner, she sat down on the edge of the large water bed and poured herself a drink. Outside the huge windows, the night desert sky was, as always, lit up from horizon to horizon with dozens of simultaneous red, yellow, and orange flashes going off. Occasionally the windows would rattle as a result of either a particularly close "explosion" or the roar of a jet airplane, helicopter, or God-knows-what tearing back and forth overhead.

She got up and pulled the window drapes closed, effectively shutting out the bombastic holographic display.

How long can this go on? she wondered again, as she sat back down and took a sip of her drink.

The money was terrific. The work was easy. But she just couldn't continue with the strange arrangement. She knew it now. It had to end – soon. Before she went crazy. Or her client did.

She knew getting out wouldn't be easy. Her "handlers" – for the most part they were unseen voices on the other end of her phone – routinely monitored her every move. They listened in on her phone conversations. They opened her mail. They even disposed of her trash, but not before searching it thoroughly. She knew Vegas girls who worked for Mafia dons who didn't go through half as much as she did.

But then, they didn't get paid anywhere near what she did.

But then there was the question of the old man himself. Exactly *how* did she feel about him? Was it pity? Was it love? Was it something in between? Either way, her feelings were much too strong for him. She had broken the number-one rule of her profession. Try as she might, she just couldn't stop thinking about him. *Worrying* about him. Those were the warning signs. It could only end badly if she didn't put a stop to it first.

She finished her drink and began pulling out her costume from her suitcase. Something had to be done. She had to talk to her handlers about getting out. Soon. Within a few weeks.

If the old man lasted that long.

Thirty minutes later, she was drunk.

It took a third of the bottle of Glen Livet, but a warm feeling had finally settled inside her, edging out the earlier fretting. She brushed her hair back into two pony tails and made some final adjustments to the costume the old man had requested for the night: that of a young high-school cheerleader. Then, with iced glasses and the rest of the Glen Livet in hand, she left her dressing room and climbed up into the observatory.

The old man was sitting at his telescope, his slightly trembling hands carefully turning the focusing knob.

"Christ, look at that thing . . ." he was mumbling, totally to himself. "That's a new one . . ."

"You're out of champagne," she said, announcing her arrival.

He took his eye of the telescope and squinted in her direction.

"Hey, is *that* my favorite outfit?"

"You always said it was," she replied, patting down the short, pleated skirt and adjusting her tight sweater. "Don't you like it anymore?"

"Yeah, sure I do," he said in a totally unconvincing tone. "Come over here, I want to show you something."

He pulled her small frame up onto his lap and directed her eye to the eyepiece.

"See it?"

She found herself looking at the full moon. It was so clear and focused, she felt like she could reach out and touch it.

"It's really beautiful," she replied sincerely.

He pulled her a little closer to him, gently squeezing her breasts as he did so. She suddenly hugged him, very tightly.

"You know, when I was a kid I dreamed of going there someday," he said wistfully. "I even thought these bastards would let me do it, sometime. It was the least they could do. But now . . . now, there's not a chance in hell of that happening. I don't think there's a chance in hell that *anyone* will ever go there again. Do you know why?"

She quickly pulled her eye away from the telescope, her carefully constructed aura of good feeling draining out of her.

"Please, don't start again . . ." she pleaded with him. "Can't we just have one night without this?"

He nudged her off his lap, stood up, and began pacing quickly around the circular room.

"If I don't tell you, who can I tell?" he asked, his tone desperate.

"But you've already told me everything!" she said to him, tears welling up in her eyes. "You tell *me* too much . . ."

"I can't keep all these things inside of me," he continued, desperately. "It's eating me up inside."

Angel stood in front of him and drunkenly pulled up her sweater, revealing her white cotton bra with calculating allure. Whenever he started with this, usually the sight of her daintly covered, small pert breasts was enough to distract him, to stop him from talking.

But not this time . . .

"It's getting worse," he told her, close to breaking down again. "I see signs of it everywhere. Out on the Range. In the sky. In my books. Even out in the stars. It's never been like this before. Not in the forty goddamn years I've been out here. I see omens, Angel. Hundreds of them—every day. They are messages to me. Telling me that something is about to happen!"

Angel pulled down her sweater and retreated to the room's huge leather couch, sitting down in a huff, wiping her eyes.

"Tell *them*," she told him despairingly. "They're all scientists and big brains, aren't they? I mean, they created all this. This *fake* war place. It must have taken geniuses to build it, to design it."

"I have told them," he said, choking up. "I've been telling them everything. But they claim they just can't make the connection. They can't see what I see. I know they're lying to me. I know they only keep me here for one reason—and everything else I tell them, they just ignore it."

He sat down beside her and put his face in his hands.

She couldn't let this happen again. Pulling off her sweater completely and unsnapping her bra, she put her arms around him and hugged him.

"Please forget about it all," she whispered, nuzzling her bare breasts into him. "Please forget what you've seen. Just do what they want and enjoy yourself. You've got *everything*. You've lived a good life . . ."

He pulled himself away from her and walked quickly into an adjacent room, soon returning with a huge box filled with scrapbooks.

"Oh, no, please . . ." she implored him. *"Not again."*

He ignored her and, instead, began pulling out the scrapbooks.

"Just look at this," he asked her, "it's my latest one."

He got down on his knees and dumped a pile of news clippings on the floor. Many had to do with the *Challenger* space-shuttle disaster; others were about various problems NASA had in getting the shuttles back into space after the accident. There were stories that documented military missile launchings that failed for one reason or another. There were at least fifty different stories on the initial failure of the Hubble Space Telescope, and another couple dozen on the problems of another telescope carried into orbit on a space shuttle in December of 1990.

Other stories were about factories that made solid fuel for rocket boosters blowing up—one of them in nearby Henderson, Nevada; one in Russia. Another batch of clips detailed accidents at the Soviet Union's rocket-launching centers; still another batch was devoted to problems with the French government's *Ariene* missile program.

"You see all this?" he asked her. "All of it is devoted to one topic: the consistent prevention of human beings being able to leave this planet in ways that we would accept as conventional. The space program of this country is moving *backward,* not forward. It has to be part of a plot. And if you would only take the time to read all this, you would see that it is all connected."

Angel now had her head down, her hands over her ears.

"They have stuff that makes all these fuel-assisted projectiles look like Model T cars," he said, more to himself than to her. "They *have* to by this time. They're just keeping it from me."

"Stop it!" she demanded. "Don't tell me any more of this. *I don't want to know . . ,*"

She had screamed so loudly at him that he finally had to take notice.

"All right," he said, gathering up the news clips and stuffing them back inside the scrapbook. "I'm sorry. I won't say any more about it. But you have to promise me something . . ."

"I'll do anything," she said hopefully, "if you just put that stuff away."

He looked at her for a long time and then said, "I saw an omen last night. It was in a new star formation I discovered. The stars tell me things, and this was a message that came through loud and clear.

"Someday – maybe soon, maybe years from now – someone will come here. They will know about some of this. They will understand. Maybe not at first, but eventually. In some ways, this person will look like me, but they'll be battered, bruised, and scarred. They may even be insane.

"Promise me, Angel, that if I die before this person gets here, you'll give all this stuff – give *everything* – to them. Okay?"

She looked up at him and felt more tears come to her eyes. He was old, crazy, and failing fast. Why did she care about him so damn much? . . .

"Okay," she said. "I promise."

He put the box back in the other room and then joined her on the couch.

Soon she was wrapped in his arms. At last, she felt safe. Secure. Warm. Wanted. *Needed.*

They shared a drink and together watched the holographic war rage outside the huge picture window.

19

Tango Base

The man they called the Boss walked into the briefing room and casually threw his notebook onto the lectern.

"Mission seven-seven-five-two has commenced," he called out to the room's half-dozen hidden microphones, his deep voice immediately activating them. "Time is 1935 hours, this date . . ."

The briefing room was dimly lit. Its dark paneling and red-bulbed track lighting gave it a mysterious hue, an entirely intentional effect. The walls, once adorned with various paraphernalia of the Soviet Air Force, were now bare, a reminder of how things had changed on the world political stage. The only leftovers of the Us-versus-Communism days were the red stars embroidered onto the seat covers of the two dozen chairs remaining in the room. There were once as many as fifty chairs, but most of them had been taken away as Cold War souvenirs.

Ryder, Woody, Williams, and Katt were the only other people in the briefing room. Each was dressed in his black zoomsuit and carrying his futuristic black crash helmet at his side. Each also had his detachable lap computer with him. Information on the upcoming mission would be inputted into this computer, which in turn would be plugged into the data flight hookups inside their individual airplanes.

The Boss cleared his throat for effect and then began the briefing.

"Gentlemen, your next mission is called ECC One. That is C-Two's acronym for extraordinary-contingency conditioning, program one.

"This is a brand new program. It was just loaded into the Cray supercomputer. The people at C-Two are very anxious to test it out, and therefore it will take precedence over any other operation.

"That's a direct order from C-Two. So from now until further notice, I guess you'd say, you're working directly for them."

Ryder and Woody shot knowing glances at each other. A mission coming down directly from C2 was highly unusual. This could be it, they both thought. The beginning of the ISC's gambit.

"According to this prospectus, anything can happen during ECC," the Boss went on. "It's a total-environment program. In the words of the C-Two programmers, ECC was written to assist the pilot to 'expect the unexpected.' Studies indicate that being a pilot doesn't improve your perception of identifying what's flying around up there. ECC was created to test methods of improving that perception, or, in their words, 'to improve a pilot's subjective decision-making capability . . .'"

All four Tango pilots stirred at the mention of these phrases. All of their missions in the past week had been relatively straightforward "turn and burns": ground attack, scramble intercepts, dogfights. But buzz phrases like "total environment" and "subjective decision-making" indicated the upcoming mission would involve psychological operations, known as psy-ops.

"We'll go on two-ship staggered launch," the Boss continued, reading from his notes. "Once you are up and mission-available, you will receive your individual vector points and further instructions directly from C-Two. There will be no nonemergency communications except with C-Two . . ."

The Boss then went into the long, involved process of reciting the relevant commands the pilots should input into their detachable airplane computers. When he was done, about fifteen minutes later, he put his notes away and removed his reading glasses.

"Any questions?" he asked.

"Yeah, how long does this program last?" Ryder asked. "One hour? Two? Until we land?"

The Boss rechecked his notes, whipping through the pages looking for some indication for the ECC time frame.

But it was quickly evident that there wasn't any.

"What can I tell you?" the base commander finally said. "There is no time limit. It appears to be an open-ended exercise.

133

No clock on it at all."

"That's strange," Teddy Williams observed.

"It sure is," the Boss agreed. "First time I've ever seen it. But it *is* a psy-ops mission and it *is* coming directly from C-Two. So, you never know what those guys are up to . . ."

Ryder nodded grimly toward Woody.

"Amen to that," he said under his breath.

An hour later, the first two black F-15Xs roared down the runway and streaked off into the night sky.

Colonel "Teddy" Williams was in the lead, his wingman, Commander "Crazy" Katt, close behind. They quickly reached their primary altitude of 10,000 feet and went into a slow orbit high above Tango Base. It was a clear night; the last rays of the sunset were just now fading in the west. With the emerging starlight and unlimited visibility, the conditions were perfect for night flying.

Exactly one minute into the flight, Williams's radio crackled to life.

"Tango One, this is C-Two . . . How do you read?"

Williams quickly cued his lip microphone. "C-Two, this is Tango One . . . I read you five-by-five . . ."

"Tango One, vector to coordinate Six-Romeo-Four," the disembodied voice told Williams. "Establish radio contact on arrival and prior to commencement of EEC program."

"Coordinate Six-Romeo-Four," Williams confirmed, punching the coordinate numbers into his flight computer. "Will establish radio contact on arrival . . ."

The voice of C2 then relayed a similar message to Katt, directing him to a coordinate nearly seventy-five miles in the opposite direction from Williams's mark.

As Katt broke away toward the northeast, Williams throttled his own F-15X up to 600 knots and roared off to the south. Vector Six-Romeo-Four was about eighty miles from Tango, and fairly close to the center of the Range itself. He knew it would be easy to locate, even at night. According to his terrain- guidance map display, a deep valley nicknamed Big Snake Wadi dominated the area, and a small lake called the Cassidy Sink was also nearby.

Williams was a little apprehensive about what C2 had in store for him this night. Flying a psy-ops mission was always a little nerve-wracking, even for a War Heaven veteran like himself. They were never dangerous per se – he'd flown during the Gulf war, so he knew what real danger was. Rather, a psy-ops flight always managed to tweak the pilot's psyche in such a way that it sometimes took weeks to stop thinking about it.

He reached his coordinate about nine minutes later, and immediately put the F-15X into a long, looping orbit at 12,500 feet directly above Cassidy Sink. Though only about a half mile in diameter, the lake was nevertheless one of the largest bodies of water out on the otherwise arid weapons range.

"C-Two, this is Tango One . . ." he called into his lip mike. "I am now at the Vector Six-Romeo-Four . . ."

"Roger, Tango One . . ." the monotone voice of C2 replied. "Hold your position . . . and report any traffic in your area."

Still orbiting above the half-moon-shaped lake, Williams searched the night sky but saw nothing flying in his immediate area. He routinely checked his fuel; it was holding steady. He checked his flight systems; everything was green. He checked the time. It was exactly 2100 hours.

That's when he saw it.

It appeared suddenly, up around 16,000 feet, about fourteen miles to his northwest. It was moving very slowly to the south, almost as if it were drifting toward him. Right away he knew he'd never seen anything quite like it before.

It was not an airplane. Rather, it was a bright blue light – the brightest blue he'd ever seen, almost neon in intensity, but with an odd sparkling quality, too.

He quickly checked his APG-65 radar set, and it confirmed his visual sighting with a corresponding blip on his readout screen.

"C-Two, this is Tango One . . ." he called into his lip mike. "I have visual and radar on unidentified traffic. At sixteen . . . about fourteen to my northwest. I have no IFF reading."

"Roger, Tango One," the toneless voice replied. "Input ECC One program now."

Williams quickly acknowledged C2's instructions and punched the ECC program command into his flight computer. Instantly the special radio-ready light on his instrument panel blinked on. This told him that from that moment on, his only line of communication would be with C2. He could no longer use his radio to call back to Tango or anywhere else, unless his flight computer judged it to be an

135

absolute emergency.

At the same time, his two-patch flight recorder light came on. This meant that the entire ECC would be recorded by the videotape camera located in the F-15X's nose and that his audio communications with C2 as well as his personal comments would be registered on an audio-tape recorder patched into his lip microphone.

It took only a few seconds for everything to be set; then he pushed his radio send button.

"C-Two, this is Tango One . . . ECC program is inputted. I am awaiting further instructions . . ."

"Roger, Tango One . . . Commence intercept and VISID of bogey."

As Williams acknowledged the order, he knew the first motive of his ECC was now revealed. C2 wanted him to get close enough to the strange blue light to attempt a VISID, or visual identification. It was more or less a routine command, though in the past he'd performed it only with other airplanes posing as enemy fighters.

He banked hard to the left, pushed his throttles forward to 750 mph airspeed and aimed straight for the bright blue light. It was still moving to the south, but very slowly. At this rate of speed, he estimated, he'd be at close visual range inside a minute.

As he closed in on the bogey, he realized the light was actually emanating from a diamond-shaped object that looked a huge toy top. It was about twenty feet from top to bottom and slightly wider from side to side. It was also spinning very rapidly, and this action was responsible for giving off the shower of bright blue sparks.

He was immediately fascinated by the object. The big blue top was obviously supposed to be a UFO—the billions of dollars' worth of holographic projection equipment scattered about the Range could create just about any kind of an illusion. But this Zoot projection appeared to be much more elaborate than anything he'd even seen before.

He booted up his throttles to near full military power, anxious to get a closer look at the projection. But when he closed to within four miles, the blue top suddenly began vibrating, throwing out even more sparks than before. When he got within three miles, the top suddenly accelerated away from him at an incredible speed.

"Holy cow!" Williams heard himself exclaim. "Look at the mother go . . ."

The blue top rocketed away to the south at a speed of 5000 mph or even more. Williams immediately kicked in the F-15X's afterburners, boosting his own speed past 1000 mph, but he knew it would be but a snail's crawl compared to the speed of the diamond-shaped blue light.

Then, in a heartbeat, the bogey came to a sudden halt. It was now about twenty-five miles off to his left and slightly above his present 12,500-foot altitude. Once it had settled in this position, it began spinning rapidly again.

Once more Williams banked the F-15X directly toward it and kicked in his afterburners. But once he came within three miles, it zipped away again, this time following a lightning-quick flight pattern directly across his nose and stopping ten miles off to his right.

"Incredible . . ." Williams whispered for his own benefit, his words duly recorded on the plane's voice cockpit recorder.

He decided to reduce his rate of approach this time, hoping to get in further on the flying top. Cutting back to a 210-knot crawl, he steered a course direction slightly higher and to the right of it. The idea worked. With this approach, he was able to study the projection longer.

Its detail was simply amazing. It looked like a huge aerial toy, something that might be part of an elaborate amusement-park attraction. A lot of things in War Heaven looked that way – but this holograph was different. It was truly enthralling to him – in a strangely personal sort of way. The way it moved, the way it would spin, the way it was throwing off long streams of lightning-blue sparks.

What was it about the object? It was almost as if he'd seen it somewhere before.

Then it suddenly came to him: He'd been married, more than twenty years before, and had had a young son. Tragically, both his wife and child were lost in a boating accident while he was deployed overseas. The boy was only three years old when he died, and the last toy Williams had given him had been a blue spinning top, the kind that would emit sparks when you cranked it up. Now, as he watched the strange blue top blazing in the night sky above Cassidy Sink, the veteran pilot couldn't help thinking fondly back about his son and that toy.

When he passed over the three-mile threshold again, the projection flitted away once more, this time to a point six miles ahead and about a mile below him. He tried an approach that was further off-angle, and managed to close to within two point eight miles. But then the bogey simply reversed itself, rocketed by him at tremendous speed, and wound up back at its former position, now far off his tail.

It went on like this for the next ten minutes. Sometimes he got tantalizingly close – to within a mile on two occasions – only to have the bright blue bogey accelerate away from him at the last moment. Throughout the pursuit, it performed an outstanding repertoire of maneuvers, spinning, tumbling, shooting away at extreme angles and extreme speeds with little warning or effort. Williams found himself pulling seven, eight, and sometimes nine *g's* just trying to keep up with it.

But despite the gut-wrenching turns, he was enjoying himself immensely. The projection was so strange, so intricate – it was almost religious in appearance. He found he had a hard time taking his eyes off it; it was truly hypnotic. He found that his entire thinking process was dedicated to getting as close to it as possible so he could see it clearer, study it further, appreciate it more.

But then, at twelve minutes into the exercise, his radio clicked on.

"Tango One, this is C-Two . . . Please give us a flight-condition read and then stand by for further ECC instructions."

Keeping the blue top in view, Williams ran a quick check of his flight systems and then reported back to C2 that everything was in order.

"Roger, Tango One . . . You will continue pursuit of bogey and initiate offensive action, all weapons . . ."

Williams was stunned. He asked C2 to repeat the command.

"Continue pursuit . . ." the monotone voice of C2 said once again. "Initiate offensive action . . . all weapons."

Williams couldn't believe what he was hearing.

Did they really want him to shoot at it?

More than a hundred miles to the northeast, Navy Commander Larry "Crazy" Katt was chasing his own "UFO."

He too had some trepidations about flying the ECC psy-op. Though his wartime experience was limited only to the last days of the Gulf war, that violent burst of actual combat was enough to put the fear of Mars into him. Before shipping to Saudi Arabia though, he'd worked for a secret Navy unit that had created psy-ops programs for Desert Storm.

So he knew what psy-ops could do.

His original vector point was located above a particularly rugged and desolate part of the weapons range nicknamed "Bumps and Scrapes" for its almost inaccessible terrain.

It was fairly unusual for anyone to be vectored to this point—flying over the sharp rocky hills of Bumps and Scrapes was usually avoided, because they would make any unforeseen air-search-and-rescue operation very difficult. Plus it was rumored that Bumps and Scrapes was the least "wired" section of War Heaven. The Fitzies in this area were few and far between, again because of the inhospitable terrain.

But oddly, Katt felt a connection to the place. He'd grown up in the Black Hills of South Dakota, and Bumps and Scrapes reminded him of home.

As soon as he arrived over the series of sharp, jagged hills, he spotted the Zoot UFO hovering close to the deck.

It was bright red and looked like a large lampshade attached to a hubcap. He estimated its base measured about 50 feet in diameter with the lampshade portion rising about 20 feet above the hubcap. There was a series of blinking yellow lights around the top of the lampshade, with another circuit of white lights at the base.

Upon first spotting it, he immediately contacted C2, inputted his ECC program, and saw his nose-camera and cockpit-audio-recorder lights switch on.

He'd been in pursuit of the huge flying hubcap ever since.

Like the vast majority of pilots—military or otherwise—Katt had never seen a "real" UFO. So he doubted that such things actually existed, simply because he couldn't believe what he'd never seen.

But this was ECC—a psy-ops test in extraordinary contingency conditioning. Many times the key in psy-ops was to *not* believe one's eyes, to trust the other senses more. He knew that the UFO was actually a holographically simulated projection, but it was probably meant to be much more than that. There was almost a humorous edge to it, like it was a big cartoon that had been elaborately drawn on the night sky. He found himself admiring it as it streaked back and forth across the sky, playing a high-speed game of tag with him. As a boy he'd devoured comic books of all kinds, and now, looking at the strange lampshade on a hubcap object, he felt as if all those child-hood comic book dreams had come true, if just for a moment.

So he was astonished when he received C2's orders that he should fire on the object.

Suddenly the exercise wasn't that much fun anymore.

But orders were orders. He powered up his Zoot Sidewinders and then activated his Zoot cannon.

The object was moving at about 50 mph, 2500 feet above the southern end of Bumps and Scrapes. Katt screeched the F-15X into a tight turn and lined up the object in his HUD display. The object was moving so slowly, it presented an almost obscenely easy target.

He keyed his HUD's target square on the center of the lampshade and launched a Zoot Sidewinder.

"Tally One . . ." he announced strictly for the flight recorder. "Missile away . . ."

He blinked as the Zoot flash from the holographically projected missile erupted from under his left wing. The Zoot missile streaked away and zeroed in on the center of the object. Katt found himself keeping his eyes closed for a second longer than he should have; something deep inside him wouldn't let him watch the missile impact on the colorful, cartoonlike projection.

He waited to hear the cockpit target-hit tone buzz on – but the sound never came. He opened his eyes to see that the missile had hit nothing and had dissolved in the night sky.

The object had disappeared.

He yanked back on his control stick and put some air between him-self and the dark ground. As soon as he leveled off at 7000 feet, the projection appeared again, this time hovering about a mile from the eastern edge of the jagged hills.

Once again, he streaked toward it and launched a Zoot Side-winder – this time he was determined to watch the missile during its full flight. But once again the flying hubcap blinked out just as the holographic missile was about to hit, only to reappear in another part of the sky.

"What the hell is this?" he whispered, just loud enough to be picked up by the audio recorder.

He spotted the hubcap a third time, hovering almost directly above him, at about 8200 feet. He flipped the big F-15X over on its back and launched a third missile as he was climbing at a very steep angle.

The missile homed in on the object fast and true. But once again, just as it was about to impact, the projection blinked out, only to reappear about four miles to his south.

"What's the point of this?" Katt said in a pique of frustration.

The pattern repeated itself one more time: he loosed his fourth and final Sidewinder, and missed the object, only to have it blink out and appear tantalizingly close-by.

"I wish it would stop playing games," Katt said suddenly into his lip mike.

But then another thought came to him: *Maybe that's the whole idea . . .*

20

Ryder and Woody received their launch orders forty-five minutes after Williams and Katt.

Once they took off and reached the prescribed altitude of 10,000 feet, they went into their slow orbit above Tango, checking that their aircraft and their myriad of high-tech flight systems were all working properly.

Once all of his key systems came back green, Ryder did a quick visual scan of the landscape below. For the most part, it looked dark and lifeless. But it was still early in the evening.

"Tango Three, this is Four," he radioed over to Woody, who was flying off his right wing. "Not much going on down there tonight . . ."

"A slow night on the reservation," came the reply.

Or maybe it's the calm before the storm, Ryder thought.

Suddenly his radio crackled to life.

"Tango Four . . . this is C-Two . . ."

Ryder hesitated a moment before keying his radio switch. At last, he was going to speak directly with the enemy — or at least someone very close to them.

"This is Tango Four, C-Two. Go ahead . . ."

"Tango Four, your vector is point Seven-Voodoo-Five," the slightly-echoing voice told him. "Establish radio contact on arrival."

"Roger, Control. Tango Four out."

Ryder tapped the coordinates for his mission into the flight computer. In the meantime, Woody was receiving his own instructions from C2.

"Heads up, Ghost," Woody radioed over, as he turned to the southeast toward his vector point.

"Roger, partner," Ryder replied. "Keep the faith . . ."

Ryder's vector point, Seven-Voodoo-Five, was located in the northwest corner of War Heaven.

The terrain below the point was mountainous and, in some parts, thickly covered with scrub brush and pine trees. Thus it was nicknamed "the Ponderosa."

It took Ryder nine minutes and change to reach the assigned position, and once there, he leveled off at 12,500 feet and did a quick visual scan of the sky around the area. He saw nothing but stars and the nearly-full, bright moon. He switched on his supersecret APG-65 radar, but an electronic sweep of the area came up empty, too.

He keyed his radio switch.

"Control, this is Tango Four. I am at Seven-Voodoo-Five and holding . . ."

He never heard the reply. Suddenly right above him there was a tremendous flash of light. He banked the F-15X hard to the left, spinning away from the burst of illumination. Quickly regaining his bearings, he pulled out at 6000 feet and checked to make sure everything inside the airplane was still working. Only then did he loop back around and get a good look at the source of the light.

He quickly realized that the flash was actually a Zoot projection of somebody's idea of a UFO. The object was hovering up around 15,000 feet about four miles off his left wing.

He had seen many things projected by the Zoots—bomb blasts, shellfire, missile hits. But this was by far the strangest. It was bright orange and shaped just like a huge tea saucer. There was a string of lights running around its lip with a large flashing red beacon on center top. There was even a double line of portholes around its middle, each with a series of blinking yellow lights surrounding it. If there was such thing as a generic design for a flying saucer, then this was it. He wouldn't have been surprised if the letters "UFO" were emblazoned on its side.

The whole idea would have been amusing for Ryder—if it weren't

143

for what Moon had told him earlier about the crazy UFO tabloid stories and their link to the ISC. What could be the connection between a Zoot UFO and C2's seditious agenda? He had no idea.

But he couldn't dwell on the big picture at the moment. Not when his every move would be monitored by C2 and the ISC. One moment's hesitation on his part might tip his hand and lead someone back at C2 to suspect that he knew something they didn't.

And that would be disastrous.

So an instant after cueing in on the projection, he quickly snapped on his APG radar and then keyed his lip mike.

"Control, this is Tango Four. I have unidentified traffic above me and four miles to my left. I have a visual on it, plus a reading on the APG."

"Roger, Tango Four," the voice of C2 responded. "Input your ECC One program now and go for VISID on unidentified traffic."

Ryder quickly acknowledged the order, again knowing that a second's delay might cast suspicion on him. He inputted his ECC command, and saw the appropriate radio and video-camera lights blink on his control panel.

Then he took off after the saucer.

For the next twenty minutes, he chased the Zoot UFO up and down the length of the northwest quadrant, trying to get as close as possible to the projection.

Although its design looked like a reject from a bad sci-fi movie, the Zoot was able to perform some astounding aerial maneuvers, sometimes emitting a dull red glow when it did so. It was almost crafty in the way it allowed itself to be chased. Anytime he brought the F-15X within three miles or so, it would accelerate away at tremendous speed, winding up ten to twelve miles away in the opposite end of the sky. There it would stop, hover, and taunt him to chase it again.

He tried everything to get close to the flying holograph: approaching it from above, from below, from the side. He flew long, looping circles around it, cutting in at the last second at full power in an attempt to catch the thing off-guard. He tried approaching it at near-stall speeds, or at radically unpredictable angles of attack. But none of his strategies worked. As soon as he came very close, the Zoot

UFO would rocket away from him.

He finally slowed the F-15X down to 250 knots and considered the situation for a moment. The VISID exercise was somewhat typical; closing in and identifying unknown aircraft was a rote exercise for most U.S. fighter pilots. The only difference here was that the object was suppose to be something other than the normal adversarial aircraft.

But did this necessarily mean that C2 wanted to change all of the rules of engagement?

That's when Ryder got an idea.

"C-Two this is Tango Four . . ."

"Go ahead, Tango Four . . ."

"C-Two, unidentified traffic is evading my efforts at VISID. Request permission to use offensive action . . ."

Not quite knowing how his request would be received by C2, he had expected somewhat of a longer delay at the other end of the line.

But no sooner were the words out of his mouth when C2 eame back on: "Permission granted, Tango Four . . . Use all offensive weapons at your disposal."

The Green force supply truck pulled to the side of the mountain road and its driver and passenger got out.

It was close to 2200 hours. They'd been on the road for nearly five hours, moving a load of Zoot-system battery rechargers from a warehouse near the southern part of War Heaven all the way up to the northeast corner of the weapons range. Now it was time for a stretch, a whiz break, and a smoke.

They went about their bodily business and then walked across the road to a small area that looked out over a twisting river canyon. It was a clear, warm night, the breeze blowing through the canyon providing a cool relief for the pair of soldiers. They each lit up a Marlboro and sat down on top of a flat boulder that offered a spectacular view of the large canyon below.

A few puffs into their smoke break, they saw a flash of light off to the north, near the far entrance to the twisting river valley. The men barely stirred; the night sky above the Range was always lit up with all types of Zoot explosions. This one looked no different.

Not at first, anyway.

After another couple drags, they saw the light again. This time it was closer to them by a half mile or so, and it was clearly nearer to the ground than when it had first appeared.

"What the hell is that?" one soldier asked the other.

"Beats the shit out of me," his companion replied. "It's a Zoot, I guess . . ."

They watched now with gaining interest as the light stayed on. It looked like a huge Fourth of July sparkler set on its end. It was moving very fast and leaving a trail of bright red embers in its wake.

Suddenly, they saw another light coming right up on the sparkler's tail. This second light was bright red and it was mimicking the twisting and turning of the large flying sparkler. At the same moment, they heard a noise that sounded like far-off thunder, along with a loud explosive popping.

Just seconds later the rumbling and popping increased dramatically, so much so that they could feel the boulders beneath them begin to shake. All the while, the pair of lights were rocketing through the winding canyon and coming right for them.

"What the fuck is going on?" one of the soldiers cried, as they both dropped their smokes, stood up, and instinctively backed away from the ledge.

"They've *got* to be Zoots . . ." the other trooper replied nervously, having to yell now over the ever-increasing racket.

"They'd *better* be Zoots!" his partner yelled.

Five earthshaking seconds later, they watched with mouths agog as the blazing sparkler streaked by them no more than a hundred feet in front of their position. It looked like a huge flying cigar, thirty-five feet in length and emanating a variety of bright yellow and white sparks.

Even more incredible, a jet fighter was right on its tail, its nose cannon blasting away.

"Jesuzz Christ!" both men yelled at once.

The two objects had rocketed by them at such a high velocity, they were gone in just an instant. But in a freeze-frame of the moment, both soldiers recognized the jet fighter as one of the famous black F-15X Tangos, specifically Aircraft No. 3, according to the markings on its tail.

"Crazy motherfuckers . . ." one of the troopers said as they watched the two objects twist and turn away from them and pass over

146

the horizon.

His partner had to agree. As they walked back to the truck, still shaking from the experience, the other trooper shook his head and said, "Those Tango guys are all nuts . . ."

21

"Tango Base, this is Tango Four . . . come in."

Ryder was about ten minutes away from landing back at Tango, his fuel low, his strange flight coming to an end.

As it turned out, he never hit his Zoot UFO with any of the F-15's holographic weapons; never even got close with his simulated missiles. Every time he fired one of his Zoot Sidewinders at the target, the "flying saucer" would blink out—just disappear—only to reappear seconds later in a different part of the sky.

He'd wasted two Zoot missiles on the ghostly projection before switching over to his Zoot cannon, and he had come closer to finding the mark with this holographic weapon. At first he had tried firing straight on at the stationary target, just as he would have if it were a hovering helicopter. But after lining up the Zoot UFO and pushing the cannon trigger, the target would shift just enough to get out of the way of the simulated cannon shells. Then, as soon as the barrage passed by and dissipated into nothingness, the Zoot UFO would either resume its former position or blink out and show up in yet another part of the sky.

The closest he came was when he fired a burst of Zoot shells slightly ahead of and above the Zoot UFO just before it disappeared. "Leading the target," is what they called it, and he had done it just on a hunch. But because the flying saucer would blink out and then reappear, it was next to impossible to lead it in the right direction. So Ryder guessed during one strafing run, and saw, just barely, a series of red mini-explosions on the edge of the craft's auralike glow, before it blinked out and disappeared for good.

His fuel-warning light came on soon afterward; and a quick call to

148

C2 confirmed that he should head back to Tango. The radio connection between him and C2 was thus broken—to his relief, he couldn't call them now if he wanted to.

Just what the weird exercise all meant was mystifying. Intercepting fake UFOs was one thing; but asking for and getting permission to fire on them was another. The ramifications were even stranger. War Heaven was a training ground; its function was to prepare the soldier for real combat out in the real world.

So what the hell did using Zoot UFOs as target practice have to do with the real world?

He checked his position and found himself about 40 miles and eight minutes north of Tango. He'd just made another routine call to the Tango tower when he felt an odd chill run through him.

Suddenly, up at his eleven o'clock position, he spotted a string of colored lights reflecting against the star-filled sky. There looked to be nine in all: three reds, three whites, and three ambers.

His first thought was that the lights were those of a formation of aircraft passing overhead. But when he turned his APG radar on, the screen showed no indications.

He quickly made a note of the time: it was 2125 hours. He checked his position. He was flying due south at 11,500 feet, cruising at 450 knots. A rough calculation told him the unusual lights were six miles to his left, about three miles above, and slowly moving southeast.

Strange things moving through the sky were certainly nothing new in War Heaven; his ECC program just minutes before had proved that.

But as he kept the strange lights in view, he was surprised to see another string of colors appear next to them. These too were red, white, and amber and numbered nine. Together with the first line of lights, they moved to form a massive V shape.

What the hell is this? he thought. Now the lights definitely didn't appear to be Zoot-generated. They actually seemed to be attached to something solid. Something that had mass and weight.

Something that *looked* real.

He estimated that nearly a half mile separated one end of the boomerang shape from the other. This meant that if the lights *were* attached to some kind of aircraft, then it was enormous.

He tried to settle himself down by taking long slow breaths of the cool oxygen. Was this an optical illusion? A reflection of some Zoot battle taking place somewhere below? Could the appearance of the strange lights be part of his ECC program? Or could he have blundered into someone else's ECC exercise?

He pulled his throttles back almost to a stall position, never once taking his eyes off the strange lights.

His first instinct was to climb to altitude and investigate, but once again the essence of his deep mission came back to him. It was imperative that he avoid any move that would lead C2 to suspect he was acting on something other than their orders.

And the last order he'd received from C2 before their radio connection was terminated had been for him to return to base. Plus he was running out of fuel.

He increased his speed slightly as the lights passed directly overhead.

Suddenly, a beam of light shot out from the bottom of the object, bathing his airplane just for an instant in dull crimson. The action startled him for a moment; this *was* out of a bad sci-fi movie.

But as soon as the red light was gone, he looked up—to see that the boomerang of lights had disappeared.

Suddenly he was all alone in the empty sky, sucking on his oxygen mask and feeling very strange.

I should have stayed in show business, he thought.

22

Four hours later

The road from Tango Base to Jacks was little more than a dusty path burned through the dry brush of high Nevada desert.

The only thing moving on this road at the moment was one of the beat-up Hummers that served as a do-it-yourself taxi for the pilots at Tango. Ryder was at the wheel of the vehicle; Woody was strapped into the passenger seat, trying his best to sip from a flask of brandy. For the most part, he was losing the battle to the bumpy roadbed.

It was now almost 0200 hours, the dead of night in many places, but possibly the busiest time of the day for War Heaven. The sky was filled with the glare of hundreds of red, green, and yellow flashes from Zoot explosions going off throughout the Range. Fighter jets roared overhead with routine frequency, on their way to some assigned action elsewhere on the Range. Occasionally an Apache attack chopper could be seen making its way through the rocky hills of the west, looking for targets of opportunity. And several times they saw heavily-armed patrols of Gray army troops moving through the valley below, using the cover of night to deploy to some secret destination.

All this activity was lost on the two pilots, though. In many ways they couldn't have cared less. They'd just endured the most bewildering debriefing session in their short but intensive assignment with the War Heaven Aggressors – one that made even less sense than the ECC mission they'd flown earlier that evening.

All four Tango pilots had known something was up when they walked into the briefing room after landing to find that the Boss, who

151

was their usual postmission officer, was nowhere to be seen. In his place was a trio of almost faceless men, each one with dark complexion, each one wearing an ill-fitting black business suit.

There were no introductions, no explanations, not even the usual postflight spread of hot coffee and doughnuts. The three men simply wanted to hear about the just-completed flight.

In great detail.

As the senior pilot, "Teddy" Williams went first. Typical of his rather quiet, dignified manner, he coolly and dispassionately told of his first sighting of the flying bright blue diamond, of his attempts to get close to it for a VISID, of receiving his orders to fire on it, of his subsequent failure to hit the target, and of its eventual departure out over the western mountains.

Katt went next. He described his interception of the flying lampshade-on-a-hubcap in almost clinical terms, reciting precise altitude levels and airspeeds of each of his close encounters, as well as his four unsuccessful attempts to shoot at the "object."

Woody then regaled the briefing with his tale of chasing the hypersonic flying cigar through endless canyons and twisting riverbeds, graphic in his description of the earth-scraping peril. It was revealed that he hadn't even asked C2 for permission to fire on his Zoot UFO. He had simply assumed it was okay because he was following the rules of standard unidentified-aircraft interception to the letter. These indeed said that any unidentified aircraft should be fired on as a last resort.

By comparison, then, Ryder's description of his pursuit and engagement of the "generic" flying-saucer Zoot was dull and businesslike. That was his intention. As soon as he set eyes on the three strangers, his gut told him not to reveal anything about his sighting of the second V-shaped object in the skies over War Heaven that night – not unless they asked him about it first.

It would turn out to be a very wise decision.

Once all four pilots gave their reports, the three men, standing ramrod straight next to the briefing podium, made a strange request: They wanted to hear it all again.

The baffled, caffeine-starved pilots couldn't believe it. But at the civilians' stern insistence, they went through the entire debriefing again. The blue diamond, the lampshade, the cigar, and the generic flying saucer. The only things changed were the cadence with which the reports were spoken. It took only about half as long the second time around.

But just when they thought they were finished, the unsmiling civilians insisted they do the briefing a third time. The pilots raised a brief complaint, but when told that it was all part of the ECC, they repeated their stories a third time.

And then a fourth.

And then a fifth.

When the pilots threatened to walk out upon the sixth request, the trio of black suits relented—but only a little. They simply switched strategies and began interviewing the pilots individually in a side room usually reserved for video- and film-projection equipment, while the others were forced to wait in the still-coffeeless briefing room.

As before, Ryder went last. He had no idea what the other pilots had told the strangers, but when it was finally his turn, the debriefers concentrated not on specifics, but on trying to find inconsistencies in his previous story of the encounter with the Zoot flying saucer. Oddly, the fact that the object was a holographic projection didn't seem to matter a whit to the questioners. They just wanted him to tell his story over and over again. Each time he did, they attacked points that he had quite innocently left out.

The questioners used many tactics during this hour-long inquisition. Good cop-bad cop. Nonverbal intimidation. Even bribes. Hints of thousands of points or transfer for TDY in places like Hawaii were dropped frequently. All Ryder had to do was agree that he recognized some holes in his story.

But through it all, he just told the same tale, many times, as close as he could, never once tripping over his words to indicate that something else had gone on that night.

When it was over, the three men in black suits had one last odd request.

They produced a single, typed page that they asked him to sign.

It read: *I, the undersigned, as an officer in the armed forces of the United States, do adhere to the principles concerning activities following the detection of extraterrestrial intelligence.*

Ryder barely read the document before signing it. If it meant getting away from the strange trio, the quicker the better.

Then, once the four pilots were reunited again in the briefing room, the Boss had finally made an appearance.

The Tango Base commander had had a quick whispered talk with the three men in black suits, and then he'd taken the podium to drop his own bombshell.

"I just have a short announcement," he had said, nervously eyeing the three men sitting at the back of the briefing room. "Although no timetable has been set, you should know that you will be leaving here and moving on to your deployment soon. Just where that is, and what your mission will be, is classified, of course. You are on stand-down until the orders come through . . ."

And that was it.

Williams and Katt set out immediately for Jacks, intent on getting in as much boozing as possible before shipping out. Woody was conveniently delayed, allowing him and Ryder to leave in the second Hummer about twenty minutes later.

Both of them knew they had to talk.

Now, as they reached the end of the high valley road, Ryder slowed the vehicle at the top of the hill. Spread out before them was the vast weapons range, lit up in every direction with continuous Zoot flashes.

He slipped the Hummer into neutral and rolled it to a halt.

Because they were forced to operate on the principle that every building at Tango was bugged, he and Woody had had very few opportunities to discuss their secret mission. But now, so far out in the middle of nowhere, that fear was lessened considerably.

Still, they had to be sure.

"How's this place?" he asked Woody, scanning the nearby terrain for any indication of hidden listening devices. "Is it clean?"

"Looks okay," Woody confirmed. "Unless they're bouncing us with a long-range electronic ear . . ."

"We'll have to take that chance," Ryder replied, keeping the Hummer's engine turning to help mask their conversation.

He took a swig from Woody's brandy bottle and then, in smooth, measured tones, he told his friend about the second flying object he'd spotted that night.

Woody listened intently, but, by the end of the story, was hardly surprised.

"It could have been a lot of things, I suppose," he told Ryder. "Though it doesn't sound like anyone else's Zoot, there's always a lot of strange shit flying around out here."

"That's for sure," Ryder agreed, taking another slug of the brandy. "The thing is, I don't know what would be worse: C-Two knowing about this thing or them *not* knowing. Either way, I just thought it was best not to mention it to the Three Stooges back there.

"Besides, we might have more important things to worry about."

"That's for sure," Woody replied. "Like where the hell are we going, and what will happen here once we leave here? You know that if the Boss goes through the trouble of telling us we're deploying soon, then we must be deploying *damn* soon . . ."

Ryder had to agree. Once one was immersed in the strange world that was War Heaven, it was difficult to keep in proper perspective what the place was all about. It was a training ground, plain and simple, a means to an end. Any soldier assigned there was getting trained for something off in the future. The last time he and Woody had left the Range they had gone to fight the superterrorist Colonel Toon in the wilds of Burma.

Just where they were slated to go this time was anyone's guess.

But it was even more complicated now. In order to maintain their cover for Moon, they *had* to go along with whatever their deployment orders were, simply because they had to assume the men of ICS were the ones writing those orders. And if that meant shipping out to the Middle East, or Asia, or wherever, they would have no alternative but to go.

On the whole, that was a rather disconcerting prospect.

"We can't do much about the ICS here if we're eating sand somewhere on the other side of the world," Woody said, encapsulating the situation perfectly with a slug of brandy. "And without the Moon Man around to direct traffic, for all we know, we could be out of this game before the first quarter is over."

"We'll just have to do what Moon and I talked about when he first briefed me," Ryder said. "Where ever we go, we have to remember that the problem with the ICS is here. On the Range. Right down in Area Sixty-one."

"Right," Woody confirmed.

"So," Ryder continued, "no matter where the hell they ship us to, when the time comes, and we're sure that the shit is about to hit the fan, we've got to try like hell to get back in here. Either together or separately. And when we do, we go through with Moon's mission, no matter what . . ."

Woody slapped him a weary, ritualistic high-five. "I hear you, brother," he said. "Under the circumstances, it's really the only thing we can do . . ."

They worked on the flask again and watched a particularly spectacular rocket attack between two Fitzies about ten miles to the south of their position.

"But I'll tell you something, partner," Woody said, capping the flask and putting it back in his pocket. "We really fucked up by becoming heroes last time."

"You can say that again," Ryder replied.

With that, he slipped the Hummer in gear and set out down the road to Jacks.

23

The Eye

The wind was blowing so hard on top of the mesa that the hard-nosed troopers of the L-10 protection squad had to take cover in their vehicles, lest they suffer painful face and eye injuries from the stream of sand blasting the summit.

It was now 0315 – the L-10s had been deployed atop the desolate butte since midnight, and from the looks of things, they would probably be holding the position until the sun came up.

It was obvious to these multiservice soldiers that something very important was going on inside the concrete bunker known as the Eye. The distinctive dark blue helicopters used by the men at C2 had been shuttling in and out all night from Area 61, their pilots braving the high winds atop the mesa to unload their cargoes of anonymous nondescript men.

So far, seventeen of them had airlifted in, and what was going on inside the Eye was known only to them, the handful of bunker technicians, and the old man from Casa Fantasica who L-10 had escorted here.

"We are about to play the main program," the amplified voice boomed inside the Eye. "Will everyone punch in their security codes . . . now."

There was a brief flurry of button-pushing as the dozen and a half men entered their individual 21-digit security codes into their armchair computers.

"Security code verification complete," one of the three men inside the control room announced. Suddenly the Eye's huge room-length video screen was alive with a dazzling color bar.

"Commencing main program . . ." another voice, that of the meeting's narrator, called over the room's speakers. "Here we go . . ."

The color bar disappeared in a brief burst of static. Then came a jittery shot of the full moon against a star-filled night sky.

Everyone in the room recognized the view right away as coming from the nose camera of a jet fighter.

"This is ECC One by the first Tango aircraft," the control-room narrator continued.

"Is this the pilot who lost his family?" someone asked.

"Yes it is," was the narrator's reply, adding: "You'll see the BT-One coming into view in a few seconds . . ."

As promised, the distinct, bright-blue, diamond-shaped flying "object" edged into view, a spray of bright sparks emanating from its top and middle.

Several of those in the audience applauded, so vivid was the sight of the Zoot projection known to the men of C2 as BT-1, or "Blue Top One."

"As you can see, the target was extremely well constructed," the narrator continued. "The psychological profile was very accurate. As a result, Tango One's intercept program went well – though some initial hesitancy was detected."

The group watched in silence as the twenty-one-minute tape of "Teddy" Williams's ECC intercept played on, from his first sighting of the blue light, through his unsuccessful attempt to fire Zoot missiles at it, ending with a long shot of the BT-1 disappearing into the starry night.

Once again, there was a smattering of applause.

"So far, so good . . ." the narrator intoned. "Here is Tango Two . . ."

The eighteen-and-a-half-minute video of Katt's intercept program was shown, his nose camera recording the high-speed flying lampshade, which was officially known at C2 as the GB-Alternate, GB standing for "Gulf Breeze."

"Notice the very systematic approach to this intercept," the narrator went on. "This pilot was involved in developing psy-ops earlier in his career, so he had, let's say, a head start on the others."

When Katt's tape was over, the narrator announced, "Once again, another textbook mission . . ." to another brief round of applause.

The group then watched Woody's hair-raising, low-level chase of the object the C2 men knew as the RTC – for Red-Tipped Cigar. Several times there were slight, absolutely unintentional titters at Woody's unconventional maneuvering through the narrow canyons as he chased the RTC, his Zoot nose cannon blasting away.

"The interesting thing about this pilot was, he initiated offensive fire *on his own,* without first asking for permission," the narrator explained. "Now, while this does suggest a kind of trigger-happy profile, it also scores very high on the initiative scale, not to mention the complete lack of the 'innate sentimentality factor' we saw with Tango One . . ."

There was a hardy round of applause as Woody's tape ended.

"And finally, gentlemen," the narrator intoned, "here is Tango Four's intercept . . .

The twenty-three-minute tape from Ryder's F-15X nose camera elicted several more outbursts of applause, especially toward the end where he was able to score several hits on the target Zoot UFO, which was known in C2 jargon as the ACME Flying Saucer, for its generic looks.

"This pilot performed the best of all for a number of reasons," the narrator explained. "One, he tracked the target superbly. Two, there was little or no sentimentality involved. Three, there were high marks for initiative. Four, he *asked* for permission to use his weapons without any prompting. And five, as you can see, he was the only pilot to actually score any hits . . ."

"Was that by design or just luck?" someone asked.

"According to the postmission briefing," the narrator explained, "the Tango Four pilot came up with the notion to lead the target, after he was somewhat frustrated with the target's evasive tactics."

"It's amazing, when you think about it," a voice from the dark said. "Is it a replay of the famous 'one in a billion shot'?"

"You'll have to ask Einstein that question," the narrator replied, to the laughter of the others. "But it's a big step in the right direction . . ."

Finally the tape ended and the lights came up.

"That was extraordinary . . ." someone said above the immediate din of whispered voices. "Four pilots. Four different profiles. Four near-flawless performances."

"Have we really found our perfect pilots?" another voice asked.

"We must still discuss it . . ." still another voice cautioned.

At that point, the C2 members left their seats and broke down into smaller groups, each one immediately becoming involved in an animated conversation.

There was really only one question to debate. Some members counseled patience, arguing that time should be given to allow further programs. Others advocated moving ahead boldly, citing a drastically-shrinking time-to-action frame, the expenditure of many resources to get to this point, and the outstanding performance of the Tango pilots.

Finally, as the sun began to rise and two hours of group discussion died down, the C2 group voted that the four pilots should advance to phase two of what was known as ISC Program Ten, code-named Project Rapture.

The vote was seventeen to one. Only the old man in the long gray pony tail and the battered Army uniform, and who had feigned sleep throughout most of the presentation, cast a dissenting vote.

24

Jacks, two days later

Ryder woke up to a sunbeam hitting him square in the face and Colleen's lovely naked body draped across his chest.

It took him a moment to figure out where the hell he was. Then it came to him: the second-floor room at Jacks, the small apartment that had become a home away from home for the Tango pilots. Formerly spare on the inside, the room was now crammed with items like a portable icebox, a small microwave oven, a couple dozen half-filled liquor bottles, empty beer cans, and a pile of duffel bags that held most of the living necessities for each of the Tangos. The place had become so crowded that a second, even smaller apartment across the hall that had to be rented to take care of the overflow.

It was the morning of the second day after the weird ECC mission flight, and the four Tango pilots had done little more than eat, drink, and bed their favorite Jacks Girl in the time between. As far as they knew, they were still on stand-down. With nothing to do but wait for their deployment orders, the pampered Aggressor pilots had decided to stay at Jacks.

That was just fine with Ryder. He needed some time away from "turn and burns," the psy-ops, the secret-missions-within-secret-missions, Zoot UFOs, and worrying about the location of his next deployment. He was very happy to concentrate on other matters.

Colleen was one. He'd grown very attached to her, though he knew that she had to be someone's agent, whether it be the CIA, the DIA, the NSA, FBI, or even the ISC. He was also finally getting to like the way the cooks at Jacks scrambled their eggs—an important consider-

161

ation, since it was the only decent food put out at the saloon. And even the cheap booze was tasting better.

He brushed Colleen's long hair back from covering her award-winning breasts and gently stroked her awake. His reward was a sleepy smile and a soft, probing hand under the covers.

Only a fool would miss out on this, he told himself. *Enjoy it while you can . . .*

"What's on the schedule today, fly-boy?" she asked him, cuddling closer.

Ryder stared at the ceiling and smiled. "How about eating, drinking, and—"

She put her finger to his mouth and smiled. "I get the idea," she said. "What do you want for breakfast? I'll go get it for you."

"Eggs," he replied, completely deadpan.

"Scrambled? Poached?"

"Cooked," he replied. "And do you think they have a slab of steak or ham down there? My body is screaming for some cholesterol."

Colleen got up and draped his service shirt over her lovely naked body. "I'll see what I can do . . ." she said. "And you'll want coffee? Tea? *Beer?*"

"Either one with a shot of whiskey will be fine," he said, stretching out in the empty bed. "See you back here in, what?—two, three hours?"

She gave him a feigned hurt look. "Try ten minutes, wise guy."

Reaching inside his shirt pocket, she came out with a wristwatch. "Here, you can time me . . ."

She threw it to him, then went out the door and headed down toward Jack's busy kitchen.

Ryder caught the watch in midair, knowing it was the busted item the kook had given him several days ago down in the Jacks bar. He hadn't given the incident much thought since he'd been so bombed at the time, he barely remembered what had happened exactly. Officers on exchange programs from foreign allied armies had passed through War Heaven before, and from what he recalled, the guy had looked like he was from the Dutch Marines or some other weenie army. He'd probably gotten caught up in playing spy, and . . .

But just then, Ryder noticed something was different about the watch: It was working. The hour, minutes, and seconds all had digital numerals flashing.

162

But the strange thing was, the digital seconds were going backward.

He watched the seconds count down and was surprised to see that once they reached 00, the minute numerals went backward, too, in this case switching from 17 to 16.

"What a piece of crap," he thought, finally tossing the watch into the overflowing wastebasket.

Just then there was a knock on the door. It was Wendy, Woody's lovely lady friend. Softly opening the apartment door, she peeked in.

"Colonel Long?" she asked shyly. "Colonel Woods would like to see you . . ."

"Tell him I'm busy."

Wendy slipped into the room and walked a few steps toward him.

"It's important," she said in a way that further convinced Ryder that she too was somebody's undercover agent. "I know it is . . ."

He knew it was useless to argue. He thanked her, then crawled into his ragged zoomsuit and stumbled over to Tango room two.

Woody was sitting on the edge of the bed, washed, shaved, and packed to go.

"What are you doing?" he asked his partner.

"I just talked to the Boss downstairs," Woody replied, forcing a handful of items into his flight bag.

"And?"

"We got our orders," he replied, dejectedly zipping up the bag. "We're shipping out . . ."

Ryder felt his stomach flip. The words he had dreaded hearing had finally arrived.

"Damn . . . where?" he asked.

Woody shook his head while at the same time trying to comb his stubble haircut into place.

"You ain't going to believe it, pards," he replied with an ironic smile. "But he said we're going to Rome . . ."

25

New Mexico

The helicopter circled the small pond twice before coming in for a landing.

The aircraft, a UH-1 Huey from the New Mexico National Guard, set down with a spray of water and dust about a hundred feet from the old watering hole.

· A single uniformed U.S. Army officer and two men in civilian clothes climbed out of the Huey. They immediately walked over to the Ford truck camper that was parked near the edge of the crystal clear pond.

The Army officer reached inside the truck's cab and retrieved its registration slip.

"It's a rental," he told the two civilians. "Out of Roswell. Paid out to someone named Vanessa Martin."

One of the civilians checked a small notebook he was carrying.

"Vanessa Martin," he repeated. "She was on the list."

The keys to the truck were still inside the ignition, so the officer gave them a twist. The engine responded with a single groan and then died completely.

"Battery's dead," the officer said. "Sounds like it's been that way for a few days anyway . . ."

They walked around to the back of the truck camper and the officer knocked twice on the back door. There was no reply.

Using a jackknife, he quickly sprung the door's flimsy lock, and pulled it open.

"Let's take a look inside . . ." he said.

164

* * *

The Army officer was a captain assigned to a Pentagon post as part of the secret Delta Force. The two civilians worked for the National Security Agency.

All three were looking for Maureen O'Brien.

The pair of NSA agents had received orders for this mission three days before, from one of the NSA's top operatives, a man they knew only as Lieutenant Moon. The Delta Force officer had been on the case just as long.

They actually knew very little about the particulars of the matter, other than that the famous *Post* reporter was missing, and that two top-secret government agencies were looking for her.

They did know that it had been almost three days since the reporter had called her contact at White Sands. Understandably concerned, the man called the national editor at the *Washington Post*, who in turn called the missing reporter's father, who happened to be a retired general and Pentagon big shot named John O'Brien.

The Delta Force officer became involved because he was a specialist in finding missing persons, mostly foreign agents or U.S. intelligence operatives lost while on duty. His boss was a good friend of the missing woman's father. One phone call was all it took for his superior to determine that he was a natural to be assigned to look for the reporter.

Coincidentally, at the same time that General O'Brien began working with Delta Force, he'd received a call from the NSA. They had a simple request to pass on to his daughter, a message from a friend of hers. The general informed them his daughter was missing, that he couldn't waste time talking to them because he had to mount a search operation for her, and then abruptly hung up.

The NSA called back an hour later to say they would be glad to assign two men to the case.

Working together, the general, the Delta Force officer, and the NSA men began making phone calls. Within hours they'd learned from officials at the *Washington Post* the gist of what kind of story Maureen had been working on; they had secured a list of names belonging to the University of Chicago's dig party; they had obtained the latest, most detailed satellite maps of the Roswell area; and they had located the helicopter pilot who had deposited the general's daughter out in the middle of nowhere in the first place.

A call to an old war buddy of the general's at the New Mexico Air National Guard put the Huey and its crew at the disposal of the searchers for as long as it took. The Delta officer and the NSA men caught the first flight out of Washington to Holloman AFB near White Sands, where they met the Air Guard Huey and began the land search.

Locating the spot where Maureen had last been seen, the Huey followed a flight path due south for about forty minutes. That's when one of the chopper crew spotted the pond and the truck camper. Maureen had mentioned in one of her reports to the White Sands contact that she was sleeping in just such a camper, thus prompting the Delta officer to ask the pilot to land so they could investigate.

Now, as the officer and the two NSA men searched the camper, they stumbled upon some very intriguing items.

They located some of Maureen's clothes—easily identified by the name tags and the Washington, D.C.–area store labels—and her two-way radio. No items essential to a reporter—notebooks, cameras, tape recorders—could be found, though.

It was obvious that two people had been sharing the camper, so the men carefully searched the bunk they assumed belonged to Vanessa Martin. They came upon the usual items owned by an educated college-age woman: some textbooks, homework binders, three dozen ballpoint pens, some cosmetics, five pairs of jeans, two pairs of sneakers, several fashion magazines, an old pack of cigarettes, and an unopened box of Lady Free condoms.

However, upon lifting up the bunk in order to get to the storage space below, the three men found items that would belong to another type of person altogether.

They found a small metal box, similar to what troops in battle would carry ammunition in. The box was literally stuffed with women's lingerie—body stockings, teddys, low-cut wired bras, garter belts.

But there was also a small two-way radio hidden in the box, wrapped up in the racy undergarments. All three men quickly recognized the radio as being a state-of-the-art piece of technology.

"It's a military-issue microwave bouncer," one of the NSA men explained as he examined the device. "It can bounce off one of several satellites and make contact with a compatible microwave system just about anywhere in the world. It's so new and so secret that not even the Desert Storm commanders had access to them."

A Macy's shopping bag at the bottom of the storage compartment proved even more baffling to the three men. Inside were three dozen issues of the most scandalous tabloids on the market: the *Star,* the *World News*, the *Globe*, the *World Reporter,* among others. Each one was meticulously hand-labeled and categorized in an alphanumeric system none of the three men recognized.

Yet the tabloids all had at least one thing in common. Each one featured an outrageous story of some kind concerning UFOs.

"Weird reading for someone who's supposed to be so educated," one of the NSA men said.

"Very weird," the Delta officer replied.

But they discovered something even more unusual a few minutes later. While checking in a storage compartment above the bunks, the Delta officer found a small video camera hooked up to a tiny battery pack. It too was wrapped in various pieces of lusty lingerie. When a small panel in front of the lens was moved, it was evident that by the way the truck itself was positioned, the camera was set up to surreptitiously take videos of the small pond or whatever was happening near it.

"A hidden camera? On this rig?" the Delta officer said, shaking his head. "This is getting stranger . . ."

They took photos of everything and then carefully replaced each item in its former location.

Once this was done, they locked the door of the camper, climbed back aboard the Huey, and took off.

Ten minutes later, they had located the main dig site.

From the air they counted seven Winnebago-style vehicles plus a Ford pickup truck parked in a circle. Not too far away were a series of trenches, covered by screens and cordoned off by bright red ribbons. Several outdoor cookers surrounded a campfire and a pile of trash bags, indicating an eating area.

But despite all this evidence of civilization out in the middle of the beautiful desolation of the New Mexico range, the place was clearly deserted.

The Huey set down and the three men once again began a systematic search of the immediate area. It was quickly apparent that whatever had happened, the dig crew had left the site in a great hurry. Tools were found next to the holes, as if they'd been dropped in place. Field notes, each one carefully inscribed with figures and written information, were blowing freely in the wind. Food, prepared but not eaten, was found near the cookers, providing a feast for the local insects and scavenger birds.

An inspection of each Winnebago yielded only mundanely typical academic items and field clothes. In one camper, though, an intriguing Polaroid photo was found. It clearly showed Maureen O'Brien sitting on the passenger side of the truck camper found at the pond, smiling as the truck appeared to be leaving the dig site.

"Well, we know for sure that she was here," the Delta Force officer said. "The question is, where the hell is she now?"

Part 2

26

Griffiss Air Force Base — Rome, New York

The B-52 Stratofortress rumbled down the runway and, with a great burst of power and exhaust, defied gravity and rose up into the cloudless sky.

The crowd of more than 85,000 roared with approval. The spectacle of the enormous veteran bomber taking off was always a favorite at any airshow; the fact that for years Griffiss had been home to a B-52 air unit only added to this day's adulation. The crowd never stopped cheering as the bomber made a wide bank and thundered back over the throng at a heart-stopping altitude of only 500 feet, its eight engines screaming for more height.

Ryder and Woody watched the huge strategic bomber pass overhead before they resumed their conversation.

"Okay, what was that again?" Woody asked.

Ryder scanned the menu board posted over the small concession stand one last time.

"Chili dog with extra sauce, large onion rings, and a beer. Better make it a light beer . . ."

Still grumbling about losing the coin flip that had led to this painful duty, Woody grudgingly took his place at the end of the long line of spectators who had cued up to get lunch. In the meantime, Ryder set off to find a shady spot where they could eat their meal.

The hot sun and blazing heat made such places a premium at the vast, wide-open air base. With the tens of thousands of people on hand, most of the good shadows were already taken, so Ryder knew that he'd have to employ a particularly sharp eye in order to secure an adequate location.

He was no stranger to airshows. His dad had taken him to various fly-ins and air races when he was a boy. These, and the fact that his father was a career Air Force pilot, had led him to want to fly for a living, too. Walking past the various static displays and concession stands, the sights and smells brought back memories from his boyhood.

This is where it all began, he thought.

The display next to the long line of concessionaires amused him the most. It was simply a roped-off area, containing nothing other than a sign declaring that a F-117A Stealth fighter was on display. It was an old gag – especially since the F-117A had been public knowledge for some time – but still a funny one.

Down from the "invisible jet" was a line of World War II airplanes, again one of his favorite sights. Besides the usual gang of P-51 Mustang variants, there was a trio of magnificently restored P-38 twin-tailed Lightnings, a pair of P-47 Thunderbolts, and a single P-40, sporting authentic Flying Tiger colors.

Next came an international display of famous old fighters including a Spitfire and a Hurricane, both in full RAF Battle of Britain dress; a rare Royal Navy Hellcat, and, most surprising, a pair of sleek Yak-11s, courtesy of the Soviet Air Force.

To the left of the Yaks was a foursome of elegantly painted, bright-yellow Harvards, courtesy of the famous Canadian Harvard Aircraft Association. Next to the Harvards was a Starduster biplane flown in by the boys from the Pearson Air Museum of Vancouver, Washington.

On the other side of three tee-shirt concession stands was a four-acre roped-off area devoted to World War II–era bombers.

There were two B-17 Flying Fortresses, one in factory-fresh silver paint, the other covered with a coat of dull European-theater green. A B-24 Liberator sat off the wingtip of this second Fort. It was painted in the desert-sand camouflage reminiscent of some of the famous Ploesti bombers based in Libya during World War II.

Next to the B-24 were three twin-engined B-25 Mitchells, all three splendidly restored. A seldom-seen B-26 Marauder and an even rarer A-20 Havoc completed the display.

The gang of old bombers was one of the hottest attractions at the airshow, and the line waiting to get a closer peek at the famous aircraft made the queue at the food concessions look puny by comparison. But next to the display was a line of tractor-trailer support trucks, and it was here that Ryder staked out a semishady place to eat lunch.

After a whistle and several long-distance hand gestures, Woody spotted him and arrived soon afterward with a huge cardboard tray of high-caloric food and drink.

"Bigger crowd today than yesterday," Woody said as he settled in next to Ryder in the slim shade of the trailer truck. "They'll get a hundred thousand here tomorrow if the weather stays this good."

Ryder took a long sip of his beer. "What time do we go on in the morning?" he asked.

Woody checked the airshow performance schedule he'd diligently kept taped to his uniform's right sleeve.

"We go up at 1035. First maneuver at 1040. We'll all have to get here by at least 0730 . . ."

"Too damn early," Ryder lamented.

"That's show biz," Woody replied.

Ryder could only shake his head in resigned agreement. The last thing any of them expected after the three weeks of intense and grueling training inside War Heaven was to be assigned to an airshow, easily one of the most confected of Air Force missions.

But that's exactly what had happened.

They'd left the Range five days ago, moving briefly to Nellis AFB and then doing the cross-country hop to Griffiss, which *was* located near Rome—not the world capital of love, food, and women in Italy, but the city in upstate New York.

Once there, the base commander relayed orders to the effect that Ryder, Woody, Williams, and Katt were now a kind of traveling aerial-opponent force—the Black Hat Squadron, as they were called in the advertisements. Their role in the airshow was twofold. One was to delight the crowds with a series of formation flybys and mock ground-attack maneuvers in the sleek F-15s. The other was to stage mock air-combat duels with local National Guard fighter aircraft. In true traveling-circus fashion, these aerial contests would always be won by the local white hats. But just barely.

The Griffiss airshow was only the first stop. They were also slated to perform at Homestead AFB in Florida, at the famous Fly-in at Wittman Field in Oshkosh, Wisconsin, and then, finally, back at

NAS Fallon in northern Nevada.

They'd been at Griffiss for four full days now, with another two ahead of them. Each day they'd been expected on the flight line early, and each day they'd answered the call in various degrees of post-inebriation trauma. Drinking the bar dry at their nearby Ramada hotel had been about the only diversion in the curious assignment .

Just how did it all fit into any plans the ISC men at C2 had for them? Ryder and Woody discussed just what was happening any chance they got — but their long conversations only led to more questions. Were they still involved in trying to solve the ISC problem? Had there been a problem in the first place? Or could the assignment to be part of the airshow simply a way of getting them out of War Heaven just when things were heating up?

They didn't know. And unless they were contacted by Moon or someone similarly in the loop, they would have absolutely no way of finding out.

"Got any ketchup?" Ryder asked Woody, finishing off the chili dog and plowing into the box of onion rings.

Woody flipped a couple packs of ketchup to him, then emptied a few more onto his second cheeseburger.

"Maybe we should try the officers' club at the base tonight," Woody suggested. "I think that bartender at the Ramada will quit if we show up again."

Ryder shrugged. "I doubt we'll see anything good in a skirt at the OC," he said. "But at least the drinks will be cheaper."

At that moment, one of the handlers for the World War II bomber display walked up, his hands full of concession food.

"You Black Hat guys are sure putting on a great show," the man told them, identifying them by their unmistakable black flight suits. "Making the local air jocks score some points, too . . ."

"That's the whole idea," Ryder told him.

The man introduced himself as Andy Sunn, retired USAF major, now a member of the Texas Air Corps, one of the warbird display groups. He gratefully accepted Ryder's offer to join them.

"Can you believe these crowds?" Sunn asked in a thick southern accent after settling in. "Word must be getting around about you guys."

"I'd say your airplanes would win the popularity contest," Ryder replied, gesturing toward the ever-growing lines stretching past the

World War II bombers. "Must be a gas flying in one of those babies . . ."

"They're not all ours," Sunn replied, draining a tall Coke and attacking his own foot-long cheese dog. "We own the Mitchells, the Liberator, and the green Fort. The rest of them are free-lancers."

They continued to eat and talk about the hot weather, the crowds, and the best places to drink, their conversation interrupted on several occasions by the racket of various aircraft flying over.

"Have you boys ever been up in a warbird?" Sunn asked them.

Both Ryder and Woody shook their heads no.

"Well, then, let me put forth an invite," Sunn told them. "We're all going up tonight. Us and the free-lancers. It's a full-moon flight—a happening, y'know? Weird things been known to happen up this way. I'm sure we can find a place to squeeze you boys in. Are you interested?"

"You bet," Woody answered for the both of them. "Got room for two more? Our partners are back watching our aircraft . . ."

Sunn nodded, finishing his quick meal and getting up to leave. "No problem," he said. "Be down on the flight line at 2100 hours. We'll be going up around 2130 . . ."

They thanked him and then quickly finished their own lunches. They were scheduled to relieve Williams and Katt at the Black Hat static display in five minutes.

As they got up and began to make their way back through the crowds toward their F-15s' display, something stuck in Ryder's mind.

"I wonder what he meant by 'weird things' happening around here?" he said to Woody.

His partner shrugged once. "Whatever he meant, could it be any stranger than what we've been through?"

"Not even close," Ryder replied.

173

27

At the stroke of nine o'clock, the still night air around Griffiss Air Force Base exploded with the sound of twenty-two piston-driven engines being cranked to life.

The full moon was rising over the mountains to the east, and the bluish shadows it cast around the darkened flight line lent themselves more to 1945 than to the present day.

The flying fortress named *Fort One* led the way. It was owned by a free-lance warbird group out of Nevada. The Texas Air Corps' own B-17 was lined up right on its tail, and would be flying in the two spot. Their engines coughing with smoke and crude power, the pair of B-17s jerked forward and headed for the nearby taxiway. The three B-25s were next, lined up in single file, their engines cutting through the exhaust trailing behind the big Forts. The odd couple of the pack—the A-20 and the B-26—were hard on the heels of the Mitchells.

The B-24 Liberator—its nickname was *Dallas Alice*—provided the rear guard and would serve as the flight leader for the group. Andy Sunn was its pilot. Ryder and Woody were strapped into seats in the nose compartment of this airplane, peering out the yellowed Plexiglass windows as the line of bombers in front of them moved to one of the auxiliary runways on the far edge of the sprawling air base.

One by one, the eight World War II bombers pulled out onto the air base's auxiliary runway and took off, the *Dallas Alice* being the last to go. Both Ryder and Woody found themselves hanging on in a varied state of anxiety as the understandably-creaky bomber rumbled down the runway and groaned its way into the air. It was a far cry from the smooth takeoffs they were accustomed to in their high-tech F-15X fighters.

Once the entire bomber fleet was airborne and formed up, it turned as one and headed east.

The two-and-a-half-hour flight would take the eight bombers on a roughly triangular course. They would first fly in a southeastly direction, toward the Schenectady-Albany area, about 82 miles away. Once there, the flight would turn south and follow a course roughly coinciding with the Hudson River. When they saw the lights of the city of Newburgh below, they would make a 170-degree turn to the northwest and head back for Griffiss.

The night was clear and the weather was perfect for flying. There was an undeniable festive feeling on board the B-24 as Ryder and Woody unstrapped and climbed up into the flight compartment to schmooze with the crew. The *Alice* was a rare airplane indeed. It had seen action not only over Nazi Europe, but also in the Pacific in the last days of the war against Japan. It had flown more than five hundred missions in all, and the Texas Air Corps had a documented report on each one.

"It lost power to all four engines over Schweinfurt," Sunn told them. "The crew was ready to go to the silk when the copilot bucked the reserve fuel tank activator switch. The engines restarted about ten seconds later.

"It took six flak hits on a mission over Berlin. One of them ripped off half the tail plane, another one took out the right outside engine. Blasted the prop right off it. The plane made it home, no problem. They fixed it, shipped back to the states for engine refit, and then sent it to Guam."

The pilot showed them a register of confirmed or probable kills by the Liberator's gunners. The number added up to twenty-three Messerschmidts, Focke-Wulfs, and Zeros, an outstanding record.

The airplane was later saved from being blown to bits in an atomic bomb test in Bikini by a concerned pilot, who, noting the airplane's connection to Dallas, wrote to the city's mayor and convinced him to have the city buy the airplane. He did, and it sat practically untouched in a private hangar at Love Field until 1980, when the Texas Air Corps got a hold of it. It had been showing off at airshows ever since.

"You've heard about airplanes that will carry you home no matter what?" Sunn asked them. "Well, you're flying in one of them. This baby's got nine lives . . ."

Ryder and Woody took their turns behind the controls. Ryder was at the wheel when the lights of the huge Schenectady GE plant came into view. A few minutes later, with the even brighter lights of Albany to his immediate left, he performed the long sweep to the south, lining up the B-24's nose with the Hudson River two miles below.

Woody took over as the eight bombers climbed to 15,000 feet and spaced out to five and a half miles between planes, a safe separation when flying at night. Being in the "coffin's corner," the men on the B-24 had the spectacular view of the seven other aircraft in front of them. Outlined by the bright moonlight, and detailed by their blinking red and white navigation lights, the small air fleet stretched like a long, blinking electric ribbon across the sky.

Ryder couldn't imagine it looking very much different than fifty years before.

The radio inside the *Dallas Alice* was hooked into a network that linked all of the airplanes, and a steady stream of good-natured, interplane chatter was going on. Ryder and Woody talked by radio with Williams, who was riding way up ahead in *Fort One,* and Katt, who was in the second B-25. They both reported soon after the turn south that they could already see the glow of the lights of Manhattan, now about a hundred and fifty miles away. The streetlights of the riverside cities of Kingston, Poughkeepsie, and Newburgh were also visible.

"West Point is just about ten miles south of Newburgh," Sunn told Ryder and Woody. "It would be a blast to buzz the place . . ."

Ryder and Woody offered only a mild laugh of approval. After all, they were still on a sensitive mission—or at least they thought they were. In such cases, there was an imaginary line drawn. Taking a joy ride in the old bomber was one thing; buzzing West Point was another.

This didn't deter the pilot of the B-24 from putting up the proposition for a vote, though. The replies were tallying up five for, none against, when they heard an alarmed voice cut in over the network.

It was the pilot of the lead B-17, *Fort One.*

"Jesuzz, what was that?"

Sunn was the first to respond.

"What do you have, One?" he called up to the lead B-17.

"We're not sure," came the reply. "Stand by . . ."

Something was definitely wrong in the tone of the lead B-17 pilot's response. It was uncharacteristically muted; the usual self-assured-ness that was second nature with the warbird pilots was gone.

"Fort One," the B-24 pilot persisted, "are you okay?"

"Stand by . . ." came the answer again.

"Tighten up," Sunn called out to the rest of the group, at the same moment pushing his bomber's throttles ahead so he could catch up with the formation.

"This is One . . ." finally came the message from the lead B-17. "We've got an unusual situation up here. Do you have indications of other traffic on your radar?"

Sunn quickly checked his nonregulation TACAN equipment.

"That's negative, *Fort One*," he replied. "Do you have a closing problem?"

"What we have is something right off our nose," came the response from *Fort One*. "About five thousand above us – right on our twelve o'clock. Can someone check Newburgh Tower and confirm this? We're kind of busy at the moment . . ."

The pilot of the second B-17, whose radio call name was simply "Two," volunteered to do this. Meanwhile, Sunn continued to talk to the lead Flying Fortress.

"Are you in collision danger, Fort One?"

"Negative, Flight Leader," came the somewhat-relieved reply. "This aircraft is, well . . . *pacing* us."

"Give me a description, Fort One," Sunn asked, pulling a pen and paper from his flight suit pocket.

"Okay, Flight Leader. We've got what looks like a series of lights. Or should I say, a string of lights. Two sets, actually. Multicolored. I'd say about eight, no, make that nine of them on each side . . . It's V-shaped . . ."

Ryder and Woody looked at each other, their eyes as wide as half dollars. *Multi-colored? V-shaped?*

"This thing looks really huge," the *Fort One* pilot continued. *"Really* large. I can't say that it's an aircraft. Even though it's flying. Or, it's more like floating. Yet, it's keeping up with us . . ."

"Fort One, this is Two . . . Newburgh Tower reports no other scheduled traffic in the area. They request you open up to their channel."

Sunn pushed his mike button. "Flight Two, can you see any of this?"

"Negative, Flight Leader . . ." came the response from the pilot of the second B-17. "We're about three miles behind now and closing .

"This thing is coming down . . ." *Fort One's* pilot anxiously reported. *"Jesuzz, here it comes . . ."*

There was a burst of static.

"Christ, it's going *right* by us . . . right now!" *Fort One's* pilot reported. He was doing his best to keep his composure, but not quite pulling it off.

There was another, longer burst of static and then *Fort One's* radio cut out completely.

"Fort One? . . ." Sunn called ahead.

". . . that's a new one on me, Flight," *Fort One's* pilot came on, his message being picked up well into the transmission. "That thing was the size of an aircraft carrier . . ."

"Texas Flight, this is Newburgh Tower . . ." a new voice broke in. "Switch over to frequency three-three-one to report the traffic in your area . . ."

"Flight Two, this is Flight Leader . . . What is your position?"

"We're up on *Fort One's* tail right now. I'm moving off his left wing."

"Two, did you see anything? Anything at all?"

"Negative, Flight Leader, I've got people at every window. It's clear skies for all we can see."

"Two, this is *Fort One* . . . Can you check me for any structural damage . . ."

"Roger, Fort One. We are doing that now. We see no damage. You look very airworthy."

There was a minute or two of further communications between Fort One and Newburgh Tower. Then, a strange silence fell upon the flight.

Finally Sunn keyed his microphone.

"Texas Flight, this is Flight Leader. Let's head for home,"

Ryder and Woody, having quietly watched the entire episode from a respectful distance, now retreated back to the nose section, where they both put a finger to their mouth and nodded a silent agreement not to talk about what had happened.

Woody couldn't resist one comment, though.

"I guess this means they're not going to buzz the Point . . ." he said.

Less than an hour later, the entire group had landed back at Griffiss.

The flyers naturally crowded around *Fort One* and waited for its crew to emerge. When they did, Ryder and Woody pulled Williams aside.

"What the hell happened up there?" Ryder asked him.

"Don't ask me," Williams replied with a shrug.

"Come on, Teddy," Ryder pressed him, "did you see anything?"

The pilot just shook his head and looked at the ground.

"I didn't see a thing . . ." he said. "Not a damn thing . . ."

28

"Black Hat One . . . Black Hat Two . . . you are cleared for take-off . . ."

Ryder acknowledged the message from Griffiss Tower, then ran his F-15's engines up to full power. Although it was only nine in the morning, the air was already hot, which meant he'd have to take the F-15 on a longer takeoff roll. That was okay—the crowd of close to 100,000 had been waiting for something to happened for nearly an hour. An extra long, extra noisy takeoff, capped with a steep vertical ascent once airborne, would start the airshow off in properly exciting fashion.

He did one last check of his instruments, then looked at the F-15 poised off his right wing.

"Ready, partner?" he called over to Woody.

"The show must go on," Woody replied.

They released their brakes at the same moment, and within seconds both were roaring down the runway, trailing two streams of hot brown exhaust behind them. On Ryder's count, they pulled back on the control sticks and became airborne, immediately putting their jets into a screeching true vertical climb.

The bombastic takeoff all but drowned out the massive ovation from the huge crowd as it watched the two F-15s spiral straight up until they disappeared from sight.

Ryder and Woody leveled off at 12,500 feet and went into a long wide circle. They would loiter here for three minutes and then begin the first part of the performance.

Ryder leaned back in his seat and sucked in a long breath of oxygen. He was glad that this was their last performance at Griffiss. Between the hot weather, the cardboard food, the bad hotel booze, and the strange incident the night before, he was more than anxious to bid the place *ciao!*

There had been little discussion among them concerning whatever it was that happened to *Fort One* over Newburgh. Teddy Williams was buttoned up, skipping the near-mandatory nightcap once they'd returned to the Ramada bar and the showing up late for the preflight performance check earlier that morning.

"I was on the phone," was all the pilot offered by way of an explanation.

No one questioned him—no one was really in authority to do so. And being pilots, they all knew better than to press the issue, especially before a flight. The world could be falling in and it would go without discussion among pilots who were ready to take off and needed their full mental capabilities to be focused on the flight ahead.

Privately, however, Ryder was planning to pull Williams aside later that day, get a few drinks into him, and then try to get a straight story on just what he saw—or didn't see—during the *Fort One* incident. The fact that what the men on the Flying Fortress claimed they saw sounded a lot like what he'd spotted over War Heaven a week before was mystifying, to say the least. Was it a coincidence? Or could it be some weird part of their mission? A little bit of both?

Once again, he just didn't know.

"I read twenty seconds to showtime, Ghost . . ." Woody called over to him, snapping him out of the disturbing thoughts. "How's your weapons load?"

Ryder did a quick check of his weapons delivery computer. There were four canisters attached under his wings. Two held 100 pounds each of a white powdery substance which when dropped would create the illusion of smoke. The second pair contained a similar powder, colored red, as well as several dozen tiny "poppers," which were akin to small blasting caps. When these canisters hit the ground, the combination of the poppers going off and the red flash smoke simulated an explosion.

"Yeah, sure, weapons look good," Ryder reported to Woody less than enthusiastically. "Computer is keyed. Fuel is nine tenths . . ."

"Ditto, here," Woody responded. "Ready for count-off."

Ryder checked the clock on his HUD. The timing of their first approach was very important, matched as it was with the script of the air show's narrator.

"Four . . . three . . . two . . . one. Let's go."

They put the F-15s in a pair of screeching dives and were soon streaking directly over the vast crowd. Turning west and then south, they reduced their altitude to 500 feet and zeroed in on the pair of surplus, rather-antique tanks that had been placed way out on the base's far runway as their targets.

With a precision and grace that came only from much turn-and-burn practice and brainpower, they both deposited a "red" bomb on the first tank. With their communications now linked with the air-show narrator, they could hear him extolling the virtues of the F-15X as a fighter/attack bomber while the enormous crowd cheered in the background.

They turned again, bore in on the second tank, and each dropped a second bomb. Once again, both of them scored direct hits. Another turn, another low-level run, and they dropped both of their white powder bombs directly into the smoking red cloud rising from their previous runs.

They went true vertical again as the announcer screamed their praises to the wildly applauding crowd.

"Your Air Force at work!" the narrator bellowed.

"Yeah, big deal . . ." Ryder called over to Woody. "A flying dog-and-pony show . . ."

They returned to their loitering altitude of 12,500 feet and leveled off.

Here, they waited for Act 2.

The two F-16As arrived over the airshow crowd at precisely 0930 hours.

Streaking in from the southeast, the pair of gray camouflaged fighters did a wide turn out and then performed a slow flyby for the crowd. Both jets were part of the New York Air National Guard's 138th Tactical Fighter Squadron based at Hancock Field in nearby Syracuse. Formerly a unit made up of the slow A-10 ground-attack airplanes, the 138th pilots had switched over to the faster, sleeker, sexier F-16s shortly before the Gulf war. Therefore they were anxious to show off their stuff.

After being properly introduced to the crowd by the show narrator, the F-16s cleared the area, disappearing over the western horizon. A minute later, the crowd saw the pair of black F-15s approach from the south, flying at 1000 feet and apparently heading for the target tanks again.

Suddenly the F-16s flashed out of the north, "pouncing" on the two "unsuspecting" F-15s. The Black Hats spiraled straight up, each with an F-16 on its tail.

The "fight" was on . . .

For the next five minutes, the crowd watched in a mixture of awe and excitement as the simulated dogfight between the two fairly matched pairs of airplanes played out.

But the outcome was never really in question.

First Black Hat One pulled down to 2000 feet and flew by the crowd at a suicidal speed of barely 300 knots. The lead F-16A swooped down on its tail and, via a puff of smoke from under its right wing and a corresponding wavering of the F-15's wings, "shot down" the enemy fighter. A release of white smoke from a tube attached next to the F-15's landing-gear door completed the illusion. The F-15 cleared the area, smoking heavily and apparently heading to its doom.

The charade was reenacted a minute later between the two remaining players. The second F-15 roared by crowd at a 300-knot crawl only to be jumped by the other F-16 and dispatched with the same harmless pyrotechnics. The crowd roared its approval as the F-16s took their victory lap around the base perimeter and then darted back toward the west, heading back to the base.

Five minutes later, Ryder and Woody quietly landed on the base's auxiliary runway, unnoticed and nearly out of sight of the crowd.

Their work for the day was done.

29

Maureen woke up to the sound of seagulls fighting.

She immediately sat straight up on the bunk, her fists tight, her teeth clenched, her mind groggy and confused.

But then she saw the thick, gray concrete walls, the dozens of empty water bottles next to her bed, the small bathroom, the collection of dusty American Indian artifacts scattered around the room.

And she heard those damn seagulls.

"Another day in paradise," she murmured angrily.

She had dreamed about her abduction again during the night, as clearly and vividly as when it actually happened. One moment, she was bathing in the clear pond; the next, she was surrounded by dozens of men, all dressed in nondescript white uniforms and armed with machine guns and two-way radios. Suddenly helicopters were circling overhead. People were shouting. Vanessa was being led away.

And then the men came after her, jumping right into the pond, pulling her out, and throwing her onto a helicopter that was hovering a few feet from the ground.

It had all happened so fast, they didn't even give her a chance to get dressed.

She still had no idea what they had injected into her as soon as she was aboard the helicopter. Whatever it was, it had knocked her out cold for at least a day and a half. Long enough to bring her to this place — this concrete room with old Indian paintings and rugs and pottery and the echoes of seagulls fighting.

She got out of bed, opened a new bottle of water, and took a long drink. Then she used the cap to scratch a line on the wall behind her bunk, adding a seventh mark to the crude calendar she'd started on her first day of captivity.

She didn't know where she was being held—not exactly, anyway. The only one of her captors that she'd seen in the past week was the young man who knocked on her door three times a day and delivered her meals, occasionally passing her a fresh bundle of laundry. He never said much beyond asking whether she needed more food or water or towels. He consistently ignored her more-pointed questions, never smiling, never chatting, never offering more than subsistence and clean socks.

But she was a good reporter and she could tell much about this man. His haircut—short, neat, without a hint of anything but soap—told her he was either military or federal government. His hands—soft, clean, manicured, and without calluses—told her that he worked inside some kind of controlled environment. And the way he looked at her—in spite of the baggy coveralls she'd been given to wear—told her that he hadn't been with a woman in a very long time.

If she was being held by the military, it would not be the first time. When she stumbled upon the preparations for Operation Distant Thunder more than a year before, the U.S. Navy saw fit to snatch her, and keep her aboard one of its aircraft carriers until the top-secret mission was under way.

She had resented it greatly then—but as it turned out, her abduction had led to her magnificent scoop on the covert action against the terrorist Colonel Toon. And this had led to her subsequent notoriety.

She could only wonder if this kidnapping would turn out half as well.

She lay back down on the bunk and for the next ten minutes repeated over in her mind the events leading up to her present condition. She had no pencil or paper to take notes, so it was crucial that she conduct this mind exercise at least once a day, so as not to forget a single critical point. Like a prayer, she evoked her long walk to the dig site. Meeting Doctor Ernie and his team. Her time at the clear pond with Vanessa. The day they found the strange alloy which could very well be something not of the Earth. The lightning-quick kidnapping. Her seven days of imprisonment.

There were some things she didn't know: and she ran these through her mind as well: Had the main dig party been snatched, too? Had their location been compromised? If so, how? What had happened to the piece of possibly extraterrestrial metal they'd dug up?

And what had happened to Vanessa?

A knock on her door shook her out of these deep thoughts.

Right away she knew it was not the quiet well-groomed young man she'd seen three times a day for the past week. This knock sounded more authoritative, more direct.

She wrapped her blanket around her and opened the door to find that her perception had been correct. The man standing in the hallway outside was about fifty years old. He was small, blandly handsome with a well tanned face and a shock of gray-white hair. He was smiling broadly.

"Hello, Miss O'Brien," he said, "my name is Walter. How are you today?"

"I demand to know where I am," Maureen told him right off with well-practiced sternness.

Walter never lost his smile. "I'm sorry, I can't tell you that right now . . ."

"Are you a member of the U.S. military?" she asked.

"I'm sorry, I can't tell you that, either . . ."

"Am I still in the United States?"

Walter just shook his head. "Sorry . . ."

Maureen smiled for a brief moment, partly out of relief. She'd been around government bureaucrats all her life. They looked differently, they spoke differently, they thought differently, from the rest of humanity. She could spot one a mile away, especially ones connected with the military.

Walter was definitely one of them.

They were also lousy liars, and Walter was no different in this respect, either. By denying answers to her questions, he was, in effect, answering them for her.

"Why am I here?" she forged ahead.

"Sorry . . ."

"When will I be released?"

"That's impossible to say . . ."

"Is the rest of my dig party here?"

"I'm very sorry . . ."

She eyed him coldly. Again like many bureaucrats, she found it easy to dislike him quickly. The tan. The smile. The hair. The incredibly predictable attitude.

"Okay, then, where's my breakfast?"

"It will be along soon," Walter told her. "But I would like to talk to you first. May I come in?"

"Talk about what?" she countered immediately, closing the door a little. "You won't answer any of my questions. What's the point?"

Walter smiled wider, showing even more of his perfect teeth, if that was possible.

"Maybe you're just not asking the *right* questions, Miss O'Brien," he told her.

His statement caught her off-guard for a moment. It was such an odd but intriguing thing to say.

"Okay," she said finally. "Come in . . ."

An hour later, Maureen was fed, washed, and wearing a new set of coveralls.

She also had a new tape recorder, a package of extra blank cassettes, extra batteries, several notebooks, and a dozen razor-sharpened pencils.

"Today's tour can only last about an hour," Walter was telling her. "We've got a busy day here and we can't afford to tie up a lot of people. So let's just say we'll get the preliminaries over with, and then you can go back and speak to any individuals you want to later on."

Maureen was trying not to let her amazement show. But the truth was, she was absolutely flabbergasted at this recent turn of events.

It had taken her about ten minutes into their conversation to begin asking Walter the "right questions."

All queries about her location, her abduction, Walter's profession, and how long she was going to be held met with "no comments." But oddly, when she got around to questions about the facility they were in — what it was, what was done here — Walter began smiling again.

"If you're interested," he had told her. "Then I can give you a tour . . ."

That was the first bombshell.

The second one came when she asked for, and promptly received, permission to take any notes she wanted. The pencils, notebooks, tape recorder, and cassettes arrived soon afterward.

Now, as she sat on the edge of the bed, testing the tape recorder,

Walter completed his walk about the room, apparently finished with admiring the Native American artworks.

"Are you ready?" he finally asked her.

She slipped a blank cassette into the recorder and gave the machine a quick "testing—one . . . two . . . three" check. It worked perfectly.

"I'm ready," she declared, trying her best to sound all business. "Let's go . . ."

He courteously opened the door for her and she left the room for the first time in seven days.

She found that it was just one of many rooms located along a long winding corridor. The first thing she noticed were the walls of this hallway. Like the ceiling and floor, they were made of heavy steel and concrete.

"Absolutely blast-proof," Walter told her, reading her thoughts. "Twenty-five feet of concrete in some places; hardened steel reinforcement throughout."

"Are you expecting to be nuked?" she asked.

He just shrugged. "You never know . . ."

They continued to walk down the hallway.

"Most of the guests' living quarters are down here," Walter explained, playing the perfect tour guide. "I believe there are twenty visitors' apartments in all."

"You have visitors here often?" she asked.

"Every once in a while," he smiled in reply.

"May I see one of the other apartments?"

"Certainly."

Walter walked over to the nearest metal door and knocked twice. Upon receiving no answer, he unlocked the door with what Maureen could only imagine was a skeleton key.

He kept the door open just long enough for her to get a quick peek inside. It was an understatement to say that her quarters were not like the others. This particular apartment featured a huge bed, two TVs, a cable box, a stereo, a CD player, and a small kitchenette.

"Looks comfortable," she remarked.

"It has to be," Walter explained, "Some of our visitors stay longer than others."

They continued down to the end of the hallway and reached a large elevator, one that looked more suited to hauling freight than people.

They climbed aboard and Walter brought them down the next level.

The elevator doors opened, and the first thing Maureen saw was a sign directly across from her that read: SEASPRAY ONE.

"Seaspray?" she asked.

Walter shrugged off her question. "Silly code name," he said. "It really doesn't mean too much . . ."

They walked out into this new hallway; it didn't look much different than a typical Washington, D.C.-style government office building, except for the steel and concrete walls. There was a line of offices, and most of the doors had numbers on them. Some even had plants outside or some kind of ornament tacked onto the door itself.

"This level is the heart of this place," Walter told her. "Just about all of the important work is done right here."

"Can you elaborate?" Maureen asked, clicking the tape recorder on.

"Well, let me show you," Walter complied.

They walked up to the first door. Next to the office number, which was 3, were the initials GBP.

"It stands for Green Ball Phenomena," Walter explained. "Crack people in there . . ."

The initials on the next door were PST.

"Project Super Twinkle," Walter went on. "Another silly name, isn't it?"

They walked on to door number 5. The letters read FFS.

"This is the office for the Foo Fighter Squadrons," he explained. "Lot of veterans. People have been around for twenty, thirty years or more."

The next door, number 6, was identified as The Zoo.

"Self-explanatory," Walter declared before moving on to door number 7, which held the initials SLO.

"Self-Luminous Objects," he told her. "Very exciting operation . . ."

Door 8 carried the title Los Alamos Bird Watchers Association.

"It's an old joke," Walter said with a broad smile. "But it proves that we still have a sense of humor . . ."

Maureen had walked ahead to door 9 by this time. It carried the most intriguing, if nonsensical, title of all: Project Arthur Godfrey.

"Arthur Godfrey?" she asked.

"That's what everyone says," Walter declared with a laugh.

Finally, door 10 was identified by the letters MNPC.

"This is the department's main office," Walter confided. "And all these other offices are its support units. MNPC stands for Morbid National Psychology Cultivation. Isn't that a wonderful name?"

Maureen could take it no longer. Nothing was making any sense. Was this for real or was it some incredible joke? She stopped Walter in his tracks.

"Morbid National Psychology? Bird Watchers Association? *Arthur Godfrey?*" she said with exasperation. *"Just what the hell do you do here?"*

Walter smiled broadly one more time; he was a bureaucrat's bureaucrat.

"You're the reporter, Miss O'Brien," he said simply. "I think it's your job to find out . . ."

30

Near Griffiss AFB

Ryder couldn't remember the last time he'd taken a nap in the middle of the afternoon.

Yet here he was, stretched out on the hard bed in his Ramada room, flight boots off, TV blaring, a ninety-minute postlunch slumber leaving him even more exhausted than when he'd first lain down.

Now that he was awake and cranky, all the commotion accompanying the airshow sounded like it was right outside his window: the din of traffic, the cheering crowds, a siren blaring off in the distance, the thunder of airplanes of all types taking off and landing at the air base, which was a half mile away. It was a wonder that he'd fallen asleep at all.

He buried his face deep into the mountain of hard pillows, trying to fight off the vague empty pain stirring deep in his stomach. He knew it wasn't caused entirely by the concession food. Rather, it was his morale. In two words, it was damned low.

And with good reason.

After the excitement and mystery of being out on the Range, the last place he wanted to be now was crapped out on a bad bed in the middle of upstate New York. He couldn't imagine any two places being more opposite than this all-too-American Rome and War Heaven. It was like they were on two different planets.

But there was also an ego thing banging away at his insides. Only the cream of the crop made it into War Heaven. Despite what happened to you once you got there, it was considered a privilege just to be asked to go, just like selection for Top Gun, or space-shuttle training. It could be in many ways the pinnacle of one's military career—especially if you survived the authentic mission higher authority had intended for you after you left the obscenely-expensive training ground.

On the other hand, no real pilot would consider being assigned to perform in this airshow to be anything more than a small entry on the bottom of a service record. Being with a regular performing team like the Blue Angels or the Thunderbirds was different, of course—that was playing for the major league team. But providing fodder for weekend pilots from Air National Guard units was something else again. It was single-A minor league ball—bad bus rides, cheap motels, and all.

What bothered him the most was this: the airshow gig was the type of assignment actually given to someone with his kind of service record. His "real" file—the one that hadn't been sanitized by Moon's confederate—was rife with less-than-honorable notations, most having to do with showing disrespect to higher officers, and a tendency not to follow orders to the last letter. It was little consolation that Woody's record was not much better.

As he lay on the bed, groggy, and pissed at himself for falling asleep in the first place, his greatest fear was that somehow, someone had resurrected his authentic service record and discovered the last place he should be was in War Heaven. With the push of a computer button, this invisible bureaucratic enemy had signed him up to be an act in an airshow, the absolute dead end of flying assignments, and unknowingly booted him out of the dangerous yet intriguing world of cloak and dagger. In this scenario, Woody, Williams, and Katt were dragged down with him, innocent bystanders caught in some paper-pusher's ire.

He tried to shake away the creeping paranoia that had been percolating inside him now for six days. He tried to concentrate on the fact that despite his surroundings, there was at least some evidence to suggest that he was still on his secret mission—one to save the entire country, no less. But the bad hotel room wallpaper and the coffee-stained bedcovers did little to reinforce this notion. He had to believe that potential world-savers slept in better accommodations.

His only consolation was that they were scheduled to fly out of Griffiss at 1730 hours—now barely 90 minutes away. His things were already packed, and checking out promised to be quick and

192

painless. So he still had some time to kill.

He chose to stay immobile for at least another half hour, watching the mindless game show on his crummy television and wallowing in self-pity. But the sirens outside his window grew louder, so much so that he had to exert himself and reach all the way over to turn up the TV.

That's when his telephone rang.

It was Katt.

"There's been an accident," he said. "Come down to the lobby right away . . ."

A minute later, the elevator doors opened and Ryder rushed into the lobby.

Katt was standing in the middle of the baggage area looking both angry and bewildered.

"Jessuz, where the fuck have you been?" the normally-unflappable Navy pilot asked him.

"Why? What's the matter?"

"Williams plowed in," Katt told him straight out. "He's dead . . ."

Ryder was stunned. *"What?"*

"It happened at the end of our show," Katt went on, trying his best to be unemotional. "We finished up and I headed in. But for some reason, he turned west. I called him and the tower called him. But he never replied. He went into that big lake out there – Lake Oneida. The plane just disintegrated. Witnesses say it blew up when it hit the water. They're all over there now, but there's nothing left but a bunch of little floating pieces . . ."

Ryder just couldn't believe it.

"God damn," he said, "Did they recover his body?"

Katt looked up at him, his eyes hard and watery.

"What body?" he asked coldly.

31

Griffiss, the next day

The four F-16A Fighting Falcons approached the near-empty air base, flying in the staggered chevron formation that had served as a tribute to fallen American airmen for many years.

On the ground, lined up on the tarmac where more than 100,000 people had stood the day before, were no more than a few dozen, all but one of them U.S. Air Force personnel.

The memorial service for Colonel "Teddy" Williams promised to be painfully brief. The Griffiss Air Force Band had turned out, as had most of the base's top brass. A grave registration unit had flown in from Maryland, bringing with them a ream of accident forms, an authorized military-personnel casket, and a box of American flags.

There was no need for the casket.

Ryder and Woody stood at attention as the F-16As roared overhead. One of them suddenly broke formation and soared straight up into the sky until it was out of sight. This was the Air Force's way of symbolizing that one of their own was now flying at the Ultimate Altitude.

Once the F-16s had left the area and the scream of their engines had faded away, the base commander of Griffiss walked out of the rank of assembled officers and enlisted men to a creaky metal podium. Through feedback and bad acoustics, he read a short prayer for a man he hadn't known and then cued the band's trumpeter who played a squealing rendition of "Taps."

Slightly ahead of schedule, the seven remaining bombers belonging to the Warbird exhibitors arrived over the memorial service, led

194

by the Mitchells of The Texas Air Corps. Flying in two staggered formations, their half-century-old engines drowned out what was left of the bugler's brave effort.

At that point, the Griffiss honor-guard unit untied their American flag from its pole, neatly folded it, and gave it to Katt, who, dressed in his khaki Navy dress uniform, stood out from the sea of Air Force blues. Williams's partner accepted the flag, saluted the base commander and the assembled troop, and then took his place back in the line next to Woody. The base commander called the gathering to order one more time, and then, with his own personal sign of the cross, dismissed the troop, thus ending the early morning service.

"I guess this is it, guys," Katt said to Ryder and Woody, sadly patting down the creases in the triangular-folded flag. "Maybe we'll see you back out on the Range someday."

Katt was flying back out with the GR unit, carrying the flag for delivery to Williams's first uncle, a man who lived in Colorado and who constituted the pilot's closest living relative.

"Good flying with you, Craz'," Woody said, shaking hands with the Navy pilot. "And you still owe me at least one round of beers at Jacks . . ."

"I hope I get to pay you off," Katt told him.

The still morning air was broken by the start-up of the engines of the Air Force transport that would carry the GR unit, Katt, and the handful of retrievable pieces of William's F-15 to Andrews AFB in Maryland. Katt would then catch an Air Force transport plane to Colorado.

The Navy officer turned to Ryder and they shook hands.

"I'm glad I wound up flying with you, instead of against you, Long," Katt told him.

"We'll do it again someday," Ryder replied.

He hadn't realized until that moment how much he'd come to admire the diminutive, astute Navy pilot. They'd flown together and drank together for only three weeks, yet it seemed more like three years.

Which made it all the harder for Ryder to ask the man one last question.

"I have to know something," was how Ryder prefaced his statement. "Did Teddy ever mention anything more to you about what happened over the Hudson that night?"

195

Katt seemed insulted by the question, as if asking about the strange incident was irreverent so soon after his partner's memorial service.

The Navy officer took a deep breath and let it out slowly, displaying his distaste for having to reply.

"No, he didn't, Long," Katt answered firmly. "He never said a goddamn thing to me about it . . ."

With that, he turned on his heels and walked out to the waiting air transport.

Less than an hour later, Ryder and Woody were reading over two faxes that had come into Griffiss communications earlier that morning.

The messages were from the officer-assignment department down in Randolph AFB in Texas and they comprised their orders for the next month. In summary, they told them that, after a two-day delay to be spent clearing up Williams's demise, the show would go on.

"I can't believe they want us to continue this circus act," Woody exclaimed, as soon as they left the communications office. "God, the Air Force is fucking heartless . . ."

"Well, it answers one thing, at least for me," Ryder said. "We ain't in the hero business no more."

"You're right," Woody agreed, disheartened. "I sure didn't see Moon out there joining in the prayer for Teddy."

They walked across the windy tarmac, instinctively heading for the officers' club and a day of somber drinking.

"You know, Ghost, there's a *real* good chance that Moon purposely hung us out to dry," Woody said, his voice lowered a notch in volume. "And we'll find out someday that it was all some kind of a weird drill. Some kind of loyalty thing."

Ryder bit his lip so hard, it almost bled. He hated to admit it, but he knew it wouldn't be the first time that small players like him and Woody had been used—or lied to—as part of some grander, blacker program. And everything that had happened so far would have fit into such a scenario.

Except for one thing . . .

"I saw something very weird over the Range that night, Pards," he told Woody suddenly, referring to the huge flying boomerang. "And the guys in Williams's Fortress saw what sounded a whole lot like the

196

same thing the other night. Now what I saw might have been part of the ECC, generated by some elaborate Zoot projector. But how about what they saw? All the way over here on the other side of the country? That would be quite a stunt to pull off, even for Moon and his guys . . ."

Woody shrugged with resigned agreement. "It beats the shit out of me what they spotted," he replied. "And it will be damn hard to ask them now . . ."

This was true. They'd hadn't spoken at all with the other men in *Fort One* since the strange sighting; they and their airplane had left several hours before Williams's accident for another appearance out west. The rest of the Warbird Exhibitors, including the entire Texas Air Corps, had been scheduled to follow them out the next day, but had stuck around for the memorial service. Just before the flyby, the president of the corps sent Ryder and Woody a note expressing his condolences and extending an open-ended offer to help them, "anytime, anywhere."

"But let's face it," Woody said, frustration mounting in his voice. "If Moon hasn't contacted us by now—even to tell us that this was all some sort of Chinese fire drill—he probably never will. And that means we probably ain't going back to the Range. And *that* means we ain't got the slightest chance of finding out what you saw."

Ryder stopped in midstep. They were just a foot or two away from the front door of the OC and all that trouble-drowning booze beyond.

"That's right," he told his partner. "But maybe there's a way we can find out what the guys on *Fort One* saw . . ."

32

The main library at Syracuse University was packed with pretty co-eds, many of them wearing the shortest shorts, and the skimpiest halter tops, thanks to the grueling heat outside.

"Good God, my summer school was never like this," Woody said as he and Ryder surveyed the situation from a corner table. "I mean, what kind of a professor would even flunk any of these babes?"

Ryder didn't even want to consider that one. He pried his attention away from the parade of young beauties and back to the matter at hand.

Their table was covered with old newspapers: the *Syracuse Journal*, the *Hudson Tribune,* the *Utica Times,* the *Rome Reporter,* the *Schenectady Gazette*. All of them dated back at least one year. Next to the table was a computerized retrieval machine, which was awaiting a hard disk that promised to contain copies of newspapers dating back to 1975. Beside *that* was an ancient microfilm viewing machine and a tray of microfilm rolls containing copies of various newspapers dating back to World War I.

It was just past two in the afternoon. The two pilots had spent most of the time since Williams's memorial service reading through the recent newspapers, looking for stories that might give them a clue to what the people inside *Fort One* had seen over the Hudson River two nights before.

As it turned out, there were plenty.

"Here's another one," Woody pointed out, showing Ryder a two-year old story whose headline read, *"Flying Boomerang" Stops Traffic on Thruway."*

Ryder quickly scanned the lead paragraph of the story.

" 'Large, V-shaped object . . . multi-colored lights . . . Startled motorists . . .' " he went on, reading just the highlights. "How many stories does that make about it being spotted over the New York Thruway?"

Woody checked their quickly lengthening list. "This makes seventeen," he replied. "And that's not counting the five stories about it startling motorists over the Taconic Parkway, a few miles away."

The quantity of news reports about the mysterious flying boomerang being spotted over the lower Hudson River valley was as mind-boggling as it was baffling for them. According to the most recent articles, more than six thousand people in the lower Hudson River area had spotted the V-shaped flying object in the past twelve years, the most active time being around 1983 and 1984, with recent spurts in the past two years. Their descriptions ran a startlingly true pattern: the phrase "a boomerang with lights running up and down its wings" was repeated over and over in the stories. Words like "enormous" and "gigantic" were also used freely, as was the statement, "It was so huge, it filled the sky."

Some witnesses claimed they saw the "Westchester Boomerang," as it was called, moving at speeds past Mach 5; others clocked it at less then ten miles per hour. Some saw it pass over them at altitudes up to three miles; others swear it went over their heads at not more than 15 feet above the ground. Some took Polaroid shots of it; others had captured it on videotape.

"How could all this go on and we never heard about it?" Ryder asked, over and over again. "I mean, this thing has been flying around the Hudson River for so long it should be pulling a Coppertone ad."

"It seems to happen so frequently, it's become sort of routine," Woody replied.

They continued scanning the newspapers, documenting the dates and publications of each news story concerning the flying boomerang. They'd just finished up with the 1989 *Schenectady Gazette*s when the pretty librarian appeared carrying their computer hard disk.

She gave them a quick lesson on how to operate the computer and its search software and soon they were flying through various newspaper editions with ease.

By punching in key words, such as "flying objects" and "Westchester Boomerang," they allowed the computer to do the grunt work for them. Within minutes they had located more than a hundred additional articles about people spotting the Westchester Boomerang, many of them quoting reliable sources such as policemen and pilots.

One story particularly caught Ryder's attention; it was, in fact, the needle in the haystack he'd been hoping for. At the end of an article concerning a flying boomerang being spotted over the Indian Point power plant—a problem-ridden nuclear plant that was located on the banks of the Hudson River—the writer had added that several similar flying boomerangs had been observed "elsewhere around the country."

"Too bad he didn't say where," Woody said after reading the article himself.

This gave Ryder an idea. He typed in the words "Las Vegas" and then commanded the computer to search all of the newspapers for mentions of the city. About fifty stories came back, but most had to do about gambling and legalized prostitution, and none mentioned enormous flying boomerangs. He punched in the word "Reno," but came up similarly empty.

"Try 'Tonopah,' " Woody suggested, a good idea, but one that produced no stories at all, as did a search for the word "Nellis."

"We can't type in 'War Heaven,' " Woody said, "I mean, you never know who's listening in . . ."

Ryder agreed, but then came up with the next best thing.

"How about 'Fallon'?" he asked, typing in the name of the U.S. Navy air training base located near Reno and not far from the northern edge of War Heaven itself.

The computer buzzed and clicked for several moments and then produced one retrieval.

"Bingo!" Woody declared, reading the copy off the computer screen.

The story came from the Hudson newspaper, reporting a flying boomerang sighting near West Point in 1988. The uncredited article included a single reference that read, "The *Fallon Register* reported a similar shaped flying object had been spotted over the Nevada city on several occasions."

"Wow," was all Ryder could say, keeping the enthusiasm under his breath. "Like I said before, it's one thing to spot this baby flying all over the Hudson River. But to confirm that something looking just like it, was spotted by someone else, so close to the Range . . ."

"Must make you feel good that you're not totally insane," Woody told him. "What I want to know is, what do we do now?"

Ryder shook his head and slumped back in his seat.

"That's a *damn* good question . . ." he replied.

33

It was exactly midnight when the single airplane lifted off from the auxiliary field on the isolated edge of Griffiss.

Rising above the line of parked F-16A fighters, above the trio of visiting B-52 bombers, above the remaining airplanes of the tragedy-marred airshow, the aircraft rumbled up to 1500 feet and then banked to the east.

Few people on the ground saw the B-25 Mitchell take off, and fewer still would see it fly over on its four-hour flight. That was fine with Ryder. The least number of people who knew about this trip the better.

He had nothing but the utmost admiration for Sunn and the other members of the Texas Air Corps for allowing them to cash in so quickly on their "anytime, anywhere" offer of help. They didn't blink an eye when he and Woody asked to borrow their valuable Mitchell to perform an important mission, the origin of which they could not reveal. With incredible professional élan, the Texans not only agreed, they gave them a quick lesson in flying the bomber and even paid for the fuel.

So here they were, in the medium-range, easy-to-fly, slow-enough aircraft, heading back to the skies over the lower Hudson River.

Woody was piloting the old bomber; Ryder was strapped into the copilot's seat. On his lap sat two 35-mm still cameras and a small video camera.

They had talked all day about this flight. What they expected to see and what would happen if something went wrong. Both agreed it was a long shot—but that they had to take it nevertheless. They were re-scheduled to fly out of Griffiss the following day, and once they did, the opportunity to look for what might be valuable clues would be lost for good.

The flight over to the Albany area was uneventful, as was the eventual turn south once the Hudson was spotted.

Just as during their previous flight, the glow from Manhattan was soon apparent off on the southern horizon, with the smaller concentration of city lights dotting the shore of the Hudson like gigantic Mohawk campfires.

The B-25 Mitchell was all over the sky, of course. The seat-of-your-pants flying that so appealed to the World War II vets only proved to Ryder and Woody how spoiled they'd become flying around in relatively cushy jet fighters that were not at the mercy of bone-rattling torque or piston-engine fuel fumes. And were those engines loud!

"Why aren't all these guys deaf?" Woody yelled over to Ryder. "My ears are killing me . . ."

"Mine, too," Ryder confessed, "And we thought the B-24 was bad . . ."

They continued south, following the Hudson River's relatively straightforward flow past Kingston, past Poughkeepsie, all the while the anticipation building as they neared the skies above Newburgh, New York.

When they finally spotted the lights of West Point, they began to climb up to 8000 feet, the same altitude that Fort One was flying when it had its strange encounter. They also checked in with the Newburgh airport, telling the control tower personnel that they were on a "shakedown flight." They were alerted to some light traffic to the west and then the Newburgh tower called over and out.

Within ten minutes they were slowly flying a circular pattern over the darkened river, just east of the lights of Newburgh.

"Well, here we are," Woody announced as they went into their first wide orbit. "Eyes up . . ."

Ryder positioned one still camera and the video job against his window and made sure both were up and ready.

"Now, let's get lucky," he said wistfully.

One hour and forty-five minutes later they were still circling.

They'd seen nothing unusual at all, not even a hint of anything strange. And they'd burned up a lot of fuel doing it. So too went their enthusiasm for the adventure.

"We must be nuts!" Ryder finally yelled over to Woody. "No one ever sees UFOs when they're looking for them . . ."

Suddenly his friend froze at the control wheel.

"Oh no?" Woody yelled back over to him. "Then, what the hell is that?"

Ryder followed Woody's pointed finger out to their one o'clock position. At first Ryder saw nothing. But then gradually he began picking out light specks from the background of clouds and sky.

"Christ . . . I see three red lights . . ." he called out. "Three whites. And three fucking ambers . . ."

Woody had already yanked back on the Mitchell's throttles, slowing the two-engined bomber to about 160 knots.

"Three more reds," he announced, "three whites, three ambers. It's a fucking boomerang! That's got to be what Williams saw . . ."

"It is . . ." Ryder declared, getting his cameras in position. "And that's just what I saw, too . . ."

The object was moving in a southeast direction and passing very slowly through some scattered clouds. Woody turned slightly to the east, putting the B-25 on a line of flight that would eventually intersect right in front of the flying V.

"Are those cameras ready?" Woody yelled as they closed in on the object.

"They are now," Ryder yelled back, clicking the video's battery-check light to on and then snapping off a few still photos using special AS-2000 night film obtained from the Griffiss base intelligence-section officer.

As they slowly gained on the object, Ryder felt a weird feeling run through him. Could one of War Heaven's unanswerables be solved two thousand miles to the east over the Hudson River and right on the doorstep of New York City?

"This ain't ECC!" he yelled out to Woody as they closed within four miles of the big V.

"You mean you hope it ain't!" Woody yelled back with a note of caution.

They droned on for a few moments, closing in on the UFO as it slowly passed into another heavy cloud bank.

"We're about fifteen seconds away from coming right up to it,"

Woody yelled finally. "Better start shooting the works now . . ."

But just at that moment, the last of the intervening clouds cleared away and suddenly both of them had their first clear, close-up look at the flying V of lights.

"Damn," Ryder swore angrily when he realized exactly what the lights were. "Dammit to hell . . ."

"I don't believe this," Woody chorused. *"I don't fucking believe it . . ."*

He put the B-25 into a dive, cutting underneath the "boomerang" as it slowly turned away from them. It was at this angle that they plainly saw that this flying V was not some huge, flying aircraft carrier or any other kind of UFO.

What they saw instead were eighteen small ultralight airplanes, flying in an incredibly-tight V-shaped formation, each with a white, red, or amber light hanging from its belly.

To add insult to injury, one of them was towing a sign that said TAKE US TO YOUR LEADER.

Ryder immediately shut off the video camera and threw the still camera aside.

"This proves it," he said. "I *am* going nuts . . ."

34

"Are you ready, Miss O'Brien?"

Maureen checked to make sure the tape recorder was working properly.

"Second day," she said into the microphone. "First interview . . ."

She looked at the man sitting across the rather ornate desk from her and made a mental note of his description. He was small, squat, with almost no hair. His face was slightly crimson with a few age spots, and his right eye appeared to be permanently teary. Maureen guessed that he was at least seventy years old.

He was dressed impeccably in a Brooks Brothers suit, and he wore several pieces of expensive jewelry, most noticeably a stunning gold tie clasp. If she had run into him in Washington, D.C., she would have guessed that he was somewhere fairly high on the political food chain, on the order of an undersecretary or maybe even an ambassador.

"May I have your full name, sir?"

He smiled and slowly shook his head. "Sorry, I'm afraid that's classified . . ."

"Then, what can I call you?" she asked.

He thought for a moment and then said, "Well, my friends call me 'Pinky' . . ."

The office itself was typically governmental. An American flag in the corner, two file cabinets, a fax, a multi-button telephone, and a Rolodex so massive it needed a separate stand all for itself.

"This department," Maureen went on, "what is it called?"

"This is the Department of Morbid National Psychology Cultivation," Pinky answered with a smile. "The Office of Doom and Gloom is what they call us around here . . ."

"And could you tell me exactly what it is you do?"

"Certainly," Pinky replied. "Our role here is to cultivate a sense of morbidity – of doom and gloom, if you will – among the citizens of this country in regard to UFOs. Now even though we've been at this location for only about a dozen years, our efforts extend all the way back to 1952, which is when our government first tackled what was called then 'the flying saucer problem.'

"At that time, we were given charge of making our citizens aware that an attack could come at any moment . . ."

"You mean from the Russians?" Maureen asked.

Pinky shook his head. "No, that's another department," he said quite candidly. "We here in the MNPC had to make citizens aware that an attack could come from, what they would call, 'extraterrestrial sources'."

"From flying saucers?"

"Exactly," Pinky confirmed. "Now, we did this in many different ways. One was by the selective release of sensitive information to various scientists, writers, and magazine publishers over the years. These people were aware of our efforts, of course, and they helped us a lot in the early days."

"You leaked classified information on flying saucers?"

"Yes, that was our job. We found that by letting out just a smidgen of information, it would propagate quite rapidly. This was the very beginning of the communications revolution, too. The use of TV was becoming widespread. Radio was very strong. Plus there were many, many magazines along the science-fiction and pseudo-science bent. Their editors were very helpful. But, of course, they were paid to be."

"You paid editors of magazines to promulgate the fear of flying saucers?"

"That's correct," Pinky replied. "And I assure you that a study of publications back then will show that the money was well spent. But as the decade wore on and we approached the coming of the Sixties, we had to adapt. So we made inroads in Hollywood and some on TV. It is those programs which continue today. We still do some work with editors and writers, but, off the record, the print angle isn't what it used to be."

Maureen couldn't believe what she was hearing, and more than once she nervously checked the tape recorder, making sure it was getting all of the bizarre, inflammatory quotes.

"Can you prove any of this?" she asked Pinky. "Do you have documentation to back up what you've told me?"

"Why, of course," he answered, reaching over to the file cabinet. He retrieved six files in all, looked them over briefly, and then handed them to Maureen.

"It's all in there," he told her. "And I can give you a tip. To cut through a lot of the repetition, key in on the OSI studies—"

"OSI?"

"Office of Scientific Intelligence," Pinky explained. "Part of the CIA . . . ."

Maureen flipped through the volumes of material, and what she read quickly seemed to confirm what Pinky was telling her.

Still, she was having a difficult time putting it in perspective. It was as if the man were talking about subjects as banal as milk-support prices or government-sponsored irrigation studies.

"Please tell me if I have this straight," she began slowly. "This office has been making a concerted effort since 1952 to put the fear of UFOs into the consciousness of the American public?"

"Yes, exactly . . ."

"And you've been doing it by leaking classified information and by paying off editors and writers?"

"And Hollywood and TV people," Pinky reminded her. "We can't forget them . . ."

Maureen was near speechless. This *had* to be a joke.

"But *why* did you do this?" she finally asked him. "What was the point?"

For the first time, Pinky's smile waned a bit. He looked confused.

" 'Why?' " he repeated. "Well, because we wanted our citizens to be prepared."

"Prepared for what?"

Again Pinky looked baffled.

"For the invasion, of course . . ." he said finally.

The Zoo

Maureen's next appointment was in room 6, the place called the

Zoo.

A tall blond man with a slight Scandinavian accent and a Sherlock Holmes pipe met her at the door and introduced himself simply at Ray. He seemed like a normal sort, unlike Pinky, who Maureen was convinced had either gone quietly mad sometime around 1961 or was an immensely resourceful, but not too amusing, practical joker.

Ray handed her a laboratory coat similar to the one he was wearing. He also gave her a pair of safety goggles, saying, "You don't really need to wear them if you don't want. But our insurance regulations say that you have to at least carry them . . ."

Room 6 was not the least bit like Pinky's office. Rather, it looked more like a wax museum in which every display had its own airtight glass enclosure. It was brightly lit by dozens of long fluorescent tubes on the walls as well as the ceilings, and it smelled heavily of antiseptic.

"Why do they call this place the Zoo?" Maureen asked Ray, clicking on her tape recorder.

Ray just shrugged. "I'm not sure," he admitted. "We only have a few animals . . . live ones, anyway."

They walked down a bright corridor and stopped at the first glass display case.

Inside were about a dozen seagulls.

"This is what I hear every morning," she exclaimed.

"They are noisy," Ray replied. "The only reason they're here is that the SLO people—that's the Self-Luminous Objects department—don't have room for them anymore."

"But why do they want them?" she asked.

Ray shrugged. "Can't say I really know," he replied. "Something about the fact that seagulls are the number-one cause of mistaken UFO reports. Has something to do with their feathers. The way they reflect the sunlight."

Maureen made a quick though confused note concerning the seagulls and then they walked down to the next glass compartment.

She glanced inside, and was immediately startled. Behind the glass partition was a hairy, yet human shape, at least seven foot tall.

"Oh, my God . . . Is that what I think it is?"

Ray nodded. "It's a *yeti,"* he confirmed. "We got this from the Red Chinese back in the early 1970s, right after President Nixon made his historic trip to the People's Republic. Their soldiers captured it in

208

the Himalayas during their war against India in 1962. It came into their camp and was stealing food. They shot it, wounded it, kept it alive for a while, but, as you can see, it died eventually."

Maureen had the microphone so close to Ray's mouth, it was interfering with his pipesmoking. At the same time, she studied the shape on the other side of the glass. Was it real?

"What are you doing with it here?" she asked him in her best reporter's voice.

Ray just shrugged. "I don't know," he admitted. "I guess no one else wanted it . . ."

They walked down to the next enclosure. Once again Maureen looked inside, and once again she was startled to her bones.

Inside the display case was a large bottle with greenish fluid bubbling through it. Inside was a head. It was puffy and pale white, but it looked just like Adolph Hitler.

"Jesus . . ." she gasped, unintentionally grabbing hold of Ray's arm.

He blew a long stream of smoke up into the fluorescent lights.

"Another gift from our Communist friends," he said, calmly dislodging her nails from his forearm. "Actually they had Nazi doctors do it, using some very obscure techniques they'd learned regrettably enough at Dachau."

Maureen stared at the floating head; sometimes, through the bubbles, it appeared to be staring right back. She felt her stomach do a complete flip. The thing looked *damn* real, like an obscene sideshow in a decrepit traveling circus.

"It's not really alive," Ray told her. "Not technically, anyway. Suspended animation is not a good description, either. I believe the official term is 'cranial coma.'"

With Maureen's knees suddenly weak and in danger of buckling, they moved to the next display. It contained the body of a white-furred monkey.

"It's a Makak," Ray explained. "Better known as a Japanese snow monkey. They're very intelligent animals. Researchers have been studying them for years. They've seen them develop ways of washing their food, separating it from dirt and sand, even seasoning it . . ."

"Why is this one here?" Maureen asked, her words having some trouble getting out.

Ray lit his pipe again. "They caught it building a fire . . ." was his ominous reply.

He steered her toward the next display, expertly holding her arm for support. Inside she saw an grossly overweight man with greasy hair sitting in an easy chair, watching TV. The table next to him was covered with prescription bottles and junk food.

Maureen put her hand to her mouth, afraid that she was about to spit up her breakfast. If this was all a joke, it was quickly becoming very unfunny.

"Do you know who that is?" Ray asked her.

"I don't want to know," she replied sternly.

Ray just shrugged and led her to the very end of the hallway to the last enclosure. Only her reporter's instincts gave her the courage to actually look inside. When she did, she suddenly could not suppress the urge to vomit.

"I've got to . . ." she said, gagging. *"Please* . . . the bathroom . . ."

Ray directed her to the door right across the hallway and she made it all the way to the sink before vomiting.

What she had seen inside the room was a bed surrounded by banks of medical equipment—tubes, wires, monitors, pumps. On the bed was the form of an elderly man approaching his eighties. His head was encased in a clear plastic bubble, which was needed because more than half the man's skull was missing. His brain and all its bloody attachments were still pumping away and the body was breathing.

But it was not the view of the open skull that had made her nauseated. It was the face of the man himself. It was President John F. Kennedy.

35

There were no smiles in the conference area three floors below the room-6 bathroom.

Thirty men, most of them military officers holding the rank of colonel or higher and dressed in various service uniforms, were sitting around the enormous table. All of them were grim-faced and sober. Together, they comprised the top echelon of the ISC.

"This is impressive . . ." the man who sat at the head of the table was saying. In a room where everyone was known only by a number, for security reasons, his was Sixteen.

He was studying a piece of metal about a third of the size of a cigarette pack. It was thick in spots, thin in others, and looked like aluminum. Yet whenever he folded it, it immediately returned to its former position. He'd held similar pieces of metal before, their textures so strange, so bizarre to the touch. He'd never arrived at an adequate definition. Was it "metallic plastic"? "Woodlike metal"? It was so hard to say.

"How much did they uncover?" he asked, passing the piece to the officer next to him and picking up a smaller fragment of the same strange alloy.

"About a half a kilogram," came the answer from the other end of the table. "But, as you know, it's so light, the exact quantity is best considered by how it measures. So, in all, they found about three square feet of the stuff . . ."

"And these archaeologists realize what they've found?" someone else asked.

"They certainly do," came the definite reply. "They were out there looking for it. They were mounting this dig for three years. Raised

211

all the money themselves, and even put everyone through a security check. Lucky for us it wasn't thorough enough . . ."

"And how does it match up with the other Roswell stuff?" someone else asked.

"Two hundredths of a second off our original mark," was the answer.

"Earlier or later?"

"Later."

"Did the four-D tests confirm this?"

"They did."

"And?"

"And, if you'll excuse the expression, you can now set your watch to the stuff . . ."

There were a few minutes of uneasy silence as the pieces of metal made their way around the table.

"Well, this certainly helps us a bit," Sixteen said, finally breaking the spell. "Those people actually did a lot of work for us."

"What it means is, we have to adjust the detonation time to this new schedule."

"Is that possible?"

"It better be. That's what the people in fusing are here for . . ."

"Where are these archaeologists now?"

"In the apartments."

"And who's getting the grand tour?"

"Just the reporter," came the reply. "Under the time constraints, we figured that would be easier on the Smile Boys to show just her the works and no one else. She's so high-profile, we'll probably get more bang for the buck this way, especially, well . . . especially if something goes wrong."

"How far through is she?"

"She's in the Zoo Room, getting the royal treatment, right now, as we speak . . ."

"And the other diggers? What did they see?"

"Just enough," was the answer. "Little here, little there. The top guy is a department head at the University of Chicago, so we figured, next to the reporter, he'd be the one to get the most exposure. So we gave him about a third of the grand tour, while we did some inquiring into his past."

"And?"

"We found the usual stuff. A couple hookers. Some porn tapes. Mostly calls to phone-sex girls about a year ago. It's looking real good as far as he's concerned."

"And the rest of the archaeologists?"

"We ran them through the abduction chamber and then did the injection series," was the response. "If our numbers stay right, one third will remember everything, one third will remember bits and pieces, and the rest will remember nothing at all."

"Just as long as we're not spending *too* much time on them," Sixteen said, reexamining the first piece of strange metal. "As we know, there's a very strict clock running here. I think all our resources should be focused on the main objective now."

"Okay, they'll all be released tomorrow. Except for the reporter, of course . . ."

"Fine . . . next item—What about the new pilots? What stage are they in?"

"Three are still in stage one. One is in stage two."

"We'll have to speed *that* up . . ."

"We can try. We're working on it night and day . . ."

"Do you realize that some of us have been hearing that for forty years?"

The comment was met by a rare laugh inside the room.

"We are getting very close, gentlemen," Sixteen said. "Very close indeed . . ." There was a murmur of agreement around the room.

"But that's it for now," Sixteen went on. "Let's do a time check . . . I read, twelve days, fourteen hours, thirty-six minutes, and zero seconds . . . *now.*"

The other twenty-nine men checked their wristwatches, each one of which was running backward . . .

36

Maureen adjusted the wet cloth on her brow and wished she'd had a hot-water bottle instead.

Her stomach was still extremely queasy, and she hadn't been able to take anything but a drink of water in nearly eight hours. She craved sleep, but everytime she closed her eyes she saw either the floating head, the dead ape or the face of . . .

She leaned over and reached for her spit bucket again — but at the last moment she was able to force back the dry heave. She had nothing left to throw up by this time. Plopping back down onto her pillows, she took a deep breath, and slowly began to regain her composure.

She felt horrible, and not just for physical reasons. Her mind was terribly confused, to the point of causing dizziness and blurred vision. What was going on here? Had she really stumbled upon one of the greatest cover-up stories of all time — one that would surely rival Watergate in scope and ramifications? Or was she just the brunt of an incredibly elaborate and ruthlessly bad gag?

She just didn't know.

After becoming sick in room 6, Ray had assisted her back to her quarters, where a smiling Walter was waiting. He seemed to be legitimately concerned in a troubled and fussy sort of way, and offered to get her anything from an Alka-Seltzer to a glass of whiskey. She turned him down, wanting only to be alone with her *mal de mer* and to be given time to think about her present condition.

He did leave her a bundle of documents from several other units which he said she could read in preparation for her interviews with various unit heads. She had read them off and on over the past few hours, making a scattering of notes. Although all of them had portions that had been inked out for "security reasons," they all seemed to support the one central thesis of this strange place: that for whatever reason, the fear of UFOs—specifically, an invasion of flying saucers—had to be vigilantly maintained in the American public's mind's eye, no matter what the cost.

The first document was labeled GBP—for Green Ball Phenomenon. It claimed that the department's role was to examine strange things in the sky that might occur naturally—meteorites, ball lightning, nocturnal lights—and how the population might react to them.

At one time, the GBP people would hire airplanes and dispense barium crystals into the upper atmosphere, which would produce the intended strange effects, sometimes hundreds of miles away. Then they would check with local newspapers and law-enforcement officials to see how many people reported seeing UFOs on the night in question. In some cases, when such a sampling was low, the GBP people would repeat the exercise and then flood police with calls themselves, setting off a firestorm of reports and thus getting a lot of "free press" for UFOs.

The report claimed the GBP people had been recently equipped with even more advanced techniques for achieving similar effects, the details of which were blacked out of the documents.

The second report was on the Foo Fighter Squadron unit. It claimed the department was made up of a dozen men, all of whom were well beyond the mandatory retirement age for civil servants. "Foo Fighters," she learned, was the name given by military pilots to UFOs they'd spotted during World War II, before the term "flying saucer" became popular. The Foo Fighter unit's role was to "provide covert education" to the nation's military personnel, sometimes by providing airborne "targets," sometimes simply sending false signals onto radar screens.

The FFS people pointed with pride to a campaign they had waged in the mid-1970s, during which a number of Strategic Air Command bases found their defense perimeters compromised by aircraft, which on the official documents were referred to as "helicopters." These "helicopters" hovered over nuclear weapons storage areas at SAC bases such as Loring AFB in Maine, Wurtsmith AFB in Michigan, Grand Forks AFB in North Dakota, Malmstrom AFB in Montana, Plattsburgh AFB in upstate New York, and even the Canadian

Armed Forces air base at Falconbridge in Ontario, Canada.

While again citing security reasons, and several paragraphs of black ink, against revealing just how this was all done, the FFS report claimed that program almost wasn't taken as seriously as it should have been, simply because it commenced on Halloween night in 1975, and many people, within the military and in the media, took the initial reports as a prank.

The report from room 4—dubbed Project Super Twinkle—was very brief. The unit was responsible for setting up literally thousands of patrol cameras, around the country on which they would capture photographs of UFOs, natural or otherwise. These photographs would then be given, or sometimes sold, to the media by an operative under the guise of being just another ordinary citizen who happened to capture something strange and flying on their camera; again, the idea was to keep UFOs in the public's mind.

The Los Alamos Bird Watchers Society turned out to be the name for the unit responsible for investigating legitimate UFO sightings over nuclear power plants and atomic-bomb manufacturing facilities, which, by inference, was apparently a common occurrence. This report led the way in inked-out passages—five pages in all had been deleted. But at least she did get to learn that the group took its name from an old, U.S. Army counterespionage outfit that had kept tabs on the Los Alamos atomic research facility by posing as birdwatchers.

The report on the department known as Arthur Godfrey turned out to be disappointingly anticlimactic. When the government first began investigating UFO reports in the 1950s, the idea came up that a well-known personality could be hired as a spokesman to state the government's point of view on exactly what was happening in the skies over the country via their radio or TV show. At the time, Arthur Godfrey was the most well known personality in America.

Whether or not he was approached for the job was not revealed in the document. But his name stuck to the unit whose job it was to "educate" selected personalities—actors (Jackie Gleason's name was mentioned), writers, sports figures, even rock 'n' roll stars—about the UFO phenomena in hopes that they would spread the word—subtly or not—to their fans.

* * *

Maureen finally drifted off to sleep, only to be awakened by a soft tapping at her door a few hours later.

She had no watch, and therefore no idea what time it was, but her body was telling her it was close to midnight.

She wrapped a blanket around her, and padded over to the door, thankful that her stomach was at last feeling settled.

Opening the door she found it was the young shy man who usually delivered her meals to her. He was empty-handed this time, though.

"You have another interview to do," he said, his eyes unintentionally straying up and down her partially uncovered body.

"This minute?" she asked. "What time is it?"

He automatically went to look at his watch, but stopped in midmotion.

"I'm not sure," he said. "But we have to do this right now . . ."

Twenty minutes later, Maureen stood outside room 7, the one with the door marked SLO, for Self-Luminous Objects. Her stomach growling but still behaving, she wondered what in hell could possibly be lurking for her on the other side.

She didn't have to wait long to find out. It was evident as soon as she walked in that this interview in SLO *would* be different from the others.

First of all, the small SLO office was a mess. There were books, magazines, and videotapes scattered everywhere. Three-ring binders, each one overflowing with ripped and dog-eared pages, were literally falling out of their book shelves. Ancient coffee cups and junk-food wrappers littered the floor. There wasn't a wastebasket to be seen.

The youngish man behind the incredibly cluttered desk was as unkempt as his surroundings. He had long stringy hair and a beard which seemed to be growing in several different directions at once. He simply identified himself as Willy, telling Maureen, as had all the others, that his real name was classified.

Unlike the other units within MNPC, SLO was a one-man shop, and that man was Willy.

"Is it true that you've either visited or read reports on all of the other units already?" Willy asked her as he cleared off a chair for her.

Maureen told him she had.

217

"Typical," he huffed. "And so they told you to interview me last?"

"No, not really," Maureen replied honestly. "That is, I don't think it was planned that way . . ."

Willy growled derisively.

"Don't kid yourself, Miss O'Brien," he said sternly. "Everything around here is planned, right down to the last detail. It was intentional that I be last on the list. I'm *always* last on the list . . ."

Maureen clicked on her tape recorder. She hoped this would be a brief talk.

"So what have they been telling you?" he asked.

Maureen gave him a quick rundown of her activities so far, leaving out the more graphic details of her stomach-churning visit to the Zoo.

"Well, you are certainly getting the grand tour," he told her.

"I consider it an incredible opportunity," Maureen told him, not quite wanting to use those precise words.

Willy laughed in her face.

"You mean you actually believe all this bullshit?" he asked her.

She froze for a moment. "I don't know . . . Should I?"

Willy never stopped laughing.

"Come on, Miss O'Brien," he said. "The yeti? The Green Balls? Hitler's brain? *JFK?* You can't possibly think it's all real . . ."

Maureen felt her head go into a slow spin.

"But I saw it all," she stammered.

"You saw what they *wanted* you to see," Willy told her. "It's a very elaborate, very expensive game they play here. They've been doing it for years. They're experts at it."

Maureen was astounded. And very confused. The man's candor was alarming. Were the things she'd seen in the Zoo real or not? Or was *this* the beginning of an elaborate scheme?

"Why would they go to such great lengths to do this?" she asked.

"The reason is simple, Miss O'Brien," he replied. "Just answer one question: When you're finally released from here, what will you do?"

"I'm going to write about this place, of course," she declared. "I'm going to bust it wide open . . ."

"Are you, now?" Willy asked mockingly. "You are going to write that the U.S. government has a secret place hidden somewhere where they keep the brain of Adolph Hitler? Where they have the body of Bigfoot? Where they keep JFK alive?"

Now Maureen was stunned. "Why, yes . . ." was the only answer she could muster.

Willy began rummaging through the piles of paper on his desk. After a few moments of searching, he came up with a large, heavily stained manila envelope. Reaching inside, he drew out three tabloid newspapers.

"Read these headlines, Miss O'Brien," he said, holding the first newspaper just inches from her face.

It was the *World News*. The headline read, *"Government Hiding Bigfoot Body."*

The next one was from *The Globe Reporter*. The headline read, *"Government Researcher Says JFK Alive!"*

The third newspaper was the *Nation's Examiner*. Its headline read, *"Government Scientists Probing the Secrets of Hitler's Brain."*

Maureen's brain felt like it was bubbling now. Yet she was still able to think like a journalist.

"Can you prove any of this?" she asked him.

"Of course I can," was Willy's reply.

"But why would they create all this?" she asked. "What's the point of it all?"

"The point is, Miss O'Brien," Willy said sarcastically, "that this place is the biggest boondoggle in history. This place isn't about UFOs and invaders from space. Or Bigfoot or Hitler's brain. It's about theft. Graft. Unparalleled corruption. They've stolen billions of dollars here, Miss O'Brien. Not millions. *Billions*. In cash. In gold. And by your buying into all this top-secret hocus-pocus, you're going to aid them in stealing even more!"

"How?" she asked.

"Simple," Willy replied, pointing to the tabloids. "By helping to add to this very clever pile of bullshit they've been hiding under for years."

Maureen bit her lip. Could she really believe this man?

"Show me your proof . . ." she told Willy point-blank.

He leaned back and smiled. "I can do better than that," he told her. "I'll tell you exactly what they'll feed you next."

Maureen flipped over her cassette and pulled out her pen to take notes.

"They'll run you through what they call the Silver Room," Willy

219

said. "They'll show you pieces of metal that they will claim came from UFOs—"

"We found some . . ." Maureen said, interrupting him.

He smiled cruelly. "Sure you did," he said.

She was crushed. Was the dig site all part of a hoax too?

"Once you've seen all these wonderful pieces of metal from UFOs," Willy went on, "they'll tell you that this stuff is actually growing younger . . ."

"Growing *younger?*"

"Yes, they'll tell you that they have this whiz-bang machine that can shoot a laser beam between the atoms of metals and thus determine their exact age. Then they'll tell you that instead of aging, like everything else in our universe does, this 'special' metal is getting younger. They'll call it 'time-reversing' . . ."

"And what does that mean?" she demanded.

"Oh, they'll tell you it fits into their theory that UFOs don't come from outer space at all," Willy replied.

"And where will they say they come from?"

Willy began to say something, but stopped at the last moment.

"I'll make a deal with you," he said. "You go and see if I'm right. Then come back and we'll talk some more. Deal?"

Maureen didn't know how she should answer. She had so many questions she had to consider, not the least of which was why this strange man Willy was telling her all this.

"Okay," she finally told him; "It's a deal."

He smiled, sincerely, but only for a moment.

"But I just have one more question for now," Maureen told him. "Off the record . . ."

"Go ahead," Willy replied. "I have all day."

She snapped off her tape recorder. "Could you please tell me where I am?"

Willy grinned once again. "They haven't told you yet?"

Maureen shook her head no.

"Well." Willy snickered. "Let me be the first. You're in Nevada, in a place called Restricted Area Sixty-one. Better known to those who care as Dreamland . . ."

220

37

Maryland

The pair of Secret Service men watched the big blue Chevrolet rental car turn into the long driveway and slowly make its way up to the main house.

"Okay, he's here," one of the men whispered into his two-way radio. "Close the gate and seal it . . ."

The Chevy pulled up to the front door of the large ski-lodge-style building and stopped. Instantly the two Secret Service men were next to the driver's door, their eyes glued on the man inside.

"Stay inside the car, sir . . ." one said to the driver. "Please pass me all your ID with your left hand . . ."

The man inside the car passed three pieces of identification to the Secret Service agent, who checked them thoroughly.

"Okay, Lieutenant Moon," the security man said finally. "You can get out and follow us, please . . ."

Five minutes later, Moon was being ushered into a small room right off the main hall of the lodge. A man was sitting in an over-stuffed chair next to the room's blazing fireplace, reading from a black notebook. He looked up as Moon entered the room.

"Come in, Lieutenant," the man said, rising to shake his hand. "Please, have a seat . . ."

Moon walked over to the second chair near the fireplace and placed his bulging briefcase beside it.

"Thank you, Mr. President . . ."

An aide appeared with a tray of coffee and small cakes and placed it on the small table between them. Moon waited for the President to take his coffee and fuss over several of the small sweets before he poured himself a half cup.

"We have a new, very troubling development in the ISC problem, sir," Moon said, getting right to the point.

"The Fort Knox situation?" the President replied, taking his first bite of cake. "I know, I just saw the report. What do you think it means?"

Moon let out a long, troubled breath. "I'm not sure, sir," he replied. "All we know is that ISC managed to airlift up to four billion dollars in gold bars from Kentucky to Nevada over the past three and half months. Just what the motive is, that's anyone's guess."

"Economic terrorism?" the President asked. "The gold reserves at Fort Knox don't really amount to much, but symbolically, well . . ."

"It might be that, sir," Moon replied. "Or they could be just stealing it."

The President took a long sip of his coffee. "Disturbing," he said, shaking his head. "Very disturbing . . ."

For the next few minutes, Moon and the Chief Executive reviewed the entire ISC problem: The initial warnings signs. The reprogramming of the Cray supercomputer. The slow absorption of War Heaven into ISC's control. The ISC's possession of a nuclear device. The inexplicable leak of top-secret data to the tabloids. The ominous blackmail threat. And now, the possible outright theft of four billion dollars in gold bullion.

By the time it was over, the worry lines on the President's brow had deepened further. He had little choice but to reach the same conclusion as everyone else who was familiar with the crisis: the ISC seemed to be holding all the cards.

"What can be done?" he asked the NSA man. "Are we certain that there is absolutely no way to shut off their power? To cut their communications? To starve them out?"

Moon gravely shook his head.

"I'm afraid not, sir," he replied. "They run on their own power, produced from a number of sources. Their communications are redundant to five times in depth. They have a five-year supply of food and water. They have their own air-purification system. Their main headquarters is reinforced with concrete that is twenty-five feet thick in most places. We figure they could detonate their nuclear device and button themselves up inside their bunkers and not have to come out for six months, or maybe even a year."

The President put his coffee aside, stood up, and threw another log on the fire.

"Are these guys screwing up anything?" he asked, the near-obscenity sounding odd coming from such a well-known voice. "Isn't there some way we can trip them up?"

Moon could only shrug. "It's just the contrary, sir," he replied. "If anything, things are running very smoothly within the Range, even under these bizarre circumstances. The units in training are continuing exercises on a record level. Their innovative scores have never been higher. In fact, the amount of supplies doled out to training units in return for their successes on the field have actually increased since the ISC made its move."

"And the commanders in the field have no idea that anything is wrong?" the President asked.

"None whatsoever, sir," Moon replied gravely. "As far as they and their men are all concerned, things have never been better inside the Range."

The President sat in silence for a long time. The only sound in the room was the crackling from the fireplace and the ticking of a clock.

"There has *got* to be a way to end this," the Chief Executive said finally. "But it has to be done very quietly. Do you realize what it will take if we have to inform our overseas allies about all this?"

"I can certainly see it as a very delicate situation," Moon replied.

"Well, then, do we have people in there on the ground?" he asked Moon directly.

"In a sense we do, sir," the NSA man replied. "But we can't expect them to function as anything more than lightning rods. In fact, their chances of having any effect are frankly pretty low. Not unless we got very lucky . . ."

"Then, if we can't count on them, what *will* it take?" the President asked, his voice becoming agitated.

Moon gulped almost audibly. "Besides trying to get one of them to talk, sir," Moon told him, "we need to identify a secure force. An army that the ISC does *not* have control over. Then we have to move them into War Heaven and reclaim it, piece by piece, using the rules that everyone on the Range is familiar with. That way, the ISC might hesitate on making good on their threats, and most of the people out on the Range itself will be under the impression that, well, that this is

223

all some kind of a security drill, sir . . ."

The President suddenly eyed him with a mild look of surprise.

"This isn't 'some kind of a security drill,' cooked up by the NSA, is it, Lieutenant?"

Moon was almost floored by the question.

"Well, sir . . . of course not," he stammered his reply. "I mean, you would be the one, that . . . well, the one who would know that, before I . . ."

The Chief Executive took another sip of his coffee. "Sometimes I wonder, Lieutenant," he said rather mysteriously.

Moon let the next few moments pass in confused silence. *What was going on here?* he wondered.

"Okay, we need a clean force," the President went on. "If we had one, I'd give the good-to-go order immediately. But where in hell can we get such an army? The ISC has a tap into every military unit in this country . . ."

Moon took a deep breath and let it out slowly. It was the question he'd been waiting for.

"All except one, Mr. President," Moon told him.

38

The Marine captain in charge of the L-10 protection unit checked his watch and spit out his wad of gum in disgust.

It was 2355 – five minutes before midnight. The wind atop the mesa was blowing at near-hurricane proportions, strong enough to whip up not only loose desert sand but also a storm of jagged rocks and pebbles. These projectiles were now hitting the top of the butte with the force of small bullets.

The Marine officer had been feeling uneasy all day. The trip up to Close to the Edge had been problematic that afternoon. First, the special combat vehicle broke down as it was climbing the hill up to Casa Fantastica. There was nothing wrong with it mechanically – rather, the Zoot mechanism had clicked off, killing the engine.

He checked the device called the HILES, which was the small computer brain that determined whether or not a piece of equipment had been hit by a Zoot shot. Oddly, the SCV's HILES screen was clear. The vehicle hadn't been hit – it had simply shut down.

The Marine had never heard of such a thing happening in War Heaven before.

He was forced to abandon the SCV and divide its crewmen between his Hummer and the Bradley, making it a tight squeeze all round. They reached the Casa only to find the old man was deep into a new batch of X-rated films and didn't want to deploy. The Marine officer had pay the old coot ten bucks from his own pocket to get his ass into the Bradley, and then only after he'd promised that he could drive the Bradley some of the way.

225

By the time they'd finally delivered the old man to the top of the mesa, it was already dark and they were more than two hours behind schedule. The final insult was that the hot meal his men had been expecting once they reached the Eye was not there. The chow chopper never showed up—again a first in his experience inside War Heaven. Tired, hungry, and grumbling, the L-10s were forced to eat some chicken a la king MREs—meals, ready to eat—the modern K-ration food that every grunt on the Range considered just one step up from eating raw sand.

Now it was four and a half hours later, and his men were getting uncharacteristically restless. Trained to stay hidden for hours, even days, on end, tonight they were rustling around in the brush patches surrounding the Eye, making noise, making mistakes. He couldn't really blame them. They were as cold, tired, and hungry as he.

And possibly they shared the same uneasiness he did: the feeling that too many little things had gone wrong this day.

The feeling that suddenly all was not right in War Heaven.

He heard the chopper long before he saw it.

It was coming out of the west, its engines causing a racket that drowned out the roar of the howling wind.

Instantly the Marine officer's second-in-command was at his side.

"The food chopper, finally . . ." the Army Green Beret lieutenant said.

The Marine captain checked his watch. It was just three minutes past midnight, extremely late for a food drop. Plus the wind wasn't exactly ideal for chopper flying.

"It ain't chow in this weather," he told the young officer. "It must be a pickup for someone inside. Get the guys on their toes . . ."

The lieutenant disappeared back into the scrub as the captain shouldered his weapon and walked over to the front door of the Eye. He pushed a red button down near the door handle and waited for the yellow light next to it to blink on. It did, twice, the signal that one of the C2 men inside was coming out.

The door opened and a man in civilian clothes stepped out.

"Sixteen. Egress. Sixty-One," he told the Marine officer.

The Marine noted the same into his small handheld computer. This officer was ISC Number Sixteen. He was heading out, going

226

back to the hardened headquarters facility at Area 61.

The chopper was now hovering about twenty feet above the mesa's concrete helipad, the violent wash from its rotor blades adding to the maelstrom of sand and dust swirling around the top of the butte.

The Marine captain gave ISC-Sixteen a thumbs-up and together they walked over to the helipad.

The blue MH-60 Pave Hawk set down with a bump and the copilot gave them a wave. Running in a half-crouch, the Marine and the ISC officer scampered to the chopper just as its side door began to open. The Marine grabbed the door's handle and helped it along, sliding it all the way to his left.

That's when he looked up to see a .45 automatic pointed at his forehead.

"Don't move, asshole," the man behind the gun shouted at him. "This is real . . ."

The Marine froze. Two sets of hands reached out of the darkness of the chopper bay and grabbed the equally startled ISC officer, yanking him inside. Instinctively, the Marine reached in to pull him back, but he too was grabbed by the collar and hauled into the chopper.

The man with the .45 – his face obscured by a handkerchief and a crash helmet – pushed the Marine's nose into the side of a small yellow box that was sitting in the middle of the chopper bay.

"Read those numbers, jarhead," the man ordered him, "or I shoot the bird."

"Weapon five-six . . ." the Marine called out, reading the lettering on the side of the box.

"Do you know what a five-six Zoot is?" the man yelled into his ear.

The Marine began nodding quickly. "Yeah, I do," he cried back, his voice nearing panic.

"Good," the man with the gun said. "If you try anything stupid, we'll drop this on you. Understand?"

The Marine never got a chance to reply. The man with the gun kicked him out of the chopper, knocking him flat on his back. From this ignoble position the Marine watched the helicopter quickly rise back into the sky.

Knowing something was amiss, four of the L-10 troopers ran forward and began shooting at the chopper. The Marine officer went berserk. He body-slammed two of the soldiers, while at the same time screaming, "Cease fire! *Cease fire!*" at the other two.

"Did they snatch that bird?" the second-in-command asked him once the firing had stopped. his voice astonished.

"They've got a fucking five-six in that chopper . . ." the Marine told them as the helicopter began to move away out of range toward the north.

The second-in-command almost choked on his tongue.

"Jesuzz . . ."

The Marine officer grabbed his number-two and literally thrust him toward the unit's Hummer. "Call in a One Red alert, now!"

The Green Beret didn't have to be told twice; he was instantly off and running toward the Hummer's radio.

This left the Marine officer and the enlisted troopers to stare up at the chopper's red taillight as it disappeared into the howling night.

"Captain?" one of them asked. "What the fuck is a five-six?"

The Marine officer was so flustered, he almost slapped the man. But he caught himself at the last moment, took a deep breath, and then addressed the trooper through clenched teeth.

"A five-six is Zoot tactical nuclear weapon," he said in stern, equally measured syllables. "If they dropped that on us, nothing would work within thirty miles of this place. For ten years . . ."

39

Gate 72 was the code name for an isolated outpost that guarded the most northwesterly entrance to the Nevada Special Weapons Testing Range.

Straddling the California-Nevada state line, Gate 72 was little more than several buildings, a guardhouse, and a movable barrier. It sat at the end of an absolutely straight 47-mile roadway that fed off State Highway 95. Anyone foolish enough to ignore the RESTRICTED AREA sign at the entrance to this road and drive the long, uncurving ribbon of seared asphalt would have to deal with Gate 72's six heavily armed, no-nonsense sentries at the other end.

No surprise, then, that the guard unit did not see many potential trespassers. The record was two in one month, and that had happened several years before.

So it was with some amazement, then, that just before sunrise on this day, the two Gate 72 guards on duty saw a column of dust and smoke coming down the road toward them.

Using long-range NightScope goggles to cut through the predawn haze, the sentrys discovered that no less than a hundred and fifty vehicles were heading toward the outpost. Some were undoubtedly troop trucks, but many of the other tracked vehicles were covered with camouflage netting, making them impossible to identify by type.

The astonished guards estimated the convoy to be about twenty miles away, but moving very quickly.

They alerted the guard-unit leader—a sergeant—and his efforts to raise someone in the convoy on the radio proved fruitless. A quick check of the duty orders for the week mentioned no supply convoys due to enter the Range at Gate 72, nor were any repair units scheduled.

Fairly certain that he was facing another unannounced security drill, the sergeant routinely ordered his men to place their unit's Hummer in a roadblock configuration and then to take up their usual defensive positions on either side of the main guardhouse. With any luck, he thought. the training session would be over in less than a half hour.

Several minutes passed as the convoy approached, still under the watchful NightScope eye of the sentries. When the lead truck reached the slightly-wider service road that led up to the guardhouse itself, the sergeant stepped forward, and using his flashlight to cut through the lingering darkness, signaled the vehicle to stop.

It didn't.

The five-ton troop truck smashed into the guard unit's Hummer going so fast, it knocked the smaller vehicle right off the roadway and kept right on going.

Stunned, the sentries raised their M-16s to shoot, but they were immediately overwhelmed by an airburst of supertears gas which had been fired from the rear of the battering ram truck.

As the guards fell to the ground gasping for breath, they found themselves surrounded by dozens of black-uniformed soldiers who were pouring out of the handful of troop trucks that had stopped at the guardhouse. The rest of the convoy—vehicles of all shapes and sizes but all covered with camouflage netting—never even slowed down. They continued to flood through the checkpoint and into War Heaven.

The sergeant of the guard unit was revived and, slightly dazed, was brought up to the cab of one of the camouflaged trucks.

There, a small man with a high-pitched voice and a southern accent addressed him.

"I'm sorry, sergeant," this man told him as the parade of covered vehicles continued to speed past unchecked. "This was unavoidable . . ."

The sergeant wiped his stinging eyes with his sleeve.

"This is a hell of a drill . . ." he said to the man. "You could have killed one of us . . ."

"You're not getting the message, sergeant," the man told him.

As if to emphasize the point, they heard a low rumbling sound, which in seconds turned into a loud screeching. Looking up into the blood-red morning sky they saw two Zoot Tomahawk cruise missiles roar overhead and disappear over the mountains to the east, right into the halo of the rising sun. No sooner were they gone when two more streaked over. And then two more. And two *more*.

"This is crazy . . ." the sergeant said, finally realizing that he was involved in something more than a security exercise.

"You're right," the small man with the southern accent said, "It *is* crazy . . ."

The large C-130 Hercules supply ship circled the isolated airfield known only as R-5 twice and then came in for a landing.

Not much more than a single runway and a handful of storage buildings, the small air base was home to only three airplanes: two F-16 fighters and a single E2-C Hawkeye early warning-detection aircraft.

It was the responsibility of these three airplanes to keep watch on the upper quadrant of the western air border of War Heaven and prevent any aerial intruders—be they Piper Cubs or airliners—from venturing over the top-secret weapons range.

For the men stationed at this highly classified air base, the Hercules supply ship was a welcome sight. It was their only link with the outside world. Besides bringing in the necessities of life out on the high desert—food, fuel, water and lots of sunblock—the Herk crew could usually be counted on to fly in a case of beer every once in a while, as well as an X-rated video or two for the airstrip's single VCR.

As the big C-130 touched down and rumbled to the end of the runway, the R-5 supply-truck ambled out to the plane's designated parking area.

"These guys are early for a change," said the supply truck driver to his helper, a man who doubled as R-5's intelligence officer. He checked his watch. It was only 0640 hours. *"Damn* early . . ."

At that moment, the back of the Herk opened up. Suddenly a small army of armed men came running down the ramp.

"What the fuck is this?" the intelligence officer yelled as the men swarmed out of the back of the C-130.

He and the driver watched in astonishment as the men in unmarked desert-camouflage uniforms began firing their weapons at the base's gear-packed communications tower.

"Those are real bullets!" the truck driver shouted. Instantly he and the intelligence man dove for cover under the truck.

It was from this position that they watched the communications tower disintegrate from the heavy barrage of rifle and machine-gun fire.

Once the shooting had ceased, the men looked up and found six of the invaders standing over them. Five were outfitted to the hilt with equipment similar to that carried by paratroopers. The sixth man was wearing an unmarked blue coverall and a baseball cap.

"You can get up now," this man said.

"Who the hell are you guys?" the intelligence officer demanded. "And what the hell are you doing here?"

The man shook his head.

"Sorry, I can't tell you . . ."

The intelligence officer was furious.

"Well, let me tell you something," he yelled at the man. "Without that tower, we can't fly out of here. If we can't fly out of here, then a whole big sector of the Range is going to go without air patrol. Are you willing to take responsibility for that?"

The man in the baseball cap nodded yes as two more C-130s began circling the tiny, but important base.

"It has to be done . . ." he said.

40

Area 61

The zebra-striped TR-1 recon jet came in for a typically-bumpy landing and rolled into a small hangar hidden in the side of the small mountain.

Its pilot—his flight suit also prominent by its multitude of zebra stripes—jumped out of the cockpit even before shutting down many of the airplane's critical flight systems. Leaving that duty to the ground crew, he retrieved the film canister from beneath the plane's fuselage and quickly headed for the cave hangar's elevator. Riding the lift down four levels, he came out on the main floor for C2 operations and hurried into its large conference room.

Three men were waiting for him there.

"Is this as critical as first reported?" one of the three asked the TR-1 pilot.

"It's worse," the pilot answered bluntly. "I shot another forty-five minutes after I called in . . ."

The three men—two Army colonels and a Navy commander—exchanged anxious looks and then indicated that the pilot should sit down.

"Start at the beginning," the Navy officer told him.

The pilot took a deep breath and let it out slowly.

"I was flying a routine surveillance sortie over sector northwest seventy-one," he began. "I've flown that pattern a dozen times before. My usual pickup consists of activity around the Fitzies near the Ponderosa, maybe an Aggressor air strike, or some chopper training by the Green force. It's a fairly isolated area, as you know, and the flight is usually — well, should I say, uneventful."

"It's the least developed area of the Range," one of the Army officers said, referring to a folder in front of him marked *Classified*. "The terrain is extremely rugged, and access to the area is limited because it's at the very end of our supply pipeline."

"To say the least," the TR-1 pilot continued. "I was turning over my pattern when suddenly the Ripple meter began clanking out at ten-plus . . ."

The worried expressions on the faces of the three senior officers now became looks of mild horror.

"Your Ripple went off at ten?" one asked.

The pilot nodded gravely. "I've never seen it go half that high," he said.

"The Ripple Line" was the universally-used nickname for the system of personnel sensors that surrounded the entire border of War Heaven. The sensors, many hidden in the ground, others camouflaged to look like bushes, small trees, and even rocks, were configured to detect any human movement across the perimeter of the Range. Specifically, the sensors would "feel" anyone coming across the border who was not wearing his Zoot badge, the small electronic dog tag worn by everyone inside War Heaven.

The system was set up to identify and intercept anyone moving onto the Range from the ground, who, for whatever reason, were able to get past the series of guardposts that were located at key points along the border.

The TR-1's Ripple meter was an airborne electronics package that could detect movement anywhere on the Ripple Line and instantly determine just how large an intrusion it was. A reading of "one" on the Ripple meter meant that anywhere from one to a dozen people had penetrated the line. The degrees of penetration went up exponentially from there. A "two" reading could mean up to 24 people. A "three" could mean 48 people; a "four" as many as 96.

By this measurement, the "ten" reading meant an intrusion of more than 6000 people.

"Your Ripple device must be off," the Navy officer said.

"But I have videos, too," the pilot replied. He passed the cassette over to the Navy commander who solemnly put it into the room's VCR. Within ten seconds, they were all watching an aerial view directly above the mountainous territory known as the Ponderosa.

Even with a slight cloud cover, it was evident there was much activity on the roads to the immediate west of the mountains.

"Trucks, tanks, personnel carriers . . ." the pilot said, pointing out the various moving vehicles. "All of them covered with camouflage netting, and not one person down there is wearing a Zoot tag . . ."

The three officers all shifted uneasily in their seats. One picked up a phone, punched in three numbers, and was soon talking to the bunker's communications room.

"Call the guardpost for Gate Seventy-two," he said into the phone. "Get a status report . . ."

"We should contact R-Five while we're at it," one of the Army officers suggested.

The officer on the phone relayed that message and ended the conversation with a terse "Yes, immediately . . ."

"Could this be a training mission by one of the Range forces?" the TR-1 pilot asked. "They could really screw up a lot of things if they were walking around without Zoot badges and—"

The Navy commander quickly turned back to the pilot.

"You're dismissed," he told the man. "And don't say a word about this to anybody."

Crushed by the sudden snub, the pilot got up and left the room in a huff. What he didn't realize was that three men in the room were among a select group who controlled every single aspect of what went on inside the Range. They not only had computer access to information on every mission carried out on the Range—big and small—they actually drew up the plans for the vast majority of them. In this way, a movement of six thousand people would be a very big event for them indeed.

"Who could they be?" the Navy officer asked once the pilot was gone. "And what the hell are they doing up there? We've got a line on every single military unit in this country and overseas. The computer would have been buzzing like crazy if a force of six thousand men made any sudden movement toward us . . ."

The other two officers could only shake their heads in worry.

"This is very serious," the Navy commander continued. "And it couldn't have happened at a worse time, so close to the countdown . . ."

"We should get Sixteen in here," the Army officer said, punching a set of numbers into the phone and then turning on the instrument's squawk box. "He's the expert."

There was an unusually long wait for someone on the other end to pick up, and when someone did answer, it wasn't the officer they knew as Sixteen. It was his aide.

"Sixteen is still up at the Eye, as far as I know," the aide reported. "He's been up there since last night."

"That can't be . . ." the Army officer replied. "The Eye has been shut down for two hours. I put through the computer lock command myself."

The Navy commander quickly punched a series of numbers into the nearby desk computer. He was asking the main computer for the whereabouts of Sixteen.

The computer churned away with screen upon screen of numbers, but its conclusion startled the three officers.

"Sixteen is non-effective . . ." was the message flashing on the screen.

All three men knew what this meant: Sixteen was missing.

41

Homestead AFB, Florida

Ryder rolled his F-15X up off the main taxiway and onto the runway called four-right.

A half mile away, he could see the crowd that had gathered for this, their first performance at Homestead Air Force Base. Located in deep southern Florida, south of Coral Gables and close to the approach to the Keys, the air base was a large patch of sweltering asphalt surrounded on three sides by the steaming Everglades. It was no mystery then that on this brutally-hot summer day, the crowd was much smaller than the one they'd seen the first day at Griffiss.

Woody pulled his all-black F-15X up beside him, settling in off Ryder's right wing. They exchanged halfhearted waves—they were both weary of the airshow, the travel, the bad food and expensive booze. The only thing still vibrant in either one was their feeling of betrayal on the part of the mysterious Lieutenant Moon.

It was burning a hole so deep in Ryder's gut he'd almost committed a serious national security breach the day before. After several hours of boiling away the afternoon at their Holiday Inn bar, he'd toyed briefly with calling the NSA in Washington and demanding to talk to Moon.

Luckily Woody had advised him against it. It would have been a mistake of historic proportions—anyone involved in War Heaven was schooled over and over in security procedures, and direct contact between trainees and trainers was high on the *verboten* list.

After a few more drinks, Ryder had also been tempted to call Maureen at her office; but this, too, would have been a mistake. Before leaving the Range for Griffiss, all of the Aggressor pilots had been told not to have any contact in any way with any personal acquaintances, again for security reasons.

So instead, he and Woody had spent the afternoon drinking, eating, cursing Moon, cursing the Air Force, then drinking and eating again. It was a routine that was getting very old, very quickly.

They remained parked at the end of runway four-right for twenty minutes, revving their engines and waiting for other airshow traffic to clear the area. Finally they got the go word from Homestead Tower. On Ryder's count they both hit their throttles, released their brakes, and began rumbling down the runway.

The 97-degree heat and the thick muggy air demanded a long take-off roll. There would be no straight-up, eardrum-busting takeoff for this show. As he attempted F-15X liftoff, Ryder could almost feel the heat and humidity conspiring to keep the airplane out of the air. More throttle and an extra goose of the tail planes were needed to finally get airborne.

They headed west and climbed to 10,000 feet. High up and out of sight of the crowd of about forty thousand, they went into a wide, slow orbit and waited.

Two Florida Air National Guard F-16s roared in below them buzzing the crowd twice before departing off to the east. At that moment, Ryder heard the narrator's cue in his headphones.

"Now ladies and gentlemen . . . may I direct your attention to air-show center . . ."

"Okay, partner," Ryder called over to Woody. "Time to jump through the hoops . . ."

Five seconds later, they put their F-15X's into identical power dives, screaming down out of the cloudless sky and pulling up over airshow center. Two aging M-60 tanks were their targets for the day. With enviable precision, they laced the tanks time after time with the red and white smoke bombs launched from underneath the F-15Xs.

As planned, the pair of Air Guard F-16s returned and the mock dogfight ensued. Although the heavy air cut down on the theatrics somewhat, the ersatz ACM was thrilling nonetheless, and, as always, extremely noisy.

In real combat, the bigger, more powerful F-15Xs would have been a good matchup against the smaller, nimble F-16s, but the script called for them to lose. Woody went first, spinning the big

Eagle fighter above airshow central after taking two direct "hits" from one of the F-16s. With his tail canister spilling out the appropriate cloud of smoke, he exited the area quickly, flashing away off to the southwest and out of sight.

Ryder came next, and he too put his airplane into a mock spin after getting smoked by the second F-16. He yanked back on his control stick and gave the F-15X full power, rocketing off to the west, like a desperate enemy pilot trying to get as much distance between him and his attacker as possible.

Once Ryder was out of sight of the crowd, he turned the big F-15X over once and shut off the smoke canister. He was soon over Everglades National Park, the huge swampy area just west of Homestead. The place was literally a jungle — and he knew this firsthand. Early in his career he'd done his survival training inside the Everglades. It was a three-day mosquito-filled horror story that had ended up with him contracting a stomach ailment that lasted two weeks.

Since then, he had decided that the best way to see the place was from the air.

He checked his fuel gauge and turned back toward Homestead, searching the sky for Woody. The script called for them to form up and land together, just to let the people in the crowd — the kids, mostly — know that the fight was rigged and that they were all right.

"Black Hat Two, this is One," he called into his lip mike. "Let's get grouped and back down . . ."

There was no reply.

"Black Hat? What is your position?"

Still, there was nothing.

Ryder turned the F-15X back toward the west and began searching the airspace all around him. He saw nothing but blue sky and a few clouds.

"Black Hat Two . . . ?"

He felt a sudden tightening in his chest, like someone had just applied a vise grip to his rib cage.

"Homestead Tower . . . Are you in contact with Black Hat Two?"

"Black Hat One . . . that is negative . . . We may have a problem here."

Ryder felt the vise slowly tighten. "Do you have a radar fix on Black Hat Two, Tower?"

There was a painfully long delay before the reply came back:

"Negative, Black Hat One . . . Black Hat Two has left our screens . . . He may have gone down."

Two hours later

The UH-60 Blackhawk search-and-rescue helicopter hovered over a small clearing in the dense jungle near a place called Rogers River Bay.

Ryder was in the bay of the chopper, a safety harness around his waist and a winch-and-wire T-strap snug on his crotch.

"Ready?" the chopper crewman yelled in his ear.

"Yeah, go . . ." Ryder replied, squeezing the safety harness.

He stepped out of the bay and felt the jerk of the safety line as it began to lower him the fifty or so feet to the ground. There was a red smoke marker directly below him, blowing wildly in the wind of the chopper downwash. To the right of the smoke bomb were six search-and-rescue personnel from Homestead. Twenty feet beyond them was the torn and battered wreckage of an F-15X.

Ryder had the safety harness off him even before he reached the ground. Untangling himself from the winch wire, he signaled back up to the chopper crewman, who in turn instructed the pilot that it was okay to move away.

The storm from the downwash subsided gradually and the red marker once again sent its smoke straight up.

Ryder walked quickly over to the search-and-rescue team.

"What have you found?" he asked them.

"Just the jet," was the answer. "No body . . . yet."

"Show it to me," he told them.

They all tramped through the waist-high swamp grass to the burned-out clearing made by the jet when it impacted. The wreckage was fairly scattered over a two-thousand-square-foot area, and several secondary fires were still burning. Though it was half lying on its left side, the jet itself was pretty much intact. One of its tail planes was missing, and the right-side wing was ripped upward as if a giant can opener had gone to work on it. The wheels were still locked in and the air brake was up. This seemed to indicate that the jet had come in slow and fairly level.

Ryder walked around to the front of the wreck and looked into the cockpit. The ejection seat was still in place, the cockpit glass shattered. The various safety harnesses were ripped apart and several of the controls on the flight board were demolished.

"The body must have been thrown into the bay," one of the rescue workers told Ryder. "Could have gone as far as three or four hundred feet. The divers are on the way."

Ryder spent the next few minutes carefully examining the inside of the cockpit. Then he asked one of the rescue workers for a screwdriver. The man gave him a foot-long Stanley and watched with some surprise as Ryder began working on the screws that held a lower section of the airplane's nose cone to the rest of the airplane.

Refusing any help, he struggled until enough of the fasteners were gone for him to dislodge the access panel. It took some massive pulling and grunting, but finally the battered panel gave way. Ryder tossed the twisted piece of metal away and, instead, stuck his head inside the hole it had covered.

It only took him a few seconds to locate what he was looking for: a small empty space next the liquid oxygen converter and just aft of the low-voltage formation-lighting strip. He let out a long sigh of relief as soon as he saw nothing occupying this space. His suspicions from the start were confirmed.

This was not Woody's airplane; he was convinced of that now. The space was just large enough to fit a plate which was where the auxiliary battery for on-board Zoot equipment was located on the F-15. No plate meant no Zoot battery. This airplane had never been Zoot-equipped. Woody's airplane had been.

From this he had to conclude that the wreckage had been placed there—very expertly, but falsely, in order to sidetrack the search-and-rescue team.

Ryder had seen enough. He would let them search for a body, let them cart the wreckage back to Homestead for examination. But he wouldn't be around to watch.

He had other plans.

42

Maureen opened one of her water bottles, took a long drink, and then used the cap to scratch another line on the wall next to her bunk.

She'd been held now for twelve days, the first seven of which she'd been *incommunicado*.

But in those days since she'd been granted access of the place, she had filled up more than a dozen 60-minute cassette tapes with interviews, and twenty small notebooks with quotes and personal observations. She'd been allowed to roam the upper levels of the place virtually untethered. Just about everything she'd asked of Walter in the way of creature comforts and work supplies had been provided without delay.

Still, she felt no closer to finding out the truth about the place, about its people, or exactly what was done here. Was it all on the level, as Walter and the majority of people here would want her to believe? Or was it all some part of an enormous joke, an expensive disinformation campaign against the American people, as Willy, the strange man in SLO, had told her?

She just didn't know.

Some things were for certain, though: she knew that Area 61 – if that was its real name – was built mostly underground and laid out like a corporate headquarters in reverse. It went down for at least a dozen levels, and in a twist of the usual method of corporate-think, it appeared that the further one went toward the bottom, the more important the work being done on that level.

The previous morning had been devoted to a tour of the ninth level down. Code-named Red Fruit level, it was where the Cray supercomputer was located. "The brains of the place," was how Walter described it.

Walter explained that the Cray had been originally developed for the government's Defense Advanced Research Projects Agency and moved to Area 61 where the secrets it contained could be better protected.

She wasn't surprised when she saw that the machine looked like something out of a science-fiction movie. It was so large, it took up an area about a third of the size of a football field. The computer room itself was low-lit, doing little to dispel the mysterious aura of the place. The computer was painted an ominous black, and the people operating it were dressed in full-length red gowns similar to what a color-conscious surgeon might use.

She'd asked Walter exactly what made the computer so special. He replied with his usual mouthful of information. From what she could understand, the supercomputer used a radically designed "direct mesh routing system." This system allowed operating instructions and relevant data to flow freely between the computer's microprocessors instead of "bumping into each other," as in less-sophisticated models. Walter claimed that expanding on this feature gave the Cray the capability of nearly a trillion calculations *a second*.

"It can keep track of every satellite in orbit, every military airplane in flight, every naval vessel under sail, every military unit down to the lowest private, and still have 998.5 billion calculations a second left over for important duty," she had quoted Walter as saying in her notes.

He further explained that if every person on Earth wore a simple electronic ID tag, then the Cray could keep track of all four and a half billion people, and still be using only one and a quarter percent of its capacity.

"Exciting" was the word Walter used over and over in describing the machine. "Frightening" was what Maureen had added in the margin of her notebook.

Soon after she ate her noon meal, Walter came by her apartment and together they walked to the elevator and traveled down to level 6, code-named Grapefruit.

This was the tour she'd anticipated so much, a visit to the facility's Materials Investigation Unit. It was here she would learn if SLO

Willy's strange predictions would or would not come true.

Unlike the business style of the upper levels, or the out-of-this-world motif of the Cray supercomputer area, level 6 had the look of a very-high-tech laboratory. There were no office doors or hallway plants here. Rather, everything was hidden behind frosted glass and massive vaultlike steel doors.

Walter led her into a large room behind one of these steel doors. It was a laboratory complete with microscopes, computers, and dozens of automated file cabinets. A large square table made of black marble dominated the middle of the lab. Two men were standing at the far end, waiting for her.

"Welcome to the Silver Room," one of them said.

After the usual preamble about their real names being classified, they were introduced as Mike and Charlie. Spread out on the table before them were six fragments of metallic materials. Each was placed on a glass stand and was identified by a plastic name tag. Maureen read them from left to right: *Kecksburg. Eureka. Kingman. Tex-Mex. Anchorage.*

She was startled see that the sixth tag read *Roswell.*

Walter left her in the care of Mike and Charlie, and as soon as he was gone, Mike, the taller and older of the two, began the presentation.

"What we have here, Miss O'Brien, are six examples of what some people like to call AEOs," Mike said. "That stands for Artifacts of Extraterrestrial Origin.'"

Several days ago Maureen's jaw would have dropped at such a statement. Now, hearing it had become almost routine.

"We'll start with Kecksburg," Mike went on, picking up the six-inch-by-four-inch piece of highly reflective metal. "On the night of December ninth, 1965, thousands of people in the midwest observed a UFO traveling southeast toward the Flint, Michigan, area. It passed over Cleveland and then, rather incredibly, made a sharp turn and headed east.

"Kecksburg is a small city in western Pennsylvania. Many witnesses there saw an object – it looked like a giant acorn – land in the woods. Remember, I said land, not crash.

"Some of these people went looking for it and a few of them came upon this huge acorn-shaped object. It was smoking and had a flashing blue light attached to it. It also had some hieroglyphics on its side.

"A unit from the Air Force's 662nd Radar Squadron was dispatched to the scene, and after ordering all the civilians out of the area, they recovered this object under much secrecy.

"This piece of metal came from what is known now as the 'Kecksburg Acorn.' "

Maureen studied the metallic specimen for a moment. She had to admit that it looked remarkably similar to what Dr. Ernie had found near Roswell.

Charlie picked up the piece of metal displayed as *Eureka*.

"The name on this one is slightly misleading," he began. "On April eighteenth, 1962, witnesses saw a UFO touch down near Eureka, Utah. But it took off shortly afterward and commenced flying west.

"This object – it was described as being bright red and oval – had been tracked on the North American Air Defense Command radars even before stopping in Eureka. It was reacquired as it resumed its flight over Nevada. But then, minutes later, there was a tremendous explosion in the air about one hundred miles northwest of Las Vegas. Military personnel from Nellis Air Force Base were sent to the crash site. They recovered about three truckloads of material, of which this is a small piece."

Once again, Maureen was able to examine the alloy; once again, she had to admit it was very similar to the piece dug up near Roswell.

Mike continued the presentation with the piece of material tagged *Kingman*.

"Kingman is a city in western Arizona not far from the intersection of the borders of California and Nevada," he began. "On or about May twenty-first, 1953, a number of soldiers and scientists were shipped out of Springs Air Force Base to a remote location near Kingman. Once there, the group found an oval, disklike object about thirty feet across had crashed into the side of a small hill.

"They recovered much of the object, and this is a small piece of it."

Charlie was already waiting with the exhibit titled *Tex-Mex*.

"Sometime in 1950," he started, "two pilots were flying then-experimental F-94 Starfires on a mission near the Texas-Mexico border. They were informed by ground controllers that a UFO was in their area, and shortly afterward, they spotted this object. They did not chase it, but upon landing, the pilots learned that the object had crashed nearby.

"A contingent of soldiers went to the site and recovered the object, which turned out to be a large disk. This piece of metal is from that disk."

At that point, Mike picked up the scrap of metal marked *Anchorage*.

"About three years ago, there was a series of UFO sightings around the Anchorage area," he explained. "On the night before Christmas, an object crashed into the Lake Clark National Preserve. It was shaped not unlike a child's toy top, and was about twenty feet high.

"It was recovered — or at least parts of it were — and this is a piece of it."

Charlie then picked up the exhibit marked *Roswell*.

"I believe you've probably seen this exhibit before, Miss O'Brien," he said. "It was recovered on the archaeological expedition in which you participated."

Maureen nodded somewhat vaguely. She had no idea whether the piece of rubbery metal was authentic to the Roswell dig or not.

"Now, the reason we wanted to show all these to you is to explain something very, very extraordinary about all six," Mike said.

The two men gathered up the exhibits and walked over to a contraption that to Maureen looked like a cross between a computer and an elaborate microscope.

"This is a metals life analyzer," Charlie explained. "A simple explanation of how it works would be to say that by shooting a laser beam at certain alloys, we can determine the age of various metals by counting and identifying the atoms in a defined area and calculating their half-lives. What we might call 'normal metals' are in fact combinations of elements found everywhere in the known universe. If we subject a piece of normal metal — from a nail file or a house key, for example — to the MLA, we can determine, basically, when the metal was forged.

"However, when we subject these AEO exhibits to this machine, something very interesting happens . . ."

"We have found that these metals — which are all alike in composition — are not getting older, as a piece of normal metal would. Rather, it's quite the opposite."

"How can that be?" Maureen asked.

"We don't know," Charlie admitted. "But what we *do* know is that these AEOs are actually *gaining* atoms-lives. They are, in fact, growing 'younger.'"

"That's rather amazing, isn't it?" Maureen observed, trying to look surprised.

"To say the least," Mike replied. "The name for this phenomena is 'time-reversing.' It's part of a new theory in high-concept physics going around involving things like old time, new time, and even sideways time. We don't pretend to understand it all. In fact, we're not sure anyone really does. Not yet, anyway . . ."

"But we've also found something even more amazing," Charlie said. "Even though the metals are getting 'younger,' we were able to determine their date of origin simply by doing some reverse calculations."

It took Maureen a few seconds to let this sink in. Willy hadn't mentioned this part.

"Are you saying that you can predict when these materials were manufactured . . . *in the future?*"

"Exactly . . ." Mike and Charlie said at the same time.

"So?" Maureen asked, pen poised over notepad. "When is it? A few thousand years from now?"

"Hardly," Mike told her coolly.

"What we have determined, Miss O'Brien," Charlie explained, "is that all of these materials are growing 'younger' to a specific date."

"And that date," Mike said, checking his wristwatch with Charlie's, "is exactly seven days, seven hours, and thirteen minutes from right now . . ."

43

Beatrice, Alabama

Deputy Sheriff "Ham" Bolly had just picked up his usual evening coffee to go at Bud's Diner when he got the radio call.

Sadie, the elderly woman dispatcher back at the sheriff's office, was in a near panic. She'd just received a call from the police dispatcher at McKenzie, the town about thirty-five miles east of Beatrice. They said that they'd been warned that something had just "rocketed" through the town of Dozier twenty miles east of them and was heading their way.

"What kind of 'something'? " Bolly asked the dispatcher.

"They don't know . . ." she replied, her voice rising to hysterical levels. "They said it was a flying saucer!"

Bolly tossed the coffee cup into a trash barrel, slipped behind the wheel of his Chrysler patrol car, and roared off in the direction of Sotter's Hill, the highest point in town.

"What's the direction, Sadie?" he called back to the dispatcher. "How high is it?"

Sadie never heard him. She had the dispatcher from McKenzie on one phone, Bolly on the other, and she was yelling at both of them.

Bolly was able to convince Sadie to patch him directly to the dispatcher in McKenzie just as he was approaching Sotter's Hill. The man at the McKenzie end was no less frantic than Sadie. He was hanging out of the second story of the McKenzie police station, literally screaming into his microphone.

"Here it comes . . . *'Jessuzz!'*"

"What direction?" Bolly yelled into his microphone. "What alti-

248

tude?"

"And there it goes! Damn!"

Bolly screeched the patrol car to a stop in the small lovers-lane parking area atop Sotter's Hill and scrambled out of the car with his binoculars.

He didn't need them.

There was a long, low, slightly winding valley separating Beatrice from McKenzie, and just as Bolly reached the edge of the hill, he looked down into this valley and saw a bright red light moving very quickly through it no more than 100 feet above the ground.

"God damn . . ." He cried out involuntarily. "What the hell is that?"

He stood in a half crouch, almost frozen to the spot, spyglasses hanging numbly at his side as the red light roared through the valley and right by him.

He couldn't move. He couldn't even blink. It was the brightest red light he'd ever seen. It was traveling so fast and so low, it looked more like a blur than anything else. He would later estimate its speed at more than 1200 mph.

It was gone in an instant; rocketing over the western horizon and disappearing into the dark night.

Bolly finally got his feet moving. He ran back to the patrol car and punched his radio send button.

"Sadie! Call over to Thomasville . . ." he yelled, his voice now in the same octave range as Sadie and the dispatcher in McKenzie. *"Quick . . .* Patch me through to their sheriff!"

Denny Hopkins was hauling a load of fruit, nails and linoleum in his Kenworth double rig going west on Route 59 when his CB radio exploded with chatter.

"Just went over Thomasville!"

"It's over Butler . . ."

"It's heading for Kewanee . . ."

Hopkins had just passed the state line from Alabama into Mississippi and was just a handful of miles north of Kewanee.

He slowed his rig to fifty-five miles an hour and began scanning the night sky, looking for whatever all the talk was about.

That's when he saw it.

It came over the trees to his left like a fireball, a bright red light, with a smaller flashing white light slightly above and behind it. It was barely 75 feet above the highway and was moving incredibly fast.

Instinctively Hopkins slammed on his brakes, nearly locking them up and flipping the rig. He had to fight the bucking steering wheel for several hair-raising seconds, and by the time he regained control of the truck, the object was gone.

Mississippi State Police Lieutenant Vern Walters had been monitoring his car radio for the past half hour, listening in on the reports of a strange flying object heading across the Alabama-Mississippi line.

Walters had positioned his car in a school parking lot on the outskirts of Meridian and turned his radio up full volume. Walters knew something about flying objects; he was a major in the Mississippi State Air National Guard. He was hoping to get a good look at the object, and possibly identify it.

For the past twenty minutes, the oncoming UFO had lit up switchboards all across the eastern edge of the state. Complaints of television and radio interference were rife, as were reports of spooked animals. One supermarket near the state line reported that entire shelves of goods came smashing down when the UFO roared over. There had been several accidents along Route 19 up from Butler, apparently caused by motorists startled by the apparition streaking overhead.

The air base at Jackson—the home of the 172d Military Aircraft Group—was following the situation; Walters was monitoring their radio frequency. One of its C-141 Starlifters was in the air, circling the city in hopes of getting an airborne radar reading on the UFO while the air traffic controllers at both the civilian and military control towers were attempting to get the same thing on their ground-based screens.

The schoolyard parking lot where Walters had set up station was located in a wide-open area, about twenty miles away from the lights of Jackson. He had an unobstructed view of the southeast and almost as clear a line of sight to the northwest. The sky was cloudless and the moon on the wane, making the visibility ideal.

The spot was *so* ideal that he wasn't alone in selecting it. News about the UFO had traveled fast – so fast that a crowd numbering about forty was already in the parking lot when he arrived. It was made up of men, women, kids, and old people, and they'd come in cars, pickups, wagons, and on bicycles hoping to get a glimpse of the flying saucer.

They wouldn't have to wait long.

He had just checked his watch – it was 9:10 P.M. – when the crowd began stirring.

"There it is!" a kid yelled.

"Damn, he's right!" someone else shouted.

"Here it comes . . ."

Walters had his spyglasses up and focused in an instant. What he saw was a bright red light, moving extremely fast, no more than 100 feet off the deck and heading right at them.

He was on the radio in a second.

"Dispatch, this is Six," he yelled without taking his eyes off the approaching object. "I have the UFO in sight. It is heading straight for Jackson. Repeat: straight for Jackson. Please pass that information along to the base there . . ."

Now that Walters had done his duty, he could concentrate on identifying the bogey. It was now about five miles away and was really putting on the steam. He could clearly see the main red light with a smaller, flashing white one following it.

But there was more.

He could also see a streak of fire coming from behind the object, leaving a long thin trail of white smoke in its wake. It was now only two miles away and he was beginning to hear a low rumbling sound.

Now the crowd was really reacting. Some of the adults were cheering, some of the kids were crying, some of the rest were simply glued to the spot, totally fascinated by the thing.

Walters lowered the spyglasses, as the object was only about a mile away and about a half mile to their south. The roaring got louder as the flame spouting out the back of the thing became more intense.

The crowd was now cheering like crazy, yet Walters couldn't hear them. The roar from the object was too loud. In a instant he realized what the thing was. It was not a flying saucer or any other kind of UFO.

He saw wings. He saw a fuselage. He saw engine exhaust. It was a jet airplane, no doubt about it.

But he did not see the emblem of the United States Air Force or Navy emblazoned on its side and wings.

Instead, he saw a huge Red Star . . .

NORAD command post, Cheyenne Mountain, Colorado

The command officer of the watch had just returned to his desk from a coffee break when his telephone rang.

No sooner had he picked up the receiver when several warning buzzers went off simultaneously on the data screens being manned by his men on the other side of the railing from his desk.

On the other end of the phone line was a recording of a woman's voice reciting a series of numbers: "Seven. Seventeen. Fourteen. Six. Six. Zero. Six. Three . . ."

The command officer punched the numbers into his console computer, at the same time watching the two data-monitor screens in front of him that were still buzzing. In the push of his computer's confirm button he realized that the recorded coded numbers and the warnings issuing from the screens were addressing the same situation:

There was a potentially-hostile aircraft zooming at low altitudes westward across the state of Mississippi.

"Activate the main screen to full status," the command officer calmly told his second-in-command. "Bump everything up . . ."

In seconds, the large screen that dominated the far wall of the NORAD command post was displaying a computer-generated graphic map of the United States. Using data being constantly transmitted from optical and radar monitoring stations across the country, the screen was able to display in the shape of yellow, green, or blue flashing lights just about every aircraft of consequence that was in the air above the country at that moment.

"Isolate . . ." the command officer called into his microphone.

In the blink of an eye, the dozens of multicolored balls disappeared, leaving only a bright red ball flashing intermittently near the western edge of Mississippi.

"What the hell is that . . ." the command officer swore to himself. More used to dealing with unidentified aircraft flying along the country's borders; a bogey flashing its way across Mississippi at supersonic speeds was a new one on him.

The red light was blinking in such an irregular fashion because the bogey was flying below the radar net, its signature showing up on the NORAD radar screens only when the pilot was forced to come up above 250 feet.

"Whoever he is, his tail's got to be scraping weeds," the officer told his second-in-command, a reference to how perilously low the bogey was flying. "He's either a hell of a pilot or he's nuts . . ."

"Or both," the second officer said.

Suddenly it seemed as if every telephone inside the NORAD command post was ringing. Warning buzzers blared. Telexes began typing.

"It's lighting up the whole system," the second officer said, hanging up one squawking phone and picking up another. "We're getting calls from law enforcement all through the area."

Now every eye within the command post was on the big screen. They watched as the mysterious red light made its way over Yazoo City and toward Greenville and the Arkansas border.

"He's got to be out of Cuba," the second officer said. "The question is, why didn't the offshore net pick him up?"

"Where's the nearest scramble base?" the command officer asked, as the din of ringing phones and other warning devices increased.

"We've got National Guard F-16s at Fort Smith, Arkansas," the second officer replied after quickly calling up the appropriate information on his computer screen. "But it might take some time for a couple to get heated up and airborne. Should I send them the scramble order?"

"Yeah, do it . . ." the command officer replied. "They'll have a bitch of a time finding anything that's flying so low, but we've got to start somewhere."

As the second officer began making the necessary phone calls, the shift commander turned to another one of his junior officers.

"Send out the general alert message," he told this man. "Flash them a patch of the bogey's probable flight path."

By giving this order, the shift commander was ensuring that higher military authorities, including those in Washington, would be made aware that a high-speed aerial intruder was making its way across the southern tier and that jets were being scrambled to intercept it.

By this time, the flashing red light had crossed into Arkansas and was following a northwesterly course that ran roughly parallel with the Arkansas River.

"Well, this will get us in the newspapers," the command officer said.

It was now ten P.M. and the late-night shift change at the control tower of Tulsa Airport had just been completed.

Each new air traffic controller found a yellow fax message at their station, alerting them to the fact that NORAD was tracking a "high-speed, low-flying" aircraft across Arkansas and heading in the general direction of central Oklahoma. The piece of information did not seem all that unusual—airborne drug dealers were occasionally caught in the military's radar net, and it was routine for all control towers in the vicinity to be so notified. It was just one more thing the air traffic controllers would have to be aware of during their long shift.

The next thirty minutes passed without incident. The airport was relatively quiet at this time of night. Most of the scheduled passenger flights had ceased, and the majority of large aircraft now arriving or departing were cargo carriers.

The calm was suddenly shattered, though, at 10:38, when a crisis-warning indicator began flashing on all of the tower's main screens. Quickly the ATCs realized that an unaccounted-for aircraft had entered into their system and was drawing very close to the airport.

Instantly all other aircraft in the area were alerted, and those that were not already in the last approach landing pattern were requested to clear the area. At that same time, other ATCs tried to raise the mysterious aircraft on their radio gear, but to no avail.

When the unauthorized aircraft reached the five-mile point on the airport's southern approach pathway, the airport's fire and crash units were alerted and all of the airport's runways were ordered cleared. Messages to local law enforcement, fire departments, and hospitals were sent out instantaneously. A call was also made to the nearest military installation.

It was less than a minute later when the ATC got a visual fix on the aircraft's navigation lights; they were bright red with a white strobe tail flasher. It was obvious that the aircraft was attempting to land, even though the controllers could see nothing to suggest that it was having any kind of mechanical trouble.

As the aircraft drew closer, the tower personnel could tell it was a jet fighter, and instantly the connection to the alert fax was made. This was quickly passed on to the military, who were now following the situation on an open telephone line.

"He's touched down." the lead ATC announced as he watched the dim silhouette of the mystery airplane land on the airport's most isolated runway. "He just popped a drag chute . . ."

At that moment, a long stream of airport vehicles—police cars and fire trucks—raced out onto the three-mile-long runway and after the unauthorized aircraft. Several of the men on the fire trucks attempted to lock their powerful searchlight beams onto the airplane, which was just slowing up at the opposite end of the runway.

It was nearly three minutes later when the first airport police car arrived. What the officers found was baffling. They thought they recognized the aircraft as an Air Force F-15 Eagle. Yet it was painted black and bearing the Red Star markings of the Soviet Air Force.

They climbed out of the police car, guns drawn. But everything was strangely still. The airplane's engines were shut down but still smoking. The drag chute was hanging limply nearby. They also saw that its canopy was popped open.

But its cockpit was empty.

Area 61

At 10:45 P.M., the fax machine on ISC level 6 began transmitting.

It took less than a minute for the entire message to print out: it was an advisory update intercepted from the communications line linking NORAD to the Pentagon.

The gist of the message was that a specially adapted F-15 fighter, wearing Soviet Air Force markings, had made an unauthorized takeoff from Homestead AFB early that evening. After panicking hundreds of people in Alabama, Mississippi, and Arkansas with its low-level, radar-evading flight, the airplane landed and was abandoned by its pilot at Tulsa Airport. The whereabouts of the pilot and his identity was, at that moment, unknown.

The level-6 security officer scrutinized the message and then called up his daily security report on his computer. He entered most of the information from the fax onto this burgeoning document, adding that the airplane in Tulsa sounded a lot like an F-15X Aggressor aircraft.

He also noted that in light of recent events affecting ISC operations within War Heaven—specifically, the whereabouts of Sixteen, the report that a Zoot five-six nuclear weapon had been used in his "kidnapping," the subsequent One Red alert, and that a "mystery army" had literally invaded the northern part of the weapons range—the report of the abandoned F-15 should be considered a medium-to-high security threat.

He checked his watch, which was running backward, for the correct time to enter on the report: It was seven days, 8 hours, 12 minutes.

He secured the document into his computer's memory banks and then made arrangements to have it distributed electronically to the top members of the ISC.

This will be interesting, he thought, as he saw the indications that the report was flashing out to 29 other computer screens located at various levels within the facility. *As if they didn't have enough problems . . .*

44

Above Dead Man's Gulch

The pilot of the AH-64 Apache helicopter adjusted his Night-Scope goggles and peered out into the darkness.

The attack chopper—it belonged to Green forces' 2nd Air Calvary Battalion—was on a night hunt. Its prey was varied. Gray army troop columns. Blue army M-1A1 tanks. Maybe even a specialty aircraft from Spookbase.

It made little difference to the Apache pilot. Any target was fair game. Any target destroyed meant points for his unit. And inside War Heaven, gaining points was the name of the game.

The area of the weapons range below the helicopter was officially known as Area B-Northwest. Unofficially, its narrow, yet strategic passages had begat its nickname, Dead Man's Gulch.

In chopper pilots' vernacular, the Gulch was a "target-rich environment." Less than twenty miles south of the rugged mountains of the Ponderosa, all roads in the area had to move through the Gulch in order to gain access to the wide-open spaces of the weapons range to the south. Long-range training sorties, infiltration units, or forces that were just plain lost moved through the Gulch all the time. The slender passage, the surrounding inhospitable terrain, and the general isolation of the area usually made these potential targets easy pickings for something flying overhead.

The chopper pilot knew that a big hit tonight, with its corresponding largesse of points, would go a long way in helping his unit—and not just in acquiring the supplies the points would eventually bring. The Range had been rife with rumors for the past few days. Wild rumors, about crucial elements of the Range breaking down. Ripple alarms going off. Whole units disappearing. Ferocious fighting between phantom units had been claimed, especially in this northwestern sector.

Such disturbing stories were not unique on the Range; just the opposite, many psy-ops programs instituted by C2 began with the spreading of rumors and disinformation.

Yet, this time, it seemed to the chopper pilot – and many others – that the latest stories were different. They included tales of actions happening out "beyond the fence," on the other side of the border of War Heaven. Breaking the bubble like that – even in a C2 psy-ops disinformation campaign – was unheard of.

Though its environment was indeed bizarre, War Heaven was nevertheless a very stable, orderly world within. Such rumblings of *instability* made everyone on the Range uneasy. A cure for this uneasiness was to go out and kill something – and cash in on the points, which, if things *were* going wrong inside the womb, would undoubtedly come in mighty handy.

The Apache pilot's thoughts were interrupted by a message from the man sitting in the chopper's forward compartment.

"We've got a target," his front seat gunner called back to him. "A big, fat one . . ."

The pilot adjusted his NightScope goggles and saw what his gunner had spotted. There there was a line of Zoot Patriot missile batteries belonging to the Blue army arrayed on a butte that made up the eastern wall of the Gulch. The target was about three miles to their north.

But right away, the pilot realized that something was wrong.

"I read their acquisition radars as 'hot,' " he radioed to his gunner, his eye suddenly glued to his own control panel.

"Ditto," the gunner replied. "Either there's a mistake or they're expecting an attack . . ."

The answer arrived just moments later.

As the chopper crew watched in astonishment, three massive 227-mm Zoot rockets, fired by an unseen MLRS, appeared off on the western horizon, streaking eastward in a slightly uneven chevron formation.

Even before the chopper pilot could yank back on the controls to get the aircraft out of the area, a barrage of three Zoot Patriots exploded from their launchers and gracefully arched up toward the trio of incoming rockets.

In a matter of seconds. the two opposing aerial forces met with a rapid-fire series of tremendous Zoot explosions so bright, they temporarily blinded the chopper crew.

"Goddamn!" the pilot yelled involuntarily, fighting with Apache's controls, hoping that the residue from the holographic explosion would not affect his aircraft's own Zoot HILES device.

But he knew there was little chance of that.

No sooner had he steered clear of the explosion when the Apache began to lose power. Its weapons panel clicked off as its fuel warning light clicked on. They were "hit" – victims of the violent missile-versus-missile engagement two miles away.

Now they were going down . . .

The Apache spiraled down to a bumpy landing on a small hill overlooking the southern approach to the Gulch. The two crew members climbed out, disgusted, angry, and embarrassed. Neither had been "shot down" before. Yet their mortification was almost instantly interrupted by the roar of yet another trio of Blue army Zoot Patriots going up toward a barrage of 227-rockets that were streaking almost directly overhead.

They both dove for the cover underneath the disabled Apache just as there was another tremendous Zoot explosion about 500 feet above them. But this time, the crewmen saw that although the Zoot Patriots had intercepted and destroyed three of the 227-mm rockets, at least three more of the high-explosive rockets were not hit and continued to roar eastward toward their targets.

"Man, this is *huge!*" the gunner exclaimed as they watched the 227s streak over.

"It's *weird*, you mean." the pilot replied. "I've never seen Patriots way the hell up here. Or 227s, for that matter."

Just then, they heard a low rumbling sound coming from the west. Still crouched underneath their chopper, they spotted a column of armored vehicles approaching the southern entrance of the Gulch. As the parade of vehicles drew nearer, they could see that they were not painted in one of the three primary colors of the Range – blue, green, and gray. Instead, these mobile weapons were covered with camouflage nettings, thus hiding their type as well as their allegiance.

"God, I count a hundred of them," the gunner said. "Maybe a lot more . . ."

They watched the column pulled into a long flank about two miles away. Judging from the length of the gun barrels sticking out from beneath the camouflage netting, many of the vehicles looked to be similar in size to the M-110A2 self-propelled gun, massive weapons capable of hurling a Zoot shell nearly 16 miles.

With enviable precision, the men in the column dismounted their vehicles and began pointing their weapons toward the Blue army Patriot battery. Within minutes, the first Zoot shells were crashing in on the defenseless Patriot missile launchers. It took only five minutes for the mystery troops to systematically destroy the antimissile weapons.

"Goddamn, who the hell are those guys?" the gunner asked as the column packed up and began to move again.

"I don't know," the pilot replied. "But all those wild stories must be true. I mean, something very strange is going on up here . . ."

"What can we do?" the gunner asked, lowering his voice to an anxious whisper.

"We've got to get the hell out of here," the pilot replied. "Or would you rather get in the way of those guys?"

The pilot was pointing to the road further off to the west. It was suddenly clogged with more vehicles, apparently troop trucks, all of them wearing the same camouflage nets, all of them heading right toward them.

"I'm with you," the gunner said to him.

With that, they both scrambled down the hill and began walking southeast.

Jacks

It was ten minutes to midnight and the saloon at Jacks was packed.

The overflowing crowd held the usual cross section of soldiers from the Blue, Green, and Gray forces, heavy with more officers than enlisted men due to the late hour. The big clock on the wall above the bar, its hands rusty and flaking black paint, was slowly ticking down the minutes to the next "personnel fraternization period," scheduled with typical military precision for 0000 hours—

straight-up midnight.

At that time, a swarm of scantily-clad females would appear and begin sixty minutes of "stress modification" with the assembled troops.

The whole concept of Jacks was that it was a "personnel stress modifier," and the amount of booze passed over the bar provided a good barometer of the stress level within the Range. Had anyone been counting—and perhaps someone was—they would have noticed that the alcohol intake for the crowd on this night was running higher than usual.

It was yet another reflection that everything was not right in War Heaven.

As usual, the crowd ritualistically counted down the last few seconds to midnight, and when that magic time arrived, the doors to the apartments on the second floor of the saloon swung open and a crowd of bodies appeared.

But right away it was apparent that something was very wrong.

Instead of the usual army of lovely females, heavily armed troops were rushing down the stairs. Suddenly the lights inside the saloon began blinking. The sudden clatter of helicopters could be heard outside. Somewhere, a siren went off.

"What the hell is going on!" someone cried out as the unspeaking, sand-camouflaged troops quickly sealed off all the exits and surrounded the gang of astonished soldiers. *"This is Jacks, for Christ's sake!"*

The lights inside the bar finally stopped flickering and the siren outside was reduced to a low, mournful wail. A man in civilian clothes came halfway down the stairs, wielding a powerful flashlight like a conductor's baton.

"Every officer above the rank of lieutenant is now considered a prisoner," he announced.

His bizarre proclamation was met with a barrage of cries of disbelief and anger.

"You can't do this!" someone yelled at him. "This is the neutral zone!"

The civilian peered down at the crowd of soldiers, squinting as if to locate the man who had shouted at him.

"As of this moment," the civilian announced in a loud, slightly strained voice, "this area is no longer neutral . . ."

With that, he gave one grand wave of his flashlight.

"Secure them," he called out. On this cue, the assault troops began systematically pulling out any officers above the rank of lieutenant and tying their hands behind their back with strands of long plastic-like wire.

This done, the civilian waved his flashlight once again. With this signal, his troops began herding the captured officers out onto the street. Having landed during the initial confusion, no less than ten UH-60 Blackhawk troop helicopters were waiting on the street and on the fields just outside of the small town. Another ten were circling overhead looking for places to land. The chopper crews immediately came forth and aided the assault teams in loading the grumbling officers onto the Blackhawks.

It took only ten minutes to fill the twenty helicopters with captured officers. Then, with the remaining lieutenants and enlisted men watching from Jacks with amazement, the small fleet of choppers lifted off and disappeared over the western horizon.

Aggressor base Victor was located in the extreme southwestern section of War Heaven.

Like their counterparts at Tango, Alpha, Beta, and other Aggressor bases, the pilots at Victor had traditionally enjoyed the embarrassment of riches bestowed on them as a result of their advantageous missions against other forces on the Range. Victor Base boasted a particularly successful record for the past month, flying two dozen missions in that time and racking up thousands of points, mostly due to the reams of accurate advance intelligence the pilots had received from C2 on their opponents.

The mission the previous night had been typical. A report from C2 earlier in the day had tipped the Victor pilots that a large convoy of Gray army forces would be moving up Desert Highway 66 just after sundown. The intelligence report not only gave the time and position of the convoy, it also provided information on the number of vehicles, the strength of the convoy's antiaircraft capability—basically several squads of shoulder-launched Zoot Stinger missiles—and its air cover, two F/A-18s on loan from the Navy and flying out of a base in the center of the Range.

Four Victor Aggressors launched for the mission, taking off just before sundown and establishing a holding position about thirty miles west of the attack zone. The Gray army convoy arrived just as advertised, as did their air cover. Using its previously established position to the greatest advantage, the Victor Aggressors pounced on the pair of Hornets, who, though giving a good fight, were quickly dealt with. Their moving air cover gone, the Gray army convoy commanders attempted to scatter their vehicles, but the wide-open spaces made this a futile tactic. The Victor pilots proceeded to attack the convoy for thirty minutes, plastering it with an exotic array of Zoot weapons such as Maverick missiles, cluster bombs, and nose-cannon fire.

When they were done, the convoy lay scattered along the side of the highway, 95 of its 112 vehicles knocked out. Upon returning to base, the pilots learned the attack was worth upward of 5000 points. a fairly typical windfall for the Victors.

It was now 3:15 A.M., nearly five hours after the attack on 66, and the Victor pilots were still celebrating. It was traditional that they stay awake until the first C-130 supply drop took place, a practice that usually took place anywhere from two to six hours after a mission was completed.

The drink this night for the Victor pilots was coffee and whiskey, and they toasted many times their two colleagues who had been killed in the accidents of two months before, their bodies never found. As the spiked java flowed, each man had one ear cocked outside the window of the small officers' club, waiting to hear the familiar rumble of the supply ship, coming for the first drop.

At sunrise — some nine hours after the successful convoy attack — they were still waiting . . .

45

Tulsa

It was seven A.M. when the pair of Tulsa city policemen walked into the Greyhound bus terminal.

The place was dirty, smelly, and just about empty. A few people were asleep on the ripped padded chairs, several more were lying on the floor nearly out of sight beside a line of rental lockers. A bland muzak-type song was echoing on the sound system. all but drowned out by the sound of several buses warming their engines outside.

The policemen approached the main ticket booth and identified themselves to the ticket seller.

"How long have you been on duty?" one of them asked the ticket seller.

"Came on at midnight . . ." he replied.

"Any trouble here during the night?"

The man shrugged. "Nothing out of the ordinary," was his reply. "Had to roust a few homeless people, that's all . . ."

"See any unusual characters?" the officer asked.

"The ticket seller smiled. "Unusual characters? *Here?*"

Neither cop was amused. With a glance and a nod, one of them headed for the rest rooms; the other continued the questioning.

"We're looking for a guy," he told the ticket seller, "Might have come in here sometime after midnight. Dressed kind of crazy. Like in a Halloween costume. Possibly military-looking haircut . . ."

The ticket seller could only shrug again. "You're describing about half the people who come in here late at night." he replied.

"The policemen flipped open his notebook.

"Okay, this guy might have been wearing a one-piece coverall-type garment. Like what a military pilot might wear. He could also be carrying a helmet. Like a crash helmet . . ."

The ticket seller was shaking his head. "I think I'd remember someone like that." he said. "But I don't pay attention to everyone who walks through here . . ."

Just then the other officer returned and nudged his partner.

"Found something," he said quietly.

They both walked into the men's room, where the officer directed his partner's attention to the last stall.

Hanging on the backside of the door was an undershirt, a pair of wool socks, and a pair of black flight boots. Numbers printed on the inside of the boots were distinctively military.

"Well, I'd say he was here . . ." the first cop surmised.

They returned to the ticket seller to inform him that the men's room would have to be sealed off for a while, and then one of the cops radioed their station house with the news of their discovery.

Within minutes there were a dozen Tulsa police officers inside the terminal, accompanied by another half dozen security men from Tulsa Airport and a pair of military investigators.

At the stroke of eight, the ticket seller greeted his replacement and, with a breath of relief, retreated to the employees' locker room. After making sure no one could see him, he reached inside his locker and stuffed the pilot's flight suit hidden there into a well-worn paper bag. Then he took out his rarely used raincoat and wrapped it around the pilot's crash helmet that was stuffed in the very back of his locker.

This done, he quietly headed to the rear entrance of the locker room, and with the skill of a burglar, he slipped out the door, got into his car, and drove home.

46

Caesar's Palace

The girl named Angel finished her light breakfast of a muffin and a cup of coffee and then motioned for the waitress.

"Could you do me a favor?" she asked the middle-aged woman, slipping a ten-dollar bill into her open palm. "The same as before?"

The waitress nodded happily and headed out of the coffee shop and into the main casino.

Angel reached into her pocketbook and stealthily took two pills from her change purse. She expertly put the pills into her mouth and swallowed them down with a gulp of water. Though she knew it was probably an illusion, she thought she felt the two amphetamine tablets begin to work right away.

The waitress returned with a paper cup that actually contained a mix of bourbon and ginger ale, Angel's usual morning pick-me-up. She checked her watch—it was almost seven A.M. Her ride would be there soon.

She ran her fingers through her streaked hair and let out an audible sigh. She hadn't slept in forty-eight hours; neither had she seen any clients. Instead she'd spent her time inside her apartment, drinking wine, smoking pot, taking pills, and going over her financial statements.

Her combined bank account was now bulging at nearly $200,000. Her portfolio of solid blue chips was hovering around $325,000. Even her gold investments—strictly American Eagles and Canadian Maple Leafs—were going up.

And it was getting to be too much for her.

She had come to some kind of a decision during her two-day solitary bake-out. Though she enjoyed the money, and to a certain degree was very fond of her special client, she had vowed to make this trip up to Casa Fantastica her last. She would first tell the old man and then her handlers, via a message to her piggish driver.

Then she would transfer her funds to other banks and take off immediately for an open-ended vacation to Maui.

She finished her morning bourbon in two gulps and left the waitress a healthy tip. A dose of lipstick and a brush through her hair, and she was off to the front door to meet her ride.

The casino was fairly crowded for this time of morning, but as Angel soon found out, the attraction was not entirely the blame of the slot machines. She discovered that a camera crew from a well-known tabloid TV show had set up right outside the casino entrance and was interviewing members of an ever-growing crowd. She walked down the long driveway and by the crowd around the bright lights, trying her best to stay out of camera range.

But she still had to walk within earshot of the loudmouth personality speaking on-camera. When she had first spotted the commotion, she had just assumed the TV show was in town to either glorify or grill yet another overexposed celebrity.

So it was to her horror that she heard the question the on-air talent was asking one of the interviewees.

"Have you ever seen strange lights in the sky?"

The woman was nodding enthusiastically even before the man finished his question.

"Yes, my God, yes!" the women replied breathlessly. "All the time . . . for years."

"And what do you think they are?"

The woman never missed a beat. "They're from outer space," she declared. "They're spying on us . . ."

Another woman stepped forward. "I've seen them right outside my front window. Bright yellow, green, and red. I was scared to death . . ."

"And where do *you* think they come from?"

"I think the government is behind it all," the older women said with a touch of anger. "I think they're all top-secret somethings or others . . ."

Angel hurried away as fast as she could, hoping to flag down her

267

driver before he pulled up right next to the camera crew. She checked her watch. He was late. Of all days! She moved even further down the sidewalk, her eyes peeled for the familiar black Ford that he used to pick her up inside the city before switching to the more rugged Jeep for the long desert trip. But all she saw were locals' pickup trucks, tourist cars, and mobile homes heading up and down the Strip.

She moved back toward the camera crew and the now-even-larger crowd, making sure that the driver had not arrived early and was wandering around. The on-air personality was now interviewing a man who was dressed like a college professor: tweed jacket, sweater, and tie—all this despite the early morning heat. Though obviously educated, the man was ranting and raving about UFOs. "I have proof," he was saying, "that the government has proof . . ." Angel quickly moved back down the street again, blocking her ears so she wouldn't have to hear any more questions about flying saucers over Las Vegas.

She was in a complete panic by 7:45; her driver had never been this late before. The amphetamines now boiling in her bloodstream, she had little choice but to sit on the bus-stop bench and anxiously scan the roadway.

She was still there an hour later. The tabloid TV camera crew was long gone. The sun was climbing in the sky and it was getting hotter by the minute.

She was terrified. Was this just the prelude to her handlers getting rid of her? Had they somehow figured out her plan to escape the contract? Would anyone notice if she suddenly "disappeared"?

She remained on the bench all morning, waving by the buses, and ignoring the men who crudely propositioned her.

Over and over, her numbed mind asked the same question: *What has gone wrong?*

47

Area 61

Maureen was waiting for Walter when he walked into his office.

"You look unhappy this morning, Miss O'Brien," he said, settling in behind his ornate desk. "Is there something I can help you with?"

Maureen had been rehearsing this confrontation for several hours. Although she was sure that many more secrets—or elaborate hoaxes—could be found within the strange facility, she also knew that she had more than enough information already to form the basis for a bombshell story—actually, a series of bombshell stories. And just like an athlete, the mark of a good reporter was in knowing when to get out. Her instincts were now telling her that it was time to get out, or at least begin working in that direction.

"I want to say, first off, that you have been very helpful," she began, her voice determined but tense. "But I have to . . . I mean, I demand . . . to be released. And I'm serious this time. This has gone on long enough . . . I have friends and family who probably have no idea what's happened to me. I have a job, and bosses who I must answer to. Do you understand?"

Walter's normally smiling facial expression drooped just a bit.

"Of course I do," he said. "And you will be released. Today—right now, if you prefer . . ."

Maureen was stunned. This was the last thing she expected to hear. Once again, Walter had managed to surprise her.

"What's the catch?"

"There is no catch," Walter replied, apparently sincere. "But there is a choice you have to make."

269

"Which is?"

He picked up a videotape, inserted it into his VCR, and then snapped on his office's wide-screen TV.

"I have bosses I must answer to, also," Walter said. "And they would insist that I show this to you before you make any decisions."

"What is it?"

"You'll see," Walter replied. "We just picked it up off the satellite. It's going to L.A. for transmission tonight."

The screen came to life with a flash of the logo of a well-known tabloid TV show. Walter fast-forwarded through the technical data and satellite-identification messages, finally settling the picture down as the in-studio stand-in announcer introduced the opening segment.

". . . to our correspondent in Las Vegas," the man was saying.

The screen blinked and suddenly it was filled with the face of the on-location reporter.

"It's our second day here in Las Vegas," the man with the hang-ten hairdo was saying, "and this latest flap of strange goings-on here has intensified to levels that . . ."

Walter hit the fast-forward switch once again.

"I won't waste your time with the nonessentials," he told Maureen.

He finally slowed the video down just as the reporter was saying, ". . . ordinary citizens and scientists alike."

Suddenly the screen held a very familiar face. Maureen felt her breath catch in her throat.

It was Doctor Ernie. He was dressed in a suitcoat, sweater, and tie, and standing in front of a Las Vegas casino.

". . . and myself have seen them," he was saying in his unmistakable, if slightly agitated professorial way. "They do exist. We have proof. The government has proof. What's more, *I have proof that the government has proof.* We have to demand an explanation."

Walter hit fast-forward again and the scene quickly shifted to the face of another man, at another location, identified by a chromacolor tag line as a professor from the University of Nevada.

". . . we regret that some people continue to pursue this line of thinking," the man was saying. "I respect Doctor Pascullo. I consider him a leading academic. But I'm sorry to see someone like him making these kinds of outrageous claims. To think that the government would actually kidnap someone of his stature, brainwash them, and

270

then let them go, is just too much for me to believe, quite frankly . . ."

Two more talking heads appeared, both speaking in the same solemn tones, both damaging Dr. Ernie's reputation even further, though Maureen was so stunned she barely heard them.

Walter let the tape run to its end and then shut down the whole TV/VCR system.

Maureen was just getting over her initial shock. Now she was getting angry again.

"This is really sick," she near-shouted at him. "You pull us in here, violate our constitutional rights, treat us like prisoners, give us a big song and dance. And then, because people like you and Mr. Pinky and the others want to keep scaring the hell out of the American people, for what reason I still don't know, you think that—"

"You don't understand, Miss O'Brien—" Walter tried to say.

But Maureen wouldn't let him speak.

"I understand it all quite well, Walter," she continued barraging him. "You are in the business of ruining reputations and stealing millions in tax dollars in the process. It really comes down to that, doesn't it? And either I stay here indefinitely, or you'll ruin my reputation, too? Is *that* my choice?"

Walter slowly shook his head no. "It doesn't have to be that way, Miss O'Brien," he said, nervously fidgeting with his tie. "Your stay here has been different. My bosses ordered it that way from the very beginning. In fact, you can still get what you have always wanted . . ."

"And that is?" she asked him, her anger peaking.

"The story of a lifetime . . "

"And *that* is?"

Walter suddenly became very serious.

"Okay, I'll put it to you directly, Miss O'Brien," he said, leaning forward. "Do you want to see a real flying saucer?"

48

Oklahoma City

The pair of FBI agents walked into the strip joint, their pupils quickly adjusting from the bright sunshine outside to the darkness within.

It was 4:30 P.M. The early afternoon show had just finished, and a fresh crowd of cowboys, businessmen, and government workers were filing in as the old crowd of drifters and the unemployed were filing out. The blaring music had been toned down and the price of the mixed drinks cut back temporarily by fifty cents.

The agents spoke briefly with the bartender, who directed them to a small table next to the dancer's runway. Within a minute, a young, pretty exotic dancer named Tamara appeared from the dressing room and, with a long sweater hastily thrown around her scantily-clad body, ordered a Coke and then sat down with the agents.

"You did the early show here today?" one of the agents asked.

Tamara nodded. "Went on at eleven . . ."

"Big crowd?" the other agent asked.

"No, not really," Tamara replied, sipping the Coke. "There never is, that time of day. Things don't start picking up until the lunch crowd arrives . . ."

"How many people saw your early show?"

She shrugged. "Seven, maybe eight . . ."

"Were they regulars?"

"About half and half," she replied.

"So there were some people you didn't recognize."

She nodded, and sipped the Coke again. It was club policy to co-

272

operate with the authorities, but that didn't make her any less nervous. The establishment was really the only one of its kind in the ultraconservative city. Located as it was near the city's trio of major bus terminals, many of the patrons were people in transit, which was one reason why the strip joint was allowed to stay open. She didn't want to upset that delicate balance.

The agent took out a crude photocopy drawing which Tamara recognized as a police artist's conception.

"Did you see this man?" the agent asked.

She took the drawing and studied it. The face looked like that of a baseball player, though the hair was less flamboyant.

"He was here," she said matter-of-factly.

"How can you be so sure?" the agent asked.

She smiled for a moment. "He left me a big tip," she replied. "Fifteen bucks. All small bills. He bought me a drink, too . . ."

The agents sat up with renewed interest. They'd been interviewing people in the rather-rundown section of the city for two hours with little success. Until now.

"Do you remember where he was sitting?"

Tamara pointed to a side booth barely visible in the shadows.

"After my main program is over, I do individual dances for the people at the booths," she explained. "This guy was sitting over there. He was wearing a cowboy outfit that looked like he'd just bought it. He gave me the fifteen dollars and then ordered the drink for me at the bar. But by the time I got around to getting it, he was gone . . ."

The agents got up and walked over to the booth. Its ashtray was filled, not with crushed cigarette butts, but with ripped pieces of carbon paper. There was also a newspaper strewn out on top of the table. One section had been folded over and across, unintentionally calling attention to a small filler item. It was headlined: *"Air Force Plane Missing."*

One of the agents quickly read the small story aloud:

"A small Air Force transport plane was reported lost and is feared to have crashed somewhere in the Colorado Rockies. The plane, a transport craft carrying two passengers and a crew of three, was reported missing yesterday, a spokesman for the Air Force said.

"Rescue teams have been hampered by bad weather in their search for the airplane. Those on board were all Air Force personnel, ex-

273

cept for one U.S. Navy officer. His name was given as Commander Lawrence Katt."

The agents put the news story aside and then took several minutes to piece together the scraps of carbon paper. When they did, they realized that the scraps were actually parts of receipts for bus tickets—seven in all.

"Wichita. Fort Worth. Little Rock. Amarillo. Denver. Sante Fe. Omaha . . ." one of the agents read out the litany. "All one-way trips. All paid for in cash . . ."

"He knows we're on to him," the other agent said. "He could have taken any one of these buses, and he left this stuff here for us to find it. Or maybe he didn't take a bus at all. The bastard's just making it as hard as possible for us."

The younger agent ran his hand through his close-cropped hair. "What now?"

"We check the bus stations again," the other agent replied. "Try to get something that might lead us to which bus he actually got on . . . if any."

"And if we get nothing?"

The older agent shrugged, carefully putting the scraps of the reconstructed bus receipts and the news story in his pocket.

"Ever been to Omaha?" he asked.

Casa Fantastica

The old man finished hanging his latest picture of Albert Einstein and then checked his watch.

It was almost 1700 hours—5 P.M.

Where the hell is she?

He walked out to the kitchen and tried to get a look down into the valley below the cliff. Desert 66 ran right through the middle of the valley, and on the clear days with no haze, he could see traffic on the roadway up to ten miles away. But today he could barely make out the portion of the highway that was closest to him—where it curved around the small mountain he called home.

The problem wasn't haze. It was smoke.

He'd been seeing it—and smelling it—all day. Where it was coming from, he had no idea. But its existence was puzzling. In all his years on the Range, he couldn't remember ever seeing smoke, or at least this much of it. Despite the nonstop epic battles between the mélange of opposing war-gaming forces, he knew that very few things actually caught fire and burned on the Range.

So, to see this much smoke was unprecedented.

He went to his medical table and gulped down a handful of pills—some of them authentically therapeutic, others unnecessary painkillers and mood elevators. He retrieved a beer from the fridge and checked his watch again.

Where the hell was she?

He padded over to the front hallway and spent several fidgety minutes checking the latest sports scores and betting lines. There were few games he was interested in playing; but what was worse, several of his TV info-cable service lines were down. At least a half dozen of his TV screens were showing nothing more than color bars or test patterns.

He walked over to his vast X-rated video library and opened several sealed packages. They'd arrived more than a week before, but he'd hadn't the time or the ambition to open them until now. The packages held typical fare: a Stacy Lords retrospective, several new Lauryl Hill features, a half dozen new "jelly-velly" films from Denmark.

He briefly considered watching several of the new arrivals—but his heart just wasn't in it. He wasn't feeling too good, and the pills had yet to take effect.

Damn, where the hell was she? . . .

He made his way back up to his bedroom and hauled out one of his hundreds of photo albums. It was an old one; the first page contained photos of his first, full-time flight-training school in Betty, Texas. He ran his finger along the service photo of him in his first officer's uniform. His sister had taken the picture back in the early spring of 1946. It had been a Sunday, and he remembered it like it was last week. It was cold out on that field that day and his family—mother, his two younger brothers, and his older sister—had come down visit him. He'd given them a tour of the base and then they'd all gone to a local cafe and eaten Mexican food. It had been raining when they left.

It was the last time he'd seen any of them.

Feeling the tears well up in his eyes, he sadly closed the album and stuffed it away.

What kind of a life is this? he asked himself one more time.

It is Hell, the answer came back once again.

With one pull of a trigger, he'd sentenced himself to Hell. And ironically had come to live in a place some people called Heaven . . .

He nervously checked his watch again. It was now almost 1900 hours. She'd never been this late before.

Where the hell was she?

49

The Boeing 707 JSTARS aircraft roared off the runway at Area 61, climbed slowly to 20,000 feet, and then headed to the northwest.

There were twenty-two men on board: a flight crew of five, plus seventeen specialists whose job it was to operate the vast array of radar systems held in the bay of the large airplane. These systems — the most advanced in over-the-horizon and "look-down" technology — were able to detect movements of opposing ground forces from vast distances, and, in wartime situations, direct air strikes or ground bombardments of those targets.

The airplane and its crew were members of the 2235th Technical Arbitration Unit, the referees of War Heaven known to all as the zebras. Although it was equipped with Zoot HILES detection equipment, the JSTARS aircraft — for Joint Surveilliance and Target Attack Radar System — was usually far away from any simulated weapons engagements. Because its elaborate systems were able to keep track of massive troop movements from great distances, there was no real need for the big airplane to get anywhere near a fray. It was also a very expensive aircraft to operate, so it was utilized only when extra-large engagements between the weapons range's assigned forces were in the offing, mainly to help keep track of which side was scoring what points and where.

But tonight, the mission would be different.

The fact that the JSTARS airplane was in the air at all was known to less than fifty people — a closely-held secret in a place were secrets were a way of life. The disruptions in the Ripple wire detected earlier in the northwest corner of the Range had now become epidemic. What was worse, there was evidence that a large unauthorized force

277

was now operating in the northwest section of War Heaven, one that was overrunning the isolated Fitzies in that area at a frightening pace. Reports being received from forces operating near the Ponderosa area confirmed these troubling stories. What's more, many of these forces were in retreat.

The JSTARS aircraft had been ordered into the air by C2 to examine the situation firsthand.

The gadget-crammed 707 was still fifty miles south of the northwest sector when the warning devices on its banks of radar screens began lighting up. To their amazement, the airplane's radar technicians saw before them the confirmation of the most outrageous rumors.

According to their radar mapping screens, the hills in and around the Ponderosa were crawling with armored vehicles such as tanks and APCs, as well as more exotic mobile weapons like MRLS, self-propelled artillery and GLCMs units, capable of launching Tomahawk cruise missiles.

To the impartial observers aboard the JSTARS, tracking such massive movements of troops and equipment was routine. But there were two things highly unusual in this case. First, while all of the armored vehicles were undoubtedly carrying Zoot weapons, they found that just about every one of them was masked either electronically or by camouflage netting filled with composite fibers that prevented accurate penetration by the JSTARS radar beams. Thus, while they could see the various vehicles and guess their types by size and shape, there was no way they could identify them exactly.

Secondly, and even more troubling, the supply line for this huge, mysterious force not only stretched all the way back to the border of the Range, it went out beyond it.

The technicians went about their jobs, charting the approaches of the mysterious force, taking count of their dozens of high-tech weapons and assuming it was one big drill. All of their data was being inputting into the plane's large central computer as well as being flashed back to C2.

For two hours, the JSTARS airplane circled just south of the disputed area, collecting as much electronic information as possible for processing once it landed.

It was into its final turn when something went wrong.

The technicians who were used to riding in the highest level of aerial comfort suddenly found themselves being jostled around the cabin of the airplane. In seconds, their screens began blinking off. The cabin lights began to fade. There was a marked decrease in the low roar of the airplane's four engines. Suddenly the airplane's cruising speed went from 400 mph to less than 200 mph.

Up front, the pilots were as mystified as the Zebra technicians. It was only after a full minute of near confusion that they realized what was happening.

They'd been hit by a Zoot SAM . . .

50

Muleshoe, Texas

Joshua Littlejohn was feeling his way through an ancient copy of *Playboy* when the three strangers walked into his small Army-Navy surplus store.

All three were dressed in identical black suits, white shirts, black ties, and black hats. Each man had a deeply tanned complexion, almost as if they were foreigners, yet their features were definitely Caucasian. A long, black Cadillac parked outside apparently belonged to them.

At first, Joshua was certain the men were connected with his church and that they had somehow discovered that he was harboring a dirty book.

So there was some relief, then, when the men identified themselves as being "from the government," though Joshua didn't have the gumption to ask to see some ID.

One of the trio stepped forward, the other two taking up positions by the front entrance of the tiny store.

"Do you sell guns here?" this man asked.

Joshua quickly shook his head no. The man spoke with a slight accent, but he couldn't quite place it.

"Has anyone been in here lately asking to buy firearms?"

Again Joshua shook his head.

"They'd know better than to come in here," he replied nervously. "There's a gun shop right up the road . . ."

"I'm talking about someone from out of town," the man in black said. "A stranger . . ."

"No," Joshua replied quickly. "No strangers have been in here to buy guns."

The man in black eyed him suspiciously.

"Have *any* strangers been in recently?" he asked. "Perhaps to purchase other surplus items?"

Joshua nearly gagged on his next breath. He'd been caught—he was certain of it now. His standing in the community was ruined. His tenure as an elder at the church was gone. He was about to be exposed as a common thief.

"A man *was* in here earlier," he said, trying to stay calm between short, anxious breaths. "I guess you could say he bought an *unusual* item."

The man pulled a photofax copy from his coat pocket and showed it to Joshua.

"Is this the man?"

Joshua took one look and his eyes went wide. The rugged face. The eyes. The military haircut.

"It is . . ."

"Did he pay cash?"

Joshua nodded slowly. "All small bills," he confirmed.

"Exactly when was he here?"

Joshua checked the large clock on the wall.

"Four, maybe five hours ago . . ." he replied. "I opened late today and he was my first customer."

"Did you see how he arrived?" the man asked. "Was he walking? Was he in a car?"

"I didn't notice . . ."

"Could he have arrived by bus?"

Joshua just shrugged. "He could have . . ." he replied honestly.

The man turned to look back at his colleagues, who both nodded simultaneously.

"And exactly what did this man purchase from you?" the man asked, turning back to Joshua.

This is it, Joshua thought. *The end.* The items the man had purchased were not from a regular supplier. In fact, they had been stolen from the nearby National Guard armory more than ten years before and had sat all that time locked up in the basement of his store. Until that morning.

"He bought two surplus parachutes . . ." Joshua finally admitted.

With that he bowed his head, closed his eyes, and tried to whisper a prayer. It did him no good—he could almost feel the handcuffs tightening around his wrists.

But after a terrifying twenty seconds passed in silence, he finally found the courage to look up.

The three men were gone.

5 1

Area 61

Maureen couldn't believe her eyes.

She was in a room that looked like a bad marriage between an aircraft hangar and meat locker.

The walls, the floor, and the ceiling were perfectly white, as were the dozens of pipes running throughout. There were no windows, and just the one door, which was something more likely found on a bank vault. The room was well-lit with banks of halogen lights. There were no shadows.

It was damned cold inside the chamber, too—she could see a faint mist whenever she exhaled.

She had her pen and notepad ready, but she couldn't write, because her hands were shaking so much—and not from the cold.

But it didn't matter. What could she write about the object sitting in the center of the room?

There was really only one description: it was a flying saucer.

It was approximately sixty feet in diameter and fifteen feet high. Pearl white, with just a slight line of neon red around its rim, the saucer's construction appeared to be absolutely seamless. She couldn't see a bolt or a screw or a rivet or any kind of fastener, even around the single, open hatchway.

Three chrome hoses ran out of the rear of the saucer and were hooked up to a large white tank. This tank was coated with a icy frost which told her it was probably holding something like liquid nitrogen. There was also a faint but constant hissing coming from the saucer, a noise that suggested that some fairly high voltage was running through the object.

Walter was standing next to her, beaming as he read her reactions. "Do you want to go inside?" he asked.

She nodded rather numbly and together they went through the open hatchway.

Inside was a large windowless chamber. Definitely a control room of sorts, it actually resembled the hub of a wheel. Maureen could see tiny hallways like spokes, branching off into other smaller chambers.

Unlike what she'd seen in the movies, the inside of the saucer was not filled with elaborate gadgetry, nor did it feature cathedral-like architecture. It was in fact very spare, almost clinical-looking. So much so, she managed to jot down the words "sterile" and "spartan" in her notebook.

Strangely, this main room was very bright, but she couldn't locate any source of light.

In the center of the room was a small console with only a dozen or so tiny lights, like those on a Christmas tree. Several of these had very terrestrial name tags hanging from them. One said *Gravity motors disengage.* Another was labeled *Inertia damps.*

On the console next to the lights, there were several lines of very small writing. Maureen studied them intently. They looked to her like some kind of pictorial writing, a combination of Chinese ideograms and Egyptian hieroglyphics, very similar to what she'd been led to believe was found on the wreckage of the Roswell craft years before.

She walked away from the console and back toward the rear of the circular room. There was a line of small, yet elaborate metal containers against this far wall. They reminded her of hospital incubators. Standing next to them were four metal boxes that almost looked like baby cribs.

"Not what you expected, is it?" Walter asked her, his voice echoing in the cavernous main room.

"It looks like the examining room at my women's clinic," Maureen replied.

Walter lost his smile for a moment. "You might not be too far off," he said cryptically.

She continued to walk around the chamber, but actually there was really very little to see.

"Don't you have any questions?" Walter asked her.

She pretended to check her notes, as if she'd written down a host of probing inquiries.

"Yes," she said. "Does this thing actually fly?"

Walter never stopped smiling. "You're asking the wrong question."

"And what is the *right* question?"

Walter thought for a moment, then said, "You might ask, 'Does this thing operate?' "

Maureen decided to take the bait. "Okay, does it 'operate?' "

"Sorry, that's classified," he said, grinning.

Maureen gave him a long cold stare. This was not the time for Walter's stale brand of humor.

"All right," she pressed on, "Assuming it can do *something* besides just sit here, how is it powered?"

Walter wet his lips and stared at the ceiling for a moment.

"Well, that's classified, too," he began. "But I *can* tell you that it uses something called element 121 as a source for most of its power."

Maureen held up her hand immediately. "I know a little about chemistry," she told him. "There *is* no element 121."

"That's correct," Walter said, "Yet, on the other hand, it *does* exist. Or, should I say, it can be manufactured, and therefore, I guess, isn't really an element at all. But that's just semantics. I do know that element 121 is extremely powerful. In fact, if I remember correctly, one kilo equals the potential force of fifty-six 15-megaton bombs."

"You said it's manufactured?" she asked. "How?"

Walter shook his head. "I'm not a physicist," he said. "And I'm not sure that even someone who is could explain that to you. I *do* know, however, that one main ingredient of element 121, if you will, is gold."

"Gold? Really?"

Walter smiled again. "That's right," he said. "Lots and lots of gold . . ."

Once again, Maureen pretended to consult her notes.

"Assuming that this craft is what you apparently want me to believe it is," she began, making up the question as she went along, "then why in hell does this country have a space program? Why do we need NASA and the space shuttle? Why would we have to build what could only be described as obsolete crafts to fly in space, if the government has something this advanced in its possession?"

Walter's grin lessened a bit. "Well, you're assuming things again, Miss O'Brien . . ."

She was getting angry. This was no time for games.

"Such as?" she snapped back at him.

"You're assuming that a craft like this travels in space," he replied matter-of-factly.

She was rendered silent for a moment by the statement.

"And it doesn't?"

Walter shook his head; the light was actually reflecting off his teeth.

"Sorry," he said with a wink. "Now *that's* classified."

Maureen felt like slapping the smile right off his face. But instead she walked away from him and back toward the center console. There were two chairs next to it, and she ran her hand over them. They were both very hard, as if made of stone and totally unpadded. They were also both very tiny, far too small for an average human to squeeze into.

And this made her think.

Though its interior was rather strange, she'd seen nothing inside the saucer that could be described as "unearthly." There was nothing that would suggest any kind of truly advanced intelligence at work. The craft and everything in it could have been manufactured for the government by an aircraft company or even a Hollywoood special effects department. It would have been very expensive, yes. But still very doable on a terrestrial scale.

All except those small chairs.

It was a small, yet nagging question: If the government *had* gone through the trouble and obvious expense of building the saucer—as a ruse, as a mock-up, or as some kind of truly legitimate experimental aircraft—why, then, would they have installed such tiny, uncomfortable, and unpadded chairs?

They left the saucer chamber soon afterward and climbed back aboard the large, slow-moving elevator that serviced all of the underground facility.

Walter pressed a button which started the big lift on its way down, causing Maureen to tense slightly. She'd learned that the deeper one went inside this place, the stranger things seemed to get. And, as per his custom, Walter didn't tell her what their next destination would be. He simply stood next to the elevator controls, fixing his tie, wiping the lint from his short-sleeved shirt and humming some innocuous tune.

"Are you married, Walter?" she asked him suddenly.

He looked over at her and smiled. She had definitely caught him off-guard.

"I believe that's classified information," he replied.

"How about family? Any kids?"

Again he just gave her a friendly shrug. "Sorry, classified . . ."

She had to laugh. "Even your family life is a top secret?" she asked. "Or is it just another example of this game that everyone around here seems to enjoy playing so much?"

"Game? What game?" he asked, sounding legitimately insulted. "We all work very hard around here."

"That's just my point," she continued. "Just about everything is so *damned* precise. All the T's are crossed, and the I's are dotted. Whatever the hell is going on around here, there really is a human quality to it all. Yet I'm just amazed at your willingness to utterly destroy people. Just totally ruin their careers and their lives — and for what?"

"Few things in life are totally pleasant, Miss O'Brien," he said.

"But it was ruthless what you did to Doctor Ernie," she countered. "He's such a fragile sort of guy. He'll never recover."

"Did you know that your precious Doctor Ernie frequented whorehouses?" Walter shot back at her, trying hard to maintain his smile. "Or that he's carried on long-term relationships with several phone-sex women? Or that he rents nothing but X-rated tapes from his video club?"

"So what?" she replied coldly. "You've just described about half the middle-aged lonely men in America. You've probably just described yourself."

"I beg to differ with you on that, Miss O'Brien," Walter said, all evidence of his smile now gone. "And I'll break a rule or two here to tell you that, yes, I am married. Yes, I have children. And no, I do not watch X-rated films or solicit prostitutes or patronize phone-sex lines."

"So you're the one-in-a-million, God-fearing perfect man?" Maureen taunted him.

"I'm a practicing Christian," Walter answered, staring straight ahead. "If that's what you mean . . ."

"And so there's no sense in my looking for a skeleton in your closet, then?" she asked.

He turned back and stared hard at her. "I'm suggesting that it would be a waste of time . . ." he replied coldly.

A moment later, the elevator doors finally opened.

The first thing Maureen saw was a sign that read: Yellow Fruit—Disassembly Facility.

"Where are we?" she asked him.

"This is the elephant graveyard," Walter replied, his smile returning as if their unpleasant exchange moments before had never happened. "It was originally built to be used for underground nuclear tests. Now, it's the place where everything comes to die . . ."

They walked off the elevator and into an enormous man-made cavern, at least the size of a football field. Like the much-smaller saucer chamber, it was lit by rather dim halogen lights. A strange, knee-high mist enveloped the floor and, combined with the dim lights, gave the place a distinctly eerie feel.

Through the mist and low lighting, she could see a dozen or so shrouded objects of varying heights and sizes scattered about the chamber floor. The largest one sat in the middle of the room. It was at least 120 feet long, maybe 35 feet high, and was distinctly saucer-shaped. It was covered in hundreds of separate white and yellow plastic sheets.

By contrast, another object much closer to her was only about four feet high and not six feet across. It was wrapped in red sheeting.

Except for the strange fog—she supposed it was necessary to keep the floor cool—and the odd-shaped, covered objects, the facility could have been a repair shop for buses or large trucks. There were a few workers moving through the mist surrounding the shrouded objects, some carrying power tools, others portable computers and clipboards. All were wearing masks similar to those worn by surgeons. A few were sporting safety goggles.

Maureen pointed to what she considered an average-size covered object.

"May I look under this?" she asked Walter.

"By all means," he replied.

He grabbed a pair of masks and goggles from a nearby receptacle which had a sign attached that read: Wear your safety glasses — it's the law!

"Regulations," he said with a grin, handing her a mask and pair of glasses. "Always regulations . . ."

Maureen carefully put on her goggles, tying back her long blonde hair as she did so. Then she covered her face with the surgeon's mask.

Walter led her to the object. At about eighteen feet long and five feet high, it could have been a covered midsize automobile. He lifted up its yellow sheet.

Maureen felt her hand go to her mouth in surprise.

"Never seen one of these before, Miss O'Brien?" Walter asked.

The "object" was a piece of machinery that looked like a enormous Jell-O mold. What startled Maureen was that when the sheet was lifted, the machine instantly began pulsating like a big bright-red police light.

It was almost as if the damn thing were alive.

Walter smiled, and quickly lowered the sheet. He walked over to an adjacent object, which was about twice the size of the first, and lifted the corner of its protective covering. It too came alive with a flash of blue light. This object was long and thin, not unlike the fuselage of a small jet fighter, *sans* the wings and tail planes.

Once again, Walter lowered the curtain too soon, a few blue reflections bouncing off the floor mist before the light died away completely.

"You can always come back and study them more closely," Walter told her, "but these are not what we came down here to see . . ."

He steered her onto a passageway that bordered the display floor and then began walking in front of her. They passed into a hallway that was lined with large, thick windows, behind which were individual work areas. Some of these rooms were dark and empty, others were lit and occupied by technicians working over covered objects. Though Walter was hurrying her along, Maureen couldn't help noticing the activity in one of these large rooms. An uncovered object was hanging by chains from the ceiling. It looked like a typical flying saucer—or, more specifically, half of one. It was about fifteen feet across, and ten feet high, but clearly more than fifty percent of it was missing.

A jagged edge and obvious burn marks indicated where the missing pieces had once fit. Unlike the other uncovered objects she'd seen on the display floor, this one was *not* pulsating with color and life. Just the opposite, it looked quite dead.

She tried not to let Walter see her studying the damaged object, but already he was nervously looking over his shoulder. She quickened her step, but not before she got a very close look at the strange wreckage and saw that there were several irregular rows of small punctures running the length of it.

They looked exactly like bullet holes. . .

She and Walter walked along the gradually-sloping, tunnellike passageway for another ten minutes.

It was getting quite cold, and the lightweight work overalls she was wearing weren't warm enough anymore. The drop in temperature didn't seem to bother Walter any, though. He seemed perfectly comfortable in his short-sleeve shirt and blue-plaid polyester pants. What a strange man he was, Maureen thought. Able to shift emotions so quickly. To keep smiling in the midst of the bureaucratic madness of this surrealistic, underground world. To engage in character assassination and still boast that he was a religious man.

He was so unusual that a stray thought suddenly flashed through her mind: *Maybe he's an alien* . . .

They finally reached the end of the tunnel to find a pair of large, meat-locker-type doors. Only one of them was labeled. It held a small sign which read: EBE Unit — Grays.

"EBE?" Maureen asked.

"Extraterrestrial biological entities," Walter explained. "Just what we need isn't it? Another government-mandated acronym . . ."

Walter unlocked the large door and swung it open. They walked into a cold, dark room, lit only by a handful of dim red light bulbs.

Maureen instantly realized where she was; she'd seen setups like this before. The bare room. The wall holding twenty or so large drawers. The cool, clammy smell.

It was a morgue.

"Better put your mask up again," Walter told her. "Regulations . . ."

He reached for the first drawer and gave it a mighty yank. It slid out slowly and smoothly.

The drawer held a slab covered by a glass canopy. On the slab was a body.

It wasn't a human. It was small, probably four and half feet tall, more dwarfish in stature than that of a young child. It had two legs and two arms, but they were very thin and weak-looking. It had an oversized head with large slanted black eyes that were wide open. The skin was disgustingly gray, almost like that of a dolphin. All in all, the body looked fetuslike and unreal.

Strangely, though, it was wearing what looked like a uniform. It was bright red, with a series of patches stitched into it at the most haphazard and unusual places.

"I can't believe this," Maureen said, her queasy stomach turning again. "Real or not, it looks disgusting . . ."

Walter nodded in agreement. "Yes, I know," he said, almost wistfully. "That's just how I felt the first time I saw it. But, like everything else around here, you get used to it after a while . . ."

He moved to the next drawer and pulled it out. There was a similar figure under the frosted glass, this one slightly larger than the first. It too was wearing a uniform, though it was devoid of patches. But Maureen detected several designs on the being's skin that looked like tattoos.

Walter closed this drawer and opened several more. They contained nearly identical beings, all of the same approximate length and weight, all wearing variously adorned uniforms, some with tattoos, some without.

Maureen could only take a quick look inside each of the glass coffins. Her stomach was very unsettled now.

"Can we go?" she finally asked Walter. "I've seen enough."

He shrugged, and pushed all the drawers back in.

"You wouldn't believe how expensive it is to operate this one little room for a year . . ." he told her nonchalantly. "The cost to pump in the nitrogen cooling agents alone is astronomical."

Maureen couldn't have cared less about the costs at this point. All she wanted to do was get the hell out of the crypt.

With all the drawers secured, Walter punched a security code into the lighted panel next to the door, and in a second the mass of steel and wires swung open.

Maureen stepped out into the hallway and took several deep gulps of air in an effort to combat her rising nausea. At the same moment, she noticed that the second, unmarked door at the end of the tunnel was opened a crack. To her astonishment there appeared to be flakes of snow blowing in from the other side.

Suddenly the door flew all the way open, and she was confronted with three men in enormously-bulky suits and helmets. But what was more amazing was what was beyond the huge door. It was yet another vast chamber, so large she could not see the far side or the ceiling. And inside this chamber it was snowing—literally. But not just snowing. The snow was blowing fiercely, as if propelled by a tremendous gale.

Maureen had to shut her eyes and gain her wits for a moment. It was like she'd opened the front door to her house to find an unexpected blizzard raging outside.

The three men in the bulky suits began to walk into the tunnel, but stopped immediately upon seeing her. At this point, Walter had left the crypt and come out into the tunnel, and, seeing what happened, literally shooed the men back inside.

"Classified . . ." Walter was saying. "That's all classified stuff in there . . ."

But Maureen wasn't really listening. Her eyes were fixed on one of the men. She could just barely see his face inside the large bulbous helmet, but it was enough for her to recognize his features.

It took her a moment . . . he looked so familiar. And then, just as Walter was closing the door, it hit her.

She knew who the man was. The narrow, boyish face. The slightly-longer-than-military-regulation hair, a certain devilish sparkle in the eyes.

It was Ryder Long's partner in Operation Distant Thunder. It was the pilot they called Woody . . .

52

Outside Abilene, Texas

There was only one light on inside the control tower of the small airport and that was coming from a flashlight.

Andy Sunn was trying his best to find the correct buttons on the tower's main control board while at the same time keeping the flashlight beam low and steady.

Out on the darkened runway, he could hear the rumbling of two piston-driven engines. The airplane warming up out there was one of the Texas Air Corps' most prized, if little used, possessions. It was not a World War II fighter, or a bomber. Rather it was a C-119, appropriately nicknamed the Flying Boxcar. The fifty-year-old airplane could perform a variety of duties, from cargo transport to forest fire fighting. But the C-119 had just one specialty, and that was dropping parachutists.

Sunn finally located the runway light switch, and flicked it twice. A quick flash of a beacon from the C-119s cockpit came in reply. Sunn then hit the tower-to-aircraft radio switch.

"Bluebird Flight, this is the tower," he whispered. "You're okay from here. Weather lines are okay. There's no traffic in the area . . ."

"Roger, Tower . . ." came the equally muted reply. "We're off, then . . ."

Sunn wished the pilot good luck, switched off the radio, and then switched on the runway lights. The two sets of deep blue beacons instantly lit up like a pair of long ribbons. In just a matter of seconds he heard the C-119's engines go up to full power and then he saw the silhouette of the veteran airplane rumble down the strip and slowly climb into the dark Texas sky.

Sunn chuckled to himself as he began switching off the few instruments on the control board.

Just like the old days . . . he thought.

The Flying Boxcar reached 10,000 feet and turned northwest.

An authentic Texan named Buck Forrester was piloting the C-119. His co-pilot/navigator was a transplanted New Jersey man named Phil Farbaniec.

Sitting in the engineer's jumpseat, bundled from head to toe in a flight suit, helmet, and two surplus parachutes, was Ryder Long.

He'd never had any doubt that the Texans would once again make good on their promise to help "anytime, anywhere"; the whole question all along had been whether he'd be able to get to their small air base without tipping any pursuers as to his real destination. He could only hope that the misleading trail of crumbs he'd left behind had thrown off anyone trying to follow him.

Originally, one of his main concerns had been that nothing unforeseen happen to the Texans—but not surprisingly, his friends were less worried about that than he was. Most of them were combat veterans—the Gulf, Vietnam, Korea, even a few World War II bucks. A little cloak-and-dagger stuff didn't faze them a bit. Quite the opposite—it was apparent from the beginning that they were enjoying themselves.

Ryder's second concern was what lay ahead for himself. He knew he couldn't risk getting back into War Heaven by ordinary routes. Even if he had made it to either Nellis or any of the other smaller military installations near the border of the weapons range, he would surely have been prevented from crossing into the restricted area and most likely arrested—especially after making the totally unauthorized low-level flight halfway across the country from Homestead and abandoning the multimillion-dollar F-15 at the end of the runway at Tulsa.

No—he knew he'd have to be innovative. After all, those were the last *real* orders he'd received during the last *real* briefing he'd attended, that being the now-infamous ECC briefing. And when he ran the scenario of his future court martial through his mind, he saw himself saying over and over, "I was only following orders . . ." and then calling the Tango Boss as his first — and probably last — witness.

Things were rushing toward a conclusion — he could feel it. He was certain that Woody's plane crash had been faked, just as he was sure that the story he had found quite serendipitously concerning an allegedly similar fate for Katt was also bogus. He had to assume, therefore, that Teddy Williams was alive and breathing somewhere, too.

In a strange way, he felt left out. If they were all still involved in the mission, then they knew what he didn't. They had already passed over the threshold. He was still fighting it. What had they seen? What did they know? Was it good? Was it bad? Was it real? Or was it one big drill?

Questions. There were always plenty of them. But his mission, given to him by Moon so long ago, was to get answers and he had no choice now but to stick with it.

As he saw it, then, this "extraordinary contingency" called for him to get back into the Range undetected and make it to Area 61 as quickly as possible.

And that's where the Texas Air Corps came in.

They had agreed to "insert" him as close as they could to the Range without getting shot down by one of the omnipresent F-16 patrol interceptors. He'd selected the site for them — it was near a place appropriately called Coyote Pass. Just a mile or two from the furthest eastern border of the Range, it was to his best estimation the most isolated place on the eastern periphery of the place.

He'd have to hoof it over the border from there, but at the moment that was not his biggest problem. Getting from the C-119 to the ground in one piece was.

He hadn't hit the silk since his pilot training days, and at the moment he was frankly worried about how he'd hold up. The idea of parachuting — or specifically skydiving, for sport — had always puzzled him. Why would anyone want to parachute out of a perfectly good airplane? Yet in a few hours, that's exactly what he would have to do. Walk right out the back of the Flying Boxcar and hope he'd packed at least one of his two recently purchased parachutes correctly.

And even if the chutes opened, he would still have to worry about landing. Little else but flat, sandy terrain would do. Coming down on a ledge, in a gorge, or on top of a sharp boulder could prove fatal.

It was more than enough for the toughest paratrooper to handle in daytime. Ryder would have to make the jump in the middle of the night.

Near Coyote Pass, three hours later

It was his three dogs barking that woke Cowboy Bobby Baulis out of a deep sleep.

He rolled out of his cot, one hand reaching for his boots, the other grabbing his .22 rifle. His dogs—two sheps and a mutt—usually slept better than he did. When they were roused before first light, it was almost always a sign that something nasty was afoot.

At the moment, wiping the sleep from his eyes, Cowboy Bobby would have bet that a cat—a big one—was outside. His isolated line shack—the only domicile within twenty miles—was close to the western face of Coyote Summit, a favorite roaming spot for cougars at this time of year. But not this time of day. That led Cowboy Bobby to suspect that if it was a cat, then it was injured and therefore very dangerous.

He slowly opened his front door, the usual squeak easily shielded by the howling of the dogs. Walking in the shadows of the small wooden structure, he peeked around the corner, back to where the dogs slept. Immediately, he knew that it hadn't been a cat—or any other kind of prowling animal—that had disturbed them. The dogs weren't barking toward a specific direction, as they would have been doing if something was coming up the hill at them.

Instead, they were looking straight up, literally howling at the stars.

He heard it a few moments later. A deep rumbling sound coming out of the southeast. He shushed the dogs and looked up and saw it. A single red light, moving slowly, from southeast to northwest.

He was tempted to run back into the shack and get his binoculars, but in the same instant he knew he didn't have the time. The object, whatever the hell it was, would have been long gone before he got back. So he stood there and stared as it moved from his left to right, probably no more than a mile and half away.

He'd seen strange things in the night sky before. That the military ran a secret weapons testing ground just over the next mountain was well known to the scattering of civilians living on the edge of the

296

place. Streaks of light and bizarre noises coming from the west were so commonplace that they didn't disturb the dogs a whit anymore.

But this weird, slow-moving rumbler did.

Although it was now almost in front of him, he could see nothing more than the light or hear anything other than the rumbling. But then suddenly he thought he saw something fall out the back of the thing, something white. At the same moment, he thought he heard a scream—definitely human—echoing across the desert and up the rocks to his eardrums. The dogs must have heard it, too—they commenced barking again until he yelled at them to quiet down. By that time, the light and the rumbling were gone. And so was the speck of white.

Cowboy Bobby shrugged and lowered his gun. This was a odd piece of Nevada, and every resident had come to expect strange things happening every once in a while. He was no different.

So he went back inside his shack, secured the gun, and returned to his bed.

He was back asleep a minute later.

Part 3

53

Ryder counted seven major scrapes on his right leg, four in his left.

Both his shoulders were sore, though he was fairly certain neither was dislocated. His left elbow was bloody and swollen, as was his ring finger, and the two bumps on his forehead felt like grapefruits.

But all things considered, he could have been in worse shape.

It had been a rough landing. It seemed like no sooner had he stepped out of the back of the Flying Boxcar than he was being dragged along the rugged desert ground, *both* his chutes filled with blowing desert wind, all hopes of floating down and landing on his feet long gone.

His main chute had finally just shredded off him, straps and all. The reserve chute—he couldn't recall it opening on the way down, but it obviously had—had propelled him along for at least an eighth of a mile, finally depositing him against the trunk of the only tree of discernible size within twenty square miles. He hung on and the chute's straps broke. He cursed at the billowing chute as it continued its journey across the desert, looking like a ghost as it blew away from him.

He vowed at that point never to parachute out of any kind of airplane again.

He patched his wounds as best he could with the bandages and bottle of iodine he'd brought along. With the initial shock of the big bounce wearing off him, he realized just how lucky he'd been. Any broken bones—or even a sprained ankle or knee—could have meant a death sentence for him. A long, slow *painful* death sentence.

All he owned he was carrying in a small knapsack: a bottle of water, his first-air gear pack, his Zoot .45 automatic, his Zoot dog tag, and the remainder of his Las Vegas winnings, specifically $228 in small bills.

He picked himself up and tried to get his bearings. His map told him that he was less than a mile from the border of the Range.

His gut told him he was even closer.

Lance Corporal Jay Cadmus was the first one to spot the parachute as it flew across the open desert about a mile to the south of him.

He called to his sergeant, who tracked the fast moving silk with NightScope goggles until it blew by their position and continued on to the northwest.

"Who the hell could that belong to?" the corporal wondered aloud.

"I don't think I want to know," the sergeant replied, watching the parachute until it finally faded into the night. "We've already got enough problems . . ."

The sergeant, his name was Reed, Corporal Cadmus, and six other soldiers were hunkered down in a small wadi, taking a twenty-minute break before they began moving again. Two days before, the eight men had been part of the elite 332nd Mountain Warfare Brigade, a highly specialized unit formerly attached of the Blue forces. Schooled by the famous West German *Gebirgsjager* brigade, the 332nd Mountain, like that unit, was made up of highly-trained, highly-resourceful guerrilla fighters. Their speciality was deploying to snowy, high-mountain or even polar environments and conducting operations behind enemy lines.

The fifty-man detachment had been broken up two days before when their commander suddenly turned up missing. The second-in-command took over and told them that he had to make the toughest decision of his career. Due to the unprecedented conditions prevailing on the Range—the apparent breakdown of C2, the disruption of the regular points-for-necessities system, the relentless onslaught of the mysterious army from the north, and now, the disappearance of their leader—he had no choice but to break up the command into smaller, more mobile units and leave them to their own devices.

It was a difficult but nevertheless sound military determination. There was a crazy story going around that a number of Gray, Green, and Blue field commanders had been kidnapped, and that their commander was among them. The problem was that unlike most of the other units in the northern part of the Range, the 332nd had never received orders after it was apparent that something had gone wrong at C2. Under the bizarre circumstances, then, the second-in-command knew that small groups of men were better off at surviving out on the Range than large ones.

This necessary disintegration had officially taken place thirty-six hours ago. Since then, the eight men had been moving south in their battered, overloaded Hummer, half of them walking with full packs at any given time in order to preserve the vehicle and its fuel. Moving slowly during the cooler nighttime hours, and resting – and hiding out – during the hot daytime, they concentrated on avoiding enemy units of any force who would gladly savage them for the few meager points it would earn.

Hard and professional as they were, the long ordeal was still tough on these soldiers, because the conditions they faced were the exact opposite for which they had been trained. Their equipment not only included the seventy-odd pounds of field gear that a regular soldier would carry, but also another thirty pounds of artic gear, parkas, thermal undergarments, special lanterns, stoves, weapons, and communications equipment. The men were used to lugging all of this gear through blowing snow and subfreezing temperatures.

And while the soldiers found that their heavy coats came in handy on the coldest of nights on the Range, carrying them – and the rest of their stuff – only added to the misery of tramping across the hot desert instead of across the snows.

The men had a destination. They had been deployed to the Range not a month earlier as part of a special task force being trained for an unspecified mission to take place in an unspecified subfreezing environment. The first three weeks of that training had taken place in the rugged mountains of the Ponderosa in the northwest part of the Range, leading everyone in the unit to believe that their eventual mission deployment would be to a high mountain range, the only question being whether it would be the Himalayas or the Andes.

They were two weeks and a day into their mountain training when things began to go wrong in War Heaven. They were one of the first units to actually see the advancing mystery army, though only in the form of long columns of smoke and dust and exhaust off in the distance. They were long gone from the mountains of the Ponderosa by the time the mysterious invaders reached their approaches. In his last briefing before he disappeared, their commander told them he was thinking of deploying the unit south, toward the site of the second half of their training, an equally mysterious Fitzie that, so they'd been told, mimicked a TPE—for total polar environment.

The members of the 332nd had done similar duty in a secret facility at Homestead AFB in Florida. There, in an old aircraft hangar that had been fitted with various ice machines, fans, and snow-making equipment, they'd spent 45 days living in simulated polar conditions. They had been told that this was only a prelude for the training time they'd receive in the famous War Heaven.

The trouble was, the eight members of the 332nd had no idea where the TPE Fitzie was located. Before he vanished, their commander had given them the few clues he knew—that it was somewhere in the center of the Range and that it was deep beneath a low, flat, rather unusually shaped mountain.

Knowing this could describe any one of a hundred places in the thousand-square-mile central portion of the Range, the men set off nevertheless, searching for this underground Shangri-La and wondering if in fact the world of War Heaven had really gone mad, or whether they were just small cogs in the middle of an incredibly large and complex exercise.

Now, seeing the parachute blowing by their hiding place caused a chill to run down Sergeant Reed's back. This was a bad omen, he decided. At best it could mean that there could be an enemy paratroop advance party in their area. At worst, an entire airborne unit was landing on top of them.

"Let's go," Reed called to the rest of the troops. "We're moving out early . . ."

There was the usual grumbling and then the rote exercise of packing all the gear that had been carried for the previous march onto the Hummer while unleashing all the gear that had been riding free. They were ready to move out within ten minutes.

The Hummer had been acting up for most of the night and now, as the team moved south out of the wadi, the overloaded, unbalanced vehicle was belching clouds of black smoke and backfiring with the sound of an unmuffled mortar.

There was nothing they could do about it but move as fast as they could, while keeping their eyes sharp for anything from an advance recon troops to an entire airborne division.

The shot came out of the dark, and was perfect, right on the center of the Hummer's steering wheel. Suddenly the vehicle wasn't smoking or backfiring anymore. It wasn't doing anything. It had come to such a sudden stop that both the driver and the soldier sitting on the passenger side nearly went through the windshield.

Thinking the vehicle had simply broken down for good, the 332nd soldiers were still cursing when they heard their own individual Zoot beepers go off. One by one they realized that technically, by rules of the Range, they were quite dead. Just like that.

The sergeant just about threw a fit. They'd made sixty miles in two nights of moving and now it was all for naught. Playing by the rules, they set down any Zoot weapons they were carrying and put their hands on their heads. Expecting to soon to be enveloped by the anticipated avalanche of Airborne troopers, they were astonished to see a single soldier standing atop a nearby cliff, a Zoot 45 pistol in one hand, a knapsack in the other.

"Sorry, men," Ryder called down to them. "But I need some wheels . . ."

54

There was no moon above War Heaven, yet the skies were brighter than ever.

"I've never seen anything like this," Ryder was saying, "I didn't think it was even possible . . ."

The entire northern horizon was lit up brighter than day. In a huge, yawing arc across the sky, the illumination from what had to be thousands of Zoot weapons being fired and Zoot bombs exploding was so intense, it mimicked a particularly vivid sunrise.

"It's been going on like this for days," the sergeant in charge of the 332nd mountain soldiers told Ryder. "They moved into the Range somewhere west of the Ponderosa and haven't stopped yet. They're rolling over anyone and anything that gets in their way . . ."

Ryder's head was spinning and he wasn't exactly sure whether it was due to the bumps on his forehead or the incredible glare from the pyrotechnics to the north.

"Who are they?" Ryder asked the NCO. "Does anyone know?"

"No one that I know," the sergeant replied. "Whoever they are, their main force is fighting its way south, with some of its detachments enveloping the flanks to the east.

"As you can see, some regular units way up there are giving them a good fight. But believe me, it's a losing proposition for them. These new guys got all the latest Zoot weapons, and even a few we've never heard of. They're unstoppable . . ."

There were several long moments of silence as the glow on the northern horizon got even brighter.

"We're new here," the sergeant went on, "but from what everyone's told us, there's never been an exercise like this before. Everything has gone to hell since it began. Our commander might have been snatched by them. C-Two is all screwed up. All the rules are off. No more nice and neat supply drops for gaining points. No more perfect communications. We heard the zebras are completely fucked up. One rumor has it that these guys—this mystery army—shot down one of their JSTARS airplanes."

"A JSTAR?" Ryder exclaimed, never taking his eyes off the bright glow to the north. "That's hard to believe. If anyone tried that before, they would have been bounced to Greenland in a second."

Ryder hadn't expected anything like this. When he left the Range it was still a nice, neat, and orderly world of war gaming. Blues were fighting Grays. Grays were fighting Greens. The Aggressors were blasting the shit out of everybody. Now it seemed like everything within the Range was collapsing in on itself. Yet no one knew why.

The strange turn of events begged two very big questions: What did this have to do with the ISC crisis? And was this mysterious force working with them or against them? There was no way to tell either way. But judging from the direction of the invading army, they would be closing in on the center of the Range and, hence, Tango Base, within a few days. And then, there would be almost nothing in the way to stop them from moving on to Area 61 itself.

When that happened, all bets would definitely be off.

But as strange as it was, Ryder knew that the mysterious invasion force could not deter him from his mission. It would make it harder for him. And more urgent. But somehow, he would have to stay one step ahead of them.

The sergeant turned his NightScope binoculars to the north.

"We were probably about two days in front of them," he said. "That is, we were until we ran into you."

Ryder finally managed to take his eyes off the mesmerizing glow of the fierce battles to the north.

"There is that problem of you 'killing' all of us," the sergeant reminded him.

"I had no choice," Ryder explained. "I've got to get back to my base. I had to grab the first vehicle I could find. You guys were just unlucky . . ."

The sergeant leaned back against a rock and lit a cigarette. "If you don't mind me asking," the NCO said. "What the hell are you doing here, sir?"

Ryder began to formulate an answer, but was frankly stumped for a logical, "sanitized" reply.

"I mean," the sergeant went on, "it sure looks to me like you jumped into this place. Or came down nearby and walked across the border. I know I'm a newcomer, but I have a feeling that's not exactly a typical deployment."

"Nothing is typical here," Ryder told him. "You should know that by now, sergeant . . ."

"You're correct, sir," the NCO replied. "But what happens to us now? We're left out here, with no transport. And very few supplies. And the way the point-and-replenishment system has gone to hell, we ain't got no way to get just the basics, food and water."

Ryder turned back to the north. "You said it yourself, sergeant," he told the man, indicating the firestorm out on the horizon. "Whoever these guys are, they'll be here in a couple days. From the looks of things, you can hold out until then. I'm sure they'll feed you . . ."

"And wind up POWs?" the sergeant asked, obviously offended. "Then we'd be failures, sir . . ."

Ryder just shrugged. He had things to do. His plan was to get back to Tango Base, get an airplane and then somehow get down to Area 61. He couldn't see any wiggle room in there for the mountain soldiers.

"Those are the rules," he told the NCO.

The man tossed his cigarette away in disgust. "Damn the rules," he said: "All the rules are off anyway. I just hate to think that we came all this way down here just to get captured by these Huns . . ."

"What's the alternative?" Ryder asked him.

The sergeant stared at him for a moment. "We could make a deal . . ."

"A deal?" Ryder asked, almost laughing. "What kind of a deal?"

The NCO shrugged. "Pretend you didn't 'kill' us," he said. "Then we can all get the hell out of here together."

Ryder had to admire the man. He was dead, dead, and dead, caught in the barrel of Ryder's Zoot pistol, and his men were of the same status. Yet his pride wouldn't let him just lay down and die . . .

"That would be impossible, Sarge," he told the man, shaking his head. "You were walking half your guys behind the Hummer as it was. Nine of us couldn't get any farther, any faster . . ."

The NCO hastily lit another cigarette. "How about this?" he began. "We passed a chopper base a little while back. I'd say probably ten miles north of here. There weren't that many people around, but we avoided them anyway.

"How about we go back, and kidnap one of the pilots and his helo, and have him fly us the hell out of here?"

Ryder just stared at the man. The audacity of proposing such a scheme was amazing.

The NCO looked back at him and seemed to read his mind. "I mean, what the hell, sir?" he said. "When I was a kid and we played guns, we always had to quit when we got 'killed.' It used to piss the hell out of me.

"And now here we are. In the biggest playground in the world. Playing the biggest game ever conceived. A multibillion-dollar kid's game. And the only one who knows we're all been 'killed' is you . . ."

Ryder looked at the man. He was only about twenty-five years old, if that. But obviously well-trained and fiercely determined.

"Maybe you've got a point, sergeant," he said. "And maybe it will be easier to fly out of here than you think."

The man's face brightened considerably. "What do mean, sir?"

Ryder took one long last look to the north and then turned back toward the NCO.

"Well, for one thing," he said, "we won't have to kidnap a pilot . . ."

The attack on Temporary Base 127 came without warning.

The small air field, which supported three U.S. Navy SH-60B Seahawk helicopters and a larger U.S. Marine CH-47 Chinook, had only been recently established by the retreating airborne unit attached to the Green forces. Tucked away in a small, hidden valley very close to the eastern border of the weapons range, TB-127 had been home for four helo pilots and eight crewmen for only forty-eight hours, a safe, if transient haven from the onslaught of the mystery army invading from the north.

Or so they thought.

The third watch had just been relieved when the relative quiet of the predawn darkness exploded with four Zoot grenade blasts. Suddenly the air was filled with vivid Zoot tracer rounds as well as a half dozen billowing smoke bombs.

The TB-127 chopper pilots and crewmen were immediately jolted out of their bunks by the sudden, violent assault. Support troops by definition, and therefore not really front-line warriors, the men at TB-127 watched with astonished indecision as a battered, dirty overloaded Hummer screamed onto their base's main landing area, white-uniformed troops hanging off its sides pitching Zoot grenades and smoke bombs in every direction.

Six of the attacking troops jumped off the careening Hummer and surrounded one of the Seahawk helos. The driver of the vehicle then screeched the Hummer to a halt next to the pilot's side of the helo and a man in a drab Army uniform leaped directly from the Hummer into the open bay of the Seahawk.

In less than a half minute, the engines of the helicopter burst to life. Suddenly the helo's rotors began to turn, the sounds of the whining engines being drowned out by the racket of the long whirling blades. All the while the troops surrounding the helo never stopped firing their Zoot weapons; if anything, the frighteningly-realistic light show from the storm of ricocheting tracer bullets grew in intensity.

Just two minutes into the attack, the Seahawk was warmed sufficiently for takeoff. A shouted command to the troops surrounding the helo set four of them running the length of the LZ, tossing two Zoot grenades each into the three remaining helicopters. Then, with another order, all of the attackers piled on board the Seahawk, and with a great burst of wind and power, the helicopter lifted off, the troops in its bay still firing their tracer rounds and tossing out smoke bombs and Zoot grenades.

It soon disappeared over the western horizon. In all, the attack had taken less than three and a half minutes.

It had been quite a while since Ryder piloted a helicopter, but luckily the Seahawk was a fairly basic flying machine.

During his initial flight training by the Air Force, he'd been assigned to a three-week chopper orientation course. At the time, he remembered being really ticked off and disappointed at the assignment. For a young flight-school trainee hoping to drive fighters, getting trained in choppers, even for three weeks, was usually a harbinger of things to come. As it turned out, he was eventually sent to fly cargo airplanes, and only assigned to fighters after his selection for Operation Distant Thunder.

But now, he was damned glad he'd spent the twenty-one days wrestling with the helicopters.

The Seahawk was simply a naval version of the Army's UH-60 Blackhawk with a few doodads needed for landing and servicing off surface ships. Not the least of these was that the helo was equipped with wheels—for easier on-board hangar storage—instead of skids like most ground forces helicopters. Luckily for the snow soldiers, the Seahawk's bay was slightly larger than the Army version, and with Sergeant Reed jammed into the copilot seat, there was plenty of room for the seven enlisted men.

Elated by their lightning-quick assault and capture of the chopper, the troopers were in high spirits as Ryder put the chopper down to the ass-scraping altitude of 100 feet and hugged the desert floor. He spotted a fairly well hidden wadi about twenty miles from TB-127 and with quick, if slightly rusty, adeptness, he circled the potential LZ once and then set the Seahawk down with a slight, rubbery thump.

The 332nd troopers alighted, and though still feeling their oats, nevertheless deployed into a quick defensive perimeter around the chopper. Meanwhile Ryder and Sergeant Reed did a quick evaluation of the condition of the Seahawk they'd snatched.

The good news was the helo's batteries were charged and strong. The bad news was there were no Zoot weapons on board, nor did the aircraft have any kind of advanced navigation equipment.

"No NightScope gear, no electro-opticals, no nothing," Ryder told Reed as he scanned the various cockpit controls. "We'll have to fly this baby by the seat of our pants."

But even worse, the helo's fuel tanks were less than half full.

"Did we snatch the wrong bird?" Reed asked when apprised of the fuel situation.

"I doubt it," Ryder answered truthfully. "I'm sure none of those helos had much gas in them. If they had, those swabbies wouldn't have been hiding out like they were."

Reed's face and spirits visibly slackened.

"How far can we go with the gas we've got?" he asked.

Ryder did some quick calculations. "With all the guys we're carrying, maybe forty miles," he finally replied. "Probably even less."

Reed took off his helmet and rubbed his tired forehead.

"Well, it was a good idea while it lasted," he said.

"What do you mean?" Ryder wanted to know.

"What I mean is, me and my men will just get off here, sir," Reed replied. "We can't slow you up. You've got to get back to your base. And we're not even supposed to be still in the game . . ."

Ryder knew the man was right. By his calculations, he was still a good 150 miles from Tango Base. But even by stretching the helo's fuel capacity to the limit, he still couldn't make it.

"It's too late to turn back now, sergeant," Ryder told Reed. "I need you guys. I need your eyes, your weapons. Your expertise . . ."

"But how can we do it, sir?" Reed asked. "The Range is so big that flying just forty miles on the gas we got will probably just put us closer to nowhere . . ."

"Then, there's only one thing we've got to do," Ryder told him. "We've got to get more gas."

"More gas?" Reed asked, mystified. "How? Steal it?"

Ryder sat back in the pilot's seat and thought a moment.

"Maybe," he said. "Maybe not . . ."

55

Area 61

Maureen woke the next morning to find that a bundle of fresh laundry had been placed at her door along with her usual morning meal.

She was just getting her appetite back after the stomach-churning tour of the alleged EBE crypt the day before, so she only picked at the breakfast of eggs, melon, and toast.

She rather nonchalantly threw the clothes bag on her bunk, paying more attention to her first sip of coffee than to what was inside the olive-drab gunny sack. It was only after she'd set aside her half-eaten breakfast that she began emptying out the bag of clothes.

Usually the laundry parcel contained several days' worth of underwear, six pairs of fresh white socks, two sets of lightweight overalls, and two handkerchiefs, everything being of a typically-military generic style.

But today she found that the laundry bag held something very different. She couldn't believe it as she pulled out handfuls of racy silk undergarments—bras, panties, camisoles, negligees. There were several pairs of black nylon stockings complete with garter belts. There were two sheer white body stockings, a black, see-through teddy, and a tiny bikini-style sleepwear set that she couldn't have fit into if she had wanted to.

Instead of the usual coveralls, she found a black velour slip-style dress and a pair of stiletto high heels.

Inside was a typed note that read: *Darling, These are for you. Please wear them for me . . . Love, Walter.*

Maureen was furious.

"Of all the pathetic, sniveling, bureaucratic attempts at titillation . . ." she screamed at the walls, for once hoping that they *were* bugged. "I'll kill the bastard . . ."

She was almost too angry to think. She couldn't believe that he would do this. Was it another part of the mind game he'd been playing with her? Was it a retaliation to the pointed conversation they'd had concerning Dr. Ernie the day before? Was it one step on the way to ruining her own reputation? Or was it something else entirely?

She didn't know. But whatever the hell it was, she would not be a party to it. She threw all of the garments off her bed, vowing not to let a single one touch her skin.

It took a few seconds, though, for her to realize that to keep this promise, she would eventually have to go around quite naked. Her clothes from the day before had already been picked up; and all had she besides the newly arrived R-rated wear was the pair of cotton underpants she'd slept in that night.

This all meant that if she wanted to storm down to Walter's office anytime soon, she would have to do so either wrapped in her blanket or dressed like a model from Frederick's of Hollywood.

After some thought, and a bright flash of intuition, she chose the latter . . .

Maureen arrived at Walter's office door twenty minutes later, slightly out of breath.

She was wearing the slinky velour dress, the black silk underwear, the black nylons—and sneakers. Her only token of protest was to wear the scuffed-up tennis shoes and not the stiletto high heels.

Walter was eyeballs up into a huge document when she burst in. Those eyes literally bugged out when he saw her. The dress was slipping down around her shoulders by this time and her heaving chest did little to deemphasize her perfectly rounded breasts.

"Do you have an explanation for this?" Maureen screamed at him, slamming the office door behind her.

Walter was absolutely flabbergasted. "Where the hell did you get that stuff?"

"These clothes were in my clean laundry bag this morning," she told him in no-uncertain terms. "Along with this . . ."

She threw the partially crumpled note at him. He unraveled it,

312

read, and immediately blushed to a bright pink.

"Surely, you don't think . . . that I . . . This was not meant for you!"

Maureen grabbed the note back from him.

"Oh no?" she asked sternly. "Then, who was it meant for? I'm the only woman here, aren't I?"

Walter looked like he was about to expire on the spot. He started taking deep, quick gulps of air, at the same time trying to avert his eyes from Maureen's lovely figure and failing miserably. "Please— My God, use my coat to cover yourself . . ."

As she grabbed his lab coat from the back of this office door, Walter grabbed the telephone. He had a hurried, hushed conversation and then quickly hung up.

"They're sending someone down here to look into this matter," he told her.

She sat down with a huff, wrapping herself as tightly as possible in the less-than-pristine lab coat.

"You have to believe me," he stammered. "I did not send those clothes to you . . . or that note . . . It was totally inappropriate . . ."

"To say the least," she replied, adding, "especially for a God-fearing, family man like yourself . . ."

Walter's jaw literally dropped open. He tried to say something but couldn't.

So Maureen said it for him. "Let me see if I have this straight," she told him mercilessly. "You say this little scandalous bundle was not meant for me. Yet, from what I've been led to believe, I *am* the only female here. So what is it, Walter? Sending these things to one of the *men* around here?"

Walter's mouth was moving but the words were having a lot of trouble coming out. "They're certainly not for a man!" he said, horrified at her insinuation.

"Oh no?" Maureen went on, not letting up one iota, "Then, should I assume that your wife is in residence here? Or is that classified, too?"

"I can't say . . ."

"Okay, then," Maureen went on. "I'll have to ask around about this. People like talking to me. I'll start off by checking with your boss, Mr. Pinky. Maybe he'll know. Or maybe Ray at the Zoo. Or—"

"Please . . . don't," Walter managed to say. "If you only knew . . .

313

the ramifications."

Despite the office's profuse air-conditioning, Walter was beginning to perspire.

"This sure looks like one pretty big skeleton to me," she told him. "And a damn good story. Or I can turn it into one. It has something more than the usual numbers, or monsters, or UFO fragments. Something a TV tabloid show would *really* like to sink its teeth into. That three-letter word . . ."

"Are you threatening to blackmail me?" Walter asked, barely able to mouth the words.

"Yes, I am," she replied, mocking him. "Sound familiar?"

A knock at the door saved him. The clean cut man who delivered Maureen's meals to her every day slipped into the office, another gunny sack in his hand.

"I'm sorry," the man said, nervously looking from Maureen to Walter back to Maureen again. "Somehow the computer delivery system shut down this morning. The wrong packages are being delivered to the wrong people all over the building . . . and I . . ."

Unable to say anymore, he simply dropped the sack of clean clothes at Maureen's feet and beat a hasty retreat.

She looked up at Walter, who was unaccustomed to going this long without smiling.

"Do you want to make a deal?" she asked him suddenly.

"You mean you want something?" he asked, looking up at her hopefully.

"Yes, I do," she stated as authoritively as she could. "After we left the crypt yesterday – I saw two men behind the big door, in that fake blizzard. Do you know what I'm talking about?"

Walter gulped hard once. "Yes . . ."

"I want to interview at least one of them," Maureen told him sternly.

He immediately began shaking his head. "That would be impossible," he stuttered. "So much so . . . I'm afraid . . . well, it is actually quite –"

"I know who they are . . ." Maureen interrupted him. "Or at least I know one of them . . ."

Walter's face went from crimson blush to ghostly pale in a matter of seconds.

"One of them is a pilot – a military fighter pilot," she said, "He's a

314

good friend of a very good friend of mine. I want to know what he is doing here, and what his role is in all this."

"This is all very impossible," he managed to say. "Those men were in an extremely classified area, that you shouldn't have seen . . ."

"Really?" she asked, taunting him. "More classified than a garage full of broken flying saucers? More classified than a morgue full of alien bodies?"

"There are different levels of classification," he stammered. "You have to understand . . ."

As he was talking, Walter was sinking further and further into his seat. It was obvious that he had never faced a situation quite like this before. Finally, he could speak no more. He simply sat there, unable to move.

"Do you know the two sure ways to get fired from a government security job?" she asked him.

He was barely able to shake his head no.

She smiled cruelly and recited the oft-repeated line: "Get caught in bed with a dead woman, or a *live* man."

Walter's eyelids dropped to half-mast.

"So what's it going to be, Walter?" she asked him point-blank. "Do I get to speak to that pilot? Or . . ."

Walter put his hands to his face, and turned his eyes upward, as if in prayer.

"What a mess . . ." he whispered.

56

El Capitan Beach, Santa Barbara, California

The two Secret Service agents jogged around the bend of the path and came to a stop in front of a small isolated cottage.

Both were breathing hard from their two-mile run; both checked their watches.

"We've only got two minutes," one told the other between gulps of air.

His partner pulled a small radio from the belt of his jogging suit and clicked it on.

'We're here," he barked into it.

The reply came back in a burst of static: "Okay, we're starting out . . ."

The two agents walked up to the front door of the cottage and banged the screen door twice. It opened almost instantly.

"Ready?" one of the agents asked the small man on the other side of the door.

"Ready," replied Lieutenant Moon. "How's the time?"

"They're two minutes behind us," one of the agents replied. "Is the bird still sitting still?"

"Too damn still . . ." Moon replied.

Exactly two minutes later, seven more Secret Service agents came jogging up the path, and, without missing a step, plunged into the heavy bushes surrounding the cottage and took up predesignated positions.

Seconds later, a third knot of seven agents arrived, jogging in tight formation around an eighth man in the middle.

"Here we are, Mr. President . . ." the lead agent announced. "We've got about five minutes . . . six, tops."

The Chief Executive took a small towel from the lead agent and hastily wiped the perspiration from his forehead and neck.

"Will you call ahead and have some iced tea waiting for us, please . . ." he told the agent, who immediately snapped his walkie-talkie on and relayed the request.

With that, the President put the towel around his neck and then walked into the cottage.

Moon was standing a few feet from the door and saluted as the Chief Executive came in.

"Hello, Lieutenant," he said simply.

Moon led the President to the cottage's small dining room. The first two agents were already inside, stationed next to the room's single window. Sitting at the end of the rickety wooden table that took up most of the room was the ISC officer known only as Sixteen.

Moon was able to let out a short breath of relief. He had gone to great lengths to arrange this curious meeting, set in the isolated cottage on the ground's of a private Pacific-view estate. Because its topic was so secret—so incredibly sensitive—an elaborate misdirection campaign had been developed.

The goal of this plan was to make it appear that the President was doing nothing more than going on his daily morning jog, a run that usually took twenty-five minutes out of the Chief Executive's busy day. Flying to California on a previously scheduled fund-raising trip and ensconcing himself at the rambling estate of a fellow millionaire, the President had set the stage for an opportunity to disappear for a handful of minutes from the eyes of the waiting press and even most of his own staff.

Now, by simply releasing an elongated version of the jog route, Moon and the President's Secret Service contingent were able to open up a seven-minute window during which the President could bury his whereabouts.

The officer known as Sixteen looked like he was about to faint when the President walked in. He began to get to his feet, only to be firmly set back in the chair by the two Secret Service agents. In an attempt to compensate for his enforced lack of respect, the man weakly saluted.

"Don't bother," the President told him sternly. "It's much too late for that kind of thing now . . ."

Sixteen sat frozen to his seat, his upper lip visibly trembling. Though only in his early fifties, he held a rear admiral rank in the U.S. Navy.

"We don't have much time," the President told him as he sat in the wooden chair at the opposite end of the table. "So I'll be brief. I want you to tell me what the hell is going on out there in Area sixty-one . . ."

The officer looked like he was going expire right there on the spot.

"I'm sorry, sir," he began, his voice trembling. "I cannot tell you that . . ."

The President wiped his face again with the damp towel.

"Are you aware of the penalties of disobeying a direct order from your Commander in Chief?" the President asked him harshly.

"Yes, I am, sir . . ." Sixteen replied.

"Then I'll ask you again," the President went on. "What is the ISC doing out there?"

The man began to say something, but the words would not come out. He simply shook his head.

"Are there nuclear weapons armed and ready to explode out there?" the President asked him.

"I can't tell you that, sir," the man replied very meekly.

"Have you illegally taken possession of a substantial amount of this country's gold reserves?"

"I'm sorry, sir . . ." was the answer.

"Is there a military coup being planned against this country?"

Again Sixteen could only shake his head. "I'm sorry, sir," he said, his voice on the verge of tears. "Under the circumstances, I just can't tell you . . .".

The President hastily checked his watch. "We've only got about four minutes left," he said to the man. "And I find your intransigence most trying. Most disturbing. You are a military officer. You've had an illustrious career—I checked. I read your service record last night. It was very impressive. You've served your country well. Up to now.

"But in case you don't realize the gravity of this situation, let me remind you that everyone involved—yourself and the rest of this ISC group—are liable for court-martial of high treason. Sedition. The penalty for such crimes is death. Do you realize that?"

The man nodded numbly. "Yes, sir, I do . . ."

"And you still choose to be silent?"

Again, Sixteen nodded weakly.

The President checked his watch and threw up his hands in frustration.

"I've got to go," he said to Moon. "I just wish this could have been productive . . ."

"I'm sorry, Mr. President . . ." Moon said.

The Chief Executive patted Moon on the shoulder.

"It's not your fault," he said. "The question is, what's our next step?"

Moon could only shake his head. "We have no other choice sir, but to continue the ongoing operation out on the Range."

"Don't like it," the President said. "Don't like it one bit. It's too unpredictable. Could blow up in our faces."

"I know, sir," Moon replied. "But I think you agree, we really don't have any other choice. Especially since the agents we inserted on the ground seem to have disappeared."

The President got up to go. He stopped at the doorway and turned back to Sixteen.

The man's eyes were fully misted over by this time.

"Sir, I have to tell you that I consider myself a loyal American," Sixteen said slowly, but with some conviction. "What we have done is best for this country. For this whole planet. I believe this with all my heart . . ."

The President stared hard at the man and then back at Moon. Then, without another word, he walked quickly out of the cottage.

57

The Gray army artillery base known as Four-Zulu-Four went on immediate attack alert as soon as the helicopter appeared overhead.

Caught in the middle of their noon meal, the base's entire contingent of 349 troops were sent scrambling about, some rushing to man Four-Zulu-Four's half dozen antiaircraft guns, the rest diving into the elaborate set of bunkers and shelters that ringed the small hilltop fortress.

The base commander, watching the helicopter through spyglasses, estimated it was about a mile above the base. It was an odd altitude for anyone with aggressive intent.

"Hold your fire!" he yelled along the line to his AA gunners. "Don't shoot until my order . . ."

A moment later, he saw that someone had hung a white sheet out the side of the helicopter and was waving it frantically. The commander of Four-Zulu-Four got the message right away. The helo wanted to land.

"Lower your barrels!" he yelled to his AA gunners. "Lock your guns . . ."

The commander then walked out to the center of the fire base, took off his white undershirt, and began waving it. It took about a half minute before he realized that the copter was slowly descending.

There were three squads of armed Gray soldiers deployed in a rough circle around the dirt patch in the center of the fire base where the Seahawk bounced down for a landing.

Ryder killed the copter's engines immediately, and cautioning the mountain troops to stay put, he and Reed alighted from the Seahawk. There was an audible angry murmur as the Gray soldiers saw the Blue force uniforms. Out on the Range, the Blues and the Grays were traditionally bitter enemies.

Ryder took a quick glimpse around the fire base. He counted twenty-one artillery pieces in all, including two massive 175-mm M-107 mobile guns, six 155-mm M-198 howitzers, the rest being fairly standard 105-mm M-102 lightweight field guns.

More important, he spotted a fenced-off area that contained at least two dozen barrels plainly marked: AVIATION FUEL.

They walked toward the man they immediately identified as the fire-base commander.

He was a tall, massive black man – a major whose face seemed to be fixed in a permanent snarl.

Ryder introduced himself and Reed and thanked the commander for not firing on them.

"Wouldn't have done much good," the officer replied. "You would have had to put down here anyway, and then we'd just have you stuck here with us . . ."

"Can we have a talk, Major?" Ryder asked the man outright. "About the current situation . . ."

The officer shrugged, and turned briefly toward the north where, despite the brilliant sunrise, the sky was still lit up with the glare of Zoot explosions.

"A chat before the tidal wave hits?" he said. "Sure, why not?"

He introduced himself as Major John "Oily" Welles. He led them to the large, ragged tent that served as his headquarters. They accepted his offer of a cup of coffee – instant, and weak, at that – and then sat down on canvas chairs placed in the center of the tent.

"What is your situation, Major?" Ryder asked.

Welles surprised them with a booming laugh. "Ever hear of Khe Sanh, Colonel?" he asked them.

Both Ryder and Sergeant Reed nodded. Khe Sanh was the site of an ill-fated strategically-located artillery base manned mostly by U.S. Marines at the height of the Vietnam War. The base had been surrounded by Vietcong and North Vietnamese troops and pounded mercilessly for weeks. The Marines bravely held, but only after sustaining huge losses.

If Welles's laugh had a slightly bitter tone to it, it was because his

321

battered base did indeed look like a modern-day Khe Sanh.

"You seemed to be well armed, at least . . ." Ryder told him.

"We are," Welles replied. "Trouble is, we're stuck here. We lost all our transport three days ago when the Aggressors caught our regular supply convoy out on Sixty-six. We normally need seventy vehicles to move all this stuff. Now we ain't got one . . ."

"How about your air?" Ryder asked. "You got a helipad here, so I assume you had some choppers."

" 'Had some' is correct," Welles told him. "We had two Black-hawks a week ago. They flew off on a spotting mission and never came back. Someone, somewhere, stole them. I heard they were seen up near Jacks a while ago."

"How have your supply drops been going?" Ryder asked him. "Have you been able to cash in points?"

"What little we have, yes," Welles replied with a sigh. "The deliveries are all fucked up, of course. I guess the days of the nice, neat, predictable supply drops are over. We had to wait almost eighteen hours for our last drop. *Eighteen goddamn hours.* That's a long time when you've got three hundred and fifty hungry guys sitting on top of a mountain with nothing to shoot at . . ."

"Really?" Ryder asked. "You've got no targets? I thought a gun like a M-107 can toss something twenty miles or more."

"It can," Welles confirmed. "But that does us no good if we don't know what we're shooting at. We have to hit something dead-on to get any points these days. When we lost our air transport, we lost our eyes, man. We can't send guys walking out twenty miles from here and then rely on a radio contact to fix a target. These days, a bad radio call would bring all hell down on us. Especially the way the Aggressors are hurting. I hear they're hurting worse than anybody. Ever since these guys came in through the north, those fly-boys have lost all their special advantages . . ."

A rare smile spread across Welles's face at the mention of the Aggressors being cut down to size. "So at least something good has come from this . . ."

Ryder was surprised to feel a pang of hurt pride at Welles's demeaning of the Aggressors. But it passed quickly. He knew he had to concentrate on other things.

"Are there targets within your range that you could hit if you had good fire-and-adjust info?" he asked the officer.

"There's got to be," Welles replied. "I have to believe that just as we're all stuck here, there are many units hiding in the area in the same situation."

He pulled a small black booklet from his uniform pants.

"The info from our last forward patrol indicated that there were still six fixed Fitzies within our range," he said, reading from the book. "Some of them have still got to be out there . . ."

Ryder took a deep breath. It had been risky just to barge in on the isolated Gray base, but it appeared as if he'd made the correctly "innovative" decision.

Now it was time to bargain.

"What if we find some targets for you?" he asked Welles directly. "We could take one of your forward guys up in the chopper and he could direct your fire from above."

Welles looked it him like he was a sidewalk hustler.

"Blue army helping the Grays?" he asked with a very skeptical smile. "That ain't supposed to happen out here on the Range . . ."

"*None* of this is supposed to be happening," Reed said, speaking up for the first time.

Welles stared at the NCO, perhaps surprised that he would talk so forcefully to an officer.

"Let's say we do cooperate," the base commander said finally. "What's in it for you guys?"

"We need fuel," Ryder said. "Aviation gas for the chopper. You got some, correct?"

Welles nodded slowly. "We do . . ."

"Well, then, there's the deal," Ryder said. "We do your spotting for you. You hit some targets. You get points. You get supplies—eventually. We get some gas."

Welles screwed up his face in consternation. "Blues and Grays, helping each other," he half-muttered. "That's a pretty strange concept . . ."

"These are strange times," Ryder replied.

58

It was two hours after sunset when the Seahawk helicopter took off from the helipad at Four-Zulu-Four.

Rising into the star-filled, moonless night, the helo hovered briefly over the isolated hilltop fire base and then turned to the north-west.

Strapped into the copilot's seat next to Ryder, Sergeant Reed was visibly nervous.

"Damn, this is something," he kept saying over and over. "This is damned hairy . . ."

Though he didn't share his consternation, Ryder knew what was bugging Reed. It was the new paint scheme on the Seahawk.

The idea of repainting the Seahawk came up during the planning session between Ryder, Reed, Welles, and Four-Zulu-Four's target-ing officer. All agreed that the deal between the chopper crew and the Gray artillerymen would be for naught if the Seahawk was shot down while on its spotter mission. It was decided that some kind of a disguise was in order.

But what exactly? With all of the previous and fragile alliances between the various forces deployed on the Range now blown away in the face of the invasion of the mystery army, there was little sense in painting the Navy helicopter in a Blue, Gray, or Green mask. Paint-ing it some incongruous color like all black or all white would not work either. The disruption of War Heaven's former clocklike life-style had made many a trigger finger feel itchy on the ground.

"It was Ryder who came up with the eventual disguise, which Wel-les's troopers had quickly applied to the Seahawk.

It was actually a variation on the white or black incongruous scheme.

In fact, the helicopter was now painted in both black and white stripes.

"Faking like we ain't been killed is one thing," Reed said to Ryder for at least the twentieth time. "But faking like we're zebras? That's really crazy . . ."

"You said it yourself, sergeant," Ryder told him. "There are no more rules . . ."

He brought the copter up to 1000 feet and settled in at an 85-knot cruising speed. From this height they got a real bird's-eye view of the calamity up north.

It was mind-boggling.

It looked like a forest fire—an enormous, 75-mile-long string of Zoot explosions caused by the weapons of the advancing invaders battering the defiant but ultimately ineffective individual Green, Blue, and Gray defending units.

The conflagration was quickly making its way south just like, in the words of Major Welles himself, a tidal wave. With some rough triangulation, Ryder estimated that the front line of the mystery army was no more than thirty miles away from Four-Zulu-Four. If the relentless onslaught continued at this pace, he theorized the fire base would be overrun in less than thirty-six hours.

He turned his attention back to the mission at hand: targeting the unsuspecting troops hunkered down in Fitzies within the radius of the big guns of Four-Zulu-Four. According to Welles's little black book, there was a Fitzie close by whose official name was Span & Waterway Assault Position, or SWAP.

Among the troops in the immediate neighborhood, though, it carried the nickname "BTF-One," for "Bridge Too Far."

The Fitzie was as elaborate as they came inside the Range. Stuck between two low ridges with a meandering artificially diverted river dividing them, the main feature of SWAP was the quarter-mile-long bridge connecting the banks of the river.

Built of steel girders and wire, the bridge held more than a passing resemblance to the famous span at Arnhem, Holland, which was the site of one of the more glorious Allied failures of World War II. In September of 1944, a plan dubbed Operation Market-Garden called for Allied forces to capture strategic bridges behind enemy lines in

Holland in the hopes of driving a wedge right into Nazi Germany itself, thus hastening the end of the war. British paratroopers were dropped on Arnhem, which was the deepest bridge inside German-held territory at the time. Their mission was to seize the bridge that spanned the Neder Rijn River. Unfortunately, the British paras jumped right into the midst of two German SS Panzer divisions, and though they hung on valiantly, many were killed, many were forced to surrender, and only a lucky few were able to withdraw.

The SWAP bridge had been built to train modern U.S. troops on the essentials of capturing and holding a large urban span. Usually a Blue force would be assigned to hold one side while a Green or Gray force held the other. When not fighting each other, the opposing forces either lived in the small, fake Arnhem-like villages built on either side of the bridge, or in the wooded areas nearby.

According to Welles's last intelligence report, a Green urban-warfare company had taken up position somewhere near the south side of the bridge shortly before the roof fell in on War Heaven. Because a unit like this had little transport, the artillery officer figured that most of them were still hiding nearby, waiting for orders that would never come and wondering what their fate would be at the hands of the mystery army.

Ryder's plan was fairly simple. He planned to buzz the bridge itself, loading the chopper's engine with an extra-rich fuel mixture and thereby making as much of a racket as possible. Any of the Green troops on the ground who saw the zebra chopper might think that somehow their salvation had arrived at last, and come out of their hidden positions. If this happened, Ryder would simply radio the exact coordinates back to the guns at Four-Zulu-Four, who would then blast the exposed troops.

But, as with many well-laid plans, this one quickly went asunder . . .

Using Reed's NightScope binoculars, Ryder easily located the SWAP bridge from about fifteen miles out. Lowering the Seahawk to just above the water, he was able to approach the span without being spotted. But upon turning the last bend in the fake river, he and Reed were amazed to see the bridge itself suddenly light up with a series of Zoot explosions.

"Jesuzz!" Reed was the first to yell, "what the hell is going on?"

Ryder yanked back on the chopper's controls and, his fighter-pilot instincts getting the best of him, put it into a dangerous, near-vertical climb. Two of Reed's troopers and the Gray army targeting officer nearly fell out of the open bay as Ryder leveled the chopper at 1000 feet.

After checking that all hands were still fit, Ryder swung back toward the SWAP Fitzie for a closer look. Hovering at a spot a little more than a mile away, they were able to see to see the span without the aid of the NightScope.

And for a moment, neither he or Reed could believe it.

"Christ, are those guys actually fighting each other?" Reed exclaimed.

It was true. There were many small Zoot explosions going off all around the span while two forces were obviously battling each other from opposite ends of the bridge.

He went up to 5000 feet and slowly passed over the bridge. Below them they could clearly see the two opposing forces heading for a fierce collision in the center of the span.

But there was more.

Welles's information was that the Green forces had been spotted in the area recently. But now, looking straight down it the clashing units, it was evident that one was Blue and the other Gray.

"Damn," Ryder swore right into his radio mike, "this gets more complicated all the time . . ."

Although it was within the bounds for the guns at Four-Zulu-Four to join the battle for the bridge, it was impossible for them to fire on the Gray forces. It was a matter of semiconductors: the War Heaven sensor engagement computers – the near-infallible HILES – simply would not allow same-side forces to score points on each other.

Therefore, the only alternative was for Ryder to call in fire on the Blue forces – something that didn't sit well at all with Reed or his men.

"God, that would be like we were Benedict Arnolds," Reed said when the situation was explained to him. "Helping bomb our own troops?"

Ryder swung back around high over the bridge. "What choice do we have?" he asked the man.

Reed shivered once and then rubbed his tired eyes.

"God, they'll send us all to the North Pole if we get caught . . "

Ryder put the chopper into a 180-degree turn so they were facing north again. He pointed to the string of enormous Zoot explosions stretching across the horizon and said, "Do you really think it makes any difference, sergeant?"

Reed slowly shook his head no. "Guess not," he said finally.

Ryder called Welles and explained the situation to him.

"They're already out in the open," he told the artillery officer. "You just got to lay it on them . . ."

At that point, he turned the radio over to the Gray army targeting officer, who began sending back the coordinates.

Within seconds the Zoot shells from Four-Zulu-Four's big 175-mm guns came crashing down on the north end of the bridge, battering the Blue army troops.

By monitoring the Gray army radios below, Ryder was able to determine that the commanders, while not quite knowing where the help had come from, were urging their men forward to take advantage of the fierce artillery barrage.

It was over in less than five minutes. Welles gradually lifted the shelling as the Gray army troops swarmed over to the north end of the SWAP. The HILES engagement computer onboard the helo began flashing, as did its counterpart back at Four-Zulu-Four. This officially ended the battle. The computer declared the Gray forces the winner and assigned a like number of points to both the troops on the bridge and the artillerymen nearly fifteen miles away.

"Well, that's that," Ryder told Reed, who still looked quite pained. "We get our gas. The gunners get their transport and we all get the hell out of here . . ."

They flew back to Four-Zulu-Four in relative silence, and came in for a radio-silent landing just as Ryder's watch beeped midnight.

Yet no sooner had they set down when he realized that something was wrong at the base—very wrong.

Everywhere he looked he could see bodies—still, motionless bodies, scattered all over the LZ.

"Jesuzz, what happened?" Reed yelled. "Are they dead?"

Ryder put his nose outside the copter window and took a long sniff.

"No, it's not that . . ." he declared. "This place has been hit with nod gas . . ."

Reed began to say something, but suddenly his words were cut off by a frightening mechanical scream, even louder than the still-whir-ring chopper blades.

He looked off to the east to see an Aggressor F-5 bearing down on them.

"Damn!" was all Ryder was able to yell.

The jet came in low and fast, dropping two canisters which exploded no more then 50 feet away from them.

"Quick, strap back in!" Ryder yelled, pushing the copter's engines back up to full power. But it was too late for the targeting officer and both of Reed's troopers. They'd already jumped out of the chopper bay, and therefore got the full force of one of the nod-gas explosions. All three hit the ground with nasty thumps, overcome by the sleep gas before they knew what happened.

Ryder covered his face as best he could and turned to look at Reed.

"I can't go," the sergeant yelled to him, his eyes already watering. "My men are here . . ."

Ryder grasped his hand and shook it, and suddenly the man was gone, out the door and onto the LZ.

Ryder saw him collapse from the effects of the sleep gas almost instantly.

Still holding his breath he yanked up on the chopper's vertical controls and lifted off, the downwash of his blades further scattering the sleep gas.

But it was too little too late. He'd gotten a mouthful of the sleep agent and now, even though he was pulling away from the summit of Four-Zulu-Four, he could feel himself going under.

Instantly he knew he'd made a mistake. Falling asleep on the fire base, and probably being captured by any one of a number of forces, was one thing. Going unconscious at the controls of the flying copter would be definitely fatal.

He gritted his teeth and fought the overwhelming feeling for sleep, at the same time searching frantically for someplace to set down.

He managed to fly along for a minute until he swooped down to the approach to the hill and saw a small forest of pines at the base of a large, sharp-faced mountain.

He was shaking and nauseated now, the side effects of fighting off the effects of the sleep gas. With one last great effort he was able to put the Seahawk into a hover and start a slow descent down toward a field in the middle of the trees.

Twenty five feet above the small clearing, he fell asleep . . .

59

Area 61

"Okay, go ahead, Colonel."

"Where should I begin?"

Maureen nervously checked to make sure her recorder was running. She was sitting in a darkened hall not unlike a lineup room at a police station. In front of her was a small stage bathed in bright lights. They were so bright, she was certain that the man sitting on the folding chair at center stage fifteen feet away couldn't see her in the audience.

"Let's begin with your old name . . . and rank."

"Colonel Daniel Joseph Woods. United States Air Force."

"What was your previous assignment?"

"I believe that's classified, ma'am."

Maureen turned around and looked to the back of the small hall where Walter was sitting. He wasn't smiling at all today. Rather he was acting like a man whose reputation – both professional and moral – was hanging by a very thin thread.

"Are you going to allow that question?" she called back to him.

"You may answer, Colonel," Walter replied.

"Okay, my previous assignment was with the 15th Adversary Fighter Squadron, out of Tango Base, on the Nevada Special Weapons Testing Range."

"Can you tell me how you left that assignment and wound up here?"

"We had completed about three weeks of training on the weapons range and then we were assigned to participate in an airshow."

330

"An airshow? Really?"

"Yes, ma'am. We left the Range and flew to Rome, New York. Once there, we became part of an airshow demonstration team. Our job was to provide the adversary role for what we believed to be local National Guard pilots. Purely for entertainment purposes."

"Were you surprised at being given such an odd assignment?"

"Yes, I was. But, looking back on it, I suppose there was some rationale to it. After all, we were providing the same mission with the weapons range – that is, playing the role of the adversary."

"And when did you learn that the airshow assignment was just a cover for . . . well, for all this?"

"Well, I first *realized* it during my first demonstration flight for a show at Homestead Air Force Base in Florida. We had flown there from Griffiss in Rome.

"I'd just completed my first show and was heading back to the base when my radio suddenly cut out. I couldn't raise anyone on any channel. Things like this happen occasionally in airplanes, so I didn't think it was that big a deal.

"But then, as I turned back toward the base, two F-16s came up on my left side. They were the National Guard demonstration planes that we'd just flown against in the mock dogfight. At first I thought they somehow knew I was in trouble and that they were there to help. One of the pilots used hand signals to tell me to turn my radio to a specific channel."

"What happened then, Colonel?"

"Well, I turned my UHF set to that frequency, and it came back on. I now believe that my radios weren't broken at all, but that they were being electronically jammed. Next thing I know I'm talking to someone from C-Two – Command Central. They instructed me to go down to an altitude of 200 feet and turn south immediately, which I did. I knew at this height I'd be off the Homestead Tower radars in a matter of seconds.

"As I was flying out, I saw a Chinook helicopter coming in, with a wrecked F-15X in its sling. The airplane looked exactly like mine, at least on the outside. I learned later that this wreckage was placed in the Everglades to make it look like I'd been killed."

"How did that make you feel, Colonel? Knowing that your colleagues believed you were dead?"

"I felt bad at first. But, since I've been briefed on the mission here,

I can see that it was necessary."

"And how did you get from Florida back out to Nevada?"

"Well, after I reached the Gulf Coast and was totally off the Homestead screens, I was met by a KC-10 aerial tanker. I was instructed to refuel in-flight, which I did, and then given a flight plan back to Nevada. I actually never stopped flying until I got out here. I refueled in-flight three more times."

"What about the men here with you – the two other pilots. Did they come to this place in a similar fashion?

"Yes – as far as I know, they did. We haven't had much time to talk about it – or talk at all, because we are so busy. But I understand that their 'disappearances' were also very carefully orchestrated."

"Do you know why, Colonel, that it was necessary to assign you to the airshow in order to, in effect, fake your death, and those of your colleagues?"

"Well, I'm not certain of the specifics, ma'am. But I do believe the idea was that a pilot being killed in an air-demonstration flight is not so unusual an occurrence. It is dangerous work, when you really get down to it. And, to a certain degree, it's easier to cover up. No one really gets suspicious if someone dies in this kind of accident, plus, because you're not at a regular base and doing a regular assignment – well, I guess you say you're just not 'missed' as much.

"I also understand that C-Two was looking for pilots of . . . a certain profile, let's say."

"And that profile is?"

"Well, I guess you'd say pilots who have certain abilities driving the airplane. I'm not tooting my own horn here, but all four of us were highly trained, on a level you could only compare to guys at Top Gun. But the profile also called for people who've been in black programs before. And also pilots who don't have any family. Guys who wouldn't be missed, as I said before. So, I can see why C-Two couldn't just go to Top Gun, or the Thunderbirds, or the Blue Angels, and select a few pilots there."

"But you fit this profile, Colonel?"

"Yes, ma'am, I do."

"You said there were four of you originally? Where's the fourth pilot?"

Suddenly Walter's voice erupted from the back of the hall. "That is definitely off-limits," he declared. "No way can we answer that question."

Maureen decided not to fight it. It probably wasn't that important. She moved on to her next question.

"What have you been doing since you came to this place?"

"A lot of simulator work. A lot of studying. A lot of review of flight tapes. A lot of everything—except flying."

"I saw you in some kind of a polar-environment room. What was that all about?"

"I understand that our eventual mission may take us fairly close to the Arctic Circle, ma'am. We were in survival training when you saw us."

"In all of this, Colonel, has anyone told you exactly what your mission here is?"

"I believe *that* answer might be classified, ma'am."

"Walter?"

"I think it's best that we keep the reply limited to how far the training has gone," came Walter's weary reply.

"All right, Colonel? Your training has been . . . ?"

"I have been training to pilot a highly-experimental aircraft."

"Experimental in what respect?"

"In many respects, ma'am."

"You mean it flies faster, or higher, or further?"

"Well, not exactly, ma'am."

"Well, then, is it shaped like a regular airplane? Wings and engines and such?"

"No, ma'am, it certainly isn't."

"Can it fly in outer space?"

"I'm not exactly sure of that, ma'am."

"Why not?"

"Well, because I haven't actually *seen* this aircraft ma'am. Not yet, anyway. I've seen pictures. Drawings. Design plans. But all my training so far has been done on simulators, and in a classroom environment."

"Really? So as far as you know, this aircraft might not even exist."

There was a long pause.

"Well, frankly, ma'am, I guess that answer would be affirmative."

60

"Is he dead?"

"He's either dead or dying."

"What the hell kind of uniform is that?"

"It's a Zebra chopper . . . or is it?"

"Bad paint job, if it is."

"Drag him out . . . . See if we can get a pulse."

Ryder was dreaming that he was in his old F-15X Eagle, endlessly spinning out of control as a battalion of cameramen, sound men, lighting technicians, actors, actresses, and gofers applauded his incredible special-effects maneuver.

At some point, he hit the ground and the Beautiful People stopped clapping and instead began slapping his face. The next thing he knew, he was looking up at Al Jolsen.

"Damn, he *is* alive," Al was saying as Ryder slowly came to.

He was lying on the hard ground next to the battered Seahawk. He could see the sky, the stars, the glow from the north. His back was killing him, as were his fingers, which were burned. He also had a hell of a headache.

He tried to clear his vision, and saw that there were six people in blackface looking down at him.

"You're alive, man," one of them said to him. "You made it somehow."

"Good thing that chopper had wheels," another one of the men said. "You bounced."

Ryder got up on one elbow and saw that the Seahawk was in fact half-hanging from a large pine tree, suspended about two feet above the ground. Its nose and cockpit were smashed, the fuselage was

334

smoking down to the tail, and the rotor blades were twisted horribly.

Ryder felt as bad as the chopper looked. But despite his additional bumps and bruises, he knew he was suffering mostly from the effects of the sleep gas, rather than from injuries resulting from the crash. That made his survival even more incredible.

Through a sore jaw and bleeding lips, he managed to ask a question: "Who are you guys?"

"Third Squad, Third Platoon, Special Forces Company," one of the men told him, adding, "Ninth Battalion, Green force."

Ryder managed to let out a long, relieved breath. He was very glad the soldiers weren't from the Blue forces on which he'd been instrumental in calling in the artillery strikes on the SWAP Fitzie. Had they been, and if they were aware of his action, technically he could have become their POW.

"Can you stand up?" one of them asked.

Ryder gave it a try, and though a little shaky, he made it to his feet with their help.

"Thanks, guys," he said, studying the six men. "I appreciate your coming to the rescue."

"You just kind of dropped in on us," the man who seemed to be the leader of the group told him. "We were about a click from here when we saw you come down."

One of the troopers gave him a canteen and Ryder gratefully drank from it.

"I'm Lieutenant Rogers," the leader of the squad said by way of introduction. "We got here Sergeant Weekly, Corporal Ray, Corporal Ziglar, Corporal Wierbicki, and PFC Dunton."

"Colonel Long," Ryder said, between swigs of the warm water.

"Do we get any points for rescuing you?" one of the troopers asked.

Ryder stretched painfully and wiped the dirt from his face and singed hands.

"I'm not really sure," he replied, running a finger along his trio of chipped teeth.

"Not sure?" the man asked. "You're a zebra, aren't you?"

Ryder just shook his head. "It's a long story," he said wearily. "Believe it or not, I'm attached to one of the Aggressor units. Tango Squadron. I'm trying like hell to get back to my base. But with this place going to hell so quick, it's been a bitch figuring just how to do that."

"You're a long way from Tango, Colonel," Rogers told him. "It's clear on the other side of the Range."

"I know," Ryder replied, capping the water can and returning it to Ziglar. "But it's very important I get there, somehow and quickly."

Rogers rubbed his camouflage-painted face. "That will be a tall order, Colonel," he said. "You need some transport and there ain't a whole lot of that around here these days. There ain't a lot of anything, nowhere."

"How are the supply drops in this area?" Ryder asked.

Rogers just shrugged. "Not great," he replied. "We just barely get food and the basics. But at least we get something. Farther north we hear there are units that have been busting balls for days and haven't got diddle."

Ryder took a measure of the six men. They were all extremely young, but very fit and tough looking. They were all dressed in all-black uniforms, their faces smudged with black camouflage paint. They were carrying Zoot M-16s and a couple small Zoot grenade launchers.

"You're a recon squad?" he asked Rogers.

"Long range," Rogers replied proudly. "We're attached to the battalion's third company, which is a special hostage-rescue unit. The main force is bivouacked five clicks from here up in the hills."

"All nine hundred of them?" Ryder asked, astonished.

Rogers nodded again. "More like four hundred and fifty," he said. "We've been seriously atritted lately."

"But that's still a lot of mouths," Ryder said. "How *do* you feed everyone?"

"By doing just what everyone else is," Rogers told him. "Pulling off a small operation here and there. Getting some points. Getting some food and stuff and then moving a little further south. Trouble is, we've got a lot of competition in this sector. Mostly from other Green units, who we can't fight. As you can imagine, everyone wants to get as far away as possible from what's happening up north."

"I know exactly what you mean," Ryder replied.

"We were about to pull a major operation," Rogers continued. "If it came through, we were hoping it would be our ticket out of here."

"You were hoping to move your whole battalion?" Ryder asked.

Rogers nodded grimly. "It's our only chance not to get caught up in

336

what's coming this way. Our last orders from C-Two were to withdraw, in small units if necessary. But we all voted that if we're going to leave, we're going to leave together. If not, we stand and fight it out together."

"Moving a whole battalion so quickly will take some doing," Ryder told him, trying to feel him out. "I've got a feeling you're not talking about land transport."

Rogers could only shrug. "I can't really say," he replied. "You understand, Colonel."

Ryder nodded. "Sure, I do."

"We've all but given up on doing the big op," Rogers said soberly. "Our CO sent us down to reconnoiter the target again, but, tell the truth, I think he's just giving us something to do. He's . . . well, he has his problems."

"Can I go with you?" Ryder asked the young officer.

"On the recon? Why?"

"Let's just say I'm curious," Ryder replied.

Rogers pulled on his chin in thought. "I don't know, sir," he told him. "Yanking you around with us, especially after you came down in a helicopter that was painted like a zebra? That sounds like it's really against the rules."

"It is," Ryder told him. "That's the whole idea."

Two hours later, just as the sun was coming up, Ryder was crouched next to Rogers and peering out of a trench toward the west.

A little more than a mile away was the Fitzie whose unlikely official name was HOREE—for Hostage Release and Enemy Engagement facility. As with many of the exotic Fitzies, the place had a nickname: Entebbe Two.

It was an airport, or at least a full-scale model of one. It featured two terminals—one of modern design, the other slightly older—a modern control tower; a main runway; a smaller, secondary runway; and several miles of taxiways, access roads, and aircraft parking areas.

It also had three actual airliners on hand: A 727 with American Airline markings, a DC-10 with United Airlines markings and a TWA 747 Jumbojet. Most tantalizing of all, for Ryder, was the gaggle of small civilian aircraft parked along the tarmac in front of the main terminal.

"Here's the tactical situation, Colonel," Rogers told him, never taking his eyes away from the airport. "Right before the shit hit the fan, we were scheduled to do an operation here. We know that C-Two flew in some personnel to act as hostages and set up a squad of Gray forces to act as terrorists.

"That was almost three weeks ago. Our job was to sneak in, seize the main terminal, free the hostages, and then get the hell out."

"Just like the Entebbe operation," Ryder said.

"More or less," Rogers replied. "The Israelis did it about as perfect as it could be done back in 1976. But there have been similar situations since, on Malta, in Lebanon, just to name a couple, that got really fucked up. Lot of people – innocent people – got killed. Back out in the real world, our company was one of the units on call for such situations."

Ryder looked at the man. "You're part of Rapid Deployment Force on the outside?"

Rogers gave him a sly wink. "You said it, Colonel, not me."

They turned their attention back to the ersatz airport.

"We were supposed drop in with four C-130s, and run the thing just like the Israelis did," Rogers continued. "The whole idea was to surprise the guys playing the terrorists."

"Tough to do if they know you're coming," Ryder observed.

"Sure is," Rogers confirmed. "But if we pulled it off, we would have been swimming in points. Enough to deal us the hell out of here."

"So what happened?" Ryder asked.

"Well, the problem, like everywhere else out here these days, is we had no gas," Rogers told him. "No gas meant we couldn't get the aircraft up and –"

Ryder cut him off. "You mean you have the aircraft? The C-130s?"

Rogers nodded. "Two of the four," he replied. "They're sitting up at our base. Fuel tanks just about empty."

"How much fuel *do* they have?"

"As I understand it," Rogers answered, "Enough to get airborne, fly us here, and land."

"But not to take off again?"

"Right," Rogers confirmed. "And the operation guidelines call for

338

us not just to rescue the hostages, but to carry them out. So . . ."

Ryder looked out at the airport and specifically at the airliners.

"Do you know if there's any fuel in those big airplanes?" he asked Rogers.

"Hard to say," the young lieutenant replied. "They flew one of them in just for our mission. I can't imagine them draining the gas out of it. Can you?"

Ryder didn't respond right away. He was "innovating."

Finally he turned back to Rogers.

"Can you bring me back to your camp, Lieutenant?" he asked. "I'd like to talk with your CO."

"You got something in mind, Colonel?" Rogers asked him.

"Maybe," was all Ryder said.

61

The commanding officer of the depleted Green Force 9th Battalion was a major with the unlikely name of Perley Diamond.

A decorated Persian Gulf veteran, Diamond had cultivated a reputation as a stern taskmaster. A regular U.S. Marine Corps officer, since coming to War Heaven, Diamond had been in charge of a mixed force of Army and Marine troops, many of them members of such special elite units like the Rapid Deployment Force.

When he first learned of the War Heaven assignment, Diamond was overjoyed. Being deployed to the top-secret Range and being installed as the head of a unit of elite troops was a dream mission for any Corps officer.

But the dream quickly turned into a nightmare for him. No sooner had he taken command of the Green force 9th when the entire fabric of War Heaven began to come undone. His vision of accomplishing great things, with such an enviable crack force, soon devolved into just keeping the men fed, clothed, sheltered, and, for lack of a better word, "engaged."

That's why the attack on Entebbe Two had meant so much to him. And that's why, as the likelihood over the past few days that the operation was slipping away from him became more evident, his own resolve had begun to deteriorate. He hadn't slept more than four hours in the past seventy-two; he hadn't eaten but two MREs in that time, nor had he bathed or shaved. Secretly, he'd been taking prescription Percodan tablets left over from a tooth extraction a month before.

With the ups and downs of the powerful codeine, then, he'd cursed his fate of being assigned to War Heaven just when it was going down the drain.

And now, his fate, and that of his men, were about to be handed to a man who claimed he was a pilot for the hated Aggressors.

"I'm sure that this will work," Ryder was telling the commander of the Green 9th as they sat in his hillside command tent. "The Israelis faced the same problem when they went into Entebbe."

That problem was fuel. The pair of C-130s assigned to Diamond which were waiting under camouflage netting on a small airstrip just over the hill had less than a quarter tank of fuel between them. Lieutenant Rogers's assessment that the big cargo planes had enough gas to take off and land at Entebbe Two had in fact been overly optimistic. By Ryder's calculations, the pair of Herks could take off and fly the ten-minute flight to Entebbe Two, but they would have to do it practically empty of men or equipment, without benefit of much engine warmup, and with no luxury of circling the airport Fitzie once they arrived. They would have to land straightaway, and if Ryder's figures were correct, their fuel gauges would be reading empty seconds after they touched down.

"The Israelis pulled off their operation like a movie script," Diamond told Ryder. "I never heard about any fuel-problem snag."

"It wasn't a snag," Ryder told the officer. "The Israelis expected it. They flew more than three thousand miles to Entebbe. They flew through thunderstorms, they had to fly low. They burned up a lot of gas, especially their lead transport. So they figured on it."

"What did they do?" Diamond asked. "Bring extra fuel?"

"No, they brought along a big fuel pump," Ryder answered. "And a bunch of technicians. While the Israeli paratroopers were taking on the terrorists and freeing the hostages, these technical guys were pumping aviation fuel out of the tanks at Entebbe Airport, and into the Israeli aircraft."

Diamond lit a new cigarette from his old one. "And you think we can do the same thing," he said.

"I think we can try it," Ryder told him. "You've got water pumps in your tech units. One of them will do for the fuel-transfer operation, we can bring a backup just in case. It'll ruin them; but that's a minor matter."

Diamond unconsciously dragged his dirty fingernails across his unshaved face.

"Getting the empty airplanes there is one thing," he said. "But your idea of getting the troops there—well, that's another. If the wrong eyes see it—or if the guys inside the terminal catch on—then we *all* lose. Our careers will be ruined."

Ryder just shook his head.

"Let me ask you a question," he said to Diamond as the man lit yet another cigarette. "What were the last orders you received from C-Two?"

Diamond was puffing up a small storm. "To withdraw in an orderly fashion," he said with no little bitterness.

"Do you know what my orders were?" Ryder asked him. "They were for me and my colleagues to be 'innovative.' To face extraordinary situations with contingency planning. That's what's happening here."

Diamond was already chewing his Marlboro down to the filter.

"And what's in it for you, Colonel?" Diamond asked him for what Ryder supposed was the tenth time in less than an hour.

"All I want is a chance to get inside one of those small civilian airplanes out there," Ryder told him. "If one has enough fuel in it for where I want to go, then, once you guys are gone and your operation is over, I leave in the civvie."

"And if everything goes wrong?" Diamond asked.

All Ryder had to do was nod toward the permanent glare of the northern sky and quote the Gray army artilleryman, Major "Oily" Welles.

" 'Then, we tread water until the tidal wave hits . . .' "

62

HOREE

Scotty Whitman laid his Zoot AK-47 assault weapon aside and pulled out his wallet.

Hidden away among his dozen or so credit cards was an identification card encased in plastic. It had his photo on it (it was an old one, before he got his hair curled and dyed blond), his full name, height, weight, hair color, eye color.

It also contained his alias: Federwebel Baader.

It was such a hell of a name, he had to look at it once or twice a day, just to remember the damn thing.

Whitman worked for the U.S. Treasury Department; specifically he was in training for the Secret Service presidential-protection contingent. A Summa Cum Laude graduate of Yale, with a double major in law enforcement and finance, Whitman had been overjoyed when he was first hired by Treasury less than a year before. It was in many ways a dream come true. The pay was good, the work promised to be glamorous and he'd always been enamored by the Georgetown Volvo-Perrier and Brie lifestyle.

So the last place he expected to find himself was in the middle of the Nevada desert.

It was explained to him that the unusual assignment stemmed from his security check. He'd passed with flying colors, a testament to his squeaky-clean lifestyle. And that was the problem: he was too clean. When the Pentagon went scouring various computers looking for government employees who could perform unusual, high-security assignments, Whitman's name popped out.

So now he was a "situation representer" which was government-speak for an actor. His role was that of a terrorist, specifically one who had engineered the hijacking of an airliner to an isolated third-world airport, and was holding the passengers as hostages.

And that's exactly what he was doing.

He, along with eight other situation representers had been holding forty-four "hostages," including two legitimate airline pilots, at the fake airport for two weeks.

In that time, they'd been fairly comfortable – they were holding the hostages in a replica of a vast modern airport terminal, which was equipped with literally dozens of television sets, vending machines, and video games. There were several airports shops – concession stands, bookstores, even a bar, and five separate rest-room areas.

The hostages – they too were government employees with outstanding security records – were each assigned a comfortable bed (not a bunk), plenty of locker space, and clean clothing each day. There was even a twenty-five-person support group at the terminal, who cooked, cleaned, and basically looked after the participants in this strange play.

The trouble was that they'd been at it for more than two weeks now, eleven days longer than they'd been led to believe they'd be on the site.

In that time, Whitman and the other "terrorists" had entered into many discussions as to why the exercise was lasting so long. Theories ranged from a bureaucratic foul-up to suggestions that things were actually going along as their handlers had planned and that they, the situation representers, were actually being "tested," for loyalty, for endurance.

Their original plan was to keep the hostages inside the new terminal building until the rescue force arrived. When that happened, Whitman and his colleagues were to hold off the rescuers for as long as possible – using the cleverly designed weapons they'd come to know as Zoots. Then, they would eventually cave in, the hostages would be "rescued," and they would all go home.

Whitman was a follower. He was happy to go along with the script, do what he was told, kill time by reading Wingman books, and, once the rescue force arrived, put up a good fight and then "die." The sooner this happened, the sooner he'd get back to his Volvo, his girlfriend, and his Georgetown apartment.

But some of the other SRs had become more zealous as time went on. They'd begun planning ways to not just put up a good fight against the rescuers, but to actually defeat their aims at freeing the hostages.

And that's why Whitman was checking his SR-ID. After much pressure and persuasion, he'd finally thrown in with the zealots. They had changed the situation drastically that morning. When the rescue force did arrive—that is, if they were still coming—then they would find an entirely different scenario than what they probably expected.

Whitman returned his ID to his wallet, picked up his Zoot AK-47 again, and resumed his watch at the main doors of the new terminal building. Outside were the three airliners, the batch of smaller private planes, the deserted runways, and the vast empty desert beyond. Nothing had changed.

"Federwebel Baader," Whitman whispered slowly. "Feeder-We-Bell Baa-Der . . ."

Such a dumb name.

Ryder sat in the pilot seat of the big Hercules cargo plane, nervously chewing a piece of gum and checking his watch every five seconds or so.

It was more than two hours after sunset, and already the grand plan was ninety minutes behind schedule. He'd been sitting inside the big Herk since 1745 hours, doing last-minute flight checks, and bumming sticks of gum from his copilot, a "retired" CIA guy named Dack.

Dack was the one who'd flown the C-130 into the small airfield, known simply as Forward One. Like everyone else inside the Range, he'd been on this particular assignment about a week longer than he'd anticipated.

It seemed more like a year.

"I'm telling you, this entire government is fucked up," the sixtyish Dack told Ryder. "I don't get paid as regularly as I used to. I don't get my service pension checks on time anymore. I had to wait seven months for my tax refund last year."

Dack had explained to Ryder that he'd been supplementing his various forms of income by ferrying airplanes in and out of War Heaven for a half dozen years. His security clearance and past participation in covert operations made him a good choice for the relatively easy duty.

It wasn't at all difficult for Ryder to convince Dack to let him pilot the C-130. Just like his partner in the second Hercules beside them, Dack had no illusions about his role in any operations out on the Range. As he put it, he was but a "taxi driver," happy to leave the heroics to someone else.

"What the hell are Diamond's guys doing?" Ryder said, checking his watch one more time. "They should have been in position almost two hours ago."

Dack handed him another piece of Wrigley's spearmint.

"You really didn't expect them to pull this off like clockwork, did you?" he asked, unwrapping a stick for himself. "Those guys have been sitting up these hills for two weeks, just trying to keep their hands out of their pants. That major of theirs is wound tighter than a golf ball. He's a glorified second loony, dreaming of general's stars. Them's the worst kind. They're all doomed from the start. Especially with the new development."

That "new development" was shining very brightly on the northern horizon. It was the advance elements of the mystery army that had been battering its way toward the hills where Diamond's troops were quartered for the past ten hours. Just by eyeballing the intensity of the Zoot explosions, Ryder estimated that the juggernaut appeared to be right over the next hill, no more than ten miles away at the most.

"They'll probably be here before Diamond gets his guys in position," Dack said. "Maybe that's best for all of us. It's my ticket home. I don't know about all you regular-service guys, though."

Ryder was quickly coming around to Dack's way of thinking. Major Diamond had been moody at best in preparing his troops for the upcoming crucial operation. At times Ryder could almost see that dark little cloud over the officer's head as he ripped out stream upon stream of orders to this men, only to contradict them minutes later. It had slowed everything down. And while the precious minutes slipped away for the 9th and Ryder, the mystery army had been drawing ever nearer.

Ryder knew some of the blame was his. The bold plan he'd proposed to Diamond might have been just a little too innovative, especially for a stale force like the 9th Battalion.

Although the original operation plan called for the C-130s to actually be carrying a combined rescue force of ninety men, the only cargo inside the big Herks' bays were two water pumps, one in each airplane. What had taken so long was that Diamond's men had to

walk to the site of the airport Fitzie. It was but one of the rules violations that were necessary for Ryder's plan to work. Yet if they were
somehow detected, the entire operation could be rendered null and
void. And if that happened, Ryder would be virtually stranded on the
Range, far from Tango, and even farther from his eventual goal of
reaching Area 61. And standing right in front of the wave of invaders
from the north.

"He's just an unlucky person," Dack was saying, referring to Diamond. "He's got the wrong last name."

As if to underscore that point, Ryder looked past the Zoot glow to
the north and over to the west, and saw through the darkening night
what looked like a thunderstorm moving into the area.

"It actually *rains* out here?" he asked incredulously, pointing out
the cloud mass to Dack.

"It sure does," the grizzled veteran replied. "About once every
hundred years."

Just then the cockpit radio crackled to life.

"Nine in position," was the simple message.

Ryder and Dack looked at each other in amazement. It was the
message they'd been awaiting for hours.

"They made it?" Dack asked, bewildered. "They *actually* made
it?"

"I guess so," Ryder replied. "So let's get the hell out of here."

They had a lightning-quick conversation with the second C-130
and, on a given signal, started their aircrafts' engines simultaneously.

As planned, they only allowed themselves a very brief, three-min-
ute engine warmup before they moved out from under the camouflaged berms and onto the small airstrip. Each Hercules had only
enough gas in its tanks to takeoff and fly for eight minutes—and no
more. This despite the fact that just about every piece of unnecessary
equipment on each airplane had been taken off to reduce their weight
and thus conserve fuel.

The second Herk went first, its extremely-light flying weight
helping it zoom off the makeshift runway in nearly half the usual
takeoff roll.

Ryder and Dack went next. Lining up the nose of the C-130 with
the middle of dirt airstrip, Ryder gunned the engines to full power
and felt the big plane jerk forward.

347

Suddenly there were three flashes off to his left. Out of the corner of his eye he picked out the distinct shape of the trio of incoming Zoot Copperhead artillery shells, smartbombs fired by the huge mobile guns of the mystery army.

Ryder yanked back on the cargo plane's control column and literally jerked the big plane into the air. Just as the wheels were leaving the ground, the three Copperheads came smashing down on the makeshift runway mere feet from the back of the airplane.

Two seconds earlier, they would have nailed the C-130 head-on.

Scotty Chapman – aka Federwebel Baader – was standing outside near the main runway when the rain began.

He couldn't believe it – no one at the HOREE could. The last thing they'd expected on this hot night was a thunderstorm. Yet here it was, a desert tempest blowing in from the west, its crashing thunder and brilliant lightning rivaling the unnatural holographic booming and flashing off to the north.

They'd heard rumors about what all the excitement was up north; something about a huge battle of some kind between many of the regular training units and some new entity on the Range. But as far as he knew, that action had little effect on him, or on any of the people at the HOREE.

They were just a sideshow here.

Scotty took off his rather shabby cap and let the rain hit his face, his neck, his badly dyed blond hair. It felt very cool, very wet, very natural, unlike anything he'd encountered since coming to this place.

But wait a second – something was wrong here . . .

Peering across the main runway, he saw first one, then two, then at least five people, standing in the ditch on the far side of the main runway.

At first Chapman thought they might be other situation representers, but in a few seconds he knew this was not the case. He was almost a hundred yards from the new terminal building, and he couldn't imagine anyone else from the fake airport being further out than he. Besides, these people in the ditch looked like soldiers; they were wearing helmets and uniforms and carrying rifles and other weapons.

But what were they doing out there? In the rain, yet?

While he was contemplating this, he heard a low rumbling sound, which he mistook for thunder.

Turning to the north, he saw a pair of airplanes heading out of the glow of the north and heading right for him. They were big and green and moving very fast and very low. They were so low, in fact, that for one horrifying moment, he thought they were both going to crash.

But then he saw that their wheels were down, as were their flaps. Their huge propellers were still spinning, whipping through the rain so quickly that they were creating long funnels of water and smoke behind them.

Were they coming in for a landing?

He watched with slacked jaw as the two big airplanes did indeed touch down and scream to the end of the main runway. At exactly the same time, the five men he'd seen standing in the ditch leapt up onto the airstrip and began charging right at him.

These soldiers were joined by five more. And then ten more. Twenty, forty, fifty! Jumping up out of the ditch and running toward the new terminal, their Zoot weapons up and gleaming in the night from the reflection of the rain.

"Shit," Chapman cursed, trying to get his feet to move. "This is it."

But where could he go? He took two steps to his left and saw that another line of troops were coming right at him from that direction. Two steps to his right and saw that the first airplane was now taking a 180-degree turn and heading right for the front of the new terminal building.

This left him only one direction to go to get out of harm's immediate way.

With a burst of speed he hadn't enjoyed since his jogging days along the Potomac, he spun around and began running for the old terminal building.

Both Ryder and Dack were fighting the controls of the C-130 Hercules. One by one its engines died away, drained of fuel and quickly losing inertia.

With the loss of the engines, so too went much of the electrical and hydraulic power on board the Hercules. No sooner had Ryder turned the C-130 toward the new terminal building then the big airplane began to win the battle of wills. The propellers fluttered, the landing gear began to screech. Halfway to their goal of pulling up right in front of the new terminal building's front doors, the big Herk rolled to a stop.

"The fat lady just sang," Dack said, locking down the rest of the systems. "I thought we'd get a little more roll out of her."

They both unstrapped from their seats and were out of the airplane just as the vanguard of Diamond's troopers was approaching at full tilt. All pretense that the soldiers had arrived at the airport via the C-130s – a necessary technical point if the operation was to be determined "successful" – was lost in the sudden downpour and the crash of the thunder. Caught up in the excitement of the moment, the soldiers of 9th Battalion were running straight across the open tarmac toward the new terminal, instead of coming up on it from the flank, as they would have had they actually been disgorged from the airplane.

It made little difference now. Ryder and Dack fell into the stream of soldiers, who, Zoot rifles up high, crashed through the doors of the new terminal building and into its main concourse.

But there was one problem: the place was empty.

Ten minutes later

By the time Scotty Chapman reached the top of the control tower of the old terminal building, the rain had stopped.

Crouching along the outside railing of the 55-foot-high tower, he watched the rescue force burst out the back doors of the new terminal building and charge, en masse, toward the old terminal building.

"Fascinating . . ." Chapman whispered, as the first Zoot tracer rounds erupted from the old terminal building, fired by his SR colleagues toward the rescue force.

In just a few seconds, a huge, confusing holographic gunfight was in full rage. Most of the rescue force had hit the ground and were firing their Zoot weapons – and orange-colored tracers – at the front of the old terminal building. Meanwhile the green-tinged tracers from his fellow hostage-takers were ricocheting crazily around the courtyard that separated the two terminals. All the while, the lightning and the last traces of the thunderstorm boomed in the background.

350

The gambit proposed by the zealot SRs had worked. Just that morning they had moved all the "hostages" from the new terminal building, where they had spent the last fourteen days in relative comfort, into the old terminal where conditions were much less accommodating. It had taken much cajoling, and a few threats, to convince the professional hostages to make the move.

Now, from the SR's point of view at least, the effort seemed to have been worth it.

He watched the spectacular firefight for several minutes, fascinated by the controlled, rather harmless fury of it all. But then, he didn't know why, his attention was drawn back toward the main taxiway in front of the new terminal. There he saw four men struggling with a piece of heavy machinery next to the newly arrived airplanes. Two of the men were dragging the machine across the tarmac, while two more were unfurling long lengths of hose just like fire fighters preparing to battle a house ablaze.

As Chapman watched mystified, the men moved closer to the 747 airliner, struggling with both the uncooperative hose lines and the bulky piece of machinery. Finally they reached the underwing of the airliner, and with the shaky precision of a bad carnival act, two men boosted a third up to a spot near the wheel well of the airplane.

This man fiddled around with something near the wheels and then clearly gave a thumbs-up signal to the other three men. He crawled on top of the wing itself, and the other three men threw a length of hose up to him. He unplugged a cap of some sort from the top of the wing and inserted the hose in its place. This done, the men below attached the other end of the hose to the machine and then began straightening out the 150 feet or so of hose that stretched back to the first rescue airplane.

At this moment, the little sideshow made sense to Chapman.

"They need gas . . ." he whispered to himself.

There had been a few moments of initial confusion when the rescue force had burst through the doors of the new terminal building. Finding it empty after a quick search, Diamond's men at first thought that they'd either hit the wrong HOREE or that it had been abandoned.

But a check of the map told them that the smaller, older building to

351

the rear of the new terminal was in fact large enough to hold the hostages. A quick recon of the building via NightScope goggles confirmed that the hostages were in fact gathered just inside its main doors.

As the rescue force regrouped and prepared to assault the second building, Dack had pulled Ryder aside, along with the other two pilots from the second Herk and suggested that they get about the more important business of pumping fuel out of the airliners.

An old hand at getting the down-and-dirty work done, Dack began firing off orders like a drill sergeant and Ryder and the other flyers were happy to comply. Within ten short minutes, the hoses were connected, the first pump was pumping and the fuel tanks of Herk number one were being replenished.

Just as the jimmy-rigged refueling operation was winding down, there was a series of Zoot explosions in front of the old terminal building. Carefully making his way through the deserted new building to the courtyard, Ryder was somewhat surprised to see that the 9th Battalion troopers had prevailed and were now in control of the old terminal building as well.

He met a jubilant Major Diamond just as the first line of hostages were being led out of the old building.

"A million thanks," Diamond told him, with a shaky smile. "Even with the resupply system screwed up, I'm sure they'll have to give us enough points for this to get us all out of here."

"That's what everyone wants—" Ryder replied.

At that instant there was one loud crack from a Zoot rifle. Suddenly, Diamond's body began to shake.

He went down to his knees, his HILES Zoot-detection meter vibrating and beeping. He couldn't believe it: he'd just been "killed."

"God damn," he screamed. "After all this?"

There was a scattering of return fire toward the tower of the old terminal building, but even above the simulated popping of the Zoot rifles, a high, shrill voice could be heard.

"Okay, that's it!" someone on top of the tower was yelling down at them. "Stop it, right now! This whole thing is fucked up."

Ryder grabbed one of the SR terrorists and pointed to the man with the designer glasses who was screaming down from the tower, the same man who'd "killed" Major Diamond.

"Who the hell is that?" Ryder asked the SP.

The man looked up to the tower and shrugged.

"That's Federwebel Baader," he replied.

Ten minutes later, a huge argument was taking place in the court-yard between the two buildings.

There were two major combatants: the "deceased" Major Dia-mond and the SR named Federwebel Baader. Surrounding the two contestants in various stages of interest were the eight other "terror-ists," the forty-four bored hostages, and the hundred or so troopers of the 9th Battalion rescue force.

The disagreement was based on one point of contention. Baader was claiming that the entire rescue operation was null and void. Why? He'd seen the empty airplanes land. He'd seen the troopers emerge from the ditches next to the runway. He'd spied the refueling operation.

According to him, all three were clear violations of the rules of engagement for the HOREE.

Just as shrill was Diamond. With no facts to back him up, his only tactic seemed to be to outshout the younger man.

Standing off to the side, alternately amused and frustrated by the bizarre scene, were Ryder and Dack.

"Did I tell you?" Dack said, reeking of the smell of aviation fuel, pointing to Diamond. "That guy is a jinx."

The disagreement quickly escalated into name-calling and even some pushing and shoving. Many of the professional hostages drifted back into the new terminal building, back to the place they'd come to love; others simply sat out in the cool air of the open court-yard and watched the heated discussion like it was a prize fight. The other SR's found a corner and began discussing their colleague's actions, while the members of the 9th Battalion stood at ease nearby, not knowing quite what to do.

"I don't have time for this crap," Ryder finally said to Dack.

He pointed to the ever-increasing Zoot glow off to the north. "Those guys are only about twenty-five miles from here by now. They'll be able to start popping with long-range stuff at any time, and their advance units will be here by midmorning. Now, I don't want to be here when they do. No one does."

"These guys need a referee," Dack said in agreement.

Ryder stepped forward and grabbed Diamond's clenched fist just as he was about to launch it toward Baader's chin.

"Can I make a suggestion?" he asked.

"Please do," Diamond replied. "Before I'm forced to kick the shit out of the puppy."

Ryder got between the two and took a deep breath.

"You guys are arguing about the wrong thing," he said.

"What the hell do you mean?" Diamond demanded.

"You both want the same thing," Ryder told them. "And that's to get the hell out of here, am I right?

Both men nodded sheepishly.

"And while you're jawing about whether the Rescue Force won this engagement or not," Ryder went on, "you're both missing a very key point."

"Which is?" Baader asked.

"Which is this," Ryder said. "According to your rules of engagement book, what happens if the rescue force *fails* to release the hostages?"

Both Baader and Diamond took pause at the question.

"You mean if the terrorists *win?*" Baader asked.

"Exactly," Ryder replied.

Baader just shrugged. "Well, then, I guess we can do whatever the hell we want, staying within the guidelines, of course."

"And what is one of the options a real terrorist group might take?"

Again Baader could only shrug. "Kill the hostages is one, I suppose," he said. "Make more demands, I guess.

"Or . . ." Ryder prompted the man.

"Or . . . move them to another location," Baader said, as if a light had suddenly gone on.

"Bingo," Ryder replied.

It was daylight by the time all of the hostages were lined up on the tarmac, their meager baggage at their side, all of them anxious to move on.

Not 200 feet away, one of the hostage pilots was running up the electrical power on the Boeing 727 airliner, while the other was going about his preflight ground check.

In line next to the hostages were the fifty members of Diamond's rescue force who had volunteered to become "prisoners." In return for this gesture, Baader and the other SR's agreed that it would be in sync with the guidelines for the rest of the rescue force to be flown out in the newly refueled C-130s.

The final point hammered out in the plan concerned the remainder of the 9th Battalion waiting about a half mile away. They were to move overland and "attack" the empty air base. After finding nothing, they could "liberate" the fuel sitting in the two other airliners. This fuel could then be used in the C-130s to ferry them to a location in the southernmost part of the Range. This entire action was deemed "correct" by all parties as it showed innovation in the face of adversity.

In return for playing the role of peacemaker, Ryder got what he wanted all along: access to one of the civilian airplanes at the HOREE.

He selected the best of the lot: a relatively new Piper Cub PA-18. It had just about everything he needed: a full gas tank, long-range capability, and the ability to take off on short and unpaved runways. If everything went right, it would do very well to get him to Tango Base.

However, the Piper did have one thing Ryder didn't need: A HILES Zoot detector device. He was surprised when he first spotted it during his engine inspection of the airplane, but at the same time, he knew he shouldn't have been. Every piece of machinery inside the Range was Zoot-equipped. There was no reason the small civilian airplane should be any different.

The sun had been up for one hour when the 727 finally began taxiing out to the main runway.

In a cloud of smoke and exhaust, It finally lifted off, climbing steeply into the sky, its hold filled with "hostages," "prisoners," and the no-doubt-triumphant situation representers. It turned south finally, destination unknown.

Ryder taxied the Piper out on the main runway, and took off a minute later.

63

Maureen rolled out of bed and hastily scratched a line on the wall behind her.

It was the nineteenth such scratch, but she couldn't swear to the accuracy of her crude calendar anymore. So much had happened lately, at all hours, that her body clock was no longer set to the normal 24-hour period. The days were running into each other, overlapping each other. Though she was fairly certain that it was now morning, she'd lost a precise count of day and night back around scratch number sixteen.

She wasn't so sure it mattered anymore. The POW instinct that drove her to begin the calendar in the first place was now nearly dissipated. Although her apartment door was still locked—electronically, from the outside—she didn't feel so much like a prisoner anymore.

She owed it all to her "deal" with Walter. After the mysterious lingerie incident, he'd become a changed man.

Her pile of filled tape cassettes was now rivaling her pile of filled reporter's notebooks. The amount of material she'd amassed was mind-boggling. Much more than she'd ever dreamed of, just a few wall scratches ago. Her idea of producing a series of bombshell newspaper stories had already evolved into an idea of producing a bombshell book.

And though she was almost loath to admit it, she knew the idea of a bombshell movie deal was not far off on the horizon. She was certain that her agent would be all for it.

She took a quick bath, toweled off, and climbed into a clean pair of overalls. She began to dry her hair, sitting close to her door so as not to miss the knock that would signal the delivery of what she hoped would be her breakfast meal.

That was another thing that had changed; She was definitely getting her appetite back.

More than an hour later, she was still waiting.

She'd spent the time going over her notes, preparing questions for her interview later that day – this one with a second pilot of the so-called "Operation Rapture" – and wondering what the hell was wrong in the world outside her locked door.

Everything was usually so punctual in the Area 61 facility that she couldn't imagine something so important as one of her meals being so delayed.

Finally, after another ninety minutes, she heard the light tapping at her door.

She walked over and turned the handle, waiting for the electric buzz that she'd come to know as the sound of her bolt being withdrawn from the other side. She pulled the door open to find the pleasant, shy young man who had acted all along as her food and laundry delivery person.

He was empty-handed, though. No meal tray, no bundle of laundry.

What's more, the hallway, which was usually brightly illuminated twenty-four hours a day, was now dim, shadowy, ominous. A siren was blaring somewhere, and she could hear people shouting in the distance.

"What's going on?" she asked the young man immediately. "Is something wrong?"

"Everything is wrong," he told her, his voice desperate. "You better come with me."

Though he was nervous and fidgeting, Maureen could tell the young man was deadly serious.

"Where? *Why?*"

"Please, I can't explain," he pleaded with her, nervously looking up and down the darkened corridor. "If we hesitate even a minute, it may be too late."

Common sense was telling her to stay put, but her gut instinct was telling her to go. Something big was obviously going on in the facility.

She turned to grab her tapes and notebooks, but the young man grabbed her arm instead and yanked her out of the room.

"There's no time!" he yelled, almost in her ear. "Just get some clothes."

She instinctively grabbed her old laundry bundle next to the door and pulled it out into the hallway. An instant later, the door slammed shut automatically, and locked itself. Down the hall, she could hear echoes of other doors slamming in a similar fashion. It sounded exactly like a lockdown in a prison.

What is happening?" she shouted at him.

"They're ordering everything into the NBC mode," he yelled back, as he literally dragged her and her laundry bag down the dark hallway. "They're sealing everything!"

They ran down the corridor, even as more of the lights were blinking out and the sirens got louder. The young man led her to an unmarked door and forced it open. On the other side was a staircase, the only one she'd ever seen in the place. From the signs on its walls, and the banisters, Maureen gathered that it was actually a fire escape.

"They had to build it!" the young man yelled back to her. "It was government regulations."

They ran down seven flights of stairs, which by Maureen's calculations brought them one level lower than the floor where the alleged alien crypt was located.

The young man paused for a moment at another door, opening it slowly and checking the much smaller, dark hallway beyond. It was all clear. He told Maureen to follow him, and they walked down the nearly pitch-black hallway to another nondescript door.

The young man produced a key and unlocked the slide bolt. He gently nudged Maureen inside, followed her in, and closed the door behind him.

It was totally dark inside, and several terrifying seconds passed for Maureen as the young man groped for the light switch. He finally found it and snapped it on.

They were in a TV studio—large, well-maintained, well equipped.

"You'll be safe here," he told her, his voice shaky and out of breath. "At least for a while."

She grabbed his hands and held them tight.

"Please tell me what's going on," she demanded. "What the hell is an NBC mode?"

"Nuclear-biological-chemical weapons," he replied hastily. "They've sealed up the entire facility. But it can't be for a legitimate NBC reason – it's too early. It must be for something else . . . something that is happening on the outside. I don't know what, but it has to be very, very serious for them to take this step."

They walked into the studio's vast control room and the young man began flipping a series of switches. There were twenty-four different TV monitors on one wall of the huge control room, banks of telephone and computers on another.

"What is this place?" she asked him.

He replied by pushing a single button on the control board. Suddenly all two dozen TV screens came to life.

In an instant Maureen was subjected to a barrage of images. Some were outside shots, others interiors, still other displaying data screens.

"There's a place further out on the Range that they call 'the Eye,' " the young man explained. "This place, they call 'the Spy.'

"There are more than one hundred hidden cameras inside this facility. And many more out on the Range itself. You can monitor every single one of them from here, as well as almost all the data readout screens from the Cray supercomputer."

Maureen studied the screens and, indeed, on half of them she could see people rushing about in offices and hallways, some of which she recognized instantly. On another row of screens there were shots from dozens of locations from the outside: the desert, hills, buttes. Seeing these was almost like a new experience for her; she hadn't seen the outside world now in almost three weeks.

"I have to leave you here," the young man told her suddenly. "You'll be safe, believe me."

"But why? And for how long?"

He shook his head quickly; obviously he was very anxious to go.

"I don't know," he replied. "But I will be back. And when I do, I will try to get you out of here completely."

"Out?" she asked, "You can get me to the outside world?"

"I think so," he replied nervously. "But I have to go now and make sure.

"While I'm gone, I suggest you monitor these screens closely. They can tell you the truth about this place. The real truth. Everything. Where they've been lying to you and where they've been telling you the truth."

"But wait," she said, pulling him back into the control room. "How? How do I do it?"

He pointed to the long double line of buttons running the length of the control board.

"Push any one of these buttons and you can look into just about any office or work area in this place," he told her. "You can look in on them, but they won't know you are doing it. The other buttons are for outside shots."

Maureen quickly studied the control board and the monitors and then turned back to the young man, who was now almost out of his socks, he wanted to leave so badly.

"What did you mean that it was 'too early' to seal everything up?" she asked him, almost desperately. "What are they planning on doing down here? I *have* to know."

The young man was beside himself by this time. "Do you know about the Big Blast? About the Black Hole?" he asked frantically.

She shook her head no, three times.

The young man took deep breath. "They are planning on detonating a nuclear device underground, very close to this facility, very soon," he said, talking as quickly as humanly possible. "It's all part of this grand experiment having to do with making a power source for the flying saucer up on the hangar level. You did see that didn't you?"

Maureen eagerly nodded. "Is it real?" she asked him.

He shrugged nervously. "I have to assume it is," he replied. "But I am sure that this Big Blast they've been preparing for will happen very, very soon. It will be detonated in a place called the Black Hole. And when it does, it will be impossible to get out of here. That's why I have to go . . . *right now.*"

"Why are you doing this?" she asked him. "I'm sure if they find out, you'll be—"

The young man held his hand up to cut her off.

"Please, I know what will happen to me," he told her. "But it's worth it . . . at least, I hope it is."

"What do you mean?"

He stood still just for one moment and stared at the floor, painfully searching for the right words.

"I have a confession," he said finally. "And an apology. I was the one who delivered that bag of women's underwear to your apartment. And it was not totally by accident."

"You'll have to explain that to me," Maureen told him. "Who did all that stuff belong to?"

He looked at his watch, and then turned to go. "I'm sorry," he said over his shoulder. "I don't have time to explain it. You'll have to find out for yourself."

"But *wait* . . ."

"I'll be back," he called over his shoulder.

And he was out the door and gone.

64

Although War Heaven contained dozens of Fitzies, hundreds of miles of roads, and thousands of men, it was, in the end, mostly desert.

Few maps existed of the place – few items were so classified in the murky world of the U.S. military's black operations. And though Ryder had spent much time out on the Range, it was impossible to know every butte, mesa, wash, and wadi. There were only a handful of navigation guides: The mountainous northwest region, known as the Ponderosa; the barren hills of the southwest; the pure "low" desert of the southeast; and the rugged, scrub-brush high desert of the northeast.

These, and the four points of the compass, were the only road map Ryder had at his disposal.

Soon after taking off from HOREE, he brought the tiny Piper Cub PA-18 up to 1000 feet and turned due west, the general direction of Tango. From this height, he hoped to spot landmarks that would give him a relative fix on his position: a particularly robust section of Desert Highway 66 would be the first thing to look for. Once he'd reached that, he could follow it north until he reached the neutral-zone valley where Jacks was located. From there, his old deployment, Spookbase, was just over the hill and then Tango Base was about forty-five miles northwest of that.

He had no trouble at all orientating himself as to which way was north; even on this bright morning, the glow from the advancing mystery army was lighting up the northern horizon, even more brilliantly than the day before.

The sight of this glow filled his being with a renewed sense of urgency. He'd just missed getting nailed by them while taking off in the big Herk, and he was sure that the HOREE was probably under their attack by now. Tango was also close to the north sector of the Range, most of which was obviously in the hands of the invaders. Translation: He had to make it to Tango before the mystery army did.

Almost unconsciously, he pushed the airplane's throttles ahead slightly. Time was running out.

The Piper Cub was easy to fly, and the weather was perfect. The wind was blowing west to east, of course, jostling the small plane, as if it was floating on a slightly choppy sea, but Ryder didn't mind. It was like the difference between driving a Jeep and a Cadillac.

He flew for about twenty minutes before he spotted the unmistakable black asphalt of Desert Highway 66. As he spied it from a distance of about fifteen miles, he supposed it was probably an auxiliary artery, as it wound through two twin mesas. But auxiliary or not, he got a surprise as soon as he was close enough to see the roadway in detail.

It was packed. Jammed. Absolutely gridlocked with military vehicles of all types. Tanks. Bradleys. LAVs. Old APCs. Mobile artillery. Hummers. Even tractor-trailer trucks. The vehicles looked mostly to be part of the Gray army, though he could clearly see some Green force equipment mixed in. There were also hundreds of soldiers on the roadway, they too mostly Gray army, with some Green troops in evidence. And like the honking, snarling vehicles, all of the soldiers were heading in the same direction: south.

Quite involuntarily, Ryder felt a lump form in his throat. What he was witnessing was not the usual traffic jam that one saw on Highway 66 daily. This was a retreat.

And not a very orderly one at that.

He overflew the clogged highway once and then turned north and climbed up to 3000 feet. He tried to tell himself that he recognized the low range of low hills just off to his left, but in a place the size of Connecticut, that was like looking at the outskirts of Hartford and thinking it might be New Haven.

He flew on, over the hills, past another series of buttes, and across a huge dry lakebed, which could have been the place they called Big Mouse, because it looked like a small head with two big ears.

He decided to circle back around and see if it was in fact Big Mouse. If it was, then he knew he was about thirty miles east of Jacks, and that much closer to Tango.

He slowed down to about eighty knots and banked to his left, beginning a slow spiral down to 1500 feet.

That's when he saw them . . .

There were two of them.

They were just specks, almost directly above him, at about 10 o'clock but coming right at him.

"I don't believe this," he said, even as he began a steep bank back to the right.

He put the Piper into a skin-stretching dive, heading at full throttle for the cover of the low mountain range he had just passed over. He was down to just 150 feet off the deck and pushing the engine to its maximum of 200 knots. But one look over his left shoulder told him that the two specks had now grown in size dramatically.

He tried jinking back and forth, but he knew this would be a useless maneuver. He reached the hills, but found they offered little protection from his pursuers. With little other choice, he banked back out over the flat open desert and poured on the coals.

But it was of no use.

Another look over his shoulder told him that the two big F-5 Aggressors were swooping in for the kill.

"God damn you guys!" he yelled as the first barrage of Zoot cannon shells ripped by him.

He yanked the Cub to the right, and managed to dodge a second and third burst from the lead F-5. Then pulling to the left, he cut back on his power to near stall speed. The intended effect was quick: the all-black F-5 rocketed by him, its momentum carrying it past the slowed-down Piper.

As it streaked by, he was able to make out its tiny tail insignia. It was from the Aggressor Alpha Squadron.

"Fucking Alphas," he yelled again. "You pussys must be hard up."

By this time, the flight leader had recovered from his initial misses, and was lined up on his tail. One long burst from his Zoot cannon was all it took. Ryder could almost feel the holographic shells passing right through him. Their signals did impact on the Piper's HILES Zoot detector and instantly, the little airplane's tiny engine began to buck.

He felt the controls begin to freeze up, and he began to lose altitude. The pair of F-5s were long gone by this time, rocketing away to the south as soon as they determined that the flight leader's barrage had done its job. Now it was up to Ryder to find a safe landing spot — and quick.

He had just made it up and over a deep wadi when he spotted a fairly straight dirt road about two miles to his left. Beyond it was a steep line of mountains that rose up dramatically from the desert floor. Other than that, there was absolutely nothing but flat, empty scorched landscape.

It took much of his piloting expertise just to put the Piper Cub on a proper landing approach. In theory, the Zoot computer on board would prevent him from landing the airplane in anything other than a safe manner, but now as he was literally plummeting toward the roadway, his faith in the omnipotent super-duper HILES system was fading fast. He hit the road about ten feet too short, bounced up, came back down with the left wing clipping a mangled tree trunk. Another bounce, another hard impact, and the left wheel strut broke away, putting the airplane in a spinning skid. The cockpit windshield shattered in on him, and the steering yoke broke away from the rest of the control column. The airplane lurched forward, catching the sputtering propeller in the hard dirt of the roadway and cracking it in half, pitching the small plane up on its nose and finally to a halt.

Somehow Ryder was able to kick open the passenger-side door and painfully squeeze his thrice-battered body out of the cockpit. He hit the roadway headfirst, then rolled over into the trench, just as the fuel tank on the Piper blew up.

When he looked up out of the trench, the airplane was totally engulfed in flames.

Ryder had faced the desert before.

Shortly before his first deployment to the weapons range, he'd been dropped off on the edge of the Mojave Desert as part of his pre-Distant Thunder mission survival training. Ignoring just about all of the basic training tenets of how to survive in the desert, he'd simply decided to walk his way out, without eating any lizards or bugs or drinking his own urine or sucking the dew out of cacti.

Now he was faced with a walk in the desert once again. But things were different this time. He was hurt—the bumps and bruises and cuts and scraps were beginning to add up and take their toll. He hadn't eaten in a while. He had no water, not even a hat.

The sharp-edged mountain he'd spotted earlier was about three miles away. There were trees there, and trees meant shade and maybe water or food. Or lizards. Or bugs.

Either way, he knew he would have to make it before the heat of the day became dangerously brutal.

So he began walking. Channeling his negative vengeful thoughts of the Alpha Squadron into positive ones about Maureen.

With any luck, he thought, he'd reach the mountain in less than an hour.

65

Lt. Colonel Randy Wilkes unhooked his oxygen mask and scratched his three-day growth of beard.

He hated not being able to shave, or wash, or do many of the morning things he'd done every day since entering military service. There was a term for it that had come out of the Persian Gulf war. They called it "military poverty." But back then it referred to the dirty, sickly, bug-infested Iraqi troops that had been left out to starve in the trenches in southern Kuwait.

Now, that description quite nearly applied to him.

Wilkes was a pilot for Beta Squadron of the Aggressor force. His base, located almost in the exact center of the weapons range, had not had a supply drop of any consequence in almost a week. Necessities that he and his colleagues had taken for granted – soap, shaving crew, razors, even toilet paper – had become quickly nonexistent. There was little potable water, no food beyond ancient MREs, and the electricity-producing generators at the base were so low on fuel that burning lights was restricted to one hour a day.

Everyone knew why Beta Base was in such bad shape – every base and Fitzie on the Range was suffering similar fates. It was because of the mystery army that was moving down from the north and the subsequent monkey wrench it had thrown into the infrastructure of War Heaven. What it all meant was beyond discussion now at Beta Base. Whether it was some kind of an elaborate drill or whether something actually *was* wrong with C2 didn't make much difference anymore. The pilots at Beta were living in depraved conditions and they were pissed about it.

That's why Wilkes was up and flying this day. He had to score some points – on *anything* – just to ensure that Beta would get the minimal supply drop of food and absolute necessities. The odd thing was that, unlike other places, the base had plenty of aviation fuel. It also still had some exotic Zoot weapons left over. But you couldn't drink JP-8, or chew on a holographically projected cannon-shell casing. So Wilkes had to go hunting.

When he first decided that he had to go drop some bombs on somebody or something, Wilkes instructed his ground crew to strap anything they could dig up onto his F-5 up to its full lifting capacity. When he took off, shortly after sunrise, he was carrying four gas bombs under his wings, and full magazines of Zoot shells for his pair of 20-mm M-39A2 nose cannons.

He had no set flight plan, no prestrike briefing. Such things had been out of the question for days, ever since the computers at Beta stopped working for lack of power. So Wilkes had launched knowing he would have to free lance it. He had turned north immediately after takeoff. Climbing up to 40,000 feet, he hoped to get a look at the mystery army that was creating so much havoc on the Range. He needn't have flown so high – or flown at all. Climbing up to the top of the mountain near Beta Base would have sufficed.

The mysterious juggernaut was now no more than fifty miles away, and judging from the storm cloud of dust, smoke, and the flash of Zoot weapons, it was moving very quickly south, toward the vast center of the weapons range.

Even for a veteran like Wilkes – he'd flown 72 sorties during the Gulf war, 12 during Panama – the scene was astonishing. The mystery army was stretched out along an eighty-mile front, apparently firing every weapon in its arsenal to clear its path, whether it was meeting any opposition or not.

It was obvious that in some areas there were defending units fighting back. Before C2 went off the air for good, many of the larger units in the northern Fitzies were holding orders to stand and fight, and judging by the exchanging of missile and rocket fire off in the distance, some were doing just that.

Wilkes was well aware that in the past few days his brother Beta pilots had found slim pickings in looking for targets in the area south of the mystery army's advance. Hitting the flood of units retreating south was considered bad form – besides, the meager supply drops got even thinner if the Zoot engagement devices detected an attack on fairly defenseless withdrawing troops.

So he really only saw two choices for this mission. Go on a hunt-and-peck flight which would in all likelihood produce limited results.

Or . . .

It took Wilkes twenty minutes of high-flying surveillance to select the precise spot for the ambush.

Flat open ground would not do. The F-5 was loaded to the gills with weapons, and therefore its low-level maneuverability was cut down to practically nothing. Hitting something in a rear area was out of the question, too. Nailing one truck or one APC would amount to a drop in the ocean, point-wise.

He knew he not only had to carry out an attack, he had to do something that would make a lot of noise with the people who were controlling what was left of the point-supply system—assuming that was, that someone was still listening.

That's why he selected a place that he'd spotted many times flying over the Range. It was a bend in one of the northernmost auxiliary arteries of Desert Highway 66. It wound itself through a series of high rock formations, then dipped drastically onto a smoother part of the desert terrain.

Even the most reckless driver would have to slow down to a crawl to make the three tight turns necessary to pass through the rock formations and gain access to the desert floor below.

It was here that Wilkes decided he would attack the mystery army.

He knew that *they* knew he was up there peering down at them through his terrain radar and with his plain old eyeballs.

What bothered him was that they didn't seem to care.

He was flying at 27,500 feet in a tight orbit above the Three-Finger Turn, watching as a miles-long convoy of trucks, tanks and APCs rumbled across the high road, down the hill, and onto the desert road.

As far as Wilkes knew, he was the first pilot from Beta to see the mystery army this close. And he soon found out that they were aptly named.

This was not an ordinary armored column. There were tanks, sure. But were they M-1s or M-60s? He couldn't tell. They had turrets and guns and tracks and moved like tanks. But each one was covered with a long camouflage netting that trailed behind it like a woman's long flowing cape.

The same was true for the APCs. They were low and sleek and kicking out a lot of smoke through their green netting. But they moved strangely. Were they really Bradleys? Or LAVs? He couldn't be sure.

Even the support and troop trucks looked odd. They were covered with a darker-color netting, more black than green, but they seemed very low to the ground. Too low. And how the hell did the drivers see out of those windshields?

He checked his fuel load and his weapons delivery computer and knew that he had no more time for sightseeing. He had his target, and he had them at a tactical disadvantage. This meant it was time to attack.

Even as he streaked down from his perch, five miles high, he was amazed to see that the armored column had yet to get a Zoot SAM radar fix on him. He would have known if they had, because his threat-warning tone would have been piercing his eardrums by now. But all he heard was the usual confused far-off jumble of staticky messages that had been just about impossible to decipher even before things had gone down the drain on the Range.

He passed down through 15,000 feet, his weapons-release computer set on automatic, a trio of troop trucks in his HUD sight. He clenched his teeth at 8500 feet. There was still no radar-guided Zoot SAMs keying in on him, nor was he being painted with radar-guided Zoot AAA.

Down to four thousand . . . three . . . two. Weapons-launch computer is clicking. He was going to drop two canisters. He knew at least one of them contained puke gas. That's what these bastards deserved. They'd inhale it and it would be sucked into their stomachs and whatever they'd eaten in the past eight hours would start coming up within seconds. The mass nausea would have to cause some kind of a jam-up on the three-curved turn, and that would have to fuck things up all the way down the line.

And *that* would count for something.

He reached 750 feet and the computers released the laser-guided canisters. He watched them through the HUD as they traveled down the glide path.

Five . . . four . . . three . . . two . . . one.

Pow! Pow!

Two direct hits on the two lead vehicles. Perfect.

He yanked back on the control stick and gave the F-5 full power, intent on flying back around for another attack.

But suddenly the sky was filled with smoke trails. They were firing a barrage of shoulder-launched Zoot SAMs at him! Instinctively he took evasive action, spinning out of the dive and punching out a half dozen flares to confuse heat-seeking warheads on the antiaircraft missiles.

Somehow he made it through the wall of small Zoot SAMs intact. He yanked back again on the controls and went into a near-vertical climb to get out of the attack range of the shoulder-launched missiles.

He looked over his shoulder and saw the smoke rising from his attack, and that the column was in fact grinding to a halt. At that moment he made a quick decision. If he went back in and got hit by the Zoot SAMs, he would lose any points he'd just gained on the flawless attack. If he left now, the point gain would remain intact. Judging from the intensity of the enemy's AA barrage, the second line of reasoning appealed to him the most.

So, with two gas canisters still attached under his wings, he turned around and headed south.

Ryder was about halfway to the jagged-edge mountain when he heard the jet approaching.

He knew it was an F-5 right away. He'd heard that distinctive jet engine sound many times in the past and had come to both love and hate it.

This time he wasn't too sure.

The fighter streaked over, about a half mile to his south, flying up around 5000 feet. The pilot was cutting back on his engine slightly, like he was in the preliminaries for his landing approach. Ryder stopped on the dusty road for a second and strained his eyes to see the insignia on the tail of the airplane. It wasn't one of the hated Alphas. Rather it was from Beta Base. It made no difference either way – he was sure the airplane was flying much too high and much too fast to see him, and therefore there was no chance the pilot would send out a search-and-rescue message.

He turned and began walking again, his eyes set on the large jagged mountain looming before him. If he could climb it, he would set a fire and wait. If no one saw him, then he would hunt for the nearest engagement computer sensor—they were everywhere out on the Range and easy to find if you knew how to look for one. When he found one, he would destroy it, ensuring that a zebra repair party would eventually chopper out to the scene. In the old days this would happen very quickly, sometimes within minutes.

Now, even in these desperate days, he couldn't imagine it taking any more than a matter of hours. But even if he had to wait a day, maybe he could then—

Suddenly he looked up and saw the Beta F-5 bearing down on him.

"Jesuzz!" was all he could yell. He didn't even have time to jump into the ditch or even hit the ground. The fighter was in, on top of him, and releasing two canisters from its wings in the next instant.

They exploded with a great crash just behind him. But the airplane had come in so low that the jet wash served to blow most of the gas right back at him. Into his lungs. Into his bloodstream . . .

He fell over like a tin soldier.

Twenty minutes later, Wilkes landed back at Beta.

His ground crew ambled out to meet him at his hardstand, their beards scruffy, their enthusiasm sapped.

"How'd you do, Willy Boy?" the chief asked.

"Not bad," Wilkes replied with weary understatement. "Hit the bogeymen up north."

The chief was impressed. "Really now?" he asked. "That might be worth something in a drop."

"Some T-paper and soap will do just fine," Wilkes said, climbing down out of the cockpit.

He went on to describe the gas attack on the strange vehicles in detail, to the fair attention of the flight mechanics.

"Two of them right on the nose," Wilkes said, doing a quick postflight check of the airplane. "Then I saw more fireworks than over Basra."

"How about the other two?" the chief asked him.

Wilkes laughed cruelly. "Dropped them on some scrub out on the

Range," he said. "Two pukers on one guy. Looked like a Blue. That might translate into one roll of toilet paper for me. Personalized."

The chief was now sharing his laugh, but not for the same reason.

"You might get more than some crap paper," he told Wilkes. "Those weren't puke-gas canisters you dropped on him."

Wilkes shrugged nonchalantly. He'd just assumed he'd been loaded up full with puke gas.

"So what were they?" he asked the chief.

He pulled two red stickers from his pocket. They were the markers for canisters three and four on Wilkes's plane. He handed them to the pilot.

They read: *ZPG-662 – A/1 Hallucination Gas.*

66

Ryder was flying.

He was zooming along, ten, maybe twelve feet above the ground. Flaps up. Gear up. No headwind. No turbulence.

No airplane.

He liked it. He had had dreams like this when he was a little kid: going to the airshow with his father, looking at the old airplanes, and wondering what it would be like to fly without all that machinery around you. Like a bird. Like Superman.

There was a feather in his mouth – or at least he thought it was a feather. Maybe it was a flower of some kind. It didn't make any difference; this wasn't what was making him fly.

Or at least he didn't think so.

He felt like someone was making a movie of him flying. Lights. Camera. Roll 'em. *This* is what he should be getting paid for. There's a message on his answering machine. It says, Take the money, go to the casino, win some more. Okay, but he'll have to fly there. How? He hated the SLUF. He alone could fly better than that piece-of-shit airplane. The same with the F-4, but only because it was so old. Plus his father used to fly one.

Moon was the cause of all this. Everything was going great until he came along. He was really a priest – or he wanted to be a priest. Why else would he live in a church?

Why was the food always so bad at airshows? Why was the booze always so expensive in Ramada Inn bars? Why would people fly airplanes that were fifty years old? What was the name of the bargirl at Jacks? Where was Teddy Williams right now? Where was "Crazy" Katt? How much would a slightly used F-15X with Soviet Air Force markings cost? Could you get more for it in Florida than in Tulsa?

Woody should be so lucky. Flying along without an airplane was much better than with one. Maybe Woody had wings by this time, too. Maybe not.

Maybe this was how UFOs flew, then. That was it! And no one on the ground recognized them because they weren't used to seeing people fly without airplanes. God, what a good idea! God, what a possibility. It was a theory. *A damn good* theory. As soon as he stopped flapping his arms, he'd write it down.

Why was he sitting in the middle of this road? There were cuts and bruises up and down his arms. His legs looked worse? *God damn, what the hell was happening?* He was bleeding. Really bleeding. Parts of his body were falling off. The wings went first. Now his fingers were burning—burning right off his hand. He tried to put the flames out by scraping them along on the dirt, but they wouldn't stop *burning*. He tried spitting on them, but only blood would come out of his mouth.

He lay flat out on his back and stared up at the cloudless sky. If his body was still burning, he couldn't feel it. There were two airplanes above him. *Christ*—they were Spads. Spad biplanes from World War I. He could tell by their black feathers and long beaks. They were circling. Circling. *Circling.* Every once in a while, one would dip down for a closer look. He knew about these airplanes. They wouldn't eat you unless you were dead first.

It didn't make any difference. Burning fingers or not, reach down and unstrap that sidearm. Here, birdie. Here you go, little birdie . . .

Blam! Blam!

Damn—the bullets go right through them? Spads were built to be bullet-proof? *Really?*

Blam! Blam!

These motherfuckers are tough. *Tough!*

Here, birdie . . .

Blam! Blam!

Go ahead. Fly away, you chicken bastards. I'd chase you if my wings weren't falling off.

If you're out in the desert and you're hungry, what do you do? Eat a bug? Eat a lizard? Watch the lizard eat the bug and then eat the lizard? It got complicated. Just lying out on this dirt road was complicated. How about thirst? What did they tell you to do again? Drink your own urine? No way. *No fucking way.*

We'll die first. That might be the best idea of all. Just lie back and die. Die and then fly . . .

Angel had never driven a car so large, so ungainly, so incredibly hard to handle.

She didn't even know what kind of automobile it was. A Cadillac? A Lincoln Continental? She had no idea. All she knew was that it was enormous, both inside and out, and that it was the only car the man at the Hertz counter would rent to her for cash.

She was a fool—she was certain of that now. To do what she had done, and take the risks that she'd taken, made her certifiable, just like her mother.

Getting onto the Range had not been a problem. She knew the location of the secret entrances: they were disguised as line roads with their guardhouses posing as isolated gas stations and tiny casinos. There were four of them alone on the outskirts of Las Vegas. The men manning these outposts recognized her, checked her absolutely-legitimate security pass, and let her through, with barely a question about the whereabouts of her usual driver.

She'd been driving for five and a half hours now, surprised that she knew the way so well. She'd passed dozens of military vehicles, which in itself was not unusual. What *was* strange was that they all seemed to be heading in the opposite direction from her.

Also unusual was the attitude of the soldiers. Every time she'd made this trip before, somewhere along the way, some soldier had let loose a wolf whistle or something even more declarative. But there was none of that this time. The rather grim faces she'd seen on these soldiers told her that for once, they had other things on their mind.

She wasn't even sure why she was making this trip. By all respects she should have been in Hawaii by now, lying on the beach, drinking fine champagne, counting her money. Instead she was driving a battleship of an automobile through the vast empty desert, to see one more time the man who'd changed her life.

The further north she drove, the less troops she saw. A few airplanes had flown over, and a helicopter had paced her along a side road for a while, but it had gone away eventually, much to her relief.

Now, as she passed by one last butte, and turned onto the familiar dirt road, she saw the familiar craggy mountain looming up before her. Even though her destination was in sight—in fact, it was only about five miles away now—she couldn't believe she'd made it.

So she was actually feeling good—giddy, even—as she tore along the dirt road, the jagged mountain getting closer and closer with every minute.

Then she saw the body.

67

Area 61

Maureen knew next to nothing about electronic machinery.

The clock on her VCR had blinked "12:00" since the day she bought it. A cassette of songs by her favorite country-and-western group, The Tennessee Saints, had been stuck in her car's tape player for almost a year, playing continuously, but impossible to eject. She even had trouble rewinding her telephone answering machine.

So it was a formidable and time-consuming task for her to figure out exactly how the huge TV control room switchboard worked.

But she was learning.

The top row of buttons—they were colored red and numbering fifty in all—apparently controlled the smaller yellow-capped buttons below them, these numbering two hundred. Each red button activated the four yellow buttons beneath it. By pushing one of them, a specific camera shot would appear on the corresponding monitor.

Once she had cracked the code, she began experimenting. Red buttons number one through twenty-five controlled banks of cameras on the outside of the facility; red buttons twenty-six through fifty were for cameras inside the facility. A separate bank of blue-capped buttons controlled the data screens the young man had said were fed directly from the Cray supercomputer.

When she pushed red button number one, and then the first yellow button directly beneath it, she was presented on the first TV monitor with a near-panoramic view taken somewhere out in the desert. When she pushed the second yellow button she got the same scene but from a different angle. Yellow button three gave her yet another higher view, as did number four, but from an even steeper angle.

This desert scene showed a small air base, with two crossed runways, several gray buildings, and a lot of high fences, all tucked away next to a small mountain. There were no airplanes parked on the runway, no activity at all around the nearby buildings. The place looked very innocuous, yet she knew it had to be important – why else would there be four cameras trained on it?

Somehow she knew then that this view was the outside of Area 61.

Red button two with yellow button one displayed a scene on top of a butte. She knew it was quite a distance away from the first shot because the clouds in the sky were completely different. There was a small bunkerlike structure on top of the butte with a place for landing helicopters nearby. She could tell the wind was blowing extremely hard at this location by the amount of sand and small rocks bouncing off the camera lens. Red button two with yellow button two was a straight-on shot of the door to this facility There were several panels of lights and switches, apparently security devices of some type, but none of them were working, because the door to the bunker was unlocked, wide open, and actually flapping back and forth in the strong winds.

Yellow button three showed another angle on the door, and when the wind was right and the door swung open, she could see right into the bunker itself. Although the place looked very elaborate, with its huge TV screens and dozens of cushy chairs with computers hooked to them, it was now quite deserted. In fact, judging from the general disorder inside – debris like papers and coffee cups were strewn all about, several windows were broken, and more than a few computers were hanging off their chair arms – it appeared like the place had been ransacked. Yellow button number four showed all this again, from a different, further-out angle.

She pushed red button three and was presented with a scene of another air base. This one was many times bigger than the first and it was populated. In fact, as she marched down the four different angles provided by the yellow buttons, she saw that people were literally running around the place, crawling all over huge airplanes she knew were cargo carriers. There was a definite air of haste and even desperation in the way these people were moving, as if some unimaginable doom was about to fall on top of them.

The Red-button-four group provided more shots of this air base.

She could tell these were taken at the opposite end of the largest runway by determining the position of the sun. These angles showed more men, they looked like mechanics, swarming over two black jet fighters with red star emblems, obviously rushing to get them ready to fly. Off in the distance she could see flashes of light erupting every once in a while, fireworks or explosions that were sometimes so bright they staticked the TV screen for a moment.

When she pushed yellow-button-four, she was able to key in on a small sign hanging on the side of one of the base hangers. It read TANGO BASE ONE, and this name struck an immediate chord in her memory. She knew she was looking in on the top-secret air base where Colonel Woods and the other Operation Rapture pilots had first trained.

The red-button-five group brought a set of very intriguing images to the screen. It was as if she was watching a cowboy movie. The camera showed a row of dilapidated buildings that looked right out of the 1800s. The street in front of them was mud-caked and worn and full of deep furrows. Another yellow button showed the entrance to one of the buildings, obviously a barroom. Above the ragged, yet authentic swinging doors was a fading sign that simply read: JACKS.

The saloon beyond the sign was deserted, and she wasn't surprised. From the looks of things, Maureen couldn't imagine the place being open any time in the past fifty years or so.

The next group of red button banks showed her a bewildering array of highly unusual settings.

One looked like an authentic space-shuttle launch site; another looked like a full-scale nuclear power plant. There were several scenes right out of postwar Kuwait and Iraq, mostly battered sand berms and bombed-out mosques. There was another shot that could have been right out of the German Alps. Still another looked like it was being broadcast from Vietnam. Another depicted four angles of what looked like a typical small American midwestern town. It looked to her like a kind of Disneyland gone mad.

Despite the variety of bizarre locations, they all had one thing in common: they all looked like they'd just been the site of kind of intense fighting. In each scene she could see discarded military equipment strewn everywhere. Tanks, trucks, jeeps, guns, big and small, all of them abandoned. Nothing was smoking, there were no fires, and none of the equipment was destroyed or even damaged in any way. But just the jumbled and chaotic pattern of it all spoke one word: combat.

Just who and what was the cause of the fighting was a mystery — until she punched up red-button-ten.

The scene was an airport. It looked absolutely authentic, right down to the two airliners sitting in front of the terminal building. It didn't wear the signs of recent fighting, but it did have something else. On the third shot, way in the distance, she could see a line of military vehicles that stretched down the runway and off into the distance. They were tanks, she supposed, and other kinds of big hulking tracked machines, with guns poking out of them at many angles. They were all covered with a camouflage netting of some kind, and the men walking around them were wearing the same kind of unmarked sand-colored camouflage uniforms. And in front of them was a line of long artillery guns, and they were firing, rapidly, one right after another.

But something didn't look right here. The muzzle flashes looked — well, almost cartoonish. Once again, it was like she was watching a movie, this one with elaborate, yet obvious special effects. It was a totally confusing scene. The "animated" guns firing, like huge expensive toys, contrasted by the absolute seriousness of the soldiers operating them.

Try as she might, she just couldn't figure out exactly what she was seeing.

68

When Ryder woke up, he was in the ocean.

The shore, all white and pearly, was a mile or so away. But there was a storm brewing. The water in between him and the shoreline was swirling around him violently and it was foamy and warm.

Should he swim for it? Could he even swim that far?

He looked up and saw a gigantic face staring down out of the sky at him. It was thin—"reedy" was a better description—and wore a scraggly beard and long gray hair. It looked like every picture he'd ever seen of the Face of God, perhaps after the Almighty had gone on a diet.

"Who are you?" the Voice of God asked him.

"You don't know?" Ryder replied.

"How the hell would I know?" the Voice of God asked.

Ryder looked back at the distant shore and saw it didn't seem so far away this time. The water was still swirling, and it was even foamier. And those looked like two big feet—his feet—way out there near the shoreline.

He looked back up at the giant face and saw it had been joined by another. This one belonged to a very pretty young female, and it looked fairly familiar, especially the hair. It was red with a long blonde streak down the middle—or was that the other way around?

"He's coming to, Angel," the Voice of God told the young woman, at least getting the name right. "You saved this guy's life."

Ryder splashed his face, hoping the ocean water would wake him up some. He was surprised to see that he still had hands and fingers. And feet. And toes. Those *were* his feet way out there. But they didn't look that far away anymore. Nor did the faces of the man and woman

382

who were hovering over him. Suddenly his mouth felt very dry.

"Are you a soldier?" the angel asked him.

Ryder tried to speak, but suddenly couldn't. He dunked his head under the water again. When he came back up, he saw that the ocean was slowly sizing down to a large, rather elaborate hot tub. The foam on the water were suds, and the swirling maelstrom was actually caused by the hot tub's water jets.

"Are you deployed out here, on the Range?" the voice asked.

At this time, Ryder was able to nod yes. Things were beginning to make a little more sense—but not much.

"I'm a pilot," he managed to gurgle.

"A pilot?" the old man said with a laugh and a cough. "Ain't you a little off your reservation, my friend? There's no airfield around here."

"I have no idea *where* I am," Ryder replied groggily. "Or who you are."

"My name ain't important," the old man told him. "But this is Angel. She's the one who found you."

"Your *name* is Angel?" Ryder asked, confused.

"That's my professional name."

"My name is . . ." He had to think a moment. "Long. Ryder Long. Colonel. United States Air Force."

The old man laughed. "My former employers," he said snidely to Angel.

"Be careful," she urged him. "This guy might be a spy or something."

"Nonsense," the old man told her. "You think they'd leave a spy out in the middle of the desert. To die? Just like that? No, I've seen this before. He was hit with gas. Can you remember anything like that, Colonel?"

Ryder almost didn't hear the question. He was looking around the gigantic bathroom, amazed at its opulence. He saw dozens of gold fixtures, lamps, and shades made out of crystal and silver, huge mirrors surrounded by pearls.

"Am I still in the desert?" he asked.

"You bet your ass you are," the old man said, obviously delighted at Ryder's reaction to the magnificent bathroom. "Like a dream, ain't it?"

Angel began tugging on the old man's elbow. "Ask him what happened to him," she urged him. "Find out why he was so close to here."

The old man took a pitcher filled with ice water and dumped it over Ryder's head.

"Do you remember getting gassed, Colonel?" the old man asked him.

Ryder willed his body to unstiffen from the effects of the ice water.

"I think so . . ." he said slowly. "I was walking. My plane crashed. Those bastards! The Alphas—they shot me down. And the Betas! They're the ones who gassed me."

The old man threw him a huge white towel.

"I thought so," he said to Angel. "These guys have been playing with gas out here for a few years. I'd say our friend here was soaked with some hippie-dippie stuff."

"What does that mean?" Angel wanted to know, diverting her eyes as Ryder stood up and wrapped the towel around himself.

"Hippies? Love Power? LSD?" the old man asked her. "Hallucinogenics?"

She just shrugged. "I've heard of them," she said. "I think my mother was a hippie once. Or maybe it was my grandmother."

The old man cackled, and squeezed her affectionately.

"I'm so happy you decided to come back," he told her.

Two hours later

Ryder cut into the piece of sirloin and felt his knife go through it like butter.

"That's corn-fed beef," the old man said, slicing into his own top rib eye. "They ship it in for me, every day. Or at least it used to be every day. Been kinda slow lately."

They were sitting in a huge, incredibly opulent dining room, something that belonged on the cover of *Homes Beautiful* or featured on *Lives of the Rich & Famous*. Everything was either crystal, silver, or gold. Even the dinner plates. It was mind-boggling for Ryder—whose brain needed no further jarring—to contemplate that he was still out in the middle of the desert, and not sitting in some Park Avenue penthouse.

"More Scotch?" Angel asked, filling his glass before he could reply.

"That's authentic Ballantine 500," the old man said. "Forty-five years old. That will help knock that gas out of you."

Ryder took a bite of steak—it melted in his mouth. He took a swig of Scotch—it felt as smooth as velvet. More steak. More Scotch. Steak. Scotch. *Steak. Scotch.* He'd never had a better meal.

He wasn't certain if the reason the food and drink tasted so good, or that the dining room looked so elegant, had to do with reality, or the lingering aftereffects of his inhalation of the hallucinogenic gas. The whole house where the strange old man lived was something out of an hallucination. It looked as if every little bit of architectural Americana that had been popular over the past forty-five years had been somehow grafted onto it, while the inside was a cross between a technological wet dream and a repairman's nightmare.

"Your tax dollars at work," the old man called down the long table to him. "If I told you how much money the government has plowed into this place in the past forty years, you'd go out and shoot your congressman. And screw the snot out of his wife, too—just to get even."

Angel shot the old man a sidelong glance. "Is *that* language necessary?"

Ryder dug into his second steak and took another long swig of Scotch. He had yet to figure out a number of things here, and one of them was the exact basis of the relationship between the old man and the beautiful young girl. She didn't live in the strange house—he had ascertained that she'd been driving up from Vegas when she found him sprawled on the roadway. He was almost certain that she was a call girl—that hair looked *damned* familiar—and that the old guy was her most frequent customer. If all this was true, then what he couldn't figure out was how a Las Vegas call girl was able to drive her Lincoln Continental right into the middle of the most restricted area in the world.

They finished the meal and settled into another enormous and luxurious room that was decorated like an exclusive high mountain hunting lodge, stuffed moose head and all.

Angel put a log on the fire and joined them on the football-field-size modular couch, passing Ryder a fishbowl-sized snifter of brandy in the process.

"So, fly-boy," the old man said, taking a mouthful of the fine French cognac. "Let's hear your story."

385

"Which one?" Ryder asked, not at all trying to be funny.

"We know you're a pilot," the old man said. "What are you doing way out here?"

Ryder sucked down a throatfull of the brandy.

"Sorry, I can't tell you that," he replied.

"And why not?"

"Well, dad, I guess because it's classified," Ryder said. "In fact, I've got to find a way to get going—"

The old man didn't hear the second half of his sentence; he was too busy laughing.

"Classified?" he repeated, mockingly. "Who the hell you fooling, boy? Classified, *sheet . . ."*

Even the jittery Angel was laughing at him.

"It *is* funny," she assured Ryder.

He was confused—still. He took another sip of his drink. "Why?" he asked.

"Because," the old man said, lifting his frail body off the couch with some difficulty, "you didn't know the meaning of the word 'classified,' until you met me."

He walked over in front of Ryder and snapped out an ancient wallet. The only thing in it was a laminated ID card. It was yellow with two black stripes running through it. It featured a recent picture of the old man and was signed—in blue ink—by the Secretary of Defense himself. But what leapt off the card at Ryder's eyes was the phrase *Level 22—All Access.*

"Do you know what that is?" the old man asked him.

Ryder did. It was the marker of the highest level of security clearance in the country. No more than a hundred people had ever been issued one, and not even the officers on the President's Cabinet could qualify. Ryder's own security level clearance, four steps above that of a regular USAF pilot, was only a Level 5.

"You *are* a famous person," Ryder told the old man as he examined the document.

Obviously delighted, the old man cackled and pointed to Angel. "Her, too."

Ryder turned and looked at her and she smiled once again, this time a little boozily. "It's true," she said, retrieving a similar card from her small, tight bustier.

"Wow," was all Ryder could say. Was he really sitting in the presence of two of the highest-security people in the country?

"So, now, my friend," the old man said, settling back down onto the couch with a creak. "Tell us your story."

Ryder took another gulp of brandy. What the hell could he tell the guy?

"I guess you could say I got separated from my unit," Ryder said.

"Well, we figured that!" the old man bellowed. "What the hell unit were you with?"

Ryder could only shrug. How could he *not* tell him? It would be like not answering a question by the President.

"I was with Tango Aggressors," he said. "We were on a—"

He never finished the sentence. The old man had leapt off the couch with such speed and verve he startled both Ryder and Angel.

"Tango Aggressors?" the man repeated, clearly astonished. "Jesus Christ . . . what the hell is your security ID number?"

Ryder furrowed his brow. "Four-Four-Six-Six," he answered honestly.

The old man drew back two huge oak doors near the fireplace to reveal a large computer set into the side of the center wall.

Flipping switches like an expert, the old man had the computer powered up and the screen filled in half a minute.

"Four. Four. Six. Six," he said, typing the numbers into the keyboard and pushing another series of buttons. "Tango . . ."

Suddenly the computer screen blinked once and it came alive with letters and numbers. Ryder took one long look and felt his heart freeze. Of all the numbers and letters, three of them screamed at him off the computer screen. Right in the middle of the field. Slightly larger than the rest, but burning a hole in his retinas: ISC.

But he had no time to contemplate exactly what he'd gotten himself into. For the old man read something off the screen and then turned around and said:

"So *you're* the guy they've been looking for . . ."

Ryder was quickly hustled up to the second floor of the house.

The huge room featured the largest picture window he'd ever seen. The view beyond it was spectacular—a horizon-to-horizon panorama of War Heaven.

"I know who you are," the old man was saying to him. "I saw you fly. Or at least I saw videotapes of your flights."

As he was talking, the old man was rifling through boxes of photo albums, newspaper clippings, and worn-out magazines. Angel had followed them up to the observatory, bringing a bottle of whiskey with her. Now she sat in the corner of the room, pulling her ultra-miniskirt up under her, looking out the window and sipping a glass of straight whiskey. Except for the booze, she reminded Ryder of a young teenage schoolgirl, staring out the window, worried about whether her first love loved her back.

The old man finally found what he was looking for. It was a black three-ring binder book with those three dirty letters, "ISC," emblazoned on it. He sat on the floor and flipped through the pages until he got to the one he wanted.

"Yeah, here it is!" he half-yelled. "Four-Four-Six-Six . . . Tango . . . Operation Rapture."

He turned and smiled at Angel. "The prodigal son has come home."

She reached over and gently slapped his shoulder. "I don't know what that word means."

The old man took the black book on his lap and settled down on the couch next to her.

"You don't have to tell me your story now, Colonel," the old man said, "I already know it."

He opened the black book to a page somewhere near the middle.

"Colonel Ryder Long," he began reading, "Tango Aggessors. Veteran of Operation Distant Thunder. Crack pilot. Great service record. A fine officer. Never any trouble, no marks at all, not even on the interactive computer update. Boy, did *you* fit the profile, Colonel."

"You sure know a lot about me," Ryder responded.

"I'll tell you even more," the old man said, closing the book. "I'll guess that you were doing some great duty somewheres, and suddenly you got a call or a letter or something and, next thing you know, you're back in War Heaven. Am I right?"

Ryder nodded yes.

"They put you in some shitbox airplane," the old man went on. "Threw you up against a bunch of hot shots. And you beat them. So they made you one of them. And you did a week of turn-and-burns that you didn't think was possible. Right?"

"Yes," Ryder replied, stunned at the man's intimate knowledge of the last few weeks of his life. Was he really hearing all this? Or was it still the Hal-Lou gas? Somehow, the old man's words were making a strange echoing sound.

"And you worked and worked, and you beat everything they sent up against you. And then they threw you a psy-ops. Against the cartoon UFO . . . Am I right?"

"Yes, you are."

The old man clapped his hands with pure glee.

"Then, the next thing you know — boom! — they throw you off the reservation. They leave you wondering who's nuts — and you isn't . . ."

Ryder reached over and poured himself a drink from Angel's whiskey bottle. This was getting very strange. It seemed that the more the old man spoke, the larger the room was becoming.

"They were testing you, boy!" the old men yelled at him, sounding like he was at the bottom of a well. "They were testing you and watching you every damn minute."

Ryder's head was spinning. His sense of balance, proportion, orientation, was all out of whack. That damn Hal-Lay-Lou-Yah Gas!

"Beautiful . . . absolutely beautiful," the old man was saying. "You were just the kind of guy they wanted. But you didn't fall for it, did you? You didn't march in lockstep like they expected you to. You fought them. That's great! Finally someone with backbone.

"They snagged your three buddies, you know. They fought it, but not as hard as you did. And they know you've been missing. I saw a report on the computer about you today. Something about parking an airplane in Tulsa? That's outstanding! What did you do, walk the rest of the way back here?"

"Sometimes I feel like I did," Ryder replied.

"Well, believe me, they probably would have found you if they didn't already have a ton of problems facing them."

"Who are 'they,' exactly?" Ryder asked.

" 'Them,' " the old man replied. "The guys who run this place. The ISC. You know about them, don't you?"

Ryder just nodded slowly. "Yeah, I guess I do."

"Well, they've have a rough week," the old man said, obviously delighted. "First, their big boy got snatched. Then this mystery army invades from way up north. You've seen the Zoot lights all over, I'm assuming?"

"I sure have," Ryder replied.

389

"And then, you turn up missing," the old man went on. "Like they didn't enough headaches."

"Do you know where the other three guys in my unit are right now?"

"If I was a betting man," the old man said with a twinkle in his eye, "I'd say that were down at Area Sixty-one getting ready for the Big Blast."

" 'The Big Blast?' "

"Sure, don't you know about that, boy?" the old man asked him, legitimately surprised. "That's what this whole shee-bang is all about."

Ryder felt a chill go up his spine. Moon had warned him that the ISC had an A-bomb and that they were apparently threatening to use it if anyone from the outside decided to move on them. Had that happened?

"They're blowing up a nuke?" he asked. "Why?"

The old man sipped his drink and gave Angel a hug.

"It's complicated, my friend," he replied. "Maybe I should start at the beginning."

With that, he grabbed another cardboard box and spilled its contents onto the bed. Angel took one look at the stuff, rolled her eyes, and quickly poured herself another drink.

"You know, I've been waiting for someone like you to show up at my door for a hell of a long time," the old man said, his voice lowering to a whisper. "And, the way I feel right now, I might not have much time left."

At that comment, Angel looked at him with such a pained expression in her eyes that Ryder thought she was about to cry. She slapped his shoulder again, only harder this time.

"I'm leaving if you start talking like that again."

"So," the old man went on, ignoring her. "Now you're here. Like the stars said you'd be.

"And now, you can listen to *my* story."

The old man disappeared into a bedroom and could be heard rustling around in a closet.

Ryder turned back to Angel, who was now woozy with intoxication.

"What a jerk I am," she said, still staring out the window. "I could've been in Hawaii by now. *But no*. I had to come back here — for

390

him. Some old dude who's my grandfather's age."

She took another, heftier gulp of her drink.

"He drinks way too much," she went on with a self-pitying laugh. "And he's got a million things wrong with him, you know. He's got more pills downstairs than a drug store. He could drop dead at any moment. And then where would I be? I should really have my head examined. Some psychiatrist would *love* to get a hold of me. I'm sure they'd find out that this is all my father's fault."

Ryder resisted the sudden urge to hug the young girl – strictly to comfort her. It was obvious that she was in the middle of a situation that was way beyond her comprehension, her only tangible connection being an unlikely affection for the old man.

"I don't pretend to understand any of this," Ryder told her. "I know the craziest things in the world have happened on this Range. But really, what the hell is *he* doing out here?"

"I'll be glad to tell you," the old man said suddenly from the doorway.

Gone were the patch-filled coveralls and wild sneakers. Instead the man was wearing the dress uniform of a captain in the old Army Air Corps.

"It's been more than forty-five years since I put this on," he said quietly, suddenly sounding and looking more like a man his own age. "This will probably be the last time I wear it."

They went back downstairs to the lodge room, where Angel threw two more logs on to the fire.

"My name is Jess Warren," the man began, patting down the creases on his dress uniform. "Do you know how long it's been since I've said that name?

"I was too young to fight in the big war. World War Two, that is. I was just a kid in junior high on Pearl Harbor Day, in a small town named Mill, Texas. I used to stay awake nights wondering if the war would still be on by the time I was old enough to join up and fight. Back then, some people thought it would be over in a matter of months, you know. Others were saying it would last ten, fifteen years . . .

"Well, the war was over in Europe by the time I graduated high school, and though I tried all that summer to sign up to fight the Japanese, the recruiters in town just kept telling me to come back in a week. Come back in two weeks. Then, come back in a month. I finally got sick of it. My marks were really good, so I applied to the University of Texas and got accepted.

"I joined the ROTC-type program there, and that's how I learned to fly. The war in the Pacific was over by this time, so I just hit the books and flew a lot on the weekends.

"I met a girl in college—a real nice girl. We got engaged, and we made plans to get hitched when I graduated. I was studying physics and was hoping to get into some kind of atomic research program, because that's what was really hot in those days.

"So wouldn't you know it, halfway through my second year of college, and the Army calls me to active service! The war's been over for a year and I still get drafted! They need pilots like crazy in those days, with all the war vets mustered out. I had no choice but to go, of course. But I got lucky, because after I went to advanced flight school in a place called Betty, Texas, they assigned me to the 509th Bombardment Group which was located at Roswell Army Air Field, near Roswell, New Mexico. My family had moved up north by this time, but I say I was lucky because it was just a bus ride back to Texas to see my girl.

"At that time the 509th was the only air group that had atomic bombs. I guess some paper pusher saw that I was studying physics and figured I'd be a good match. So I went to Roswell, and what do they do? They put me in a F-51 Mustang chase plane, to take pictures! Of the A-bomb blasts!

"Well, it was a secret at the time, but they used to load up my airplane with live ammunition, and I'll tell you why: The brass was always afraid of what would happen if the crew of a plane carrying an A-bomb had to ditch quick. Or, even worse, if for some reason the pilots or someone on board went nutty. Hey, stranger things have happened. If it looked like the airplane was going to go down near a populated area, or if things went screwy on board, I was under orders, as a last resort, to shoot at it. Even though I knew the guys on board. I was to aim at the bomb bay and try to blow the thing up in the air, because the geniuses in Washington figured they could better deal with an A-bomb going off in midair than on the ground.

"The crazy thing is that it would have probably killed just as many people—me included! But thank God, we never had to come to any of that. I would never want to be in the position of killing other Americans. Who would?

"So one night, it was very early July, we were returning from a night mission over to White Sands. There was a very secret test range over there where they dropped A-bombs while everyone thought they were just dropping them out here in Nevada and out at Bikini Atoll in the Pacific. There was a bitch of a storm going on—these really violent thunderstorms would sweep through the area at that time of year. Almost like small tornados.

"The two B-29s I was accompanying had been having trouble all night. Their radios weren't working; they'd fought the weather the entire way. In fact, they never got to drop their bombs, because the weather over the target area was so bad.

"Things got worse on the way back. We were all having trouble finding the field. We didn't have all the super-duper navigation equipment back then like they do these days, and in the dark and bad weather, well, it was a chore just to line up with the base.

"They sent me ahead to get a fix and then double back and guide them in by radio. I found the base okay, and circled back to get the B-29s in line. That's when it happened . . ."

The man took a deep breath and looked up for the first time to see both Ryder and Angel totally engrossed in the story.

"You've got to understand something," he began again. "I've never killed anything in my life. I never went hunting as a kid, never owned a gun or a knife. I never even went fishing. My friends used to make fun of me—I was always studying or reading while they were out shooting quail or rabbits.

"Anyway, just as I was on my way back out to round up the bombers, I get a call from the Roswell Tower. They tell me that an unidentified aircraft had inserted itself—those were their exact words—had 'inserted itself' between me and the bombers. They didn't have any idea what the hell it was, only that it was well within the restricted airspace set up around the base. You have to remember, this was the only base in the United States that had A-bombs on site.

"So the tower sends me in to intercept this whatever-it-was. I was thinking—actually, I was praying—that it was just another airplane from the base that they had lost track of. That kind of stuff happened every once in a while, too, especially in bad weather. I was hoping I'd run into a cargo plane or something, or maybe even a civilian plane off course or in trouble and needing a place to land.

393

"So I vector to the area – and remember, I'm flying around in some heavy soup – and suddenly I see this damn thing.

"It was big and white, bright as hell, like a fluorescent light, but in the shape of a disk. It was acting so strangely, flying very weird. Like hopping from here to there. Sometimes you could see it move – sometimes it would just disappear and show up, a second later, about a half mile away.

"The other weird thing was that even though I was flying through the storm, and getting knocked around by the turbulence, this thing looked like it was just moving as smooth as hell. The weather wasn't having an effect on it at all.

"Now, we had been hearing about these strange flying things for a while. 'Flying disks' is what we used to call them. During the war they used to call them 'Foo Fighters.' As soon as I saw this thing I knew it wasn't an airplane – either civvie or military. I knew it must be one of these flying disks.

"I radioed back to the base and told them what was happening, and as usual, they didn't have any idea what to do. They start calling around to the big brass while I'm flying around with my ass hanging out, *plus* the two big loaded bombers coming back in! I tracked this thing as best I could, considering the weather, and kept the tower informed.

"This went on for about ten minutes, and I was going down in fuel by this time. Suddenly the thing turns straight on south, heading right for the base. I yelled into the radio and they hit the all-alert button. At that point one of the tower officers got on the horn and told me to fire on the damn thing!

"I asked them to confirm the order and they came right back and said, yes, shoot at it. *Shoot at it!* Do what you have to, just don't let it get to the base. They were pissing their pants because of the A-bombs, of course, and under the circumstances, I guess I can't blame them. This was all so new to us back then.

"So I gunned the engine and got as close as I could, and then, well, I started shooting at it. The thing was going all over the sky by this time – just appearing here and there. Moving real fast, when I could see it at all. But still going toward the base.

"All of this was happening very fast – within one or two minutes – but it was just like they always say, you know, time stood still. I was looking at this thing and all I was thinking was, How can it zip back and forth like that? And how can I get a shot at it when it's moving in such an unconventional manner? I mean, I was blazing away, but by the time the bullets got there, the thing had moved, in a flash.

"Well, call it a bolt of intuition, or whatever, but something from my college studies popped into my head. It was something Einstein once wrote. He said, 'The faster an object moves, the more it bends space.' Now, my professor always used to ask us, Where would such a hypothetical object bend to? The answers—at least by our own, let's say, earthbound terminology—would be 'up' or 'down' or 'sideways.' But he used to press us, to get us to think about what Einstein was really saying.

"Well, I didn't understand it all back then, or now. Not exactly, anyway. But the idea was that if the object was moving fast enough, it would bend itself right out of existence—move itself, not through space, but . . ."

He stopped for a moment. Enraptured by the tale, Ryder wanted to reach over and shake the man.

"But what?"

"Well, it sounds crazy," the old man continued, "but the theory would be that if it could move fast enough—I mean *really fast*—it would be able to bend itself through time. Actually move through the time dimension. It sounds nuts, I know, but Einstein wrote and thought about this a lot.

"So now here I am, flying around up there, and all this stuff comes into my head. I think, what if this thing has the ability to generate so much speed, it's actually bending itself in and out of time? It was a scary thought, especially under the circumstances. But I had my orders and I'm just thinking of a way to prevent this thing from reaching the base.

"I'm watching it, blink in and out, moving here and there in fractions of seconds, and I just come up with an idea. If the thing *was* flipping in and out of time, then that might mean, when it disappeared, it wasn't actually moving through space as much as it was moving through time. I would see it in one position, then it would disappear only to show up somewhere else a second or two later. The only thing that was happening, to my eye, was the thing had changed position. But actually some time had passed—just a few seconds, yes—but time *had* passed. If this was happening, it would, according to Einstein's theory, create such an optical illusion.

395

"So I figured, what do I have to lose? The object was still there, it just wasn't in my time frame. So what I did was plot a quick course, and as soon as the thing would blink out, I'd fire a burst halfway along the course where I thought it would pop up again. It was one hell of a long shot, believe me.

"But on my second try, I hit the damn thing . . ."

At this point, it almost seemed like the man was about to cry. He was getting very emotional. Angel rose and fixed him a drink, which he gulped down too quickly.

Then he went on.

"As soon as I pressed the trigger, I saw the bullets hit. They looked like they were exploding in midair, but I knew right away what was happening. It was cause and effect. It was like doing an experiment and seeing the results right away. The object was there, in the time dimension or just coming out of it, and just not the three other dimensions.

"As I later figured it out, it was an incredibly lucky shot. More than one in a billion. That's probably the scariest part of all. That's what I've had to live with ever since. That nagging question: *Why me?*"

"I know that feeling," Ryder said.

The old man sipped his drink and let out a long sigh.

"After I hit it, the thing blinked back on," he continued, speaking slower, softer, his voice just above a whisper. "It was wobbling, and kind of fading in and out. I knew I had hit, had damaged it. It stayed still for a moment, and then it went down.

"I was running on gas fumes by this time, so I headed back to the field as fast as I could. I just made it. The people at the base had no idea what had happened, so I told them. In detail, physics lesson and all.

"Well, right away, they think I'm nuts. Crazy. Gone around the loop. I thought they'd give me a medal, and the bastards sent me to the infirmary! Can you believe it? Is that typical of the Army? They practically forgot about the bogey they sent me after. I remember one guy saying that it was just a weather balloon. Something that got caught in the storm. No big deal. The two B-29s landed safely and all the A-bombs were okay, and that's all they really cared about at the moment.

"So they had the doctor talking to me, the regular flight surgeon.

He tells me he's an expert in battle fatigue; he's seen this type of thing before. Then they send in the chaplain, and he tells me that I've been working too hard and that I should come to services more often. Of course by this time I knew I should never have opened my big mouth – but it was too late. I wrote a report on it, but they filed it with the doctor, not with the operations people. Only about a few people talked to me afterward, and everyone just kept quiet about it. No official reports, no nothing.

"Then, a few days later, this local rancher, his name was Brazel, found a bunch of debris out on his place. He called the base, and they sent some guys out to pick up some pieces of this stuff. They bring it back to the base, where it's examined. Right away everyone knows it's nothing we built. Not this stuff. It's like nothing anyone has ever seen. So right away, they claim they've recovered a real 'flying disk.' They even release the story to the newspaper and it runs as the lead story!

"But then, someone starts to put two and two together. Whether it was the doctor or the chaplain or the guys in the tower, I never found out. But they remember my story and then they look at the wreckage and they realize that maybe I'm not so crazy. I'm just a guy who's flying chase planes who happens to know something about physics and shot down something that was definitely *not* a weather balloon.

"Well, right away – boom! – they put a real clamp on the whole kaboodle. They try to yank back the news story, saying that what they found *was* a weather balloon, which was a laugh for anyone who'd seen the debris.

"The media back then wasn't like it is now. It was nowhere as widespread or powerful. So the Army was able to pull back the news story. Then they threatened some people in Roswell – like the rancher and his family – and got everyone to believe the weather-balloon crap.

"But meanwhile, they moved me and the debris up to Wright-Patterson air field in Ohio. All very hush-hush. While they studied the material, they put me under a microscope, too. They debriefed me over and over, on how I hit the damn thing, and why, and mostly, could I teach people to do it again . . ."

At this point, the old man broke down completely. He was drunk *and* emotional. Angel moved over very close to him, and put her arms around him.

"They promised me everything, the bastards," he continued bitterly. "Rise in rank. Pay scales like you wouldn't believe. Under-the-table payments. No taxes. The works. But what they didn't tell me – not at first, anyway – was that just like they put the clamp on the whole Roswell story, they put the clamp on me. They put the clamp on my life. They moved me around from air base to air base, always shutting me away, not allowing me to talk to anyone except some general who wanted to meet the guy who'd shot down a flying saucer. I was Top Secret. I had no life. I was never allowed to go back home. I never saw my girl again. Damn them, I never even went to my own mother's funeral!

"Finally, around 1957, they moved me out here. They put me in a Quonset hut, just down the hill. By this time, I knew that I'd never get out. The strange thing was, I'd been hidden away so long, part of me didn't *want* to get out. Everything had changed so damn much.

"They'd ruined my life, and not because they were geniuses, either. Far from it. They just didn't know what to do with me. So I started making demands on them. Blackmail, they call it. I made them give me everything I wanted. First a house – a livable place. That was the beginning of this joint. This room was the first. Then I made them start adding things on. I told them I wanted TVs, radios, movies. Women. At first, they blinked every time I wanted something. They'd yell and scream. But they always wound up giving in because they knew that if my story ever got out, they'd all be screwed for keeping such a significant event from the public and then lying boldfaced about it.

"The funny thing was, they never did figure out just what they'd found on that guy's ranch in Roswell. Not really, anyway. People in this country have always thought that the government was keeping the truth about UFOs from them. The truth is, for years the government didn't know any more than the regular Joe on the street. Obviously things were flying around in the skies. But they didn't know where they came from. So to them, it was like the Russians, you know? The invaders. Like they were coming over the next hill at any minute. So the government decided that if this thing is going to happen – if flying saucers are some kind of national security threat – then the people must be warned. They must be educated. They must be ready!

"But exactly how do you accomplish something like that? Well, it ain't as easy as giving people civil-defense drills and telling them how to build bomb shelters. But you can't allow them to let their guards down, either. So you keep them always thinking in the backs of their minds about flying saucers and that they might be evil—just like the commies! An invasion from outer space! Movies. Books. Pulp magazine stories. TV. It was everywhere during the Fifties—and people just lapped it up. But what the government didn't realize back then is that people *like* to get scared sometimes. It's fun if it doesn't last too long. And all these CIA bozos just thought they were doing a hell of a job. What a laugh!"

"But did they listen to you?" Ryder asked him. "Did you tell them what you thought the saucers were doing?"

"Sure, a few of them studied my theory," he replied, "They considered that these things could be moving not through space but through time. But how the hell can you prove something like that? In fact, in a lot of my debriefings, the questioners tried to get me to admit that I had shot the thing while it was in my sights, and not while it was, well, invisible. But I just stuck to my story, no matter what they wanted to believe."

He took another long swig of his drink.

"Then things began to change a little while back," he said. "About two years ago, they took an interest in me again. I mean, before, I used to just sit out here day after day, doing nothing. Seeing nobody. I was a well-off hermit. But then these new guys began coming around. They began asking all the same questions again—but a lot of new ones, too. They were very interested in my angle on the physics of the whole thing.

"That's when I found out that they'd made some kind of a breakthrough in studying the original debris found at Roswell, and at others places, too. They were able to determine its age, among other things. And that's when everything went crazy."

"What do you mean?" Ryder asked.

"Well, let me show you," Warren replied. He got up and retrieved a small metal box from a wall safe.

He opened the box and took out an irregular chunk of metal about the size of a golf ball.

"This is a piece of the Roswell debris," he said. "Specifically, they believe it might actually be part of the craft's power source."

He gave it to Ryder, who felt like he was being handed the Hope

Diamond. The thing *was* odd; it looked very solid, yet it was extremely lightweight. He rubbed his fingernail along it and felt its texture to be a cross between wood and plastic, yet it looked like metal.

"Strange, isn't it?" Warren asked. "Its main ingredient, if you will, is actually gold, they tell me. 'Supergold,' some of them call it. But it's not like anything found here on Earth. Apparently its atomic structure is incredibly atypical.

"One physicist they sent up here told me that one kilogram of this stuff is equal to dozens of 20-megaton bombs. So, you hold in your hand, Colonel, the potential for enough destructive force to obliterate every major city in this country."

Ryder imagined he felt the thing burning a hole in his hand.

"But you see, this material obviously has more potential than just destructive value," Warren went on. "That's what the people I've talked to lately have been working on. Or at least that's what they tell me. Apparently they are trying very hard to duplicate it. One idea is to put a lot of gold in the proximity of a certain kind of nuclear blast, and then somehow quickly reconstruct the atoms into a small amount of supergold. Or maybe it's the other way around. Obviously, there's a lot of high-concept physics involved in that kind of operation."

"Why are they doing it?" Ryder asked, wondering if in fact he'd stumbled onto the ISC's true agenda. "Are they building their own flying saucer?"

The old man shrugged. "Exactly why, I'm not sure," he admitted. "After they pumped me for information, they kind of forgot about me again. Oh, they let me sit in on the meetings in which they were selecting you guys—the pilots. Drove me around in all their tanks and stuff, trying to make me feel important. And they'd ask my advice every once in a while. But basically, it was just paying me some lip service. You know, throw that old dog a bone. I did my best to make trouble for them—just to keep them on their toes."

Ryder gave the chunk of material back to Warren and then got up and poured himself a drink.

"Every time I look at this," Warren said, rolling the fragment around in his fingers, "I think of the great man himself."

" 'The great man'?" Ryder asked.

"Einstein!" both Warren and Angel answered simultaneously.

"As absolutely brilliant as he was," Warren went on, almost wistfully, "I can actually say that I know more than he did. Simply because I can touch this stuff and know what it is. Or, more realistically, what it probably is."

He sat back down and slumped his shoulders.

"Except for Angel, you are the first one I've told the entire story to, Colonel Long," he said to Ryder, tears once again welling up in the corners of his tired eyes. "It's a great burden off me. I'm so lucky you came upon us today."

He slipped further down onto the couch. Suddenly he looked very, very old.

"And now . . ." he stammered. "And now . . . I guess, I have other things to do . . . Thank you, Colonel."

Ryder stared at the old man as he slipped further down into the soft couch cushion.

"Are you okay, Captain?" Ryder asked him worriedly.

The old man looked up at the girl, sitting a few feet from him now, and shakily wiped a last tear away. "And good-bye for now, my Angel . . ."

With that, he leaned back, closed his eyes, and then slowly fell face forward onto the couch.

Angel was stunned. "Oh, please *no* . . ."

Ryder was up and at the old man's side in a flash. The man's face was almost pure white and his eyes were closed tight. Ryder gingerly went to feel for a pulse. But when he did, the old man's eyes suddenly popped back open.

"Fooled you, didn't I?" he said with a grin.

69

The Spy

Maureen was getting worried.

She'd been cooped up inside the TV studio for hours now, alone in the cold room, watching the banks of monitors with their flickering shots of the night falling in the desert, while feeling another kind of darkness begin to envelope her.

Just what was going on here? Had she been duped by the strange young man? He'd mentioned that the people inside the Area 61 facility were planning on detonating *an atomic bomb*. Walter had never mentioned such a thing. No one had—until now. Just where was this explosion going to take place? Somewhere further out in the desert? Or somewhere dangerously close-by?

She tried to shake away the disturbing thoughts. It was no use creating more problems for herself—she had plenty already. At least she had felt somewhat safe inside her spare living quarters, spending her time trying to figure out what the hell was going on inside Area 61 as well as inside Walter's head.

Now she was alone—*really* alone. Left here by a man who had hinted about an impending nuclear explosion, who had admitted that he'd deposited half the Frederick's of Hollywood catalog in her laundry bag, and then mentioned he had something to apologize for.

Was he ever coming back?

She tried to kill some more time by watching the TV screens. But with the encroaching darkness, she was hard pressed to find any further exterior views.

So she began pushing more buttons further down the board, discovering that some of them controlled cameras inside the place. Soon enough she was looking at some very strange interior shots.

One was of a large low-lit chamber that was similar to the cold storage hangar where she'd seen the alleged flying saucer. This room contained two aircraft that looked almost as unusual as the disk, though there were some characteristics that told her they were somewhat more conventional.

They were jet fighter planes of some kind, of this she was certain. She could clearly see a cockpit, a tail plane, landing gear, engine intakes and fuel tanks on each. Also evident were the long, red-tipped missiles slung underneath their wings, six on each airplane.

The angle of the camera didn't give her a good perspective on the shapes of the airplanes themselves, but they looked slightly flat and oval, almost like a pair of elongated pancakes. The tips of their wings were folded up, suggesting they were in their storage mode.

What was strange was that Maureen couldn't figure out how the airplanes had gotten into the chamber. Although there was much support equipment surrounding the two aircraft, there were no large doors anywhere in evidence. How then did the airplanes find themselves there? Even more intriguing, how were they expected to get out?

She punched some more buttons and was able to obtain another shot inside the aircraft's hangar. This one partially answered her question. The angle was lower and facing upward, and she could clearly see two elaborate sliding doors attached to the chamber ceiling. With this new discovery in mind, she switched back to the first shot, and examined the two aircraft more closely.

She knew about the Harrier jet—the Marine attack plane that could take off and land vertically by redirecting its jet blast. Could these two airplanes work on the same principle? Each one *did* have two spoutlike devices under the wing that appeared to be movable. What's more, the floor underneath them was scarred black with soot and oil, indicating perhaps that the airplanes were designed to take off and land vertically. But there was no way she could tell for sure.

She bounced around to more camera shots, seeing many empty corridors and padlocked doors and little else. She'd almost given up, when she pushed red button thirty-four with yellow button three. It took a long time for the camera to focus, but when it did, Maureen found herself looking in on a grand sitting room, complete with crys-

403

tal chandelier, a roaring fireplace, and a massive leather coach.

"Where the hell is this?" she wondered, thinking at first that it might be somewhere within the Area 61 facility itself. But then, by studying the landscape outside the huge picture window at one end of the room, she could tell that this place was nowhere near Area 61. The terrain in the background was completely different. It was flat and at a lower perspective, indicating that the room sat in a house that itself was on top of a mountain or a butte.

She was fascinated that this place would be on the Spy network, and she spent much time studying the splendor of the room.

Then, rather suddenly, she saw shadows moving down a stairway and toward the room. People were coming. Three of them. She pulled her seat closer to the monitor and waited with curious anticipation.

The first person entered the room. It was a very elderly man, skinny, bent over and wearing some kind of an ancient Army dress uniform and a long gray pony tail. He grabbed a glass from a nearby table and then plopped down onto the couch. Right behind him was a young girl, too young to be his daughter, even too young to be his granddaughter. Yet when she sat beside the old man, she hugged him and kissed him right on the lips, passionately.

This is very strange, Maureen thought as she watched the odd couple.

But the real shock came when the third person walked in. Tall. Rugged. The unmistakable face.

She couldn't believe it.

"Oh my God . . ." she gasped. "Is that really him?"

70

Outside Tango Base

The Blue army company commander hastily lit a cigarette and then checked his watch.

It was 2240 hours — one hour and twenty minutes to midnight.

He and his field staff were hunkered down at the top of a small rocky plateau, about two miles north of Tango Base. Strung along for a half mile in the desert below him was what remained of his highly-regarded unit, the 4th Battalion of the 77th Blue Army Division.

Once a highly-mobile force of 950 light infantry, 4th Battalion, also known as Charlie Blue, was now a sparse 411 men in total. In their glory days, the hardcore light infantrymen had carried highly-portable, sophisticated weapons, like shoulder-launched, laser-guided Zoot SAMs, silencer-equipped 50-mm Zoot mortars, and short-range, all-terrain surface-to-surface Zoot missiles. Riding in stripped-down, souped-up Hummers, their *forte* had been to move out quickly, penetrate enemy territory, seize an objective, hold it for long periods of time, and then get out fast.

But now, like every other unit in this part of the Range, Charlie Blue was in retreat. They hadn't received supplies in more than four days, hadn't pulled off an operation in six. All of their whizbang weaponry was gone, discarded for lack of ammunition and Zoot batteries. Most of the men were armed with only simple Zoot M-16s. And they had lost their fleet of hot-rod Hummers more than a week ago for lack of fuel.

That's why Charlie Blue was now taking part in a very desperate mission — perhaps its last.

The Charlie Blue commander had been first contacted by the chief security officer of Tango Base early that morning. The man from Tango had a big problem: his intelligence people were telling him the

405

unstoppable mystery army would be within five miles of Tango Base inside of twenty-four hours. The brass at the Aggressor air base — once considered the jewel of War Heaven in many respects — had no other choice but to evacuate the place.

And quick.

The Tango security chief wanted to make a deal. If the Charlie Blue commander joined the security perimeter around the Aggressor air base this night, while the Tango squadron bugged out, they would be guaranteed 1000 points, enough to feed and equip each man in Charlie Blue for about three days.

Charlie Blue would be but one of seventeen units making up the protective line around Tango. Hodgepodge groups of retreating Blues, Greens, and Grays, all of them starved for supplies, would also be up on the line — mercenaries for one night while the haughty Tango Base folded its tent and slipped away.

At first the Charlie Blue commander felt that such a patchwork security perimeter could hold — at least for a while. First of all, according to the Tango security chief, the seventeen units combined would equal a force of close to 2500 men. Second, there were near-impenetrable defenses already surrounding Tango Base. Though the air base was on a plain that was open on three sides, with only a small but inaccessible mountain range protecting its rear, it was nevertheless well-protected from attack. It was surrounded by thousands of remote-controlled antipersonnel Zoot mines, as well as a ring of automatic "trip-wire" SAMs — Zoot Hawk missile batteries that could be programmed to send dozens of antiaircraft missiles at any approaching aircraft that wasn't transmitting an appropriate IFF (Identification Friend or Foe) signal. This necklace of protection was complemented by another, highly automated ring of standard Zoot antiaircraft guns, including long-range Zoot Gatlings and radar-controlled AA guns which could be lowered and used against ground troops.

But the commander of Charlie Blue grew slightly apprehensive when he studied the Tango security officer's map of the proposed defense line. He found that his men would be deployed in positions right up along the edge of the Zoot-mine apron itself.

This told the Blue army officer one thing: if the mysterious army launched an attack and breached the far outer defense perimeter around Tango, the men of Charlie Blue would be the first to take the brunt of the hammer blow. And if they failed to hold, then the attackers would have a gap wide enough to pour through and get into Tango Base itself.

In this worst-case scenario, the patchwork defense army flanking Charlie Blue's positions could probably put up enough resistance to allow the Aggressors to evacuate. But just like Charlie Blue, most of those units would be wiped out in the process.

In other words, it had the potential to be Custer's Last Stand, Dien Bien Phu, and the Alamo all rolled into one. What was worse, if the mystery army was able to overrun Tango itself, then they would be in a perfect position for taking over the entire midsection of the Range, including its heart and soul, Area 61, not that far to the south.

Still, the Charlie Blue commander thought it was worth the risk.

His men were getting desperate. They were hungry, low on field supplies, and, worst of all, they were demoralized. Joining in a security line for a few hours was just about the only mission remaining that his depleted unit could accomplish. And they needed the points. Even if his unit received one half—or even just one third—of the 1000 points, then at least they would eat and get enough supplies to keep moving south.

So he had accepted the Tango security man's offer.

The eight-mile walk to the Tango base defense line earlier that night had carried them through areas heavy with retreating Gray and Green forces, many of them without arms or ammunition at all.

Once Charlie Blue made it to the destination, the commander deployed his troops over the half-mile-long portion of their line in standard fashion—ten-man units, each set up to give the other covering fire. On one side of Charlie Blue there was a six-hundred-man unit of Gray army combat engineers, now turned infantrymen. On the other side was a two-hundred-man Green army airborne assault unit—pilots, troopers, mechanics, and door gunners—that hadn't seen a helicopter in six days. They too were now turned into grunts.

Other units along the ten mile defense line included Gray army sapper squads, Green army special-ops units, Blue army mountain troops. There were forty tanks in all adding to the defensive ring—Blue Army M-1A1s mostly, though more than half of them had no fuel and had to be towed into position.

There were also a dozen Green army attack choppers flitting around—AH-1W Sea Cobras mostly, though several AH-64

Apaches had also been spotted. All in all, the defense was pretty deep, and in the old days it would have constituted a fairly impressive force.

But these weren't the old days.

Once Charlie Blue was in position and set, the commander and his staff had secured their position atop the small plateau. Its clear field of view made it an ideal location from which to command his troops.

Now, all they had to do was wait.

Trouble arrived exactly at 2300 hours.

They'd been settled in for nearly an hour when the Charlie Blue commander got a "20-17" report from one of his forward squads about five hundred yards north of him.

It was the last call the Charlie Blue officer wanted to hear: a 20-17 meant "infiltrators in the wire."

He scanned the area himself via a long-range NightScope and did indeed see about a half dozen heat sources slowly crawling through the vast Zoot minefield that lay like an iron sheet in front of Tango. It was evident by their slow but steady progress that the infiltrators were clearing a path through the mines. A quick call to the commanders on either side of him confirmed the oncoming enemy action in the middle of his sector.

The Charlie Blue commander was thus faced with his first dilemma of the night. Should he have his men open fire on the infiltrators and thus draw attention to himself? Or should he wait until they were through the minefield and then subdue them in a quieter fashion?

Keeping his positions unrevealed was at the moment the highest priority. Thus, he opted for option two. He ordered his forward unit to silently deploy to the point where the infiltrators would break out of the minefield and then ambush them. He waited twenty minutes and then called the forward unit. What in the hell was happening? he asked. Nothing, came the reply. The enemy sappers had stopped about five hundred feet in front of the ambush spot. Now they were silently slipping back the way they had come.

This raised the second dilemma for the Charlie Blue commander. His men were now facing a large swath that had been successfully cut in the mine apron. What to do? Should he send some of his men tiptoeing into this breach, only to have them steamrolled by the massive force that might be poised to attack through the clearing? Or should he mass his men at the critical spot on the edge of the nearly depleted minefield and meet whatever attack head-on?

While he was trying to make up his mind on this decision, he was introduced to his third dilemma. A call from the Gray unit on the farthest right flank reported that their listening devices had detected the sound of heavy equipment coming their way.

"Launch a drone," the Charlie Blue commander told his troops, who quickly complied. Watching the video signals being sent back from the small airborne camera on his own portable TV monitor, the Charlie Blue commander was astonished to see that a force consisting of no less than two hundred-fifty tanks and five hundred APCs was waiting just over the sight line. Each one was covered by camouflage netting, thus defying identification. But one fact was certain: if each APC was carrying a normal complement of eight men, then the Tango defense line was facing a force that was at least twice the size of theirs, and that didn't count the tanks.

It went from bad to worse a few minutes later, when the sound of jet engines suddenly cut through the tense night air. The first inclination, that the noise was caused by incoming attack jets, was quickly dispelled. Actually, the airplane noise was a harbinger of something worse. High above the perimeter line, the distinct outline of the Boeing 707 JSTARS aircraft came into view.

He had a hasty conference with the other perimeter line commanders, and with the Tango security chief as well. All of them agreed that with the huge army waiting just out of sight, and the captured sophisticated targeting airplane overhead, an attack was imminent.

The Charlie Blue commander checked his watch again. It was now exactly midnight.

"Call down along the line," he told one of his staff officers. "Tell the men to get ready."

The first Zoot shells from the mystery army came crashing down on Blue Charlie's position two minutes later.

The tidal wave had finally arrived.

71

Casa Fantastica

"Are you sure you don't want to take a bottle of Scotch with you?"

Ryder checked his small knapsack. It was packed with several steak sandwiches, a six-pack of Coke, a bag of ice, a box of Oreos, his Zoot .45, and the remainder of his Las Vegas winnings a total of $228. The supplies were enough to carry him for several days. Truth was, he was only going about 65 miles.

"I don't think I should take any booze," he told the old man. "I'm hoping I can steal a plane somewhere and get the hell down to Area Sixty-one before, well, you know . . ."

But as far as the Scotch was concerned, the old man wouldn't take no for an answer. He stuffed two bottles of the fifty-year-old Ballantine into Ryder's already overflowing knapsack.

"You should sip it for medicinal purposes," he told Ryder. "You might think that all that hallucination gas is out of your system, but I guarantee you it ain't. That stuff will stay with you for days. Weeks. Months, even."

Ryder was in no position to disagree. Although he felt much better since eating the two steaks and loading up on brandy and Scotch, he'd already experienced what could only be described as Hal-Lou flashbacks.

There had been two of them. The first came shortly after the old man scared the hell out of both him and the young girl by faking that he was dead. No sooner had the old man popped back up on the couch than Ryder saw his face turn fast into that of a devil and then that of an angel, halo and all. He shook the disturbing vision out of his head, and quelled the panic rising in his chest by convincing himself that it was just the Hal-Lou gas coming back to haunt him.

The second flashback was no less frightening, but at least had a pleasant edge to it. Angel had walked into the kitchen to get a bucket of ice, and when she came back she was, to Ryder's eyes, totally naked. He'd seen it all. The small, pert breasts. The slim, curvy waist. The delicate, innocent, milky-white thighs. He was able to shake this hallucination away, too, but only after enjoying it for a second or two longer than he should have.

So now here he was, some hours later, his bag packed, the Lincoln Continental warmed up and ready, wondering when he'd suffer his next flashback. Would it happen while he was driving to Tango? Or while he was looking for an airplane to steal? Or while he was flying that airplane?

He had no idea. So he didn't put up much of a fight when the old man stuffed the two bottles of Ballantine into his sack. Maybe the old guy was right, maybe the Scotch would keep the Hal-Lou flashbacks to a minimum.

"It's already past midnight," Ryder said to the old man now as they stood out in front of Casa Fantastica. "I've got to get going."

The old man nodded slowly, sadly. "We could talk for hours, Colonel. Days," he said. "We are alike in many ways."

"I know," Ryder told him. "Maybe we'll do it again someday."

The old man coughed, and in doing so he almost lost his balance. He was saved from toppling over only by Angel's steadying grip.

"Maybe," he said, his voice both raspy and drunk.

He hugged Ryder and Ryder hugged Angel. It was getting very emotional and Ryder wanted to get the hell out of there. But just after he climbed into the big Lincoln, the old man staggered over to the window.

"Here, you should have this now," he said, handing him a small black box. "They never did tell me what it was for, exactly, but you never know, you might find it will come in handy."

Ryder took the box, shook hands with him again, waved to Angel, and then was gone, screeching out of the driveway and down the dirt road off the mountain.

It was only when he got out onto the open road that he opened the black box. Inside was a very expensive digital watch.

It was running backward.

72

The Spy

Where the hell is he?

Maureen had spent the last three hours punching up cameras, bouncing around from scene to scene inside and outside of Area 61, trying to find another view into the strange, ornate house where she was almost certain she'd spotted Ryder.

But try as she might, she could not find the right combination of button pushing to give her anything other than that one shot of the now-darkened room.

She still couldn't believe she'd seen him. Whoever it was had stayed in front of the camera for only a few fleeting moments before sitting down with the other two people on the huge couch that was just about out of camera range. Later on, the trio left the room completely, and though Maureen stayed glued to the TV monitor for another two and half hours, she never saw any of them again.

Now the doubts came creeping in. Had the blurry figure really been Ryder? Or were her eyes just playing tricks on her? She knew that one of the Operation Rapture pilots was "missing," and the presence of the pilot named Woody did lend some evidence that Ryder might be somehow connected to all this. But as time passed and she watched the flames die inside the fireplace on the edge of the luxurious room, so did her belief that it was him. And with this, came crushing disappointment.

What a cruel trick for fate to play on her . . .

She turned her misery into anger. Where the hell was the young man with the manicured hands? What was *his* game? Could this be part of it? Had it all been arranged?

The studio seemed to be colder by the minute. The more she examined it, the more she realized how little it had ever been used. Some of the equipment still had instruction tags attached to them. Other stuff had never even been plugged in.

She could hear a constant pounding noise above her. It sounded like massive hydraulic pumps. It made her think about the young man's claim that the people in charge of Area 61 were planning on detonating an atomic bomb. As time passed and her resolve began to buckle, she worried about how close she was going to be to this exposion if it occurred, whether she had been actually placed here, in harm's way, intentionally.

She turned back to the TV control board, telling herself that it was her only hope of uncovering more clues. She found it much more difficult to operate the interior cameras than those on the outside. Unlike those exterior cameras, some of the interior ones took up to ten minutes or more to come into sharp focus, due she supposed to some kind of warming-up action.

She eventually found a clear shot of Pinky's ornate office, though the bullet-headed bureaucrat was nowhere to be scene. She also located a camera shot from the Zoo. It was also deserted, each of the glass displays covered in plastic sheeting. Still, just the sight of the glass cells, and what was contained inside them, made her shiver. Had they been real? Or just part of a big hoax? Maureen wondered if she'd ever find out for sure.

She managed to punch up shots of other important units throughout the facility: the supercomputer room, the Silver Room, the Elephant Graveyard. All were empty, as was the office for SLO—the Self Luminating Objects Room where she'd met the strange, unkept man named Willy that one and only time.

She was also able to spy in on chambers that she'd never seen before. One of them contained dozens of inflated silver weather balloons. Another room looked like the interior of a flying saucer as it would be represented in a grade-B sci-fi movie, all instruments and lights and gadgets tacked to the walls, nothing at all like the interior of the "authentic" saucer she had toured. A small sign on the outside of this garish mock-up read Abduction Chamber One.

Still another shot depicted a large storage room which contained several dozen small airplanes that looked like hang gliders with small engines on them. She'd seen similar flying machines before at a small airport outside Washington, D.C.: they were called ultralights. They were parked in neat rows of twenty apiece. Some had large lights hanging off their bottoms. Although they were not illuminated, Maureen could tell some were colored red, some white, some amber.

As she worked her way through the buttons, it was easy to realize that all of the work spaces in the facility were in fact sealed tight. So where were all the people?

Her answer came when she began pushing buttons further down the line. These brought her views of the individual living apartments. Suddenly she was able to spy in on people sitting in their rooms, some alone, some with another person or two. Some people were reading, some were on the phone. One man was poring over a calculator and reams of paper. Another man was typing furiously into a computer. Still another was reading the Bible.

She was able to cue up a scene in a large apartment where she recognized the two men within to be "Mike" and "Charlie" of the Silver Room. It was apparent that they had simply brought their work with them; she could clearly see the six chunks of metal that the men had claimed were from various UFO crash sites lined up on a dresser top.

Another long wait for another office camera to come to focus answered another important question. The camera was spying on a small anteroom, a place that was obviously a hallway that led to a larger room. There was a coffee machine steaming away in the corner of this room about ten feet away from a set of massive steel doors.

As she watched this view, she began to recognize some of the people who were coming out from behind the large steel doors simply to get a cup of coffee. Each person looked haggard, tired, edgy. They were all drinking their coffee black and often.

She recognized Pinky right away; it would have been hard not to. He came out for two cups within twenty minutes. Then Ray, the curator of the Zoo came out, poured himself a cup, drank it on the spot, poured another, and went back into the room. She saw three technicians from the Elephant Graveyard take turns making new pots of the coffee, and then, to her surprise, she recognized two men who had been aboard the helicopter that had snatched her from the clear pond near Roswell so long ago.

It was one of these men, in a moment of clumsiness or disinterest, who unintentionally answered one question for her, and posed another vexing mystery. This man, carrying two cups of coffee into the room, failed to close one of the large doors behind him. In the five minutes or so that it was left open, Maureen had a straight-on view of the meeting room beyond.

It featured a huge elliptical conference table with thirty seats around it. Only one was unoccupied, it was in the middle, and clearly marked: seat 16.

The twenty-nine men around the table were obviously involved in some kind of marathon discussion. The table was covered with scattered papers, books, small computers, even a few old-fashioned slide rules. At any given moment, any one of the men could be seen nervously checking his watch, and several times it appeared as if all of the men checked their watches at the same times if synchronizing them.

Despite the hubbub, her eye drifted back to the single empty chair. Just from its center position, she got the definite impression that whoever filled it was a higher among equals, if not the chairman of the board itself.

But there was something bewildering about the man sitting in the next seat over—it being either chair 15 or 17. It seemed like most of the people in the room were deferring to him, as if he were now the person in charge due to the absence of the man belonging in seat 16.

But this authority figure seemed an unlikely choice: It was, unmistakably, scruffy Willy from SLO.

415

73

Tango

Lieutenant Bobby Tiffin couldn't believe what he was seeing.

He was flying a Green Army AH-1W Sea Cobra attack chopper supporting the defense line around Tango Base—or what was left of it. At this moment, he was watching the mystery army flow through as many as ten breaches in the formerly solid Zoot minefield that had stretched out in front of Tango. The camouflage-netted tanks and APCs were firing nonstop at the patchwork of defenders strung out along the crumbling defense line, overrunning their positions with fair ease in most places. Only those parts of the perimeter where the defending troops had managed to depress the barrels of their antiaircraft weapons—AAA guns and Zoot Phoenix Gatlings—to fire point-blank at the invaders were proving any problems for the attackers.

Tiffin had been at it now for two hours and was surprised that he'd lasted this long. He'd already seen a handful of other choppers go down, over the line, most knocked out by Zoot SAMs launched from the mystery army. Several others had expended their ammunition or fuel and had simply dropped out of the fight. Now only Tiffin's aircraft and two Apaches were left.

The intensity of the battle was so incredible, and the expenditure of Zoot weaponry so massive, that even though it was now two in the morning, Tiffin had no need for his night-vision equipment. It was as bright as high noon around the embattled base.

He landed quickly next to a hangar at the far end of Tango and helped the ground crew members fuel up his chopper and charge what was left of his Zoot weapons. The base was practically empty by this time—Tango Squadron and most of the support personnel had bugged out just as the opening shots of the battle were being fired, taking their secret documents and personal effects aboard four C-130 Hercules which had left in the company of two auxiliary F-15s. Tiffin had no idea where they were headed; but judging from the size and the seeming-invincibility of the mystery army, he didn't think it really mattered.

He lifted off again, his gunner cueing up the last weapons they'd had taken on: two Zoot Hellfire missiles and a single Zoot TOW antiarmor rocket. Just as they cleared the top of the hangar, two Zoot Tomahawks came crashing down on the end of Tango's main runway, zapping the base's remaining radar set and killing all of its landing assistance devices. Under the rules of Zoot engagements, the base was now technically destroyed, incapable of handling aircraft taking off or landing.

"That's it," Tiffin's gunner radioed back to him. "The ball game is over for this place."

"Let's get rid of these fireworks and get the hell out of here, then," Tiffin told the crewman.

He swung the chopper up and around the small mountain range to the rear of the air base, intent on attacking the mystery army's far flank. This way, once their weapons were expended, he'd be able to get out of harm's way quickly simply by turning west and booting up the throttles.

He put the chopper down to 75 feet and screamed along the edge of the protective mountain toward a stream of tanks pouring in on the base's battered northwest barrier. Tiffin's gunner selected the lead tank and let one of the Hellfires fly. It impacted right on the turret, the resulting holographic explosion momentarily illuminating the design of the tank under the camouflage netting.

"We got it," the gunner reported, seeing his HILES engagement sensor light blink on, indicating a direct hit. "Whatever the hell kind of tank it was . . ."

Tiffin pointed the Cobra at a line of APCs roaring across the now-defunct minefield, and his gunner let loose the Zoot TOW missile. Directing the powerful weapon via its wire-guided system, he was able to impact it on the second-in-line APC, killing it instantly. It screeched to a halt immediately nearly taking out the pair of APCs that were plowing through the field right on its tail. Once again the tremendous Zoot explosion gave light to the shape of the APC under the camouflage disguise.

417

"That's the damnedest APC I've ever seen," Tiffin's gunner commented.

"It sure ain't no Bradley," the pilot agreed.

They picked out their third target – another attacking tank which was firing on two of the stationary Blue Army's M-1A1s on the end of the defense line near the base of the mountain.

Suddenly something caught Tiffin's eye, something that was so out of the ordinary on the fierce battlefield, it actually drew his attention away from the matter at hand.

He pulled the chopper up and out of its attack dive, and swung around to the east, fascinated at the strange sight.

"Do you see what I see?" he radioed ahead to his gunner.

"I see it," was the reply, "but I don't believe it."

He too had forgotten about launching their final Hellfire.

Coming through the middle of battlefield, oblivious and unaffected by the storm of streaking Zoot missiles, shells, explosions, and gun fire, was a huge Lincoln Continental convertible.

There were only twenty-two people left within Tango Base itself – volunteers who agreed to stay behind and service the helicopters that had been contracted to help protect the base while the rest of the Tango squadrons evacuated.

These mechanics now knew that the glorious history of Tango Base and the Tango Aggressor squadrons was about to come to a rather inglorious end. The hired helicopters were now long gone, either shot down or out of weapons or fuel. The air base itself was officially inoperable – it had been plastered by Zoot Tomahawks nonstop for the past ten minutes and there wasn't a Zoot-generated device still operating anywhere.

The twenty-two mechanics gathered in front of the largest hangar at the end of the base, the aircraft barn where the infamous black F-15Xs were once kept. Now it was empty, dark, useless. From this vantage point they could see the titanic battle raging out on the perimeter about a half mile away. It was so obvious that the mystery army would break through at any moment that the mechanics were in the midst of a discussion of what would happen to them once they were taken POW by the strange invaders.

The consensus, which was *the* rumor making the rounds on the Range in the past few days, was that War Heaven was actually about to be shut down for budgetary reasons and that this was the Pentagon's way of letting it go out with a bang. Others couldn't believe that, instead arguing that the invading army and the whole scenario that they brought with them was authentically an OBD—"one big drill."

Either way, the point they did agree on was that, judging from the ferocity of the battle and the racket it was making, they would know the answers very, *very* soon.

They shielded their eyes as another barrage of Zoot Tomahawks came crashing in, followed by a string of bright, holographic artillery shells.

Then, just as the Zoot images were dissipating, they heard a strange sound. Not a tracked weapon or an aircraft, it sounded like . . . like an automobile?

They looked to the sand wall protecting the far end of the runway just in time to see it burst away in an explosion of dust and smoke. From this cloud emerged a screeching, dented, dirty, and battered Lincoln Continental.

The enormous car ran the length of the runway, turned around, and came to a screeching halt in front of the astounded group of mechanics.

"Who the fuck is this?" one of them yelled over the thunder of the nonstop Zoot explosions.

"Jesuzz Christ," someone else yelled, "It's Colonel Long!"

Ryder knew most of the mechanics; they'd serviced his airplane during the vicious turn-and-burn week, as well as all the other ACM flights before and after.

They were simply amazed that he'd driven *through* the titanic battle now raging less than a half mile away.

"Hertz cars don't have HILES tags," was how he answered their barrage of questions of how he did it.

But when they asked him why, he had no ready answer, just another question.

"What do we have here that can fly?"

They laughed—all twenty-two of them.

"Are you kidding?" a chief named Joe Gaffney said to him. "This place is plastered. Closed. Out of action. Look around you, Colonel. Now you know how the Iraqis felt."

Ryder didn't have any time to dally.

"I mean, something real, *not* something with a Zoot on it."

The mechanics looked at him with a mixture of horror and be-

419

musement.

"You're not serious?" Gaffney asked him.

"I'm damned serious, Chief," Ryder said.

He jumped back in the Lincoln and screeched down to Hanger 5-T, the second largest barn on the beleaguered base. There was nothing inside. He continued on his way, down to Hangar 4-RW, which was a cargo plane barn. It too was empty.

He took a U-turn and went down the narrow passageway between the two large hangars. There was a small air barn attached to 5-T and accessed at the rear. It was a repair facility, usually reserved for airplanes in transit.

He skidded the car to a halt and jumped out. The hangar door was closed but not locked. He gave the sliding door one great yank and it slid back. He took a look inside.

"I don't believe this," he said, hoping the vision before him was not a flashback from his inhalation of Hal-Lou gas.

It was the old Tennessee Air National Guard F-4 Phantom from Spookbase.

Ryder was already up in the cockpit of the airplane when about half of the ground-crew mechanics came running up.

"Colonel?" Gaffney was calling out to him. "What are you doing, sir?"

"I'm trying to get this thing fired up," Ryder yelled back down to them.

They were staring up at him like he was out of his mind, which wasn't that far from the mark.

"Colonel, you need a ground start-up unit for that old bird," Gaffney explained to him. "You just can't turn the key."

Ryder shook his head and tried to clear it, just a little.

"Okay, then, let's go," he called down to them. "Start me up."

The mechanics looked at each other, not quite believing what they were hearing.

"Colonel, are you okay, sir?" Gaffney yelled up to him. "Do you know what's going on out there about a half mile away?"

"Dammit, of course I know," Ryder yelled back down to him, "I just drove through it."

"But nothing can move on this base," Gaffney insisted, believing now that the pilot was simply drunk. "It's been canned."

420

"I've got to launch in this airplane right now!" Ryder angrily screamed down at the baffled mechanics.

"Colonel, are you serious?" Gaffney yelled back up at him. "Nothing can move here. We've been wiped out by the Zoots."

Ryder blew his top.

He climbed out of the cockpit, down the ladder, and grabbed a huge screwdriver from a nearby toolbox. Then, like a man possessed — again, not too far from the truth — he began unscrewing one of the access panels underneath the Phantom's long snout. He literally ripped the panel off after removing only half the screws. Reaching inside, he grabbed a bunch of wires he knew were connected up to the Zoot battery and gave them a yank. They all came out in his hand — wires that to him looked like they were flaming yellow, neon red, and bright, bright orange.

"Does this show you how serious I am?" he yelled at the mechanics, shaking the handful of wires at them.

They were astonished. Ripping out Zoot wires? It was as if he'd desecrated the American flag or done something equally malicious.

"Sir, the base is out of operation," Gaffney said. "Nothing can take off. The Zoots . . ."

"Fuck the Zoots!" Ryder screamed at them. "This is the real world I'm talking about. Not all this *nonsense.*

"Now, get this airplane up and charged and running. *Now.* That's an order . . ."

Still the mechanics were frozen to the spot. All the while the thunder of the mystery army was getting closer.

Even in his partially deranged state, Ryder knew that something had to be done to get the men off the dime. With the Hal-Lou gas still coursing its way through his system, there was an undeniable new dimension to his decision-making capability. He'd found a new talent of getting right to the point.

He reached down into his flightsuit and came up with two massive fistfuls of dollar bills, the last of his Las Vegas winnings.

"Will you do it if I pay you?" he asked the men.

Ten minutes later, the F-4 was rolling out onto the base's perfectly-good main runway.

The Zoot explosions were now only about a football field away from the far end of the airstrip, and Ryder could already see the first line of net-covered tanks breaking through the inside perimeter.

He gunned the big Phantom's engines, kicking up a noisy storm of black exhaust that almost rivaled that of the oncoming tanks and APCs. He turned the F-4 around, its nose now pointing toward the tanks and other armored vehicles that were flowing through the base perimeter and were racing toward its main buildings.

He did one last very quick check of the flight systems; everything seemed okay, though the F-4, which had somehow made it over from Spookbase for repairs, only had about a third of a load of fuel. He knew it was much too late to worry about that now. He snapped the brakes, pushed the throttles ahead to full power, and felt the corresponding kick in his ass as the F-4s dual engines obeyed.

A few seconds later he was rumbling down the runway.

The eleven mechanics who had taken the bribe had reached the main runway by this time.

They were ready to simply throw up their hands and surrender to the mystery invaders who were now swarming all over the far end of the base. But they had one last spectacular sight awaiting them.

It was the F-4 taking off.

As the huge fighter-bomber roared down the runway, it seemed as if every invading soldier began firing at it. At least two dozen separate Zoot SAMs streaked up from all directions toward the lumbering airplane as it lifted off – and all impacted somewhere on the venerable Phantom. But to the invaders amazement, the airplane just kept right on going. Holographic rifle fire, AA guns, more Zoot SAMs, followed the big fighter-bomber as it slowly gained altitude. Though sometimes lost in the storm of simulated 3-D explosions it continued to climb, invulnerable, plowing its way through the bombastic yet completely harmless explosions.

Without wavering a bit, it finally leveled out, turned, and roared off to the south.

It took the mystery army soldiers about five minutes to systematically search every building at Tango before they came upon the passive mechanics.

A squad of ten soldiers ran up to the group, their Zoot M-16s up and ready, indicating that the men should keep the hands raised high.

"Lighten up, men," Gaffney told the sand-camouflage uniformed soldiers. "The big game is over and you guys won. Now when can we go home?"

None of the soldiers said a word. They expertly, if roughly, searched each mechanic for weapons, studying their newly-earned greenbacks for a few moments longer than they should have, before returning the money to the men.

"Come on, guys," Gaffney yelled at them. "Fill us in. What the fuck has been going on out here for the past two weeks? Where did you guys come from? Is it one big drill or not?"

The soldiers did not reply.

The Spy

Maureen had seen the whole thing.

The titanic battle around Tango. The explosions on the runway. The helicopters. The tanks. The missiles. The rockets. The strange explosions. The men surrendering.

And she had seen the automobile. It had driven right through the fury of the weird battle, apparently impervious to the cartoonish explosions caused by the elaborate toy weapons with which the soldiers on both sides were battering each other.

And by manipulating the TV control-board buttons, she was able to follow the car as it crashed through the sand barrier and onto the beleaguered base itself. She watched as the man behind the wheel stopped just long enough to talk to a group of mechanics, then went screaming down the runway, right toward one of the hidden cameras. And as the car whipped by, she had gotten a crystal-clear video image of the driver.

And it was definitely Ryder.

Tears were flowing down her cheeks as she saw him reappear a few minutes later, in the cockpit of the ungainliest jet fighter she'd ever seen, shouting orders to the other men, completely unaffected by the growing number of colorful explosions going on around him.

And then she saw him take off, screaming down the runway, into the face of the battle itself, finally disappearing from her view in a hail of aerial explosions and bomb blasts.

And through it all, she had only thought: *Is he coming to rescue me?*

74

The unglamorous name of the butte was T-2.

Three miles to the north of Area 61, the mesa had a commanding view of the airfield and nondescript buildings known as Dreamland.

At that moment, three armored columns consisting of tanks, APCs, and troop trucks were streaming past T-2 and heading for Area 61. Their only opposition were the depleted remnants of the Blue, Green, and Gray armies. Fighting in small unorganized groups, their Zoot batteries running down on their weapons, these retreating troops could perform little more than delaying actions in the face of the huge onslaught of the mystery army.

The blue UH-60 Blackhawk helicopter had just landed on top of T-2. There were five other helicopters on the mesa's summit, all of them supporting the small command center that had been established near the southern edge of the butte.

Lieutenant Moon jumped out of the Blackhawk, followed by a man who was dressed in a suit coat and tie. It was just sunrise, but a wickedly hot wind was blowing across the top of the stark mountain. The man in the business suit was quickly soaked in sweat.

Behind him came two heavily armed men in more appropriate lightweight desert gear. Between them was a man in prison-blue overalls. His hands cuffed, his legs in shackles, his eyes blindfolded, the man known as Sixteen had finally returned to the Nevada desert.

Moon walked over to the small command post and nodded to the four military officers who were busily coordinating communications between the three advancing columns. One of them handed him a message just received over a portable fax machine. It read simply, *Confirmed: Tango Base taken.*

424

This was good news for Moon. A large obstacle had been eliminated. Now he could concentrate on the climactic battle at hand.

The officer who had handed him the message was the overall commander of the so-called mystery army, which was known officially as the "Sanitized Forces."

Below them, they could see that the remainder of the defending Blue, Green, and Gray forces had now cohered into a ragged line that stretched across the desert for about two miles. But this line was anything but solid. Rather, it was continuously collapsing back toward the Area 61 airfield in the face of the overwhelming armored columns.

The desert was ablaze with Zoot flashes and their corresponding sound effects, but it was clear that the advancing Sanitized Forces were the ones doing most of the shooting. Behind their armor were two more large groups of soldiers, walking north. These were the prisoners of the Sanitized Forces: Blue, Green, and Gray soldiers who'd run out of ammunition and supplies and were now POWs.

"How much longer do they think it will take?" Moon asked the man in the business suit, who in turn whispered something into the ear of the Sanitized Forces' commanding officer.

"He says forty-five minutes," came the secondhand reply from the man in the suit. "One hour at the most."

"That might be too late," Moon said.

He turned and gave a signal to the guards holding sixteen to bring him forward. Clanking and rattling, the men slowly led the prisoner up beside Moon, removed his blindfold, and then retreated.

Pointing out over the edge of the precipice, Moon directed Sixteen's attention to the action below.

"It's over," he told the man simply. "There's no sense in anyone inside Area Sixty-one to delay in giving up. This book will be closed in a matter of minutes."

Sixteen squinted in authentic horror as he saw the three advancing armies moving toward the small mountain range that housed the underground Area 61 facility.

"Now wouldn't it be just plain smart for you to call those people holed up inside there and tell them to come out?" Moon asked Sixteen. "Before someone gets hurt—*for real?*"

"I . . . I can't do that," Sixteen replied. "You just don't understand."

Moon took a battered, cheap wristwatch from his pocket and

shoved it under Sixteen's nose.

"Why is this thing running backwards?" Moon demanded of the man. "Is this the countdown for the detonation of your bomb?"

Sixteen looked at his captured watch and saw that the numerals now read: 1 hour, 12 minutes, 11 seconds.

"I can't tell you," he said, bracing himself nevertheless. "I just can't . . ."

Moon yanked the man's collar sharply, holding his head firmly in place so he could not help but stare out at both the advancing and retreating troops.

"Can you see that?" Moon yelled at the man. "Can you see that there will be about six thousand people all over that airstrip in less than an hour? And if this watch is a countdown to your explosion, that they might all be killed?

"Do you really want six thousand homicide charges thrown at you, too?"

Sixteen was now sweating profusely.

"You just don't understand," he said, gasping for air in the dry Nevada morning. "No one has to get killed. But you have to let us do what we have to do. If we don't, then everything will be . . . will be . . ."

The man's words died off and were replaced by the sounds of him trying to catch his breath.

Moon was furious. "They're going to throw you in a hole so deep, mister," he growled at the man, "it will make solitary at Sing Sing look like a sun room."

Moon motioned for the two guards to remove the man.

"Bind those handcuffs tighter," he told the guards angrily. "And gag him, too."

Moon looked at the backward-running watch again and swore lightly under his breath. The man in the suit was up beside him now, as was one of the commander of the Sanitized Forces.

"How long does he think it will take to bust into the place once his troops get there?" Moon asked the guy in the suit, who once again whispered into the ear of the commanding officer.

"Using real explosives, about a half hour," came the reply. "They have four helicopters waiting nearby. The men inside are the special troops. They have the real explosive charges. They are armed with real weapons."

Moon wiped the perspiration from his own brow. He was running out of options just as quickly as he was running out of time. He knew his next decision could very well result in a major loss of life on both sides. He turned directly to the military commander of Sanitized Forces.

"If some of your men get killed – for real," he asked the man, "are you concerned that the others won't be able to keep it a secret?"

The commanding officer had the message whispered in his ear again and then took a long moment to think it over. He, too, was in a difficult position. Like Moon, the last thing he and his ten-thousand man force had expected to be doing a month ago was fighting as close as one could get to a real war in the middle of the American desert. After all, he and his men had come to make movies. Still, they were professionals, in more ways than one.

He turned back to Moon and answered his question with one word: *"Nyet."*

75

The Spy

Maureen froze when she heard the door to the TV studio opening. There was nowhere to hide in the vast control room, no weapon of convenience. She prayed that the person coming through the door was the strange young man who first brought her to this place.

It was.

"Where have you been?" she asked him with equal parts of scorn and relief. "I thought you would have been back hours ago.

"It's very confusing up above," he told her. "They are in a total radiation protocol. Everything is sealed up tight. Every place except the Black Hole. They've got soldiers everywhere. Real soldiers, from the L-10 protection squad. They have orders to shoot on sight, and they will do it, believe me. So, it was very difficult for me to move around."

"But have you found a way to get out?"

"I think so," he replied. "But there are a few things that have to be checked first. We'll have to figure out a clear route from here to the exit door by using the hidden cameras. It might take a while."

"How long do we have?"

The young man checked his watch. "One hour, two minutes, and a few seconds," he replied. "When the blast goes off, then it will be absolutely impossible to get out . . . that I know for sure."

The man began working the TV control console like an expert, pushing buttons both red and yellow with learned aplomb. Then he took out a pad and pen and began making crude drawings of the various levels of the facility.

"They've got L-10 soldiers stationed at all the critical points," the young man told her. "See for yourself."

He pointed to the first line of five TV monitors. Sure enough, Maureen could see that heavily armed troops had taken up positions at places like the doorways on Level 3, the elevator entrance down in the Elephant Graveyard, and outside the Silver Room.

"They've been preparing for this moment for a very long time," the young man said. "Even though they know as well as anybody that this whole place could go up."

"It can?" Maureen asked, startled. "How?"

"It's one of a number of scenarios," the young man said. "But the detonation they are planning might set off a chain reaction that may be impossible to stop."

" 'Impossible'?"

The young man nodded grimly. "It's similar to what the scientists who exploded the first atomic bomb faced. They had determined that there was about a one-in-a-hundred chance that their chain reaction would spread to every atom on Earth, literally destroying the entire planet."

"And where did you say this explosion was going to take place?" Maureen asked.

"In the Black Hole," he replied. "And that's a very appropriate name, believe me."

He began flipping a series of switches and punching several buttons down near the end of the console.

"This is the loading tunnel," he explained, pointing to the monitor which was displaying what looked like a typical coal-mine tunnel. "It's about a mile from here, deep underground. They have a small particle accelerator at the far end that's been working on special gold fragments for about three weeks. On the other side of *that* is the Black Hole. It's a hollowed-out cavern originally intended for underground nuclear testing."

"A particle accelerator is a very complex piece of machinery," Maureen observed.

"And this one is no different," the young man replied. "You see, the whole idea is to first separate the atoms in a small amount of gold—that's where the particle accelerator comes in, then fuse them back together in the correct reconstructed order, via the nuclear explosion. That's where the bomb comes in.

"If the Cray supercomputer's calculations are correct, then the explosion will begin a chain reaction. The result should be an acceptable amount of supergold."

Maureen was immediately confused. The young man was getting ahead of himself.

"Acceptable amount of what?" she asked. "What are you talking about?"

"Supergold," the young man replied. "Enough to power up that craft you saw up in cold storage."

"So that *is* an authentic UFO up there?"

"Authentic in design as re-created by the Cray," he answered.

He pushed one of the blue-capped buttons, the ones that controlled the data screens for the Cray supercomputer.

"They replay this readout twenty-four hours a day," the young man explained. "The computer is constantly updating it, but it gives you a good idea of what their plans are."

What Maureen saw was a computer-generated, three-dimensional drawing of the flying saucer she'd inspected with Walter a few days before. The detail was so crisp, it almost looked like a photograph. But as she was watching it, she realized that the design was actually an animated sequence that was slowly but constantly re-drawing itself.

"You have to explain this," she told him. "Are you saying that they built a flying saucer from plans that came out of the computer? How did the computer get them?"

"The quick answer is to say that it studied the various pieces of recovered UFO wreckage and reconstructed it from there," the young man replied. "Like forensic scientists can reconstruct a person's face just from a fragment of their skull or jaw, the Cray was able to get the design down pat, inside *and* out. The various molds, if you will, were all stored down in the Elephant's Graveyard. What they got was a kind of generic flying saucer."

Maureen's reporter instincts were flowing again. She'd get a story yet.

"Okay, if that's the short answer," she said, "what's the long answer?"

The young man settled back in his chair and checked his watch.

"Okay, long but quick," he began. "It all started back about two and a half years ago. The story goes that right after the Cray was put on

430

line, they started asking it questions. And—"

"Wait a minute," Maureen interrupted him. "Who are 'they'? I mean, who is behind all this? The CIA?"

The young man gave a nervous laugh. "Hardly," he said. "It's a group called the ISC."

Maureen shook her head; she was hearing the term for the first time.

"Intelligence Security Committee," the young man told her. "They are the people who really run this operation."

"Never heard of them."

"Very few people have," the young man said. "They started out as a very small group of representatives from all of this country's other intelligence services. They were put in charge of running Area Sixty-one, all of its secrets, and the Cray. They were actually formed as a budgetary move—you know, all the consolidation after the Cold War supposedly went away.

"But things started to get out of hand almost immediately after the Cray began operating.

"As I said, they began feeding it questions. So-called 'impossible questions.' Unanswerable, paradoxical things like 'How can two parallel lines meet?' or 'If a spaceship is moving at the speed of light and turns on a spotlight in its nose, what happens?' It would usually reply with some long complicated set of equations. Useless stuff, really.

"Well, somewhere along the line, someone inputted, 'Where do UFOs come from?' Instead of the usual lengthy, convoluted response, the computer surprised everyone by coming back with a rather austere statement, which basically said, 'Give me more data and I'll give you an answer.' "

"Well, the ISC people running the computer thought this was very strange, almost as if the Cray was displaying some kind of intuition on its own."

"Artificial intelligence?" Maureen asked.

The young man half-nodded. "Maybe not that artificial," he replied. "That was the surprise. But in any case, the people running the Cray thought this would be a great exercise for their big expensive toy. So they began feeding raw information into it. Everything they could get their hands on concerning UFOs. Government files. Scientific studies. Reports of sightings, going all the way back to the Bible. Every possible theory that had ever been written about. They dragged in some of the top scientific minds in the country, picked their brains about everything from quarks to superstrings to Saint Elmo's Fire, all in relation to UFOs. They were just shoveling all this stuff into the Cray."

"But that seems like a lot of people working on a very strange idea," Maureen said.

"It was," the young man replied. "And the security concerns were enormous. Because the end result, whatever it might be, had the potential of changing everything. World history. Science. Religion.

"So, in a very clever, very devious way to protect themselves, the ISC simply let most of these very learned people go back out into the world after giving them the 'Grand Tour,' as they called it. Some of them were drugged beforehand or convinced that they were crazy. Some weren't. They also snatched normal ordinary citizens, too, and did variations on the same plan, though they used the abduction chamber on them, this to better poison the waters, so to speak.

"Then, as you probably know, some of these people claimed they'd seen all this crazy stuff in Dreamland. Looking back on it, it was really a very cruel thing to do, especially to these scientists, because right away their credibility was shot. Their reputations were ruined. No one could believe *all* of these stories. It turned out to be the perfect cover for the people in charge here."

"So, in other words," she said, "by revealing a bit of the portal, they were protecting everything inside."

"Exactly," the young man replied. "And you see, the people who had been working in the Morbid National Psychology Cultivation unit had been unknowingly sowing the seeds for this for years; that's why the ISC latched onto it so quickly. Through their rather misguided efforts to protect the citizens from what they themselves didn't understand, they were actually able to form one, nearly monolithic national opinion on UFOs. And that was that they belonged in the same category as ghosts, the Loch Ness Monster, Bigfoot. Fantastic stuff. *Fascinating* stuff. *Mysterious* stuff. But not something that so-called 'rational' people would really believe."

"And so, in the end," Maureen said, "it didn't make any difference if UFOs existed or not. The majority of people would still believe they shouldn't be taken seriously."

The young man nodded in firm agreement. "Not unless one landed on the lawn of the White House," he said. "Quite an example of mass conditioning, don't you think? On a smaller scale, it's rather similar to the idea that, thanks to movies, TV shows, and books, most people believe that the Native Americans were the 'bad guys' during the opening of the American West, when, in many ways, quite the opposite was true."

"It *is* fascinating, in a frightening kind of way," Maureen said. "So what happened after all of this UFO data was fed into the Cray?"

"Well, they asked it the same question: 'Where do UFOs come from?' And again, its reply came back that it needed still more information. The problem was, there wasn't a whole lot of data left. Finally, after a lot of arm-twisting and back-room dealing, someone allowed the ISC access to fragments of UFO wreckage. Not just from Roswell, but from the other locations as well: Klecksburg, Anchorage, the Tex-Mex site. That was the big breakthrough.

"They had already developed the four-dimensional materials analysis device in the Silver Room by that time. By hooking up that machine to the Cray, they were able to study all the UFO fragments together. And that's how they came up with the 'growing younger' theory that I'm sure they told you about.

"Now, frankly, this stumped the Cray. For only about ten minutes or so, but that's a long time for a machine like that. I mean, how could something be growing younger? It didn't make sense, unless . . ."

"Unless what?"

"Unless the material was created *after* the time period in which it appeared."

"After. . . ?"

"That's right. And when the Cray figured that out, then the floodgates really opened wide. Because in all instances, it determined that this UFO material—or more specifically, its atomic structure—was created on a certain date. At a certain time."

"And that time is . . ."

The young man looked at his watch. "Forty-eight minutes and sixteen seconds from right now."

Suddenly a few more things began to make sense to her.

"So when I asked Walter if their flying saucer flew through space and he led me to believe it didn't . . ."

"And he was apparently telling you the truth," the young man said. "Because, what the Cray told them finally was that flying saucers aren't space vehicles at all. *They are time machines*."

Maureen was stunned. "Time machines?"

"But what's even more important," the young man went on, "the Cray declared that the beings that pilot UFOs, the beings that build them, aren't space aliens at all. That's the myth."

"Then, what are they?"

The young man looked at her for a long moment. "The reality is that they are us," he said. "They are human beings—from another time."

Maureen suddenly felt a tingling sensation run through her body. "My God . . . you're not serious . . ."

"I'm very serious," the young man replied. "And it makes perfect sense. Einstein himself believed that it would probably be easier to move through time than to build rocket ships that would be fast enough to make it worthwhile to fly vast distances in space. Such crafts would have to go at the speed of light, at the very least."

"But human beings?" Maureen asked, "How can that be?"

"You saw the bodies in the crypt, I assume?" the young man asked her.

"Yes, I did," she replied distastefully, "and they were disgusting . . . not human-looking at all. In fact, it makes me sick just thinking about them."

"Me, too," the young man admitted. "But again it fits into this scenario.

"There's a hell of a theory about how advanced cultures evolve into fetuslike beings. I'm sure you'll agree that's what those characters in the tomb looked like: This theory is called Neoteny, and it addresses the genetic shift which causes some advanced species to maintain some fetal characteristics into the adult stage. It sounds crazy, but look at the difference between an ape and a man. One is definitely more fetal-looking than the other. Take the human race and project it several hundred thousand years, or even million, and—"

"This is just too, *too* much for me to comprehend," Maureen declared.

"I know," the young man replied. "And don't feel bad. It took the Cray about an other half hour of burping before it was able to sort all this out."

"But how can something move through time?" Maureen asked. "I mean, despite what Einstein said, I would think it's just impossible."

"People thought flying was impossible, too, at one time," the

434

young man replied. "And I'm not an expert, but let me tell you what they told me."

He took a clean piece of paper and drew a circle in its center.

"Let's say that we think of our existence right here, right now as 'now-space,' " he said. "From our perspective, this 'now-space' is all that exists. We live here. Time seems to move forward. Everything is in one, constant flow.

"But that's like assuming that the world is flat. All the evidence seems to be there, but that doesn't make it so."

He began drawing a series of circles around the one in the middle and connecting them with straight lines.

"What the Cray figured out was that there were things called 'intimate singularities.' These are like windows to what they call 'then-space,' which, for lack of a better description, is everywhere else other than our 'now-space.'

"These 'intimate singularity' windows are outgrowths of a theoretical entity called a wormhole. The computer itself labeled them 'Super-Wormholes.' You can best imagine 'ordinary' wormholes as being infinitesimal tunnels, way down in the subatomic level which connect and disconnect random points in the universe. A Super-Wormhole is the same thing, only larger and much, much rarer.

"Now, according to the Cray, if one end of a Super-Wormhole is spinning very rapidly in space and the other end is stable, then the moving end is in a different time. That apparently is a mathematical fact. If you can locate the stable end of a Super-Wormhole, then you've found the entrance to a tunnel into another time . . ."

"Incredible – if it's true," Maureen said.

"What's even more incredible is the supergold," the young man said. "Not only does it produce the energy needed to allow the craft to move through the Super-Wormhole, it turns out that a small amount of supergold can irradiate any other kind of material, virtually mutating its atomic makeup into its own, in a very slow atomic reaction. For lack of a better term, they call this 'an atomic infection' process.

"The Cray figured out that once a craft powered by supergold passed through the Super-Wormhole, then this reaction – this 'atomic infection' process – is immediate. Instantaneous. This is what baffled the Cray for a few seconds, too. Why was *all* of the metal found at the crash sites not only growing 'younger' but also pointing to the exact same date and age?

"It finally realized that what it was reading was the effects of the supergold irradiation.

"It's natural, then, to understand how going ahead in time would accelerate and complete this 'infection' process in an instant. It's similar to the Big Bang, the commonly accepted beginning of the known universe. Everything happened in billionths of a seconds. But it takes that one entity to start with."

"And that's what the Big Blast is all about?"

"Exactly," the young man said. "They determined that the first batch of supergold *began here. With this explosion.* That's what the countdown is all about. A new beginning. A new epoch."

"They *are* playing God, aren't they?" Maureen said in a hushed tone.

"They certainly are," the young man answered. "And how do you keep something like *that* a secret? Who do you tell? Who do you *not* tell? I know for a fact that the President doesn't know anything about all this. The people here were actually afraid to tell him, because they considered him a security risk. They knew that if the politicians and the regular military ever got involved, then they would miss this very important countdown deadline."

"But what about the Operation Rapture pilots?" she asked cautiously. "Where do they come in?"

The young man took a deep breath and let it out slowly.

"Well, you have to understand something about this whole scenario," he went on. "There were always several options of what could happen. One of them, of course, is that the grand experiment would be successful and that supergold would be forged and that the Cray was correct all along. Then, with this material, they would be able to power up the flying saucer immediately.

"Of course, there would have to be a test flight. Now, I don't pretend to know how that saucer upstairs works, or how you operate it, or even what it's made out of at this moment. But they do. And they knew that it called for a pilot of extraordinary talents—both physical and psychological—to fly it. If he were to actually travel in time, what would he be like when he came back? How long would he have been gone? What would he see? Who would he meet? The possibilities *and* the paradoxes are endless.

"So, just like when they were selecting the first Mercury astronauts, the natural place to start the search was in the country's military pilot corps. And the natural place for these people to be tested and trained, both physically and psychologically, would be here, around Area Sixty-one, again because of the highest security surrounding this matter."

"But that flying saucer," Maureen said. "It has only two seats. And they're damn small at that."

The young man smiled. "I told you they built it *exactly* to the Cray's specs," he said. "Even the small seats.

"In any case, the original plan called for two pilots in the saucer and another two pilots to perform a more ominous task."

"Ominous?" she asked. "In what way?"

"Well, it was like developing an insurance policy," he replied. "Strictly because they were really tinkering with Nature in a big way here. They had no idea what the condition would be of someone who'd actually returned from traveling through the time barrier. *If* they returned.

"So they trained two pilots to accompany the saucer once it was airborne, flying in specially adapted jets to some point near the North Pole. Once there, they would watch him 'blink out,' as they call it. Then the plans called for the saucer pilot to return to that *exact time frame* and place, and immediately contact the pilots in the waiting airplanes. When this happened, he was to read to them a list of agreed upon code words. And if the pilot of the saucer didn't comply, then . . ."

"Then what?"

"Then the pilots in the airplanes had orders to shoot down the saucer."

"Shoot it down?"

"I know it sounds crazy," the young man said, "but there is a rationale to it. Back when they were testing A-bombs out here, anytime they sent an airplane aloft with a nuclear weapon on board, they would secretly send up an armed fighter plane. If something went wrong with the airplane carrying the A-bomb, or, frankly, if something went wrong with the crew, and they were starting to act crazy. well, these armed chase planes had orders to shoot them down before they were able to do any significant damage.

"It's the same idea here. They know how to shoot down a UFO. And I'll let you in on a major secret: the UFO that went down at

Roswell didn't crash. It was shot down. There's a technique to it, and they've been drilling it into the heads of the pilots who were selected for this mission."

"But how could they be sure that these pilots would actually fire on this saucer?" Maureen asked, this being just one of a million questions racing through her mind. "That's a very tall order, especially if they think they know the person who's flying it."

"They were *conditioned* for it," the young man explained. "Every facet of these pilots' makeup was taken under consideration. Including one called 'the sentimentality factor.' It comes down to this: 'You do what you've got to do, no matter what.' Everyone around here thinks that way, from the ISC guys to the L-10 soldiers. They're almost religious about it. For good reason, I suppose . . ."

"It's all so crazy," Maureen said.

The young man laughed softly. "You really don't know the half of it," he said.

Now Maureen was split on whether she should mention that she'd seen Ryder. She wasn't sure if she could trust this strange young man. But she couldn't resist probing him a little bit.

"You said that there were four pilots selected for this," she said. "But I know there's only three, here, now at this facility. Do you know what happened to the fourth one?"

The young man shook his head no.

"Who knows? Maybe he was the smartest one of us all," he replied with a wan smile. "Maybe he just figured it all out a long time ago."

76

It was just a few minutes before sunrise.

Ryder estimated he was about 40 miles from Area 61 and the Phantom was flying — but just barely. It had obviously been in the repair barn for good reason. It was borderline operational: the engines were running okay, the necessary life support systems were working. But things like the cockpit heater, the air brakes, and the drag-chute switch were busted. None of the navigation lights worked, neither radio could send or receive, and there was no remote compass. The tail-plane controls were all fucked up, as were the rudder pedals, which were alternately sticking and spongy.

"Only a Phantom," Ryder said more than once. The airplane he'd bitched about several weeks before was fast earning his respect for ruggedness, if nothing else.

He had no idea what the hell was going to happen once he got to Area 61. He would try to land the jet, and then . . . then what? Crash the front door of the place? Sneak in somehow? Call the cops?

There was always the "play dumb" option. Knock on the front door, tell them he was the missing fourth Tango pilot, that he'd been misguided and delayed, but was now here to do their bidding. Though it was probably the most logical approach, that scenario appealed to him the least.

Five minutes later he saw the low mountain range that he knew housed Area 61.

It was quickly coming up on decision time.

Could he really just blow in on the place and land? The most restricted area in the world? The headquarters of the people who were disobeying direct presidential orders?

He didn't know. And the way his thought processes were acting, he wasn't even sure he could think that deeply about it. He was still experiencing bouts of trembling, was still sweating buckets, and was still sucking on the oxygen pipe, trying to clear his lungs of the nasty residues of the Hal-Lou gas. But it wasn't doing him much good. Every once in a while he'd see sharp, vivid colors just explode out of nowhere. By the time he was able to shake them away, he'd find himself flying at a different altitude, or a dozen degrees off his course heading. It was wild, frightening, and unintentionally amusing. Like the ultimate drunk driver, he had trouble concentrating on the subject at hand, yet his instincts were allowing him to go through the motions of flying the plane.

Obviously this was no condition for the person assigned to save the day to be in.

He was now about two minutes from getting a visual on Area 61. Hal-Lou aftereffects or not, he needed a plan—*now*. A good one. But his wacked-out brain cells just wouldn't cooperate. He was a hero, wasn't he? It said so in the newspapers. So it seemed like he should have an answer to anything.

But at the moment, he didn't.

But after the long two minutes passed and he finally got a clear visual of the place, he found, once again, that events were making up his mind for him.

It was apparent right away that he wouldn't be able to land at Area 61, for one simple reason: the runways were too crowded.

He couldn't believe it. He didn't know whether he *should* believe it. As he overflew the place at a height of 5000 feet, cutting back on the F-4's engines so he could get a good long look, he could see at least two dozen aircraft clogging the pair of airstrips. And what room they weren't taking up was being hogged by tanks, trucks, and APCs—all belonging, no doubt, to the mystery army.

So he had lost the race. It was that simple. The mysterious invaders had reached the secret base before him.

Now what?

Fly back to Tango? No way. Fly to Nellis? And wind up in a psychiatric ward, like the old man, Jess Warren? No fucking way.

He turned around and flew back over the secret base, fairly certain that there were no *real* AA weapons around. He tried to let the moment sink in—he knew he was witnessing history of sorts. The end of War Heaven, at least in its present form. The ISC members were either giving up at that moment or sealing themselves inside their survivalist tomb, locking themselves away for six months to a year, continuing their weirdo agenda, whatever the hell it was.

All good and strange things come to an end, he thought. *Even in a place like this.*

He turned and overflew the base a third time, this time foolishly low at 1500 feet.

From this shallow height he was able to get a good read on the types of airplanes clogging the runway. There were fighters, and some attack airplanes. Were those F-15s? Were those A-10s? He couldn't quite tell.

But there was one airplane he instantly recognized. Parked at the end of the shorter runway, it was silver, had stubby wings, a Plexiglas nose, and four propellers. In the sea of modern weaponry scattered all over the base, it stood out like a ghost from the past.

It was the B-17 Flying Fortress nicknamed *Fort One*.

"Those bastards!" he cursed. "They *were* watching us all along."

All of sudden his eyes were filled with the colors again, as if his turn of emotion had triggered the flashback. He began shaking. Were they Zoots? Were they fireworks? Could they be real explosions?

He shook them away, but then found the F-4 picking up speed. Why? Because his hand was heavy on the throttles.

"Jessuzz, Ry," he screamed at himself. *"What the hell are you doing?"*

He yanked back on the throttle, but at the same instant his radar started beeping.

Something was up there with him. He searched the sky and saw two specks heading right for him out of the south, moving fast on full afterburners.

"Who the hell can these guys be?"

He got his answer a few moments later.

Booting his own engines up into afterburner, he banked away just in time as the pair of oncoming Soviet-built MiG-29 Fulcrums streaked by him.

"MiGs?" Ry said, shaking his head violently from side to side.

"Out here?"

He twisted in his seat and saw that, yes, those were two MiGs. At least he thought they were . . .

He instinctively did a full overhead loop, which effectively placed him behind the Fulcrums. He took a good, long look. They *were* real. Weren't they?

"Goddamn, what is happening here?"

Probably expecting a well-placed burst or two, the MiG pilots broke off in opposite directions, one up, one down.

In an instant, Ryder found himself pulling the F-4 up on its tail.

"Where have I done this before?"

The Fulcrum thundered straight up and out of sight, leaving behind only a whisp of white exhaust and a pair of wingtip contrails.

Ryder pulled back further on his own control stick, at the same time opening up his own throttles and boosting the F-4's powerful engines past Mach 1. In an instant, the Phantom was rocketing straight upward, chasing the twin vapor trails of the Fulcrum up to 20,000 feet.

"What the hell am I doing?"

He leveled off somehow and found himself so close to the Fulcrum's tail that the exhaust from the big Soviet fighter's engines was actually soiling his own canopy with dots of oil.

The Fulcrum pilot—no doubt a long way from home—had had enough of this football game. He put his airplane into a screaming dive and rocketed away to the east, a natural reaction to get away from the crazy F-4 pilot.

Ryder found himself performing a series of tight circles, yelling wildly as he went.

"Is this the movie?"

Then his radar began beeping again.

"What now?"

He turned to see a chevron of six MiG-27 Floggers coming right toward it from the north.

"What the fuck . . . this has all happened before . . ."

Suddenly the air was filled with streams of frighteningly-bright yellow light flashing out at him from the opposing airplanes. For one paralyzing moment, Ryder thought it was real ammo. But then half of the Zoot cannon fire struck his airplane head-on to no effect.

Ryder screeched the big Phantom up and over, and turned back

442

and headed right for the formation of Floggers. No doubt startled, the MiG pilots scattered frantically.

The next thing he knew, the F-4 was roaring straight down.

Ryder took two deep gulps of oxygen and tried to shake away the frightening hallucination – if it was a hallucination. He yanked back on the control stick, nearly killing himself in the gut-wrenching pull-up maneuver. By the time he leveled off he was at 100 feet.

An entire battalion of camouflage-netted battle tanks was waiting for him. Confusion reigned. What were they doing? They were firing at him, but the holographic missiles and cannon shells were passing right through the battered F-4's fuselage.

"This has all happened before . . ." Ryder kept telling himself over and over, in an effort to calm himself down. *"I know it has . . ."*

Leaving the confused armored column in its wake, the F-4 continued its low-level supersonic flight.

Ahead of it waited a line of portable SAM batteries. To Ryder, it appeared as if all the SAMs launched at once, each one streaking toward him. Yet he weaved his way effortlessly through the antiaircraft missiles. Not a single SAM even came close to hitting his jinking fighter. But what difference did it make? They couldn't harm him anyway.

Beyond the line of SAMs, a squadron of Soviet Hind helicopter gunships rose up from the protection of a red-sand butte. They were armed with air-to-air missiles, and instantly commenced launching barrages at him. But again, the holographs simply went right through the F-4 and quickly dissolved into the atmosphere.

Finally he was able to yank back on the control stick and get up to a safer altitude. He was bathed in sweat right down to his boots.

"Jessuzz," he said, praying the frightening flashback was over. "I should have drank that Scotch."

He settled down and came back over Area 61. The air was just filled with aircraft. Cargo planes. Fighters. Helicopters. Most of them of Soviet design.

What the hell was going on here? Had the Russians taken over the U.S. while he was inside the Range?

Just then another problem arose. His fuel light clicked on.

That was it. The end of the free ride. Now it was time to proceed. He'd fought it long enough. It was his job to fulfill the original mission and that's what he would do. Get to Area 61, sniff out what's going on. If nothing else, his curiosity would be satisfied.

There was just one last detail, now that he was running out of gas. How was he going to get down there? With the runways clogged and the air above Area 61 positively lousy with Russians, there was only one last viable option left.

It was time to punch out.

77

The Spy

"Okay, I think I've got it."

Maureen turned away from the main bank of TV monitors and back toward the young man. He was hunched over the control board, scraps of tape everywhere, a red ink pen hanging out of his mouth.

"If the L-10 soldiers stay in their positions," the young man began to explain, "then not only we can follow this route up and out of here, we can set off a diversion, too—it might help somewhere along the way."

Maureen turned back to the TV monitors, which were now trained on the nearby Area 61 exterior shots. Everywhere she looked on the monitors she could see soldiers, tanks, other tracked vehicles, helicopters, airplanes. There was obviously some kind of a fight going on right outside the front entrance to the underground facility, although all the weapons being used were those unexplainable cartoonish devices.

"But what happens when we do get out?" she asked him, pointing toward the monitors. "We walk right into all that?"

The young man was shaking his head no. "That's why we're going out the back door," he said.

He began punching buttons and soon had an array of interior scenes on the first five monitors.

Maureen recognized the first shot as focusing on a door near the Elephant Graveyard. The second and third shots showed the long tunnel that led toward the alien crypt; the fourth shot showed the two large doors, one of which belonged to the crypt itself.

445

"We're going to hide in that awful tomb?" Maureen asked him, horrified.

"No," the young man said. "We're going through the other door."

He pointed to the fifth monitor. Maureen had just assumed it was white with static; now, upon closer examination, she realized it was really filled with snow.

"It's the polar-environment chamber," he explained. "There's an emergency exit far on its other side, again because of government regulations."

"How long will we have to be in there?" she asked. "The place looks gigantic."

"It's six hundred yards from that door to the emergency exit," the young man explained. "Two football fields. Then it comes out right on the side of the mountain. But I'll be honest with you, it's rough in there."

"After this place, I'm ready for anything," Maureen declared.

"You'd better put on as many clothes as possible," he told her, picking up her laundry bag and handing it to her.

She began dumping the contents onto the control board but immediately realized that it did not contain her usual coveralls, socks and handkerchiefs.

It was, in fact, the bag containing the women's lascivious underwear . . .

The young man was instantly mortified.

"I think it's time you explain this," Maureen told him, her hands full of the lingerie.

"I have a terrible confession to make," the young man said, his voice low.

He reached over and began pushing TV monitor buttons. It took a few moments, but then the picture on monitor eight finally came into view. Maureen immediately recognized the scene as her former apartment, the place she'd spent the last nineteen days.

She quickly put two and two together.

"You were spying on me?" she asked, her voice so angry it was barely above a whisper.

The young man could only stare at the floor and shake his head.

"I'm terribly sorry," he murmured. "It was not every night. But, yes, when things just got to be too much around here . . . I did. I know who you are. I've watched you on TV, many times. And . . ."

"So it was you all along that delivered these clothes?" she said. "And I blamed Walter."

"Well, he's not totally without fault," the young man said.

"What do you mean?" Maureen asked.

"That stuff *did* belong to him," the young man replied. "I just switched laundry bags, hoping . . . well, hoping you'd at least . . ."

Maureen was almost too tired, too confused, to be angry. All she was concerned about was getting out and finding Ryder.

But there was a nagging question.

"Walter owned these clothes?" she asked the young man. "But why? I was the only female up there. Wasn't I?"

The young man replied by hitting a pair of console buttons.

The scene was inside one of the apartments. The place had two TVs, a CD player, a large bed. Maureen was surprised that she recognized it. It was the room located just down the hall from her former quarters. Walter had shown it to her on the first day she was let out.

Two people — a man *and* a woman — were moving about the room, their images blurred and ghostly as the hidden camera sought to adjust itself.

Maureen watched with growing fascination as the two people on the screen took shape. The man was pacing back and forth in front of the bed, his hands gesturing wildly. The woman, who appeared to be wearing a miniskirt or some other kind of brief women's wear, judging from the amount of her leg visible, was reclining on the bed, not moving much, either listening intently to the man or totally ignoring him.

After ten seconds or so of adjusting, the camera finally came into focus. At the same moment the man turned face-full toward the TV to make himself a drink.

Maureen was stunned. It was Walter.

Now she became very intent on identifying the woman reclining on the bed.

After making his drink, Walter walked over to the bed, leaned down, and kissed the woman full on the lips. When he moved out of the way, Maureen got her first good look at her face.

She couldn't believe it, but suddenly another few pieces fell into place.

The woman on the bed, decked out in racy women's underwear,

was Vanessa.

Maureen felt the breath catch in her throat.

"So it *was* her," she said. "She's the one who compromised the Roswell dig site."

"She's been in on this whole project from the beginning," the young man said. "She's a very mysterious woman. None of us is even sure whether she's Walter's wife or not. But she is just the strangest lady — in fact, both of them are pretty weird."

"But why are they even here?" Maureen asked. "I mean, I could never really figure out what Walter did exactly."

"He did exactly what his job was," the young man said. "He was the 'tour guide' here. Both of them come from very deep security backgrounds. Both of them were hired to be responsible for the security of the facility. Whenever we would have guests staying in the apartments, either she or Walter would act as the 'tour guide.' She would take care of the men; he would take care of the women.

"When word got out that your dig team was going to Roswell, it was decided that Vanessa would infiltrate the group, because she looks so young and she can play that innocent act to the hilt. She enrolled in the school and was part of the dig group almost a year before it even left for Roswell."

"Very clever," Maureen said, watching the woman. "And insidious."

They watched Walter and Vanessa move from what looked like a heated discussion, to a period of cuddling, back to arguing again.

Suddenly Walter got up from the bed, walked over to one of the TVs, and snapped it on. Then he inserted a videotape into a nearby VCR.

The TV screen came alive with a blurry picture, much too small for Maureen to see.

"Is there any way we can see what they are seeing?"

The young man pushed another series of buttons and suddenly five more monitors came to life, all of them showing the same scene.

Maureen was absolutely horrified. It was a grainy, slightly-out-of-focus video of the clear pond. She and Vanessa were standing near the edge of the water, taking their clothes off. There was no sound, but Maureen remembered exactly when the incident had taken place. It was the first day Vanessa had brought her to the watering hole.

"Oh my God . . ." she gasped.

The video played on, jump-cutting to a scene where she and Vanessa were both naked and sunbathing beside the pond.

"This is what they were going to use to blackmail me," she whispered.

The young man nodded gravely. "They have something on everybody," he said. "But you'll notice that now that this place is shut down, and the important people are at their jobs, those two are locked inside their apartment, waiting for whatever is going to happen to happen."

"Please shut it off," Maureen said. The young man quickly complied.

At that instant the entire facility suddenly began shaking violently. *"What is that?"* Maureen yelled.

"I don't know," The young man said.

They both turned back to the TV screens monitoring the action outside Area 61. There were explosions, rockets firing all over the runways and near the buildings themselves. It looked violent, yet, to Maureen's eye, still very fake.

"Let's go," the young man said, gathering up all his notes. "We've got to get the hell out of here."

78

Ryder felt like he was stuck inside a Salvador Dali painting.

He was dangling far off the edge of a high cliff, his parachute inextricably caught on the branches of a prickly overhanging Joshua tree.

Five hundred feet below him was Area 61.

He didn't know whether to laugh or cry. His situation was so absurd. After a near-perfect ejection, he'd come *that* close to dropping right in the middle of the chaos of Area 61 itself. But at the last minute, his chute was blown into the large, jutting tree, leaving him hanging fifteen feet out from the ledge, like a wounded marionette, his safety harness, his parachute straps, and parachute cords all wrapped tightly around him.

Way off in the distance he could see the twin fingers of black smoke rising from where the venerable F-4 had gone down, its gas tanks empty, its work done. While he hoped it hadn't hit anything, he wondered whether he should have stuck with it longer. It was not like him to jump too soon.

The colors and bright lights continued to flash before his eyes as he swayed back and forth in the hot morning wind, and in a strange way he seemed to be getting used to them. Through these tinted eyeballs, the scene below him looked like something out of a living comic book. Dozens of soldiers belonging to the mystery army were running around, some firing their Zoot weapons, some herding POWs away, others directing in more helicopters, others trying to make some sense of the jumble of airplanes on the base's two tiny airstrips.

There were helicopters – American-made, Soviet-made, even types he did not recognize – flying about, some passing so close by him, he could see the soldiers on board looking out at him. But none stopped to help him.

Maybe they thought he was dead.

He could see a traffic jam of tanks and APCs further out on the air strip, and even from this height he could tell they were definitely not M-1A1s or Bradleys. With their camouflage nettings now removed, they sure looked a hell of a lot like Soviet T-72s and BMPs.

From somewhere deep in his Hal-Lou-soaked mind, a stray notion bubbled up: *Maybe this was all part of the movie he'd worked on.* For an instant that idea made the most sense. But it was quickly blown away by a particularly strong gust of desert wind, one that served to further entangle him in the hellish mesh of parachute straps, cords, and harnesses.

Still, he couldn't help but remember the story of one paratrooper dropped on Normandy the night before D-Day. The man had come down in a small town occupied by the Germans. Like Ryder, he never made it to the ground either. His chute had caught on a church steeple, suspending him above the village square. Unable to move, he'd played dead and watched the battle for the village rage below him, a fight the Germans won by brutally firing on the other paratroopers as they floated down. He remained there, hanging by *his* cords, until American troops liberated the town some time later.

Or at least that's how it happened in the movie.

The serpentine escape route the young man had charted out of the Area 61 facility consisted of short cuts, double-backs, slow, quiet movements through dimly-lit stairways, and terrifying full-out sprints through pitch-black corridors.

Though necessary to avoid the fierce soldiers of the L-10 protection squad, the roundabout trip proved to be a nerve-wracking dash for both Maureen and the young man. Any time they came upon a dim lamp – and they were few and far in between – he would check his backward-running watch and call out the time they had left to get out of the mountainside bunker before the Big Blast sealed them inside for a half year or more.

Their last time check, taken as they sneaked right past the Level-3 elevators themselves, was down to seventeen minutes even.

"We still have one stop to make!" the young man told her in a hurried whisper as they ran down a flight of fire stairs and turned out into another dark passageway.

The detour was behind an unlocked, nondescript door halfway down a corridor on Level 4.

Quickly hustling inside, Maureen discovered the place was a computer whiz's dream come true. It was much more elaborate than the dingy, cold TV studio; warmer and more human in dimension than the spooky Cray supercomputer chamber. Its main features were the rows upon rows of colored tubes, brilliant reds, greens, and blues. Inside each tube, there seemed to be a constant, pulsating bubbling action, exquisitely beautiful in form and just a delight to look at.

"What is this place?" she asked.

"It's called the Zoot Room," the young man said, quickly punching up a number of screen on the main control board next to the door. "It controls all the holographic projections throughout the Range. The instruments in this room can simulate just about anything, though their specialities are things having to do with weapons training."

This is what I was seeing on the TV screens?" Maureen asked. "Those cartoon things out in the desert?"

"Almost forty billion dollars' worth of 'cartoons,' " the young man answered hastily. "And I guarantee that no congressional appropriations committee ever delegated a penny of it."

He spent the next crucial thirty seconds inputting orders into the control-room computer. Finally he locked the command in and nudged Maureen back toward the door.

"This might work, but it might not," he told her. "But should we need to distract anyone on the outside, it will happen in about five minutes."

With that, they were out the door and back to running down the darkened corridor.

T-2

Lieutenant Moon checked the backward running watch. It now read

0 hours, 14 minutes, 13 seconds.

Down below him, three miles away, the scene around Area 61 was utter confusion. The Sanitized Forces had taken possession of the two runways and the outlying buildings, but many Zoot flashes could still be seen bouncing around the main buildings as well as the entrance to the mountainside facility itself. By using his high-powered binoculars, he could see that most of the last-gasp resistance was coming from a small pocket of Green army troops.

"Goddamn jarheads," he muttered with angry admiration. "You'd think they'd know when to give up . . ."

Though he knew the men were just doing their job, their valiant display was also very dangerous. A very, very critical clock was ticking here. Even when the last of the surface resistance was overcome, the Sanitized Forces still had to break into the mountainside facility where they could very well meet *real* soldiers with *real* weapons firing *real* ammunition.

The ten Soviet-built fighters that had taken part in this final push had now exited the area, although a cloud of smoke forming about fifteen miles to the south seemed to indicate that one of them might have crashed.

But Moon had other things to worry about — one plane down would be a small price to pay for this day's madness.

He had one last trick up his sleeve — it was sitting in the bay of the Blackhawk. But he was extremely reluctant to use it, though he had full presidential authorization to do so. For if he did, it would cause catastrophic side effects that would last for years on the Range, and especially in Area 61. There was also a huge economic concern. By quick calculations, if he decided to play his ace, it would be a decision that would cost no less than twenty-five *billion* dollars.

And he wasn't even sure whether it would work or not.

He checked the watch again. It was now down to 13 minutes, 47 seconds. He checked the battle area again; if anything, the fighting looked to be growing in intensity.

That was it. He could wait no longer.

He turned toward the Blackhawk helicopter and gave the pilot the signal to start the engines. Then he looked back at the confusing battlefield.

"If only we had more time," he muttered to himself, picking up the

453

radio nearby.

He pushed the send button, cleared his throat, and gave a single, unmistakable order.

"All units . . . evacuate the area."

What the hell was happening down there?

As Ryder twisted and turned, trying to squirm his way out of his increasingly precarious position, he noticed that something very strange was happening 500 feet below his flight boots.

The invading troops were no longer advancing. Quite the opposite, they were most definitely retreating.

Quickly.

Some were jumping on the backs of tanks, some onto the APCs, a lot into the trucks, or onto bumper guards, fenders, roofs, whatever. It also seemed as if every helicopter down there had gunned its engines to life simultaneously, kicking up enough sand and dust to rival any *El Niño.* Even the big cargo planes had their props spinning at a snap, some of them taxiing out onto the runway with two engines turning and two engines just now fluttering to life.

This was all very confusing to Ryder's strained synapses—at first, anyway. What had happened? Had everyone decided to give up on this enormous game of guns and go home? What was it, time for supper? Had someone run out of film? Or Zoot batteries?

Or . . .

Then it came to him. Spinning around uncontrollably in the early-morning, hot desert breeze, it came to him.

The bomb. The ISC atomic bomb. That's why the old man's wristwatch was turning backward. It was the countdown. And word had just reached all the troops below. And now they were getting the hell out of the blast area as fast as they could.

He began yanking like crazy on the parachute straps, but succeeded in only tangling himself more. He had no knife, nothing even sharp enough to try and cut through the heavy canvas straps and fiberglass cords. And if he did, what difference did it make? The next stop was 500 feet, straight down, not a handhold or even a place to bounce in sight.

The sky was suddenly alive with aircraft again—the choppers taking off and staying low, the cargo planes screeching up and going high. All of them were heading north, as were the majority of the withdrawing troops.

He managed to take the backward clock from his flight-suit pocket. The face had been cracked in the bail-out, but it was still running. It read: 11 minutes, 26 seconds.

He finally stopped struggling and allowed himself to hang loose for a moment.

"I wonder if they'll ever find my body?" he thought.

79

The sergeant of the L-10 protection squad couldn't believe his eyes.

He had just checked on two of his men who were standing guard outside the elevators that led to the Elephant's Graveyard when he heard the slightest noise down the darkened hallway off to his right. He had immediately flipped on the NightVision scope on his authentic M-16 and scanned the nearly-pitch-black tunnellike corridor. Within seconds he picked up two faint figures making their way down the hallway—a man and a woman—hurrying along about 200 feet in front of him.

The L-10 soldier—actually a member of the U.S. Army Green Berets—made a quick, hushed radio call to his commanding officer up on the next level, reporting his find. His officer told him that there were two people unaccounted for inside the facility. Two people who could have a huge effect on what was happening at that moment down in the Black Hole.

His return orders, then, were difficult to accept, but nevertheless necessary. He was to stop the two people from leaving the facility—using deadly force if he had to.

The sergeant reached into his belt, came up with a full clip containing real bullets. This is what he'd been trained for, he told himself. To act on orders even when the worst-case scenario came up. *To do what he had to do, no matter what his feelings.*

He didn't like it, though.

Still, he grimly locked the clip into his M-16. Then with his NightScope on full power, he plunged into the pitch-black tunnel in cautious, yet determined pursuit.

Running down the pitch-black corridor was like a nightmare for Maureen.

She expected to crash into a brick wall at any second, and if not, then trip and fall into some bottomless pit. Even worse, she could not shake the feeling that someone was following them.

But after what seemed like hours of flat-out running, they finally saw their goal up ahead. The two doors, illuminated in the dimmest of red lights, one of which led to the alien crypt, the other into the polar-environment chamber, and possibly freedom.

"How . . . much . . . time?" Maureen gasped as they ran the last fifty feet to the doors.

"Seven minutes . . ." the young man called back over his shoulder. ". . . and fourteen seconds . . ."

They both skidded to a stop right underneath the red light, and the young man began trying his long rings of keys.

Suddenly Maureen grabbed his arm and dug in her nails.

"Listen!" she hissed.

They both froze.

"Can you hear it?"

There was the constant pumping noise way in the background, plus the general hissing that permeated most of the facility at these levels. But there was also something else.

Footsteps. Coming closer to them in the dark.

"Damn," the young man cursed, frantically working the keys into the unmarked door. "This is not good . . ."

The footsteps were not running; that would have actually been better. Running indicated someone who didn't know what the situation was, someone out of control, perhaps. No, these footsteps were from someone walking evenly, consistently. In control, one right after another.

And getting closer.

"Hurry," Maureen urged the young man. "God, *hurry.*"

A second later, he found the key that fit. He thrust it into the lock, turned it heavily, and the huge door swung open.

Immediately the tunnel was enveloped in a blast of snow. The sound of the wind was deafening. Maureen was instantly covered with ice particles, her eyes stinging, her ears nearly flash-frozen.

"Go!" the young man was yelling to her. "Get going!"

The next thing she knew, they were inside the chamber. It was like being tossed into the middle of the worst blizzard imaginable. She couldn't see. She couldn't breathe. She couldn't cry out. Her hands and feet felt like they were instantly becoming frostbitten.

"Which way?" she screamed to the young man.

He couldn't talk—his face was already completely covered with snow, making him look like a horror-movie snowman. He just pointed, and grabbed her arm and began dragging her along with him.

At first, she was glad that she had put on all of the pieces of lingerie before leaving the TV control room; she thought they would provide a small modicum of warmth. But her coveralls were already totally iced up and pressing against her bare skin, stinging with ice-cold pain. She could just barely breathe, and she couldn't see very far due to the blowing snow.

Still, she was amazed at what was inside the chamber. She had just assumed that it would be one big empty room with snow, but it wasn't. There were at least two big airplanes inside. Frozen over and packed solid in ice, they looked like coffins. There were different kinds of gun emplacements, several ice-coated tanks, and a long line of iced troop trucks that looked like they'd been flash-frozen during a traffic jam.

They continued dragging themselves through the ankle-high snow, fighting against the howling wind and cold. What made it all the worse, they appeared to be walking up a steep incline.

"Two football fields," Maureen kept telling herself. "It's only two football fields long . . ."

"Halfway!" the young man yelled back to her, pointing to a barely visible metal sign that displayed the fraction "1/2."

Maureen tried to take a deep breath and buck up for the second part of the journey when suddenly, above the howling wind and blowing snow, she heard a very distinct *crack!*

In an instant, the young man's left shoulder exploded in blood.

"Oh my God!" she screamed. "They're shooting at us."

Lieutenant Moon finished strapping himself into the Blackhawk's copilot seat and then checked the backward watch.

It read: 5 minutes, 58 seconds.

He pushed the send button on his radio. "All clear?" he asked.

"All clear," came the barely audible reply.

Moon turned to the chopper pilot and yelled, "Okay, let's go . . . fast!"

They immediately lifted off T-2. The chopper was barely airborne and out over the side of the butte when the pilot pointed it nose down and screamed toward the Area 61 facility.

It was just Moon and the pilot aboard the Blackhawk—everyone else involved in the operation was heading out of the area as fast as possible.

Perfect, Moon thought grimly as he watched the ground rush up to him. *No witnesses.*

The runways were almost entirely clear by this time. All of the soldiers on both sides were gone. Some of the Sanitized Forces equipment—about a half dozen tanks and one large cargo plane—had been left behind. But that was of little consequence now. What Moon was about to do would make the loss of a few million dollars' worth of equipment seem petty by comparison.

Reaching an altitude of twenty-five feet, the Blackhawk circled around the abandoned runway once.

"Where do you want it?" the pilot called over to Moon.

"It doesn't make much difference," Moon yelled back. "Put it about two hundred feet out, I guess."

The pilot circled one more time and then headed down to the spot where the two runways crossed together.

"How's that?"

"As good as place as any," Moon replied, unstrapping from his seat and climbing back into the copter's bay.

But suddenly the pilot grabbed his arm and twisted it.

"Jesus Christ!" he yelled. *"What the hell is that?"*

Moon looked up into the part of the sky where the pilot was pointing and felt his jaw drop.

Hovering directly overhead were three, incredibly bright flying saucers.

Just how close to death do you have to get before your life flashes in front of your eyes?

459

That was a strange, morbid question, Ryder thought as he continued to entangle himself further in his twisted parachute straps, fighting a losing battle to somehow break free.

He knew it was practically hopeless. Even if he did get loose and was able to swing over to the cliff, how far could he get? Certainly not far enough to get away from the results of a nuclear blast.

But he'd be damned if he was going to go passively.

He checked the backward watch. It read five minutes exactly. He tried yanking himself up a little on the straps, but because of the hopeless knotting of the shoulder harnesses and parachute cords themselves, this turned out to be yet another self-defeating maneuver.

More morbid thoughts filled his head. If a twenty-megaton atomic bomb went off in the front lobby of the main building at Area 61, would it kill him instantly?

Definitely.

How about if the bomb went off somewhere underground nearby. Would it bring the mountain down with it?

Probably.

If he was thrown clear of the blast, would an autopsy find elements of hallucinogenics in his body.

Maybe.

He began yanking on the parachute cords again when his line of sight was distracted by a single helicopter that was hovering above the deserted airfield.

Are those guys crazy? he wondered, now biting into one of the several dozen parachute cords.

Suddenly he felt a slight twinge of vindication run though him. Would he feel better if the people in that helicopter went up in the blast with him?

Most definitely.

The chopper landed and two men got out. They were just dots on the desert landscape to his eyes, but nevertheless he could see them pointing off to the northwest. He twisted himself around so he could face in that direction.

That's when he saw the three UFOs.

Maureen was one frozen step away from complete panic.

She was packing snow onto the young man's nasty shoulder wound, at the same time half-carrying him up the incline through the blowing, freezing snow.

What a place to die, she thought. In the middle of a blizzard. In the middle of the desert.

She had no idea how far away they were from the exit. She had no idea how many people were shooting at them or how far back they were. What she did know was that the man's wound was leaving a trail of blood in the snow that would clue those in pursuit in to their every move.

So she had to think quick.

Obviously there was nowhere to hide. And stopping completely would mean certain death. But was there a way to delay the pursuers, even for a few crucial seconds?

The L-10 Protection Squad sergeant reached down and scooped up a handful of snow.

Even in the blinding, artificial wind he could see the dabs of blood in the snow. It was his first indication that he'd actually hit something up there.

He checked his M-16 and continued walking against the wind. He was dressed in a somewhat heavy uniform, and the Kevlar helmet was fair at protecting his head. But he cursed his mustache; it was now so heavy with ice, it was clogging both his nasal passages and his mouth. Every time he wiped the snow away, it just built right back up again in a matter of seconds.

He found another patch of bloody snow, this one displaying a much bigger stain. Five feet away was another patch, and then another one about four feet away from that.

He stopped for a moment and aimed his NightScope up ahead. It took a few moments, but he was nevertheless able to make out two very faint images on lens. It wasn't a clear picture, but he was amazed that the scope worked inside the polar environment at all.

He squeezed off another three shots and then resumed trudging through the snow.

After another six feet he found another bloodstain. But then he spotted something right next to it. It was a pair of coveralls, the same type worn by all the visitors in the Area 61 facility. The garment was stained with blood from the shoulder to the knees. He could not find the bullet hole, but it was yet another indication that at least one of bullets had found its mark.

He fought his way against the wind and snow for another five yards and then spotted yet another piece of bloody clothing.

He reached down and picked it up but was startled to see that it was a white negligee, hideously smeared with blood.

That's when it hit home with the L-10 soldier. He'd shot the woman.

Maureen had read once that when you die, you see a long tunnel with a bright light at the end of it. Everything swirls around the light and there is music and you see the faces of loved ones passed on and you feel a great, soothing warmth.

She saw the light. It was red and there were swirls of snow around it. But there was no music and she didn't see any of her deceased relatives.

And there was certainly no warmth.

I must be still alive . . .

She was dragging the young man now, staying low and waiting for a bullet in the back of her head. But it never came. Maybe her attempt at – what did they call it? psy-ops? – had worked. Maybe the people doing the shooting back there *did* pause a moment because they thought they'd shot a woman.

The light ahead was actually an illuminated sign, and maybe in the end it would be the government's obsession with regulations that would save her. How else could she explain the bright red lit sign that said Exit that was now standing out in the furious blizzard like a beacon.

Only twenty feet to go.

She helped the young man to his feet, washing his face with snow to keep him conscious. He was near completely covered with ice, the only part of his body not encased being his bloody shoulder.

Ten feet to go.

She had no feeling in her toes, no feeling in her hands up to her elbows. She couldn't even feel what she was wearing. Was it the body stocking? Was it the remains of the velour dress? Or the three teddys? She didn't know.

Five feet . . .

Her ears were as hard as ice, and she feared that if she even touched them, they would break off.

Two feet away.

She felt like she could not go another step, but she did. On determination and Irish will alone, she lunged forward and grabbed the door handle and twisted it. If it was locked, they were both dead.

Please . . .

It opened without the slightest resistance.

She pushed the young man right through it and he fell, rolling down a slight incline and coming to stop at the edge of a small sand dune.

Then she straightened herself up and walked through the door.

She was out. Just like that.

80

The world came to an end at least three minutes ahead of schedule.

Ryder had just checked the backward-running watch and he distinctly remembered it reading: 3 minutes, 33 seconds.

He had twisted back toward the place where the helicopter had been, and saw that it had taken off, and was shooting straight up into the cloudless morning sky. The UFOs had moved over and were hovering above the spot where the helicopter had set down.

He'd continued to struggle with the straps and the cords and the safety harnesses, intent on going down with a fight. But he couldn't help but looked at the UFOs, too, and wonder: Were they real? Or had someone set off a Zoot device inside? Did it really make any difference?

That's when the bomb went off.

He saw it before he heard it, heard it before he felt it. But only billionths of a second separated the sensations. It was white – hot, pure white light. Then it turned yellow, instantly, and then to orange just as fast. The colors were incredible. He stared at them and they burned his eyes.

Then the sound arrived. Like a police whistle going off next to each ear, the sound quickly mutating into the roar of waves crashing and then thunder – booming, nonstop thunder.

The blast pressure hit him next. Instantly he was slammed against the side of the mountain, and, just as quickly, sucked back out. The tree which had been holding him like a spiny hand holds a puppet was ripped up by its roots and hurled over the top of the mountain, Ryder and his chute going with it, cords, straps, and all.

* * *

Maureen saw the blast.

She also heard it, felt it, even tasted it.

It rose – a huge mushroom cloud – over the mountain and up into the cloudless sky. The colors were red, orange, yellow, even blue and green. The noise was tremendous, and the wind it created rivaled that which she had just battled inside the polar environment chamber. Debris of all shapes and sizes was flying over her head, and a rain of rocks and sand was falling on her and the wounded young man who she was protecting with her body.

But then, just as quickly as it had started, it was suddenly gone. She looked up and was just able to see the enormous, frightening, fiery cloud simply vanish, dissipating into the early morning desert air.

At that moment it dawned on her – this wasn't the Big Blast. It had been, instead, one of those cartoon explosions, the things that the young man had called the Zoots.

"Are you okay?" she asked the young man. "Can you stand up?"

The young man struggled to his feet, and caught his breath.

"God, we made it," he said, forcing a smile, and turning his face to the bright, hot morning sun.

They both looked at each other and suddenly laughed. His shoulder was bloody, but the wound was not life-threatening. The skin on his hands and face was already cracked and peeling, the result of the sudden change from the hard-blowing cold to the blistering Nevada heat. The result was, he looked like he'd gotten an instant sunburn.

Maureen looked no better. She too was red with some skin peeling. Her hair was frazzled and dripping. Her clothes, only the two remaining layers of lacy, low-cut underwear, were literally falling apart.

"Jesuzz, *we're alive* . . ." they both yelled at once.

The L-10 protection-squad sergeant collapsed as soon as he fell out of the door from the polar-environment chamber.

He had just regained his footing when the huge blast went off, knocking him back against the heavy door and breaking his left knee-cap in two places.

The pain had not hit him yet, so he staggered to his feet a second

465

time, picked up his rifle, and hastily wiped the sand from its critical parts. Then he half-crawled up the side of a large sandy mound and looked down to the flattened part of the mountain's summit below.

He saw them right away. The woman, her clothes literally in tatters, and the man, his shoulder bloody. They were stumbling along, with their backs to him, about 150 feet away. He had to stop them. There was no middle ground in his orders. When things went wrong, you did what you had to do, even if it meant shooting someone in cold blood.

He began to go over the mound to catch them, but took one step and felt his knee crack. He looked down and was astonished to see that part of a bloody bone had ripped right through his uniform leg.

Staggered by the sudden pain, and close to going into shock, he dropped to a kneeling position and rested his M-16 barrel up against his shoulder.

He knew the man wasn't going to get very far. Not with that wound. So he lined up the woman in his sights. He took a deep breath and began to squeeze the trigger . . .

Suddenly he was gasping for air. Something was tightening around his neck, cutting off both his breathing and his blood supply. He began to gag, dropping his weapon and instinctively grabbing for his throat.

Then a boot landed hard on his cheek. Another one fell heavily into his chest. The rifle was kicked away. He fell over onto his back. Through blurry eyes he saw a man standing over him, his hands bloody, his body wrapped in a mass of ropes and cords and straps, dragging a shredded parachute behind him.

The man was down in his face in a second. Grabbing his collar, the man yanked him up off the ground and growled: "This is War Heaven. No one gets killed in this story."

T-2

It was the supreme irony that neither Moon nor the Blackhawk pilot knew what time it was.

Neither one had a watch—not one that ran forward, anyway.

They were both lying flat out on top of T-2, looking out over the edge of the butte down at Area 61 three miles below.

The last wisps of the tremendous holographic explosion were just now dissolving, leaving only the bare outline of the Zoot A-bomb blast.

"Did it work?" the pilot asked.

Moon checked the backward-running watch. It read: 1 minute, 1 second.

"We'll know soon enough," he replied.

His twenty-five-billion-dollar bet had been laid. The Zoot Five-Six tactical nuclear bomb had exploded at precisely three minutes before the backward-running watch would hit zero. The resulting explosion had been incredible; he and the pilot had watched it from a height of two miles, and still, the brilliant holographs had stung their eyes.

But would it work?

The Five-Six was the most powerful Zoot weapon ever detonated inside War Heaven, of this Moon was sure. Just like a real nuclear weapon, the Five-Six had the ability to obliterate everything for miles around—just as long as it was connected to a Zoot device. Moon's gamble was simple: If anything inside the Area 61 mountain facility having to do with the ISC's A-bomb was Zoot-connected—a power booster, a laser fuser, even a simple data card—then maybe the massive Zoot explosion would zap it, and thus prevent the ISC from touching off its own, very authentic nuclear blast.

"According to this, we've got forty seconds," he said to the Blackhawk pilot, holding the backward-running watch right between them.

The downside, of course, was that by unleashing the Zoot atomic bomb, Moon had just ensured that nothing with a Zoot device could work within a twenty-mile radius of Ground Zero for at least ten years. This meant that no matter what happened, no matter what the outcome of the ISC story, this part of the Range would be dead, lifeless, for the next decade.

He looked back at the strange wristwatch.

"Thirty seconds . . ."

All of the thousands of Zoot sensors, all of the laser support gear, all of the Fitzies, all of the military equipment jammed on the nearby Route 66, all of the weapons left over from the titanic last battle, and everything left inside Area 61 that was Zoot-connected was now frozen in time for ten long years.

His calculator had told him the night before that it all worked out to be $2.5 billion in losses a year, for ten years.

"Twenty seconds . . ."

But if he was able to stop the ISC's real bomb, then it would be a small price to pay. With their own nuclear device disarmed and War Heaven in a shambles, the majority of the ISC's power base would be gone.

"Fifteen seconds . . . twelve . . . ten . . ."

It had been a rather hurried affair, though. Now he wished he knew whether the ISC had their bomb at ground level or below.

"Nine . . . eight . . . seven . . ."

He wondered if he and the chopper pilot were a safe enough distance away.

"Six . . . five . . . four . . ."

He wondered whatever had become of Ryder Long.

"Three . . . two . . . one . . . *zero*."

Nothing happened . . .

Not for another billionth of a second.

Ryder was near suffocating when the Big Blast went off.

It was not due to any injury he'd sustained, though he had plenty all over his body.

It was because Maureen was squeezing him so tightly, she was actually preventing him from breathing.

She was crying when the real nuclear bomb went off. Crying and screaming the same things over and over directly in his ear. *I can't believe it! How did you know I was here? How did you find me?*

And he was saying things right back to her, like, *I don't believe it, either,* *I didn't know you were here,* and *Why are you dressed like that?* But he just about gave up saying anything more. In the flash of time that elapsed before they were both thrown to the ground, he remembered thinking, *If she thinks you're a hero, let it be.*

A fraction of a second later, he literally saw the mountain move. First it went up. And then it came crashing down. The noise alone was enough to make their ears start bleeding. As it turned out, both the young man and the L-10 soldier were in the best position—both were flat out on their backs when the Big Blast went off, and thus were spared being tossed head over heels to the ground.

468

But just like the first, fake blast, the aftereffects of this one didn't last too long, either. Ryder was able to pick himself up on one elbow and look up at the sky. He expected to see a monstrous mushroom cloud—the real McCoy, this time. But there was none.

He crawled to a nearby ledge and looked down to the desert floor below, and saw that an gigantic crater had formed where the runways of Area 61 used to be. There were wisps of smoke and dust coming out of the crater, just as all of the abandoned nearby military equipment was falling in, including the priceless B-17 named *Fort One*.

But other than that, there was nothing. Nothing but a barely-discernible golden halo that surrounded the entire area.

"I think we're okay . . ." he whispered to Maureen. "It was an underground blast."

"I knew that," she told him, crushing him in her well-intentioned body hold again. "I knew that all along."

The UH-1H Huey helicopter of the New Mexico Air National Guard was moving east over the rugged area of War Heaven known as Bumps and Scrapes.

Sitting untethered inside the passenger bay was the Delta Force officer and the two NSA agents. They'd spent the past two and half weeks searching for Maureen O'Brien, and now, all three felt they were nearing the end of their mission.

It had taken an order from the President himself to allow them to fly into the Nevada Special Weapons Test Range. They'd heard deep, dark rumblings of things gone wrong inside the super-secret war gaming area. But they had also heard that there was really no trouble at all, that it was just one big drill, a final blowout for the place before it was closed down because of a shrinking Pentagon budget and a change of the world's balance of power.

Just how the famous daughter of the retired but still powerful General John O'Brien had managed to get herself into the place, they didn't know. In many ways, it made no difference. All three men knew better than to ask questions that they knew were probably unanswerable, at least to them.

They had seen some very odd sights since entering the airspace over the weapons range, though. When they first flew in, they saw that the roads were clogged with military equipment—M-1A1 tanks,

Bradley APCs, Marine Corps LAVs. There were no soldiers around. Just the equipment, it had all broken down at once and had been abandoned there wholesale. Except for the lack of mass destruction, it looked like the road out of Kuwait, circa 1991.

Moving deeper into the range, they began to see more military equipment, some of it moving, but most of it not. Oddly, a lot of this stuff was covered with camouflage netting. But some of it wasn't. And it was easy to see that this uncovered equipment was actually of Soviet design. They wound up seeing hundreds of T-72 tanks, BMPs, and other Russian military vehicles.

"Either they are making this stuff to exact Russian specs in Detroit somewhere," the Delta officer observed, "or someone bought a lot of this stuff, dirt cheap."

"Any price for realism," one of the NSA agents agreed.

The deeper they pressed on, the more soldiers they saw. Many were simply walking, not in any ordered columns, but just walking. Then they saw more military equipment of Soviet design. But none of this was moving, either.

"This is weird," the Delta officer said. "I thought these guys are supposed be fighting each other. You know, simulating war?"

"Who knows?" the Delta officer said. "Strange stuff always goes on out here."

About a half hour into their flight they felt the Huey go into a brief but violent fit of shaking. A quick check with the pilot revealed that something had happened, maybe an electrical charge of some sort that had blinked all of the flight systems for a few moments. But everything looked okay now.

After that, the two NSA agents and the Delta officer strapped into their safety harnesses.

The pilot called back and pointed out their initial destination about fifteen miles out. It was a nondescript mountain range, very small and low by Nevada standards. But it was here, they'd been told, that they might find yet another clue to the whereabouts of Maureen O'Brien.

Ten minutes later they were circling the small range.

Below were four people, three of whom were waving at them wildly. The pilot put the Huey into a hover about 200 feet above the flattened-out summit. From this height, the three men in the back were able to study the small group of people trying to flag them down.

"Two wounded guys, another guy trying to get out of some ropes, and a woman in a ripped nightgown," the Delta officer said, reporting exactly what he saw through his binoculars.

The NSA agents had their spyglasses up too.

"I know it's strange," one said. "But I think the babe in the nightgown is our package."

They yelled to the pilot to land on the mountain and pick up the small group.

"Is it really going to be this simple?" the Delta officer asked.

"They look like they've been waiting for us," the second NSA agent said. "Maybe it's just some kind of wild publicity stunt."

81

Hollywood, three months later

The line of empty limousines stretched for two and half blocks.

One by one, the limos inched forward to pick up their passengers in front of the spotlight-lit theater. With each one that moved into position, another celebrity couple would run the gauntlet of photographers' strobe flashes and autograph-hungry fans, happy to dive into the back of their assigned stretch Caddy.

The premiere of the $100-million fighter-pilot movie epic was the biggest thing to hit Hollywood in a year. The film had already received rave reviews during the critics' preview sessions, and now, after this special showing for the cast and crew, it would open in general release to eagerly awaiting crowds.

"We're next," Ryder told Maureen, tugging at his tight tuxedo shirt collar and eyeing their limo as it cozied up to the curb. "Are you ready? Can you run in that outfit?"

Maureen straightened her black nylon miniskirt and stabilized herself on her ultra-high heels.

"Why run?" she told him. "Let's be dignified."

The outrageously uniformed concierge was now waving frantically at Ryder.

"Okay, dignified," he said. "Let's go."

They made it about halfway down the red carpet leading to the stretch. Suddenly a hand reached out and grabbed Ryder by the sleeve.

He turned to find a leathery-faced woman of about fifty, bleached blonde and wearing makeup that had apparently been applied with a putty knife.

"Colonel! Do you remember me?"

Ryder did. It was the tabloid reporter who had tried to hook him during his last day of work on the film.

"Yeah, sure I do," he replied, trying to be as polite as possible.

"Well, how was the film?" the woman asked, her small tape recorder now parked under his nose. "Did you enjoy it? Did you spot any technical flaws? Does it look like the most expensive movie ever made?"

Maureen hastily whispered something in his ear.

"All the money is right up there on the screen," he told the reporter, repeating Maureen's suggested response word for word. It was so correct, the reporter was immediately deflated.

But only for an instant.

"Is it true that there is already a sequel in the works, Colonel," the reporter barked, "and that it will be based on your own exploits in Operation Distant Thunder?"

Ryder quickly looked to Maureen for advice, but all she could do was roll her eyes and tug him gently on the arm.

"No comment," he said as they went into a gallop and dove into the waiting limo.

They were both surprised to find someone already in the back seat waiting for them.

It was Lieutenant Moon.

"Little out of your element, aren't you, Lieutenant?" Ryder asked him as the limo driver screeched away from the curb and headed down the boulevard.

"I'm just as happy to leave all this celebrity stuff to you, Colonel," Moon replied, via his lopsided smile. "You look like you're getting used to it."

"In a million years, maybe," Maureen commented, helping Ryder unravel his hangman's noose of a bow tie.

Moon produced an envelope from his suitcoat pocket.

"Thought you'd want to know," he said, reading the two-page document he'd pulled from the envelope. "They finally broke through into the lower levels of Area Sixty-one."

"Jessuz, when?" Ryder asked urgently.

"This morning," Moon said. "Took forty-five straight days of drilling. That was after we had to haul in all the non-Zoot equipment."

"So what did they find?" Ryder asked, not really sure that he wanted to know the answer.

"Nothing . . ." Moon said dramatically. "No people. No gold. No VTOL airplanes. No flying saucers. No nothing . . ."

Ryder and Maureen just looked at each other. They'd been waiting to hear something – anything – for three months. And it turned out to be yet another mystery.

Or another dead end.

"So it *was* all just a hoax?" Maureen asked the NSA agent.

Moon just shrugged. "Seems like it to me," he said wearily. "Fifty people got out somehow. Four billion in gold. Quite a heist. Quite a plan."

"Nothing about . . . the others?" Ryder asked.

Moon knew he was referring to the other Tango pilots, who may or may not have been in on the end plot with the ISC.

"No sign of them," he replied, reading from the second page of the document. "Not a boot, not a helmet, nothing. None of your tapes and notebooks were found either, Ms. O'Brien."

"*Damn* . . ." Ryder slammed his fist against the limo door. "Are you sure they checked every inch of that place?"

"They did," Moon replied. "We used the maps that Ms. O'Brien gave us. The apartments. The polar room. Even that TV studio way down the bottom of the place. The one that no one has any idea who built it. They're gone. Maybe everyone went up when the bomb went off in the Black Hole. Who knows? They're taking wall scrapings to see if they can identify any human material, but that'll take a while.

"So if they're all alive somewhere, and your buddies get caught along with the rest of that gang, then they'll have to get themselves some very slick lawyers to beat a court-martial *and* a major felony theft rap, plus about a hundred other charges."

Moon handed the document to Ryder.

"Sorry it wasn't better news," he said.

He knocked twice on the soundproof glass separating them from the driver and instantly the limo began to slow down.

"Until next time," he said as the car came to a stop.

Just as he was stepping out the door, Ryder grabbed his sleeve. "One last question, Lieutenant," he said. "If this was all one big drill, would you tell us?"

Moon thought over the question for a moment. "If it was," he finally answered, "then I'd certainly be under orders not to."

With that, he was out the door and gone.

They reached the mountaintop ranch house forty minutes later.

Owned by Maureen's agent, they'd been holed up in the obscenely-palatial retreat while recovering from their ordeal in the Nevada desert.

They retreated to the all-glass bedroom and climbed out of their evening clothes and into the his-and-her satin robes that were get-well presents from the agent. Ryder made them both a strong drink and then he climbed onto the huge leather couch which he had pulled against the window facing east.

"Waiting for your spirit?" Maureen asked as she settled down next to him.

Ryder was staring out over the San Bernadino Mountains, off into the distance where he imagined War Heaven to be.

"I still can't believe it all happened," he said. "Something inside me just can't accept it."

"My editor has that same feeling," Maureen said wryly. "God, those ISC guys had me snowed. Even that kid who led me out of there, wherever the hell he disappeared to. When I wrote down everything I remembered—or thought I remembered—it read like the worst sci-fi book ever written. I couldn't sell that story to *The Enquirer* under my *real* name, never mind the *Washington Post* . . ."

"Someone knows what happened," Ryder said wistfully. "They had to do something with all that gold. They either melted it down, or they'll try to sell it on the black market. They'll slip up, eventually."

"It would be their first mistake," Maureen said, putting her head on his shoulder. "And their only one."

She was asleep within a minute, snoring softly and using his healing shoulder as her pillow.

The pain—both physical and mental—had finally begun to heal. His body was still battered, but on the mend. He was still experiencing the occasional flashback due to the Hal-Lou gas, especially at night, but the episodes were getting fewer and further in between. Things seemed to have been getting better.

Until tonight—when Moon had opened up some of the wounds again. Ryder wondered if it would take him another three months, or maybe three years, to get over the whole strange adventure and, most important, the loss of his partner and best friend.

He fell asleep sometime soon after Maureen, drifting off from a combination of the long day, the renewed melancholy, and the stiff drink.

It was such a deep sleep that he was surprised the mellow-toned doorbell woke him up.

He gently laid Maureen down on the couch and padded down the stairs, too sleepy to wonder who the hell was at the door. Just as long as it wasn't another reporter.

He opened the door to find a tall thin man, with curly longish blond hair and wearing an odd uniform.

"Who are you? Pizza delivery?"

The man smiled thinly. "We meet again, Ghost. And you don't remember?"

Ryder stared at the man. He *had* seen him before. Then it came to him: it was the guy from Jacks. The one who gave him the watch that ran backward.

"What the hell . . . ?" was all Ryder could say.

"You didn't give up trying to figure it out, did you, Ghost?" the man asked him mysteriously. "You actually saw more than anyone else."

"How the hell did you get up here?" was the only question that Ryder could get out.

The strange man smiled once more. "I came with a friend," he said.

Ryder wiped the sleep from his eyes and looked up to see Woody standing next to the strange angelic-looking man. He looked different, too. His hair was almost shoulder-length and almost as white as the other guy. He was also wearing the same kind of uniform.

"Is . . . is it really you, Pards?"

Woody smiled beatifically. "It's me," he said simply. "I'm breaking many rules here, Ghost. But I had to come back. I knew you'd be going mad, wondering what happened."

Ryder was breathing hard, trying to talk, frozen where he stood. It was like seeing a ghost. Two ghosts.

"What the hell is going on?" he finally blurted out, wondering if he should call out to Maureen.

476

"I can't really say right now, Ry," Woody told him. "But I will, someday. I promise. And by the way, Williams and Katt send their regards."

"We have to go now," the other man said. "And next time, Ghost, when you're given a present, don't throw it away."

With that, they both turned and walked down the long driveway.

Ryder was left standing alone at the front door, in absolute bewilderment as the two men disappeared around the edge of the curve.

"Wait a minute!" he called out, finally summoning up enough saliva to talk again. "Wait . . . Woody!"

He ran down the rock driveway, cutting his bare feet on the hard gravel. He reached the bend in the curve and stopped on top of a grassy knoll that looked out over a vast south side lawn.

"What the hell . . ."

Staring out onto this lawn he saw the flying saucer—the same one he'd seen projected during the ECC mission. Woody and the other man were just walking up into it, when Woody turned around, gave him a quick salute, and then disappeared inside the huge disk.

Then, without a noise or even a rustling of the breeze, the saucer suddenly shot straight up into the night sky, up so far he could hardly see it.

And then it blinked out.

ACTION ADVENTURE: WINGMAN #1–#6
by Mack Maloney

WINGMAN (2015, $3.95)

From the radioactive ruins of a nuclear-devastated U.S. emerges a hero for the ages. A brilliant ace fighter pilot, he takes to the skies to help free his once-great homeland from the brutal heel of the evil Soviet warlords. He is the last hope of a ravaged land. He is Hawk Hunter . . . Wingman!

WINGMAN #2: THE CIRCLE WAR (2120, $3.95)

A second explosive showdown with the Russian overlords and their armies of destruction is in the wind. Only the deadly aerial ace Hawk Hunter can rally the forces of freedom and strike one last blow for a forgotten dream called "America"!

WINGMAN #3: THE LUCIFER CRUSADE (2232, $3.95)

Viktor, the depraved international terrorist who orchestrated the bloody war for America's West, has escaped. Ace pilot Hawk Hunter takes off for a deadly confrontation in the skies above the Middle East.

WINGMAN #4: THUNDER IN THE EAST (2453, $3.95)

The evil New Order is raising a huge mercenary force to reclaim America, and Hawk Hunter, the battered nation's most fearless top gun fighter pilot, takes to the air to prevent this catastrophe from occurring.

WINGMAN #5: THE TWISTED CROSS (2553, $3.95)

"The Twisted Cross," a power-hungry neo-Nazi organization, plans to destroy the Panama Canal with nuclear time bombs unless their war chests are filled with stolen Inca gold. The only route to saving the strategic waterway is from above—as Wingman takes to the air to rain death down upon the Cross' South American jungle stronghold.

WINGMAN #6: THE FINAL STORM (2655, $3.95)

Deep in the frozen Siberian wastes, last-ditch elements of the Evil Empire plan to annihilate the Free World in one final rain of nuclear death. Trading his sleek F-16 fighter jet for a larger, heavier B-1B supersonic swing-wing bomber, Hawk Hunter undertakes his most perilous mission.